The Future Weavers

A catalogue record for this book is available from the National Library of New Zealand.

Soft cover ISBN 978-0-473-58733-8

epub ISBN 978-0-473-58734-5

POD ISBN 978-0-473-59309-4

Cover design by Amanda Sutcliffe

Cover Art by Artefy

Design & layout www.yourbooks.co.nz

Printed by Ring Write Books

The Future Weavers

R. DE WOLF

Other Work

Guardians of the Ancestors Book One

Kaituhi Rawhiti – A Celebration of East Coast Writers
– Crushed Violet (a short story)

In memory of my beautiful Māori brother,
William Grennell Ngarimu,
who believed in learning, teaching,
chasing dreams and encouraging aspiration.

Characters

Ari	Woman of Marama's Chief, Marama's friend and self-appointed mother
Arihia	Younger sister of Roimata
Aroha	Marama's daughter
Atarangi	Rangi's mother
Hana	A spirit, once the best friend of Rangi's ancestor Ngaio
Huia	Daughter of Rongo
Kai	Marama, Starman and Tane's son
Kani	Woman of Marama's village from Hawaiki
Kauri	Man of the spirit Hana when she lived
Kiri	Young woman of Marama's village
Manaia	Marama's great-great-grandmother, a spirit
Maui	Son of Starman and Marama
Mihi	Captured and enslaved woman
Muru	Youngest of the Rotowhā leaders
Nani	Marama's grandmother, a spirit
Ngaio	Best friend of the spirit Hana and maternal ancestor of Rangi

Ngoi	Rongo's woman, daughter of a story-teller and master-carver
Nikau	Rongo's second in command, of his men
Piri	Senior tohunga of the village and tribe
Rangi	Chief of Rotowhā
Rongo	Second in command of Rotowhā
Starman	Master navigator, son of the sea and Marama's man
Tahu	Young warrior of Rotowhā
Tamati	Tohunga and Piri's chosen successor
Tane	Marama's first love, Kai's spirit father
Tau	Son of Ari and the Chief, leader of Kāingatipu
The Chief	The Chief who led Marama's people from Hawaiki to Aotearoa
Tuakana Marama	Girl of Marama's village and a namesake

Chapter 1

Everything in life was perfect until the prophecy foretold scythed through the normality of life, severing Marama's connection to everyone she loved.

The woman stood on the hill, high above the village. Her body limned against the sky as the easterly wind ruffled her hair. The lookout had always been her special place. The first time she came here was with her beloved *Nani* (grandmother). Their ancestors cloaked them in welcome. It was also the place where her son Kai's whale *kaitiaki* (guardian) revealed himself. The whale spoke to her, so she wouldn't fear him when he returned each year for her son. Time had flowed by, swift as the water in the stream. Four years had elapsed since they buried Nani here. Her spirit soared above their village, Kāingatipu, to watch over the people she fought to save.

Nani had received the prophecy of their departure from the island in Hawaiki - to leave if they wanted to survive. Marama missed the old woman. She thought about her daily as she completed the tasks Nani taught her. After Nani delivered Marama's second child Aroha, she confided her departure to the ancestors was imminent. Life without Nani was unimaginable for Marama, but the cooler climate in winter made her old joints ache. Nani lived a long and eventful life. When she departed the physical world, Marama could feel her comforting presence enter the spiritual realm. Their bond remained intact, simply transformed. Now she needed Nani more than ever. The day foretold was fast approaching, and Marama's heart was being ripped in opposing directions. Inside her, life was stirring as their second son clung tenaciously to her womb. A murmured promise of future joy for the family, if only she could hold him. His future was less tangible than the other children. Pain clawed at her chest.

She would soon be parted from her oldest son Kai and his father Starman, her love and saviour. Marama knew before Kai was born, he would return to Starman's home. As his ancestors had been for generations, Kai would be initiated in the sea cave to become a dedicated son of the sea. The years passed, but no word came of whether they would return from this journey. The spirit of Starman's grandfather had warned her, if she departed with them, she would lose her unborn child. If she left, Aroha would also be at risk or left behind, and Marama would leave her people with no healer or spirit guide. Going on this journey was never really an option.

It was Starman who taught her to love and live again. After losing her first love Tane, Kai's spiritual father, Marama had wanted to die as well. Kai was all she had of Tane now. Tane insisted her mortal life must be lived without him when he relinquished his role as her spirit guide. She often sensed Tane's presence around Kai. Marama was sure the two of them shared a bond, but Tane never spoke to her. Perhaps it was best. Once she let go of Tane, she was able to commit fully to her relationship with Starman. They shared a deep, abiding love and treasured their family. She sighed as tears sprang to her eyes. So much loss — her parents, Tane, Nani, and now three of the people she loved most would leave her too. A sob tore from her throat. She buried her face in her hands to staunch the torrent of tears, but her body heaved with emotional distress.

"Hush, Marama, I am here. Don't carry on so you make me

feel sad, and I shouldn't fret here," whispered Nani in her mind. Marama looked to the sky. She managed a smile through her tears, at Nani's humour, undiminished even in death.

"I need to know they will return Nani, and we will be together again," she pleaded out loud. There was no reply from Nani, and she crumpled on the ground.

"Marama, you imagine tragedy at every turn. The future is never certain, even in this realm. So many threads of fate vie and twist in perpetual motion. It is difficult to know what will and will not happen with any clarity. Still, I can tell you Kai and Starman return," Nani murmured cautiously. Marama sat upright, her heart pounding, bursting now with hope as she wiped tears from her eyes how she had longed to hear those words. She projected thanks and love to Nani, but she was already gone.

Someone approached, footsteps crunched on the path. Marama turned to see Starman clambering to the hilltop lookout. He searched for her, worry etched on his face. Marama reacted like a young girl with stomach butterflies. She pondered what she had done to deserve such a beautiful man. Starman was still lean, and more muscular than ever. The chiselled planes of the face so dear to her wore more lines at the corners of his eyes, but he was still handsome. Marama ran to him and hugged him fiercely as she couldn't bear to lose him too. The children needed them both, so she clung to him. Starman stroked her hair and held her close. He kissed the top of her head, feeling her angst, a mirror of his internal struggle.

Years ago, she made him swear he would never leave her. Starman had agreed, even though they both knew one day he would set sail with their son. That day was almost upon them, and it pained him to leave her. She was pregnant, and Aroha was still young. Kai, however, held a destiny charted by his bloodline to fulfil. He placed his finger under her chin and tilted her face upwards, seeing the tear trails on her cheeks. Starman fervently hoped she would come to love him as she had once loved Tane. The price they paid for that love was the extreme pain they were now experiencing. He brought his lips to hers and kissed her tenderly, but Marama needed more. Before he knew what was happening, she unleashed the passion of her fraught emotions. They returned to where it had all started, in a tangle of limbs on the ground. Once more, they held one another and anticipated the arrival of a child.

"I should have pretended it was time to leave earlier," he teased. Starman earned a slap on his rump for his cheekiness, but it was worth it to make her smile. He would miss her, somehow she completed him. His chest constricted as he contemplated leaving her.

"What shall I do if I want your body when you are away? Take a young lover?" she asked with wide-eyed innocence.

"I suppose you could do that. Although, I would hate to drag a poor boy from your mat when I return. Of course, you need to find somebody who is attracted to an enormous *puku* (belly) in a few months." He grinned and waggled his eyebrows up and down, but his humour earned him another slap from Marama. He did make a valid point. When she became pregnant, she remained slim for ages, then swelled like a wet sponge almost overnight. The sudden appearance of her colossal belly was an enormous source of amusement in the village. Small children thought she was hiding something in her garments. While carrying Kai, she struggled with the unaccustomed bulk of her body getting in the way as she worked. In the end, the baby stepped in, with a warning system, to protect them both from her clumsiness.

"Come Marama. Ari will look after our children this morning, and I will look after her grandson this afternoon. So we should spend some time together, make happy memories today, to hold on to while we are apart." Marama took his extended hand and allowed him to pull her up. Starman was right, and she would have plenty of time to be alone and wallow in the depths of misery soon enough. Her communication with Nani reassured her that her boys would return. Best to seize the fleeting moments time offered them.

Kai stood on the beach still as the rocks. He accompanied Nana Ari to collect *kaimoana* (seafood) from the pools left as the tide retreated. It wasn't long until Kai became distracted. When his whale brother drew near, he beat in his heart and sang in his ears until Kai's dreams filled with the ocean. Every year the whale came for him. His parents would paddle out and entrust his brother with his care. Of course, Tane, his spirit father, accompanied them. They would frolic in the waves, share their experiences until the whale called to Marama he was bringing Kai home. Sometimes the whale lingered so they could play together every day. It strengthened the bond between them. This year he would journey with his father, to be initiated as a son of the sea, and his whale brother would travel with them. The prospect of being with his brother delighted Kai, but being parted from his mother for the first time was painful. He often journeyed with his father, but his mother usually travelled with them if the trip was longer than two days. This time she would remain at home, even though he could feel her sorrow. Kai decided to ready his belongings for the journey when he returned home. It wouldn't be long now until they departed.

The whale arrived in the bay below the *pā* (fortified village) the following day. Starman steadied the voyaging outrigger he had built for longer journeys. Saying goodbye to Marama and little Aroha hadn't been easy, but the sea was calling him. His blood ebbed and flowed with the tide. Kai was unable to hide his excitement at the coming adventure. However, to his credit, he tried to suppress it for his mother's sake. Marama and Ari clung to each other on the shore. Tears streamed down their faces as they watched the men and boys they loved launch their *waka* (canoe). Aroha buried her head against their legs, unable to watch. Ari had been distressed when the Chief, her man, announced it was his duty to return to their island. He needed to see for himself if any of their people survived. Officially, he was no longer the chief. His second son Tau, who left their home island with his father at the last minute, was now in charge. Many people still sought guidance from the man they followed across the sea, including the council members, whenever they made an important decision. The journey would give Tau a real opportunity to stamp his authority on leadership. The Chief and Ari's *mokopuna* (grandchild), Koha, begged to go on the journey. Although he was young, he argued his case well. He reminded his grandparents he intended to be chief one day and therefore shared the responsibility to discover the fate of their people. On the voyage, he would learn from his grandfather and the navigator daily, along with his friend Kai who was much younger. Although Ari had other mokopuna now, Koha was special to her. He was all she had left of her eldest son Tama, who had defied his father and remained on their island to perish. The desire to find survivors warred with her instincts to protect her *whānau* (family) and keep it together. In the end, she relented, but the pain in her heart was physical as anxiety took its toll.

Marama and Ari grew ever closer as they both tried to bear the pain of separation. A temporary separation, they hoped. The other family affected was Piki's. The young man was the Chief's best pupil in weapons, strategy, and leadership. Piki successfully lobbied his family, the Chief, and Starman to join the voyage. Koha and Piki determined their fate. As children, they both refused to stay with their parents on the island. Each had decided, on his own, to voyage and survive. People were now reluctant to interfere with the choices they made. Piki regarded the Chief as his father just as Tane, Kai's spiritual father, had. He valued any time he could spend with the Chief to peel back the layers of wisdom that shrouded him in *mana* (spirit, strength, and standing). The Chief did everything in his power to groom worthy men to lead and protect their people in the future. It was a culture and attitude transplanted from their home. A chief or future leader could fall in battle, become sick, or simply be called to a different path. Perhaps a course that would lead them away from their people. It was wise for a chief to share tribal knowledge liberally with any student who showed interest and talent. Blood ties weren't the sole determinant of leadership. History proved blood selection only could cause tribal extinction. It only took one weak or incompetent leader. Piki's grandfather also pleaded to accompany the travellers, as he wanted to die on his beloved island home. The addition of a skilled sailor and fisherman to the waka was beneficial, so the final crew numbered six. The voyagers' friends and family remained on the beach long after the whale or the vessel could be seen against the horizon. Marama and Ari dreaded the return to their empty *whare* (house).

Life trickled by, as inevitable as the drops of water building the stalactites in the beach cave. The sun rose, there were chores to do, duties to attend to, meals to prepare before dark descended, and then it was time to sleep again. People felt subdued as a sadness descended like a blanket of winter fog on the villagers' *wairua* (spirit). Marama devoted herself to Aroha and her spiritual duties. In doing so, she failed to notice Kāingatipu had fallen into a passive melancholy that reflected her mood. Nani came to her in a dream; she told Marama she must always look past her own heart and nose to protect her people. Marama opened her eyes and saw the malaise. She didn't have the same connection to Tau that she shared with his father. Tau was a warrior, he wasn't a spiritual man, and although good-natured, he didn't place much value on women's opinions. His attitude surprised his parents, as he had lived through two enemy raids and the exodus from the island. He knew first-hand the critical part Nani and Marama played in saving them. Still, in Tau's eyes, the triumph belonged to his father alone. Marama decided to speak with Ari. At least as Tau's mother, she held some influence over him. However, even she would need to tread carefully, for he was determined to set his leadership course.

Ari mentioned casually to Tau during a family meal how lethargic and depressed she felt since his father departed. A whānau discussion ensued regarding how they all felt. They were a bit down, out of sorts and other villagers were in the same mood. Tau considered the matter carefully. His father would lift the spirits of his people, and this was now his role. The next day, Tau announced a ceremony at dawn to launch one of the great canoes. The men would depart on a three-day excursion to hunt and fish. When the hunters returned, the village would celebrate with a feast dedicated to the ancestors, the Gods, and the voyagers. Tau saw hunting and fishing as the perfect opportunity to bond with his men and the village boys, who he would also take. His mother and Marama both questioned the decision to leave the pā undefended. Tau dismissed the worries of the women as the village had never come under attack. Only friends visited them, and the excursion was only for two nights. Tau reassured them they were capable of looking after a few women and children. In truth, many of the women looked forward to having quiet days to spend together without their menfolk. The men hastily prepared provisions, and a buzz of excitement permeated the village. Tau's plan was working, and he was pleased with his decisive action. He asked Marama to focus her spiritual efforts on ensuring a successful hunt and catch. She marshalled the ancestors to lend the men their support. Marama and Ari were again left standing on the beach as the great canoe flew from the shore. A cloud slid across the sun, blocking the heat for a moment and making them shiver. It created a feeling of uneasiness in Marama. That night she barely slept for worrying about Kai, Starman, and the voyagers.

Marama sought Ari at first-light as the spirits urged her to honour them with a women's feast. They called everyone together and sent out foraging parties for berries, greens, kaimoana, birds, and animals. Marama went deep into the forest with a group of women and girls. She would clear the traps and snares she laid the day before. Ari took a large foraging party to the beach to dive for *koura* (crayfish), *pāua* (abalone), and *kina* (sea urchins). The girls chattered as they left the pā, but they were puffed, so they halted to drink at a stream. Marama tended to range further than most women, which meant her haul was often the greatest. Although Aroha was only a little girl, she was used to her mother's long treks up the hills and had no trouble keeping up. As the morning wore on, people became tired, and conversation faded to focus on finding safe footing. The women were relieved to reach the traps. Their efforts rewarded them with a plentiful supply of delicious plump birds and *kiore* (rats). Marama divvied up the haul somewhat but reserved the heaviest portion for herself. She realised she was more familiar with this task in the forest terrain than the others. A group of the girls went back to the stream to refill water gourds. The hairs on the back of Marama's neck prickled. Nani whispered to hide the child before she heard a squeal of alarm from the creek. Marama grabbed Aroha and boosted her up inside a hollow tree trunk.

"My darling, you must be quiet. Stay here hidden until it is almost dark, then find Nana Ari. Don't move or make a sound, no matter what you hear, understand?" Aroha nodded her head and placed her finger over her lips to show she knew what to do. Marama motioned to the other women to scatter in different directions. She shed her haul while stealing towards the stream. Holding her breath, Marama tried to still her pumping heart, crept, and saw a group of six fearsome-looking warriors. They poked and prodded the terrified girls while they tied their hands. There were crashing sounds from the bush downstream, followed by shrieking, and Marama knew they had captured more women. Two more warriors returned with a woman each. Marama strained to hear their conversation from her hiding place.

"A nice catch. These girls are all unknown to us and, therefore, foreign. Do you think they will satisfy our chief and the tohunga, Rongo?" one of the men asked. He looked to a large, stocky, fierce-looking man covered in *tā moko* (tattoo). Rongo was their party leader but not the chief. The dialect of Māori he spoke was slightly different from the people they befriended, so she surmised they must be from another area.

"Piri predicts our chief will only breed a son when he finds a foreign woman who is special enough to bear him. Although these women aren't from our village, none of them appears special to me. We dare not return empty-handed. Best to take the prettiest ones and hope our tohunga will see something extraordinary," he said with an exasperated sigh. "Move them out. We head home today, and we will send out another party." As the first warrior, and a childhood friend to their chief, Rongo desperately wanted to find the woman who could bear his cousin a son. None of his many current women had been able to produce a male child. He watched his chief become bitter and vicious with those around him as a consequence. People feared him because he was highly unpredictable. Rongo had just one woman, but already they had two sons and a daughter. A fact he was careful not to flaunt, but hardly a secret. Ironic as he was so ugly, with an ungainly body that looked unable to move with the speed and grace it did. His woman hadn't wanted him when he approached her parents. He won her over with kindness, time, love, and a bit of cunning. If only his chief could find some happiness, Rongo hoped he would return to being the friend and leader he supported to become chief. The cousin he had once loved like a brother.

Marama mulled the words over. It wasn't the information she wanted to hear. She could only think of one person who might fit their requirements—her unfortunate self. Marama was conscious, now crouched close to the warrior party, that she had hidden Aroha nearby. The captured girls needed to be set free. They couldn't be taken as captives to be used by a chief who might mistreat them. She would track them, find a way to free the girls and lead the men away from their village. Once Nani accused her of using herself as bait, and at the moment, this was her only plan. At all cost, Marama knew she must keep them away from the undefended pā and her people.

"These two were running downstream, and they might have been heading towards a settlement. Do you want us to scout ahead and see?" The warriors looked to Rongo for an answer.

"It is a good thought. People must live in the vicinity, but they scattered in all directions, and we are only eight warriors. If we haven't found a satisfactory woman, we will return with an appropriate force to find the settlement," he said with a frown. Rongo would prefer not to lose good warriors while searching for an elusive woman foretold in a prophecy. They had no idea when this woman would appear. Marama felt her heart sink, and she knew what she needed to do. She must sacrifice herself to save her people, her child, and her family, without question. A son, just a few days old, nestled in her womb, but events propelled her toward a foreign village. Marama constantly worried about her unborn son. The spirits never defined his future like Kai and Aroha's. The destiny of this baby was nebular at best. Still, her choices were limited. Marama must free the women and lead the warriors as far away from the pā as possible. She needed to be cunning. They couldn't guess what she did, or her sacrifice might be in vain. Marama missed Nani and the Chief terribly as she had never planned anything like this on her own, but they were both busy elsewhere.

Marama back-tracked as quietly as she could. She crept up the hill away from the men while they talked, inspected the women more closely, and organised their gear. Marama headed for the echoing rocks. She had used them to show Starman how she appeared to produce sound from everywhere, out of a tiny shell, when they first met. Once in place, she threw her head back in mocking laughter as loud as she could. The sound reverberated around the hills until the warriors looked up puzzled and a little alarmed. Marama threw a large rock into the trees, sending startled birds into the air as it thudded and bounced its way to the ground. She set the bait.

"Stay here with the women and guard them; it could be a trick." Rongo signalled to two of the men. The women were all bound by the hands and feet, then secured to a tree. "The rest of us will fan out and comb through the forest, to the top of the hill. Give the signal if you see anyone, and we will run them down. It was a woman's voice, but it seemed to come from many directions, so keep a lookout for caves or rock formations."

Marama threw a smaller rock further into the forest to lead the men away from the stream. She was quiet, but she also needed to be quick if she wanted to free the women. Tracking directionally opposite the warriors, she stalked down the hill on the other side of the stream before cutting back towards the women. There were two guards; she had hoped for just one. They were, however, both young and not particularly vigilant. They were probably disappointed to be assigned guard duty. Marama crawled on her belly until she was behind the tree where the women were tied. She whispered to Kiri, who was the nearest girl.

"I need you to distract one of the guards. Flirt, flaunt your body, ask to pee or for water. I will take care of the other guard and free the rest of the girls. Give me a few moments to crawl away." Kiri stretched voluptuously with her hands overhead, posturing like a *kererū* (native wood pigeon) cavorting in mating season. She had large full breasts, and she jiggled about begging to be allowed to pee. Then, with eyes widened in supplication, attempting to look both innocent and alluring simultaneously, Kiri put on quite a show. When the guards pretended to ignore her, she pouted prettily and teased them.

"Perhaps you are afraid to be alone in the forest with an unattached girl who is hunting for a prize trophy," Kiri purred. The other girls giggled and drew one of the guards into the flirtatious, suggestive banter. It wasn't long before he cut Kiri's leg ties and marched her into the forest, where she wasted no time. She giggled, gasped and moaned loud enough for all to hear as she seduced him, which distracted the other guard. The second guard became annoyed he was missing out on the fun and wanted to see what they were doing. While Kiri's groans of pleasure enthralled him, Marama crept up behind him and hit him on the head with a rock. Not hard enough to kill him, but enough to knock him out. She gagged and tied him up quickly, just in case he awoke. After she cut the girl's bonds, they helped her drag the guard into the undergrowth. Marama sneaked up behind the guard who was engrossed in his dalliance with Kiri and knocked him out as well. Kiri threw Marama a grateful smile and gave the unconscious guard a swift but satisfying kick before stomping on his hands. They bound and gagged him as well. Marama asked them to scatter in different directions stealthily and away from the village first, before finding hiding places until the late afternoon. She explained she would create a distraction, then find a place to hide for the night. Tomorrow she would make her way back to the pā, using a circuitous route to avoid the warriors tracking her. The women nodded in understanding and set off in the directions Marama sent them.

Marama closed her eyes for a moment, she didn't like deceiving her people, but she wanted them to be safe. She focused herself on what she needed to do, hurry and track below the men fanning out. Marama intended to lead the warriors on a merry chase before allowing them to capture her. Their leader Rongo seemed intelligent, which would make the capture plan she was formulating more believable. Sweat beaded her brow as she ran hard up the hill. Marama was grateful for her old running habit, taken up again, to increase her strength after Aroha's birth. Muscles answered the call as she gained her second wind and settled into a fast ground-eating rhythm. When she was halfway up the hill, she howled a primal scream at the sky. The sound carried and stopped the warriors in their tracks. They instinctively turned to the direction the sound came from, hesitated, waiting for instructions. Rongo gave a loud whistle which was the sign for his men to regroup to him. He followed up with intermittent bird calls to let them know his position until all his men arrived.

"We are being led away from the prisoners. Two of you go back to where we left the others and check they are secure. Bring them all to the top of that ridge, where the rock protrudes against the skyline," he said before indicating which men he wanted to go. The four who remained were the fastest runners. Rongo wanted to capture the woman. He felt compelled to do so and couldn't shake the feeling this was an important task. Her behaviour so far, if indeed it was one person, was unusual. Perhaps she was the woman they were seeking. Birds flew skyward in front of them, so he arrayed his men to fan out. This time Rongo sent his fastest runner straight at Marama while putting men above and below her. Rongo headed for the ridge, where he would have a good view of everything moving below, to rendezvous with his other men. When he arrived at the top of the hill, he scanned the forest below him. He was surprised to see that the woman was now further ahead of the pursuit by his reckoning. Rongo scratched his head and puffed out his cheeks to help him think. There could be more than one person. They might be running a relay, then hiding. It could have been a woman who screamed, but maybe the person running was a man, trying to lead them away or into an ambush. If it was the woman who screamed running, and he had a feeling it was, she knew the terrain but also ran like a man.

The two men he left guarding the prisoners arrived looking sheepish, while the two sent to check on them were barely able to suppress their mirth. There were no prisoners with them, so Rongo surmised what had happened but let them stutter out the truth anyway. Best they learned from the mistake. Red-faced, sore heads hanging in shame, their comrades gave in to their desire to laugh. Rongo kept a stern face but didn't berate them for their stupidity. It wasn't necessary as they learned the lesson, and he was sure the other men would tease them mercilessly. When your men respected you, letting you down was punishment enough. As he scanned ahead for the woman, he realised he could still see his men running but could no longer see her moving. She was either hiding, doubling back towards them or attempting to slip down the hill through the net. He issued orders quickly to his remaining men. Rongo sent one of them to run down the slope and track perpendicular to the stream. Two men walked in a line between the other runners, in case she was coming back between them somehow, and the last man ran along the ridge to try and sight her. Rongo would stay at the vantage point and use his whistle signals to direct his men if need be. He was almost sure she would try and sneak back to wherever the women all lived. If his men let him know they were in pursuit again, he would run the ridgeline to meet them at the rock formation atop the next hill.

The men ran, searched, looking for their quarry, but she was illusive. Then Rongo heard a kererū flying, its wings flapping noisily to carry its weighty body through the trees, just below him. He froze, listening intently. Dropping to the ground, Rongo placed his ear close to the earth and closed his eyes. Did he hear soft footfalls and a faint rustling of leaves? Yes, he had. Now she was running back towards the stream. Somehow she slipped through the net he cast with his men. His legs were fresh, but instead of dashing off in pursuit, he paused to close his eyes again and listen. The sound of splashing water let him know she was crossing the stream or walking in the water below his current position. When he reached the creek, he scanned both sides for footprints.

Marama hid in the treetops to allow the runners and following men to pass her as she headed back toward their leader on the ridge. She made noise to attract Rongo's attention; he was tracking her. Marama entered the creek, leaving the water across the rocks on the far side. Deliberately, she left soggy footprints in the dirt, heading down the hill. Then she walked backwards in her prints until she returned to the water and picked her way silently upstream. Exiting on a fallen log, she left no marks and climbed from tree to tree for as long as she could. Marama smiled to herself as he took the bait and followed her footsteps downhill. It wouldn't take him long to figure out her footprints led nowhere. By then, she would've recovered her breath and be ready to lure him to the next part of the chase. Picking up her pace, she ran away from the stream just below the ridgeline. Having lost her trail, Rongo closed his eyes again and thought he heard a noise above him, heading in the other direction. He re-crossed the stream, began climbing, and found broken twigs underneath the tree where she climbed down. A partial footprint followed. Rongo knew he had underestimated his quarry and should take care not to lose her again. He pursued her with short bursts of speed, checking in the trees and undergrowth while looking for signs he was on her trail. Rongo gave a shrill whistle to call his men to him. She would hear too, but he hoped this might cause her to panic and make a run for it. Marama did hear the whistle, but instead of running, she slowed her pace. Taking meticulous care not to leave any sign of her passage, she angled gradually uphill. If she was trying to escape, the least likely path was upwards, so that was where she went.

Rongo could no longer hear her and scouted for signs to show him which direction she was taking. He couldn't find any trace. The sun burst from behind a cloud, and he saw the glint of a long red-gold hair snagged on a branch further up the hill. Rongo gave thanks to the sun, for its rays revealed his path.

Marama made pace again. When she was close to the ridgeline, she dropped to her belly and crawled across a rock platform. Looking for a place where she could go over the edge of the ravine, she grasped the trunk of a tree. She swung herself down, dangling for a moment until she found another bush to brace her legs. Marama slowed her breathing. She was inhaling deeply through her nose, holding her breath, before gently expelling the air softly out her nose. Her pounding heart quieted. After a long morning of exertion, she waited. Footsteps sounded above her. He was light on his feet for such a large man and quicker than she anticipated. Marama knew if she remained quiet, he would never find her. Unfortunately, that wasn't the objective. Once she heard him moving away towards his men, she took a pinch of dirt and pebbles, releasing them in a trickle, down the side of the cliff. The warrior stopped in his tracks. He turned to retrace his footsteps. Standing on the rock, he noticed the tree growing out over the edge and shook his head, smiling. Rongo crawled across the stone shelf to avoid alerting her to his presence. He must be careful not to lose her, so he peered tentatively over the ledge. Marama stared up at him with round green eyes, quietly enjoying the startled look her appearance caused, appraising him. She cast a desperate glance out over the ravine to make him think she was considering jumping.

"No! Please don't!" he cried. "Grab my hand. You need to live." His plea was sincere. Rongo was aware he hadn't introduced himself properly, but he didn't want to scare her further. When she didn't move, he wriggled further over the edge and clasped her slender golden wrist in his meaty grip. "You will need to help me. Everything may seem lost to you, but you will be the mother of a great son. Take my hand and climb up."

Marama was surprised by the gentle coaxing of such a fearsome warrior. He was terrifying to behold up close but seemed quite genuine. Her hesitation panicked him. Rongo didn't know if she would throw herself off the cliff, and he was aware his appearance affected people negatively. He watched her closely, holding her gaze. She didn't look scared. The woman wasn't sweating, her breathing wasn't erratic, and her eyes weren't dilated. Rongo believed she was assessing him. He decided he should never underestimate her and harboured a slight suspicion she meant for him to find her. Marama lowered her eyes swiftly, hoping her curiosity hadn't betrayed her and grabbed his arm to haul herself up. They stood regarding each other before he bound her wrists and whistled his signal to his men. In Rongo's mind, there was no doubt that this woman fit the description from their tohunga perfectly. She was the most unusual person he had ever seen. He lifted her hair to examine it and peered into her eyes, looking for tricks, but was satisfied they were indeed green.

"Where do you come from? Are you a forest nymph?" he asked her. Marama shook her head. "You can understand me?" She nodded that she could. "Do you speak?" Marama nodded again, so he told her the name of his mountain, his river and tribe, to identify himself. "I am a descendant of Maui Potiki, Kotuku is my tīpuna, my name is Rongo," he said, pointing at himself. Then he pointed at her.

"I am the mother you seek," stated Marama. His eyes widened slightly, surprised she knew of the prophecy, but relieved to have found what they were seeking. He gave her water and gently tended to the scrapes and cuts she sustained while on the run, applying a numbing ointment from a pouch he carried to the worst of them.

"Do you have a name that people call you?" he asked.

"Marama," she replied, "the moon daughter from under the burning mountain, of the lost green island." Rongo puffed out his cheeks again, his brain engaged in assessing her name, as he was superstitious when it came to the Gods. As a warrior, he relied on the moon. He certainly didn't wish to offend any deity, so he began *karakia* (prayer and ritual) to protect himself and his men. The first of his men arrived, and he observed the impact Marama's appearance had on somebody else. Rongo hoped he hadn't gawked and looked as stupid as his men did but suspected he had. As each of his men arrived, one by one, the woman's appearance didn't fail to surprise a single warrior. Her unique appearance was a relief to them all, as their chief would be pleased when they returned. Marama was satisfied her plan had worked. Aroha and the women would be safe from further raids on the pā. Without their warriors to defend them, they didn't stand a chance. Even when they did return, there was no way of knowing the martial strength of these people or if Tau could defend the village. Her future didn't look as hopeful, but she was alive and while she drew breath, there was always a chance of survival. In time, Starman would return. She was sure he and the old Chief would come for her if she couldn't escape or win her freedom. Until then, she would do her best to hold the spark of life growing in her womb. Rongo wasted no time in regrouping his men for the trip home. Marama would always walk in the middle of the group, sleep in a circle of men with two guards to keep watch at night. Nobody was to touch her or speak with her without his permission. He didn't want to risk any of his men being beguiled and losing their captive.

They travelled south-west, trekking through the forest, crossing streams, hunting on the way and only stopping to rest before it became dark. As the stars and moon emerged, Marama noted their path. She committed her observations to memory by repeating them over and over until sleep overwhelmed her. If the time came to escape, she would be able to find her way home. Her captives fed her, gave her water, and Rongo checked her abrasions regularly. They allowed her to bathe and take care of herself. It would be best if she arrived in their village looking presentable. Nice enough to please their chief, but strange enough to satisfy the vision of the tohunga. Marama was meticulous with her grooming.

To protect her unborn son, she must seduce their chief swiftly. Not a task she was looking forward to, but she couldn't simply escape and return home. They would know where to look for her, undoing all her work to lead them away from her people. The warriors were impressed with their prisoner. Marama marched all day like a man, never complained, ate and drank what she was given and didn't try to escape or talk to them. She barely seemed to stir the forest around her as she walked, and the warriors doubted they would have found her without Rongo. There was something aloof and other-worldly about her. They tried not to stare at her unusual eyes but stole furtive glances. For a woman, she was tall, muscular, but also shapely. Maturity and bearing her children had transformed her once boyish body into a curvy, statuesque figure. Some of the warriors were quite fascinated by her. It wasn't that she was beautiful, but she was intriguing, with a presence, was meant for their chief and therefore unattainable. Rongo observed his men, noticing the effect Marama had on them and noted who was becoming infatuated. He wished he had brought the younger tohunga with him to perform the appropriate karakia. Still, he hadn't, so he did his best spiritually. Rongo started taking one of the night watches, ensuring his trusted second in command, Nikau, was awake when he was asleep. The woman was oblivious to his men, kept to herself, for which he was grateful. He knew of men doing the craziest things where women were concerned, and this woman was clever enough to outsmart them if she wanted to. Rongo warned men individually to remain vigilant. After three days of marching, they reached a fast-flowing river. The warriors retrieved two canoes hidden in the undergrowth on their journey outward. Marama travelled in Rongo's canoe, with her hands and feet bound, secured to the stern and Rongo. Nikau placed a woven flax basket over her head so she couldn't see where they were going.

The lack of sight made no difference to Marama. She could feel the direction of the sun on her skin, the movement of the canoe as they navigated through smaller tributaries against the flow of the water. Methodically, Marama stored the travel details in her memory. Healers and spirit guides were required to recall enormous quantities of information, so retaining the directions when she had nothing else to do wasn't an issue for her. The men caught fish out of the freshwater, and Marama was surprised at the delicacy of their flesh, inventing recipes in her head she thought would complement the flavour. She didn't know if she would be expected or permitted to cook food when they reached their destination. However, her interest in cooking delicious food had sharpened with the passing years, and it gave her something familiar to occupy her thoughts.

Marama worried about Aroha, although she knew she could find her way home. She fretted about Kai, even though his whale brother and both his fathers watched over him. It was a waste of time worrying about Starman; she knew how capable and content he was at sea. Perhaps it was they who should be worrying about her, she thought with a sigh. Nani had been extremely reserved when she reassured Marama the boys would return home. What Nani hadn't said was whether Marama and her unborn son would be there to greet them. While travelling, Marama didn't dream or feel Nani with her. She had asked the ancestors to safeguard the voyagers and aid the hunting trip as Tau requested. The presence of unknown spirits around her was intense. They were weaving the designs of a destiny she didn't yet comprehend but found herself playing a part in it. She needed to be patient, bide her time until she could connect with the spirits and seek their guidance. Until then, she sent silent prayers to her namesake in the night sky, supplications to the Earth Mother for her children's safety, and gave thanks to the God of the forest for sustenance and shelter.

Marama felt the motion of the canoe change and the men

around her paddling with a slightly altered rhythm. When Marama still cradled Kai in her womb, his paternal great-grandfather bestowed a gift of knowledge from Starman's ancestors upon him. During the exchange, knowledge flowed through her as the conduit, and Marama gained an enhanced set of skills in navigation and voyaging. She guessed they entered a larger body of water without the fast-flowing current. Her spiritual senses rippled as an unknown presence flowed through her, brushing against her being with a probing curiosity before withdrawing with a sigh of grudging acceptance. The encounter jangled her nerves. Were the spirits here so different, she wondered?

Marama was unsurprised when the canoe scraped upon stones as they landed on the pebbled beach of a tranquil lake. They removed her head covering, and Marama blinked as she took in the picturesque vista surrounding her. The forest grew verdant to the water's edge, abundant with ferns, in myriad shades of green. It was breathtaking, and in other circumstances she would have been delighted to be here. Rongo motioned for her to wash, drink, and tidy herself up. Four of the men took a trail through the trees with Marama sandwiched between them while the remaining men secured the canoes. They wended their way uphill, on the well-worn path from the lake, before pausing to place the woven basket over her head.

"We have reached the sacred waters and settlement of Rotowhā. You will need to wear this again. We want everyone to be as surprised as we were by your appearance. Tread carefully Marama, so you don't fall and hurt yourself. You might hear voices as soon as we are approaching our destination, our home," said Rongo. Marama just nodded her ascent and focused her attention down so she could see her feet. It slowed progress substantially but allowed the other men to catch up so they would all be part of the returning, successful, search party. They hoped to find favour with their fickle chief, although some were concerned for Marama, including Rongo. Marama could smell smoke and the aroma of cooking in the air long before they met the first villagers.

A group of excited children ran ahead to bring the news of their arrival. The families of the returning men clustered around the front of the *wharenui* (large communal building), eager to see their loved ones and the person with them. Their chief emerged from inside the building as soon as he saw Rongo. Tohunga Piri had announced in the morning that the woman would come to them. The Chief didn't want to get his hopes up too much, but he couldn't suppress the excitement building inside him. Finally, he might achieve his dream of having a son, and he hoped, a worthy successor. Rongo sent the runners to ask for a formal welcome as they brought a stranger into their midst. This action told the chief Rongo believed he had found the right woman, adding to the air of anticipation. His second in command was cautious by nature, and Rongo wouldn't dare to disappoint him. By now, most of the village gathered to witness the welcome and see what was creating such a fuss. The crowd included a sour collection of faces that belonged to the chief's women. The *karanga* (welcome) rang out, loud and clear on a still afternoon. Rongo and his men sombrely approached the chief with Marama positioned in front of them. The chief and tohunga Piri both greeted Rongo formally with a *hongi* (touching noses). Rongo looked at both men and cleared his throat to speak.

"Chief, your tohunga instructed us to seek a foreign woman, one who would be special enough, to bear the son you desire. By the will and the guidance of our tīpuna, the Gods revealed her to us. We give you Marama, moon daughter," he announced. Rongo pulled off the woven head covering and withdrew the cloak from her shoulders with a flourish. There was a collective gasp from the watching crowd before people covered their mouths as they tried to avoid incurring the ire of the chief or causing offence. The chief was speechless. She was more than he expected. Marama was spectacularly foreign but not unattractive. The tohunga thanked their tīpuna for sending such a clear message and delivering the answer to the chief's prayers.

Approaching Marama carefully, the chief looked more closely

at her eyes, for he had never seen green eyes, golden skin or red-gold hair. He took her face in his hand, turning her head from side to side to look at her better before his face split in a wide toothy grin. Marama looked right at him and didn't flinch when he touched her. Instead, she stood tall and proud. Outwardly, nothing betrayed the pounding of her heart. She could ill afford to be intimidated or dominated by this man, who his warriors feared. A fine-looking man, the chief was imposing in size, well-muscled, and his face was attractive with slightly slanted eyes. Still, he looked as hard and unyielding as stone. He was pleased with her, a relief to his men and Marama. The head woman of the chief's household, his first love Roimata, hurled barbs at Marama from her eyes. Marama perceived the intense hatred directed at her and turned to lock eyes with her new enemy. The woman paled. Breaking the eye contact, Roimata stalked to the chief's whare so he wouldn't witness her rage.

Chapter 2

The chief declared they would feast in the evening and sent everyone off to prepare for the festivities. With formalities over, Rangi embraced his cousin and friend Rongo rather than greeting his premier warrior. He congratulated the men on a successful expedition and granted them rewards or favours they desired. The men left content with their payment but cast a few sympathetic or forlorn glances in Marama's direction.

"Chief, I am nervous about taking Marama to your whare. Roimata already hates her, and I fear your women will not welcome her," warned Rongo.

"There is a private whare for her. I don't want to waste more time; I have waited long enough for my son," said the chief. "I will escort her there myself."

"Chief, this woman knew she was going to have your son when we captured her. She introduced herself as 'the mother you seek' when we first spoke. I think you are truly favoured," said Rongo sincerely. The chief smiled at his cousin to show his appreciation for the information. He would discuss it with Piri later after he inspected his strange new woman.

Marama waited while the men spoke, momentarily left in the company of the tohunga who was making gestures with his hands to the spirit world. She had learned this language from her Nani. The tohunga asked his ancestors to find a woman who could bear the chief a worthy son. Her son would be someone of great significance, and she would also play a pivotal role in the future of Rotowhā. Piri turned to her suddenly. He felt she was standing right behind him, but she was still where Rongo left her. Watching him, he thought, although she was now looking at the ground. It wasn't polite to be watching him surreptitiously, but she needed to understand what was driving the events around her. Piri decided he would have to get to know her to discover why he sensed her presence while communing with the next world.

The chief walked towards Marama, cut the bonds that secured her hands, and gestured for her to follow. He stopped in front of a small whare and motioned for her to enter before him. Marama turned to face him, and he grabbed her roughly. She completely surprised him by crushing her lips against his and moulding her body against his.

"We will conceive our son today," she murmured in his ear before biting it playfully. A shiver of pleasure ran through his body at her willing aggression. He kneaded her buttocks as he thrust his groin against her. They both pulled at each other's garments, and he was captivated by her full creamy breasts. Dark nipples stood out in contrast, demanding his attention. He felt his need for her growing, an ache as he pushed her to the ground. Before he knew it, she straddled him with a gasp, and rode him roughly. It was more than he could stand, and he climaxed quickly, crying out at the intensity of his release. Marama lay on top of him, panting slightly from the exertion but pleased she had taken his seed into her. Her son would be his son, in his eyes. She breathed a sigh of relief, but to his ears, it was a sigh of pleasure.

"The son I will bear will be special. A warrior, a leader and favoured by the Gods," Marama whispered. Many years before, her Nani confided that men see what they want to see and hear what they want to hear. A wise observation, proven to be accurate on many occasions. The chief stilled as he mulled over the words she had spoken in a prophetic tone. They were words that echoed the message of his tohunga. The wheels of his destiny were turning in his favour, and he was excited by this foreign woman. Marama aroused him in a manner he hadn't experienced for a long time. Sex had become a functional chore, rather than a pleasure, as he tried to breed an heir. The women in his whare who constantly vied for his attention or favour only disappointed him. He rolled over, pinning her beneath him and found himself gazing into the green depths of her eyes. Marama was an enigma to him. She wasn't afraid and desired their son as much as he did. The chief stroked her hair. It's texture silky to his touch, and the colour seemed to shift as he moved it with his fingers. Marama watched his face closely as he inspected her. He was curious about everything that made her different, and he seemed to have enjoyed her body. She had closed her eyes and pretended he was Starman, to fool her unwilling body into participating in the seduction, but he didn't know that. Having a son meant the world to him, and at the moment, she enjoyed his goodwill as the future mother. Finally, he pulled away and dressed, so Marama covered herself as well, not quite sure what else to do.

"As my *whakapapa* (genealogy) explained, my name is Rangi. I am chief and a direct descendant of Maui. Your arrival pleases me. I will have one of the women bring you food and water," he said brusquely, turning to go.

"Wait, please. I am the mother. My role is to nurture and protect this child with my life. Your women will not welcome the child they couldn't give you or me. I think it might best if I prepare my own food." Marama dropped her eyes in submission and to give him time to consider her request. It didn't escape Rangi that Rongo had already warned him Roimata hated Marama. He doubted any of the women would welcome an outsider who could produce an heir when they hadn't. Nodding to Marama to let her know he understood her concern, he left to speak with Rongo about organising her food. She had a point. It pleased him to know she noticed her reception and was smart enough to vocalise what she needed. To be a chief, you needed the ability to think intelligently, so two observant parents were advantageous for his son.

"I will organise a guard until you settle in and have somebody take you to bathe," Rangi said as he left. Rongo and the men who captured Marama, volunteered to feed and guard her for the moment. She was used to them, and some familiar faces might comfort her. Rongo would send his young daughter to her, for some female companionship, and to take her to bathe. After their bath she could show Marama the village while the guard watched them.

The girl peeked into the whare, her eyes round and glowing with the responsibility her father had given her. She was excited as well to be able to look at the stranger more closely.

"Hello, I am Rongo's daughter Huia, welcome to Rotowhā," she said shyly. "My father has sent me to bring you *kai* (food) and to take you to the bathing pools afterwards. Look, I have some soap plant for washing." Huia held out her hand and smiled, revealing a gap-toothed grin.

"Come in, Huia. I am Marama and thank you for bringing food. I'm hungry after the journey," she said, rubbing her belly. Huia was pleased to be invited in, began laying out the food neatly and chattering about what it was. Marama's heart longed for Aroha. She looked down at the food so Huia wouldn't notice the moisture that sprang to her eyes, but the girl was observant, and a concerned frown wrinkled her brow.

"I'm sorry," said Huia quietly, "I should have asked you what kai you like."

"It's not the kai Huia. Thank you for your kindness. I was thinking of the people of my village and how much I miss them. Just feeling sorry for myself, I suppose," said Marama with a wry grin.

"That seems normal. If someone took me to live somewhere else, I would miss my whānau terribly, especially my father. He looks pretty fierce, but he is kind and plays with us at night when we are home. I think we should be friends so you won't feel so alone here," she said with a hopeful smile.

"I would like that very much," said Marama, smiling back at Huia, a drop of fresh water in a parched mouth. Huia told Marama about her home while she ate her meal. Who was who and what sort of things they did. Huia explained she would show Marama around after they bathed, and one of her father's warriors would look out for them so people wouldn't scare her. Huia felt a great deal of pride in being chosen by her father. It meant he trusted her, and she was sure her friends would be envious. She cleared up after the meal diligently, asking Marama to wait until she came back, and reassured her a guard was just outside. When Huia returned, she held her hand out to Marama. They walked hand-in-hand through the village as if they had been friends for life, to the hot mineral pool set aside for the women to bathe. People looked at them, surprised to see Rongo had allowed his precious daughter to accompany the strange woman. They tried not to stare but failed miserably. Marama was, once again, a curiosity. She saw the steam rising from the water, and Marama hesitated by the pool, sniffed the air. Huia giggled as she waded into the water, enjoying the enveloping warmth and gesturing for Marama to come in. Marama made sure the guard had his back turned before she shed her garment and followed Huia into the pool.

The warm steamy bath felt delicious on her skin and soothed her aching muscles. Huia showed her how to make lather with the plant leaves and offered Marama some to wash. Marama cleansed her body thoroughly before turning her attention to her hair, giving it a good scrub. Huia asked if she could touch Marama's hair and help her wash it, so Marama acquiesced, submitting to the ministrations of her new friend. The collection of scrapes and cuts she sustained during the chase and on the journey to Rotowhā smarted at first, but in general, improved after the bath. It was warm beside the pool, so they sat on the rocks to dry themselves properly, and Huia produced a wooden comb for their hair. She first showed Marama by combing out her hair and moved to comb Marama's hair for her.

"Where does the hot water come from?" Marama asked.

"It comes out of the ground, a gift from *Papatūānuku* (Earth Mother). Over time we have made a series of pools for cooking, bathing and washing, by moving rocks. Don't you have hot water where you live?" she asked, her eyes wide.

"No, we don't. We have to wash in cold water. When the weather is warm, it's perfect. But in the cooler months, nobody enjoys it, so people do become quite smelly," she said, wrinkling her nose. That made the girl giggle again but didn't sway her from her task of gently combing Marama's hair. The red-gold colour, and the silky texture of her hair, were fascinating to Huia.

"Do you think I could keep the strands of your hair that have come out in the comb," she asked innocently. "I think it's beautiful, and it seems a waste to throw it away." Marama nodded to the girl, quietly amused that the child just said what she was thinking. Huia finally put the comb away and let the guard know she was ready to show Marama around. The girl hoped Marama's hair would dry in the late afternoon sun if she took long enough. Marama paid close attention to her guide, eager to learn the settlement layout and where everyone lived. Huia must have had instructions from her father as she pointed out the chief's whare from a distance and gave it a wide berth. The chief, tohunga, wharenui and supply buildings were all in the centre. Rongo, his warriors and their families surrounded them. The rest of the Rotowhā settlement fanned out inside the palisades, with gates that could be lashed shut when they were under attack. Outside the perimeter, there were communal gardens, a place for butchering or plucking after hunting, a smoking hut for preserving supplies, an exercise area for the warriors, the pools, and a lookout rock with a commanding view over the lake. Above the village, there was an imposing cave where the tohunga and chief went to speak with the spirits. Huia explained it was *tapu* (forbidden) to everyone else. Marama cast a long glance up at the cave. The memory of the cave Starman found when they journeyed to Aotearoa flashed across her mind. She wondered if she would be able to hear or see the spirits of their ancestors. For now, they paused to look at the view and Huia was rewarded with the sun shining through Marama's now dry hair. Her mouth formed a little moue of appreciation. Huia's perception was that she was looking at a nymph or a Goddess for a moment. She grabbed Marama's hand again and steered her back to the village, reluctantly delivering her back to her whare as Huia had work to do before the festivities began. Before she left, she embraced Marama and gave her a happy smile.

"I know you are sad, but I really enjoyed spending time with you, and I know we will be good friends," she said earnestly. Marama hugged her back, agreed with her, and placed a motherly kiss on her forehead before Huia raced back to her whare. One friend was one better than no friends. A long time ago, she had been a loner until Tane befriended her. The prankster who went on to become her best friend, then her first love, before another vain and ambitious man killed him. An old familiar pain lanced Marama's heart when she thought of losing Tane. Nani once told her, her mother had resented being born a woman and Marama lamented she often felt the same way. Her Chief, the real chief, not Tau, valued the skills and abilities she possessed, but so few men did. Starman respected her as well, not unusual in his culture, he told her. First, Marama had been a prize, and now she was the vessel to produce a son. Not problems she would have faced if she were a man. Tau wasn't the leader his father was. He left the women and pā undefended, so here she was fulfilling somebody else's destiny. Enough self-pity for one day, she chastised herself. Take each breath, let your heart beat, think about what you say and survive. With her thoughts back in order, she lay down and slept. Secure because the guard would stop the chief's women from killing her in her sleep, for now.

A gentle cough from outside the whare woke Marama. As she blinked the sleep from her eyes, she sat up, and the tohunga called a greeting to her before entering. His hair was greying, and his face was covered in tā moko with different patterns to those of the warriors, telling spiritual stories. He had piercing pitch-black eyes. Alive with both intelligence and curiosity, they regarded her candidly.

"Our chief has asked me to prepare you for the feast this evening Marama. I have brought you appropriate garments, adornments, oils and a cloak. The chief doesn't want his son to be birthed by a captive, so tonight, we will adopt you into our tribe as his woman. During the ceremony, I will call on the ancestors to welcome you and the child you will conceive into our midst," he explained.

"We have conceived the child already," said Marama alarmed. "The chief didn't want to waste any time." The tohunga closed his eyes gently before they snapped open wide in surprise.

"Don't worry, the ancestors anticipated his arrival, and they welcome him. He will perform great deeds on behalf of his people. I can already feel his presence," he said, not bothering to hide his amazement. "Who are you, Marama, that I can feel your presence in the realm of the spirits?" he asked smoothly, looking her straight in the eye. Marama raised an eyebrow at him as she returned his stare. She considered how much information she wanted to share with him. Honesty always served her well, and she didn't want to risk offending him or be economical with the truth.

"I am Marama, moon daughter, healer and spirit guide of my people," she said.

"Do you speak with the spirits as a spirit guide?" he asked.

"Yes, sometimes I do. At other times they come to me in dreams, with messages."

Piri looked at her thoughtfully. He knew there was something spiritual about her, and now he knew why. The tohunga was keen to understand the extent of her abilities and how they compared to his own. Could they collaborate, and could he learn skills from her, Piri wondered? Would she be privy to his communication with his tīpuna? These were all questions that he would need to explore carefully.

"I will come another day, so we can discuss the spiritual world and the plans the ancestors weave outside our realm of existence," he said. "Now it is time for you to prepare yourself. Is there anything else that I can bring you to make a positive impression on your new people?" Marama asked him for some cold black coals from the fire; she wanted to outline her eyes for the theatrical effect. She would have to work hard to win the support of people, as she would need protection from the chief's women. Fortunately, she had earned the respect of Rongo and his men while they travelled. Sending his daughter to her showed others Rongo didn't consider her dangerous. Marama dressed in the new garments with care, noting that the weaving work was of high quality. The cloak was simple but pretty, decorated with exotic feathers. She made the black paste to outline her eyes, oiled her skin to highlight its golden colour and dressed her hair with braids hanging down each side of her face. Marama waited, meditating quietly to calm her nerves before the ceremony.

"Marama, I am sorry, I couldn't prevent this path, so warning you would have served no purpose. Your son may be born here, but you need to be vigilant. I fear this chief will challenge even your will. Save your enemy to achieve what you most desire," whispered Nani from a great distance. She remained still, repeating Nani's words over and over to commit the message to memory. Finally, the guard called to her that the tohunga was approaching, so it was time to go. Marama knew she had created the impact she wanted with her appearance as she stepped out of the whare. Both the guard and the tohunga stopped to stare at her for a moment. All her life, she had been different, a curiosity. One of the lessons she learned was to make it work to her advantage. Nani had ensured Marama understood the power of theatre. It had once saved their village from a brutal raid. She stood tall, proud, unique, and prepared to face her new people.

The tohunga was pleased. Marama understood how to create

an impression, and he thoroughly enjoyed the impact she made. When she walked behind him, into the crowd, it added to his reputation. The chief sat with Rongo, surrounded by his warriors. The chief's women were banished to sit at the back of the crowd. A painful punishment and slight that the tohunga feared would only fuel their resentment. The chief invited his tohunga to come forward and perform the ceremony to bind his new woman to their village and tribe. The tohunga sang of the ancestors' deeds, following the chief's whakapapa, deep into the past. At last, he called on their tīpuna to accept Marama to become a woman of the chief and their *hapu* (village/sub-tribe).

Marama stepped into the deep of night. The spirit world surrounded her, but no familiar voices spoke. Then the muted sound of whispering spirits filled her ears. Their whispering continued for a few moments, before silence rang.

"Marama, I am Kotuku, the great-grandfather of Rangi and Rongo. We have diverted your path and brought you here, so please be welcome. Once you helped to save your people, and unfortunately, we need you to save ours. Rangi is setting us on a path to extinction, and only Rongo can turn the tide. We beg your forgiveness but implore you to be true to yourself." Marama opened her eyes with a gasp to find Piri staring at her. Did he know of the exchange? She was on her knees, wind swirling, lifting her hair away from her face in all directions. The villagers gaped as the ancestors eddied, creating a wind tunnel on a calm evening and spoke to their tohunga of her welcome. When Marama's eyes flew open, lit green by the spirit world, people were startled and drew back. The chief stepped forward and pulled Marama to her feet, claiming her as his woman and one of his people. Piri completed the ceremony, thanked the spirits, and the chief triumphantly declared the feast could begin.

Marama sat with the tohunga, the chief and his warriors as Rongo selected food from their eating baskets for her. She was painfully aware that the women of the chief's household were seated as far away from her as possible, widening the void between them, as the chief publicly showed his displeasure with them. Marama's captors now guarded her to protect her from the hostility brewing against her. If all went well, it would be almost nine moons before her son was born. That was a long time. Escaping while she was pregnant was too risky, and she was going to need more than one tiny but lovely friend to watch her back. There was singing and dancing, so Marama listened to the words, watched the actions that told their stories, to learn as much as she could about these strangers. Their ancestors travelled to Aotearoa many generations ago, in a great canoe, led to this land by their chief. Over the years, they fought to maintain the rich fishing and hunting grounds that surrounded them through battle or forming alliances by exchanging family members to create blood ties. They worshipped the Gods who heard their prayers, providing them with bounty, and the ancestors who helped them navigate their spiritual waka through time. Tales of bravery, cunning, and winning love, abounded but all the stories told the deeds of men. It was as if women hadn't contributed to tribal life at all. When reciting whakapapa, they mentioned women because somebody had to give birth to all these wonderful men. Around her, Marama saw beautiful weaving, tapestry, and smelled delicious food cooking. Children worked or ran about the village, but the work of women wasn't acknowledged, let alone celebrated. She had thought Tau dismissive of the deeds of women, but here he would be an outstanding and enlightened gentleman. Life was going to be challenging. Marama was chewing these thoughts over when the chief announced to his men lasciviously that he wished to bed his new woman. He grabbed Marama's hand and led her back to the whare. Of course, he wouldn't be satisfied with her claim she already carried the son he desired; she was now his latest acquisition. In the afternoon she had seduced him to complete her deception. Marama would pay the price for that deception for many nights to come, but she couldn't afford to lose his favour either. She would remind herself if she weren't here, Aroha, the women and children she loved, would have come under attack. Marama could have lost the unborn son as well.

To her dismay, Rangi returned to her whare with alarming frequency and sometimes snored as he slept beside her. He wasn't a considerate lover. Rangi just satisfied his own needs in whatever way he saw fit unless Marama took control which he seemed to enjoy. It wasn't the sexual relationship she shared with Starman but a master with his servant, a status she struggled with daily.

They had only been back for a few days when Rangi despatched Rongo and a large contingent of warriors to inflict punishment on a hapu that failed to honour an agreement. The hapu traded whalebone each year from their chief's brother on the coast. They had agreed to share a portion of the bone annually. The hapu would receive fishing rights, and be protected by their larger near neighbours in return. They advised Rangi that this year, they hadn't received any of the valuable bone used for weapons, utensils and adornments. Rangi's scouts already knew the bone had arrived. The other chief traded their portion with distant tribes. As the relationship soured after their chief gave his daughter to Rangi, the other village might have formed a new alliance. The daughter was unhappy living with Rangi. While she was birthing Rangi's daughter, mother and child both died. Rangi sent them back unceremoniously to her parents – a bald insult. Rongo suggested they send a large delegation to speak with the errant chief and extract a more significant contribution of wealth than usual in compensation. Instead, his chief opted to stir his warriors for battle and demanded blood to deter any future dissent. Marama listened, watched the discussions and planning when she could, otherwise gleaning information from Huia, who heard all Rongo's conversations with her mother. She pondered if this action was what their tīpuna feared. Squabbles and battles were sometimes inevitable, but when warriors were injured or killed, it created a long-term conflict that stretched through generations, heaping bitterness upon bitterness with each fresh loss. Huia confided that her mother was worried her father could be walking into an ambush. It transpired that Huia's mother was correct.

Two other hapu forged a new alliance. Both had incurred the displeasure of Rangi as his demands on them increased. Rongo and his battle-hardened men won the day, anticipating the possibility of an ambush and subjugating the rebels, but all battles come at a price. Many of the men were injured and some quite seriously, including Rongo. The head tohunga and a younger man he was training went from man to man treating their wounds, issuing instructions to the women to heat water and fetch supplies they needed while they sought the aid of the ancestors. As Marama watched what they were doing, she noticed their healing skills were somewhat rudimentary compared to her own. Between herself and Nani, they found many new medicinal plants with valuable properties in Aotearoa. They also befriended a tohunga of great skill in another village, and in the spiritual world they spoke with a *kuia* (respected older woman) who boosted the depth of their knowledge. They had been like children, experimenting with this potion or that paste to test the properties and efficacy of what they made. The thought of her Nani always made her feel better, and she heard a spiritual echo - *hold on, help is coming.*

Marama kept herself busy preparing her meals, washing her garments, cleaning her whare, weaving, doing whatever manual chores she was given by anybody—gathering medicinal plants, when she walked with Huia and the guard. She hoped that she would be of more use once people became accustomed to her. Once her belly swelled, she supposed she would present less of a flight risk. Most of the warriors seemed to recover over the coming days, except one who died from loss of blood or infection. Not Rongo, however, who received a deep wound on his lower leg and foot. Huia was deeply upset that her father seemed to be getting worse, not better, and confided that she heard her mother weeping when she thought they were asleep. Marama questioned Huia on Rongo's condition. Her brow creased in a frown after Huia left, as she knew Rongo would die if he didn't receive appropriate treatment. Two days later, Huia's mother arrived at Marama's whare instead of her daughter.

"I have seen the Healers Mark on your hand, and Huia speaks of your skill. Please, can you save my man?" There was desperation in the woman's eyes. She knew that if her warrior husband lost his leg or perhaps his life, her family would be devastated. Nani's words to Marama, to save her enemy, rang in her ears, as did the plea of Kotuku.

"Yes, I can," Marama replied. "I, however, am a prisoner. A new sex slave, although officially I have been adopted. Your man captured me, so I imagine it is unlikely your chief would allow me to treat his best warrior. What about the old tohunga, can't he treat him?" She asked the question more gently as the woman flinched.

"He says his fate is in the hands of the Gods, and he prays for his life. I am a practical woman, who has grown to love the man I once scorned, and I believe the Gods have sent you to save him. But, unfortunately, nobody gives him much hope of recovering, and I can smell the decaying of his flesh like everybody else. If you were to save him, we would both owe you our lives, and you may need people to help you one day." Enemies surrounded Marama, she was pregnant, and the truth of the words reverberated in her mind making her frown in concentration. How to approach this she mused?

"I think you should share your belief first with the tohunga. Credit his prayers with my being here, the Healers Mark revealed to you, and enlist his support to plead your case with the chief. Then you should both go to your chief and tell him only he has the power to save your man's life by ordering me to treat him. You will have to convince them you are right and appeal to the ego of both men. I will need to do the same and allay their fears that I may inflict pain or exact revenge on my captor. So that you understand, the reason I told you I could save him is that he showed me kindness. Rongo offered me water, tended my hurts when nobody else thought to do so, and Huia loves him. That's not to say I won't value your help in the future; I already know how much I will need it." Marama saw the woman's eyes widen as she listened to her plan and how she spoke of exploiting the weaknesses of each man to win the opportunity of saving Rongo. She had never heard a woman express herself so plainly. No woman in this village would ever dare to do so. It only served to cement her belief in Marama's abilities and fuel a growing admiration.

"My name is Ngoi," she said.

"I am Marama, healer and spirit guide, not a captured womb for breeding sons," she smiled wryly. The two women regarded each other frankly. Circumstances brought them together, and desperation made them unlikely allies and underlying the respect, a tiny kernel of friendship was germinating. Ngoi didn't waste any time, and she went immediately to the tohunga. She thanked him effusively for his prayers, which the ancestors had answered when she saw Marama's Healers Mark. The tohunga agreed to speak to the chief with Ngoi, but he wanted to question Marama first. As a captive, they needed to exercise some caution with her. Ngoi said she agreed, and was grateful for his caution, but feared they were only offered one chance by the Gods to save Rongo's life.

The tohunga nodded his head in agreement. He had prayed to the Gods, asked his ancestors for two specific outcomes, a son for the chief and the life of their best warrior. The strange woman did seem to answer his prayers if she could deliver what they desired. He meditated to clear his mind before he went to question her. Best to understand her motivation for wanting to heal her captor. Piri called a greeting as he entered the whare where Marama was housed, by herself, so the chief could visit her whenever he wished. Determined to father the son he so desperately craved, the chief's frequent visits to the foreign woman's whare were causing much discontent with the other seven women in his household. Five of them produced only daughters, and two of them bore no children, including his first love who ran his whare.

The petty infighting and hostile environment of the chief's whare was well known in Rotowhā and beyond. The chief didn't value his women or treat them well, they were simply vessels that failed to give him a son, so he despised them. He only spoke to his first woman as they had risen to power together. Rangi thought it a shame Roimata was unable to bear his children. Parents disciplined their daughters by threatening to offer them to the chief as his next woman, but in truth, they promised them to other men when they were extremely young to try and prevent that outcome.

"I am Piri, the village tohunga," he said, introducing himself again very informally. Marama was, after all, a captive of no rank until she produced a son. She raised her eyes to him, and their colour struck him. He hadn't been close to her often, and he had never seen anyone else with green eyes. The tohunga ducked his head in greeting to avoid staring while he composed himself. It was he who received and shared the message from the ancestors. If the chief desired a son, he must seek an extraordinary woman, and she certainly was that. As she regarded him coolly, he felt the hairs on the back of his neck rising, his skin prickled as it often did when he spoke to his tīpuna, but the spirits he sensed around him were unfamiliar. His brows drew together in a frown, and he wondered if he had underestimated her again. He felt a spiritual power around her, even more than on the night of her adoption, and he berated himself for neglecting his duties.

"Greetings tohunga," Marama said. She had thought long and hard about concealing or revealing her abilities, as there were pros and cons for both. Increasing her worth in the village would increase her value, make her more important to keep. It could also mean she and the baby would receive better care than if she remained just a mother. Marama didn't know the tohunga and decided to proceed openly but remain alert. Nani's presence wrapped tightly around Marama's spiritual core.

"Ngoi tells me, you believe you can heal her man."

"I can save him," she stated.

"What intrigues me is why you would heal him. Why would you save the man who captured you?" he asked. Marama regarded him carefully, as his question seemed to be in earnest. He is the village spiritual guide; we are equals, but women are of little value in this village, she thought. Could she cut through the gender barriers that the men in the village had erected and win him over to support her?

"There are many reasons why I would save him. Firstly, I am a healer, gifted generations of knowledge and committed to helping those in need. When Rongo captured me, I was alone, hurt, hungry and thirsty. Your warrior tended my hurts, brought me water and fed me his left-over food. Although he captured me, he also treated me as a person. He is the only adult in this village to afford me any respect as a living being until today. His woman, who doesn't know me, begs me to save him. His children cry outside where he can't see their tears. His men provide food for his family and visit his whare frequently. I ask myself if this is a man who deserves to die? Or is this a good man, endowed with enough mana to inspire love and respect? What is more, your tipuna Kotuku has asked me to save him. It seems he has a pivotal role to play in the survival of your people, a fact I think you already know. My spirit guide also sent me a message 'to save my enemy'. You have asked for two important favours, and unfortunately for me, I am the answer to both. The son he wants so badly is already growing in my womb," she said with a shudder, recalling Rangi's sweaty, grunting body lying on top of her. Piri's face paled at the astuteness of her observations, her reasons and her knowledge of tribal affairs. She left him in no doubt that she was more than just an unusual prisoner who provided the chief with pleasure.

"I will speak to the chief with Ngoi, and if he agrees, I hope you can deliver. Saving Rongo's life is important to all of us." Piri turned on his heels and left the whare, shaking his head to clear it of the strange buzzing inside.

The tohunga found Ngoi outside, wearing a hopeful look and waiting for him.

"Come, we will go and petition our chief together. We need to approach this carefully. Rangi's mood is often erratic, but ask him, and I hope he will ask for my counsel," he said. Ngoi nodded in agreement, grateful that Marama had tutored her on how she should approach the chief. Rangi relied on Rongo heavily, but Marama was right, the decision must be his choice. Ngoi knew she must request this favour in just the right way.

The chief was busy sharpening his *pounamu* (greenstone/jade) *mere* (flat hand-held striking weapon) when they arrived. Rangi was humming to himself, so at least he was in a good mood. Since Marama had come, his temperament was much improved, a relief to many who dealt with him daily. Ngoi rarely spoke to the chief. Rongo kept his family in the background, where they would be safe. He was aware Rangi's lack of sons was a sensitive point when he had two strapping boys, blessed with his fighting prowess and their mother's good looks. The chief greeted the tohunga, who explained he brought Rongo's woman with an unusual petition for his consideration. Rangi continued stroking the blade of his weapon with a frown but suddenly turned to Ngoi and gestured for her to speak.

"My chief, you know that Rongo is gravely ill from his wound, and only you have the power to save him." Ngoi fell to her knees, clasping her hands together. "Your woman Marama is a healer. The Gods themselves revealed her Healers Mark to me after I implored them to intervene. Rongo captured her, so I doubt she will help him, but I know she can. Only you can make her save him, chief," she finished looking into his face with tears standing in her eyes. Rangi looked down at Ngoi, petite and pretty, she had been unimpressed when her father promised her to Rongo to ally with them. Lucky man, here was his woman begging him for a favour to save his life. He doubted any of his women would do the same. Perhaps Roimata once, but not since Marama arrived. He agreed with Ngoi that it was unlikely Marama would be eager to save the man who captured her.

"Aren't you concerned that Marama may decide to kill Rongo in revenge for capturing her?" he asked Ngoi.

"I am, but if we don't find a treatment for his wound, he will die anyway. Marama is going to bear you a son, we adopted her, and you are our chief so we must all submit to your will," said Ngoi emphatically. This pleased Rangi. Even though she was a woman, her conviction in his total authority reflected the thoughts of his people. Marama was his woman, and she would do whatever he told her to do. Rongo was his cousin and right-hand man, so he must make every effort to save his life. He wouldn't be easy to replace. Rangi nodded at Ngoi, turned to Piri, and asked him to bring Marama. Ngoi thanked Rangi, praising his compassion and wisdom, as she wiped tears from her cheeks. Her reaction confirmed Rangi's conviction that he made the right decision. He was also curious to know if Marama could heal Rongo, as he had seen the putrid, rotting wound himself and doubted he would ever recover. So far, his new woman had been full of surprises. Perhaps she possessed a useful talent as well. All the more reason to assert his authority and ensure he bent her to his will. Rangi decided he would make her treat Rongo, whether she wanted to or not. Piri and Marama arrived, so he put his mere down carefully.

"Show me your Healers Mark Marama," he said. Marama showed him the tā moko on the inside of her wrist, a mark that Ngoi recognised.

"Tell me what it means?" he asked.

"It means that I have completed training with a skilled practitioner, and I am adept in the art of healing," said Marama.

"Does this mark mean that you should heal people when they are sick?" Rangi asked silkily.

"Yes, yes it does," she said, bowing her head slightly. He smiled to himself because this was going to be easier than he thought.

"Good, I am pleased that you bring a skill to our home. Let us test how skilled you are. You will go now to Rongo's whare, with his woman Ngoi, and heal him. Do not fail me," he warned Marama. She bowed her head to indicate that she understood and followed behind Ngoi stiffly, looking resigned but unhappy. The tohunga watched them go, the objective neatly achieved. The chief made all the decisions, and he was pleased, totally unaware of how easily Ngoi had manipulated him. Piri reminded himself again not to underestimate Marama or Ngoi, for that matter. He told the chief he would go with the women to observe what Marama did. The chief asked him to return later with a report on the health of his first warrior.

Once they were out in the open, Marama asked Ngoi if they could go back to her whare to retrieve supplies for her examination of Rongo. Ngoi nodded, and they changed direction, the guard assigned to Marama trailing behind them. Marama carefully selected the remedies she needed. Fortunately, Rongo had captured her with her healing *kete* (woven bag) intact, but what she wanted was the treatment she had already prepared in a tightly covered basket.

"You are very clever," murmured Ngoi "thank you. Goodness, what is that awful smell?"

"It is part of the treatment I have been preparing. I'm sorry, it smells terrible, but it is efficacious. Let's go. We don't have much time," Marama said. As they entered Rongo and Ngoi's whare, Marama could smell that her assessment of his ailment was correct. He had gangrene. Ngoi sent the children to stay with relatives. As Rongo's condition deteriorated, they were becoming increasingly distressed by the thought of losing their beloved father. Rongo's ability to love and discipline his children simultaneously had been a pleasant surprise to Ngoi. A revelation that helped defrost the heart which froze as soon as she clapped eyes on him. Marama asked Ngoi to heat a large quantity of hot water and began examining Rongo. She wanted to cleanse the wound to see how much flesh was infected. His eyes opened as Marama sat next to him. Marama explained what she was doing, the three options open to him, and what she would do in a simple, straightforward manner. Ngoi came to sit on Rongo's other side. Piri entered the whare but stood at a distance to observe the treatment without interference. Marama completed a quick but thorough examination of Rongo's health before cleaning the wound. Fortunately, he was a strong man. Out of the basket, she removed maggots one by one from an evil-smelling piece of meat and dropped them into the wound.

"This is the only way to remove gangrenous flesh without cutting off the limb," she explained to Rongo and Ngoi. She needed to stay, monitor the maggots' progress, and remove them once they did their work. Marama also gave Rongo a pain potion to help him sleep through the treatment and broth to keep up his strength. She treated other wounds with antibacterial washes and ointment to prevent further infection in his body. Both Piri and Ngoi were impressed with Marama's calm efficiency. Neither of them had ever seen maggots used to treat wounds, and they supplemented her efforts with their prayers. Once Rongo drifted into sleep, the tohunga left to perform his other duties but promised Ngoi he would return in a few hours. "Thank you for your support, time and most of all your prayers, which have brought Marama to us. We are lucky to be blessed with a tohunga who cares for his people so much." Ngoi's words were sincere and cleverly chosen. Marama smiled inwardly, amused that Ngoi was a fast learner. She had just secured the ongoing support of the tohunga by attributing him the credit for Marama's presence. Piri departed feeling appreciated and loved.

"You are also clever Ngoi, and you are learning how to win the hearts and minds of men. I will ask your tīpuna and mine for assistance with Rongo's healing. My descent is from generations of highly respected women, spirit guides and healers. In my village, I perform the duties of a tohunga in the spiritual world and a healer in the practical world simultaneously. Your tīpuna wish for Rongo to live. It is they who have manipulated fate and brought me here at this time. Would you like to join me in asking for their assistance? As Rongo's woman, his only woman and the mother of his children, I believe it would be powerful," said Marama holding her hand out to Ngoi. Ngoi looked a little nervous, but as she looked at Rongo, fighting for his life, she placed her hand in Marama's and closed her eyes. The whispering spirits already surrounded Marama, and although she could feel Nani's presence as well as her great-grandmother, neither of them spoke. They were politely waiting for Kotuku, Rongo's ancestor.

"Thank you for following your heart and fulfilling your duties as a healer Marama," said Kotuku.

"Esteemed old one, the disease has been festering for some time, and I would have liked to treat him earlier. The remedy is in progress, but if Rongo is to retain his former skills as a warrior, I implore you to assist his weakening body. Around me are the spirits from my line of healers. I seek your permission to ask for their assistance, but in return, I would also ask a boon for the future of your people," she said. The whispering stopped. Marama knew she was taking a risk. The spirits didn't like making bargains or being manipulated by humans, but the boon was for the benefit of their people.

"An unusual request of the spirits, Marama, but then you are an unusual person. So what is it that you desire for our people?" asked Kotuku. Some of the ancestors muttered that her request wasn't appropriate, but Kotuku's curiosity was piqued.

"I would like to share my healing skills with some of the women of this village. Warriors need their wounds tended to, and children need help to be born into the world. People need nurturing, and your tohunga have many duties already. Knowledge is a gift I have always been encouraged to share," she said. Again there was silence for a time, followed by the murmur of many whispering voices talking at once. A concern for Marama, but she knew her ancestors were there for her protection. She waited patiently while a debate took place. Finally, Kotuku spoke to her again.

"Marama," he chuckled, *"you certainly know how to create excitement, even in the spirit world. A long time ago, a woman betrayed her man, our chief, to her father. This woman told her father of the sacred hunting and fishing spots, as well as the battle plans of her new iwi. Since that day, women have been assigned to more menial tasks, accorded lowly status, confined to the home and denied any claim on deeds of renown. Your request has stirred much emotion amongst us. We question if punishing all of our women, for many generations, for the misdeed of one woman from another tribe*

was and is the appropriate action. Perhaps it is time to make amends to our women, so we grant you your boon with our thanks. Rongo must be returned to full health to fulfil his destiny. So, we ask you and your tīpuna to assist us with our blessing and humble gratitude," he finished politely.

"Ngoi, can you hold one of Rongo's hands and mine," breathed Marama.

Marama knew her ancestors were marshalling Rongo's tīpuna to help them repair his body. The women both tingled, warmth and energy flowing through them. Marama knew what was happening, but Ngoi had never functioned as a conduit before, so the spiritual energy inspired a feeling of divine ecstasy in her. When they opened their eyes, Ngoi found that she was crying but didn't entirely understand why. She looked to Marama, overwhelmed by a sense of positivity that everything was going to be okay. Marama smiled back at her, squeezing Ngoi's hand in encouragement just as Piri returned, drawn to the swarming presence of his ancestors. He could still feel them, and he immediately regretted leaving, as he would probably never know what transpired. While Marama perceived she had been in the spirit world for a short time, and Ngoi believed they had just joined hands, actually hours had elapsed. Marama rose to check on Rongo's wound and was delighted to find the maggots were bloated, performing their duties well. The wound appeared shallower than before as if they repaired the flesh from the inside out. Marama smiled and gave thanks to the spirits who aided Rongo's body. She moved her hands in the flowing gestures Nani had taught her. Piri frowned as he realised Marama was also able to speak with the spirits in this sacred language. The tohunga and spirit guide locked eyes in mutual acknowledgement of her skill. Marama cleansed Rongo's wounds and repeated the examination before announcing to Ngoi that she was hungry. Ngoi realises she is starving and thirsty, having not eaten anything since the early morning.

"Where are my manners," said Ngoi jumping up. "I will fetch

us something to eat." She scurried off to Rongo's sister's, where she knew they were smoking fish and cooking a meal, returning a few minutes later with two woven baskets heaped with food. Ngoi was ravenous. It felt like she hadn't eaten for a week, so she stuffed food in her mouth as she poured them some water. Marama was used to the energy burn of the spirit world, so she wasn't surprised that Ngoi was famished, and Piri also looked amused. Halfway through her meal, Ngoi brought her hand to her mouth self-consciously, as the need for sustenance gave way to awareness of what she was doing.

"Healing is hungry work, Ngoi," Marama said, continuing to shovel her food into her mouth at a rapid rate. Piri looked from one woman to another, surprised to observe that they were becoming friends. Was that a good outcome or not, he wondered with a slight frown? Then Kotuku spoke to him.

"This is a good result. It is what we want. We wish for Marama to share her healing knowledge with the women, starting with Ngoi and Huia. A new age is dawning for our women." The message wasn't the cryptic riddle of words his ancestors typically delivered to him but a direct instruction, so Piri immediately responded.

"It will be done." Piri glanced at Marama, who was engrossed in eating and approached Rongo to see how he was faring. Much to his surprise, Rongo's complexion had improved, his breathing less laboured, the rank odour diminished, and the injury looked remarkably better. He suppressed an inward shudder as he regarded the fattening maggots inside the wound but had to admit, they were highly effective. When he looked up, Marama was watching him with a grin.

"The first time I saw the maggots in a wound, I thought my grandmother intended to kill her patient. Two days later, I was astonished to see he was recovering. Thank you as well, because this healing wouldn't have been so effective without the help of your tīpuna. They wish to see Rongo return to being the robust man he has always been. It appears he has an important role to fulfil."

"They see more in you than the mother of our chief's son. Our ancestors want you to share your healing knowledge with our women, starting with Ngoi and Huia. How do you feel about being given that task?" he asked, expecting resistance from her. Ngoi looked up from her food, startled by the conversation and surprised their ancestors mentioned her and Huia.

"In my culture, only the selfish try to hold skills and knowledge exclusively. To do so is to invite the wrath of the Gods, who impart gifts for the good of many. I will share the knowledge of healing with your women, and it is my honour to do so," Marama said solemnly, inclining her head in acceptance. Her words couldn't have rattled Piri more. He was slightly taken aback by how often she surprised him. It was only a few days since she arrived amongst them, and he was unaccustomed to being wrong so often. Piri left the women to go directly to the chief and report on the progress of Rongo's treatment. Ngoi regarded Marama for a few moments while she picked at her remaining food. She desperately wanted to ask Marama about what she experienced this afternoon but didn't know how to broach the subject with her.

"As an apprentice healer Ngoi, you may ask me any questions to improve your knowledge, and I expect you to do so," said Marama sternly. Ngoi was startled again, and she wondered if Marama read her mind.

"How did you know what I was thinking?" she asked breathlessly.

"I didn't read your mind, Ngoi. You chew your lip when you are worrying and wrinkle your brow when you are thinking. Today you experienced for the first time how it feels to be a conduit for the work of the spirits, without any training or prior warning of what that would entail. You did exceptionally well, and I attribute that to the love you feel for Rongo. Love is a pure emotion. When the spirits flow through you, you feel an ecstasy that is so difficult to describe. The depth of the feeling is unlike anything we experience in this world." Ngoi looked thoughtful, so Marama shared the story Kotuku told her. Why women in Rotowhā were assigned such lowly status, and how the spirits wished to make amends.

"We are going to learn, from you, how to heal people?" asked Ngoi.

"That is the favour I asked of your tīpuna, but it is only the beginning of righting a wrong that has continued for generations." Marama moved to the fire, where water was warming, and she began preparing a herbal drink to restore her and Ngoi's energy. While they sipped on the brew, Marama explained what she was doing when she examined Rongo in the morning. She experienced a sharp pang of loss as she recalled giving Starman his first lesson in diagnosis in what felt like a different lifetime. Ngoi did ask lots of questions, and before long, they moved to Rongo's side to put the theory into practice. His eyes fluttered open as Ngoi was tending his minor wounds. A few heartbeats later, his vision filled with her smiling face, a balm to his tormented dreams. Marama examined his eyes, explaining to Ngoi how they should react to light. Smelled his breath, seeking to understand what was happening in his stomach and deciding what to feed him if he could take food. Ngoi hung on every word as she wasn't just an attentive pupil, but a woman trying to save the man she loved and the father of her children. Marama stressed to Ngoi that she must always hold the enthusiasm, her dedication, as the people she would treat in the future would be equally beloved to their whānau. Empathy and compassion were just as critical in a healer as skill. Rongo seemed to comprehend that there was a lesson in progress, and he looked from Ngoi to Marama, wondering if he inhabited another disturbing dream. Whatever had occurred improved his clarity of mind, and if he wasn't mistaken, he was lying on his back in his whare.

"Rongo, how are you?" Ngoi asked. "Can you understand me, my love?" Rongo gave a faint nod which was enough to bring tears of joy to Ngoi's eyes. Marama explained it would be helpful for his body if he could eat something, even if he didn't feel like it. Rongo nodded again, so Marama passed Ngoi the broth they prepared earlier. The soup was thick with sweet *kumara* (sweet potato), but the meat broth had been simmering for a couple of days now, full of dissolved bones, greens and the nutrients he needed. As Ngoi dribbled small amounts of the soup into Rongo's mouth, followed by a sip of water and sleeping potion, Marama told him what was happening to his body. She included details of the inside out spiritual healing by his tīpuna through herself and Ngoi. She lifted one of the fat maggots from his foot to show him, telling Rongo they had almost finished their work.

"The gangrene will soon be gone. There is a lot to do for you to attain optimal health again. My newly appointed apprentice healers Ngoi and Huia will be taking care of you for a while yet." Rongo's brows lifted as he looked at Ngoi, who nodded and smiled at him, her eyes twinkling with excitement.

"A message delivered by your ancestor Kotuku to myself and your tohunga means I will train the women of your village in healing. Ngoi and Huia were selected to commence training first." Rongo looked from one woman to another in disbelief. "No, this isn't a dream," said Marama, "but that's enough information for now. I will be showing Ngoi how to prepare a sleeping drink so your body will have the healing rest it desperately needs. We will also be cleansing your wounds and applying salves to prevent infection, just as we did this morning. Do you have any questions before sleep claims you again?" she asked. He shook his head slightly and squeezed Ngoi's hand.

"I love you," he mouthed to Ngoi before turning to Marama and croaking, "thank you." Then he closed his heavy eyes again as sleep enfolded him in gentle arms.

"I notice you are always honest with Rongo, informing him what is going on. Is that important to the healing process?" asked Ngoi. Marama thought carefully about how best to explain her straightforward manner when treating people.

"As a healer, you learn to read people and understand what it is that they need. Rongo, for example, is a man of intelligence.

He will comprehend the information we are giving him, and that knowledge will lessen his anxiety. Worry is counterproductive to the healing process, as is feeling out of control or helpless. To achieve the best result, we need to banish any unhelpful emotions. Circumstances can vary a lot. For example, when I was young, still learning my craft, I once helped my grandmother deliver a baby when the birth was complicated. The mother was already distressed, in pain, exhausted, and the baby was coming early. It would have only upset her further to know what was happening and what we needed to do. On that occasion, we didn't give her much information at all, just instructions for what we needed her to do to get the baby out quickly. Many layers of knowledge are involved in healing, and the wairua of each person is unique. That is one of the things I love most about being a healer, each person is different, and you are challenged on each occasion to find the best treatment that you can." Marama was already enjoying speaking about healing. Answering Ngoi's questions allowed her to return to some of the lessons she learned long ago. Ngoi's reaction convinced Marama that teaching her craft in this village would improve her skills as a tutor. When she returned to Aroha and her other apprentices, she hoped they would benefit from her experience. Marama gave silent thanks to the Gods for their wisdom, mercy, and the opportunity to make friends. The two women passed several hours in productive companionship, discussing treatment, potions, herb lore and watching the ponderous progress of the gluttonous maggots.

Chapter 3

Piri delivered his report to the chief. To Rangi, it sounded like they were making positive progress, and he was curious to see how Rongo fared. After eating and making plans for the fishing tomorrow with his men, he would visit Rongo's whare. He found the message from Kotuku somewhat strange, but it was hardly necessary to interpret such explicit instruction. When he thought about it, he could see the benefits of having more healers available to treat his men's wounds when they returned from battle. He had already lost one warrior, and Rongo hadn't recovered yet. Rangi had more important duties for his tohunga to perform than delivering babies and treating children's ailments. That work was far better suited to the women, so perhaps his ancestors were correct. He would prevent further dissent amongst the lesser villages, which meant more fighting, so he was already drilling his men. It would be helpful if Rongo were able to return to his duties soon. Rongo was second to the chief in battle prowess, and he led the men well, which enabled Rangi to split his forces with confidence.

The Gods were indeed showing him their favour. He would soon put the disappointment of so many inadequate women behind him and return some in disgrace to their people. The chief realised what a nuisance they were in his whare. After his son was born, the child and Marama would move in while the others moved out. Perhaps he would keep a few of his favourites, but he would visit them rather than have women and his wailing daughters underfoot. Rongo's life was much more attractive with his one devoted woman than his nest of problems. He would have to decide what to do with Roimata.

Once they had been young and fancied themselves in love. They dreamed and schemed together about how he would become the supreme chief of the area, with their sons following in his footsteps. The beautiful daughter of a chief, he fought to win Roimata for himself, shared all of his dreams with her. When he did become the chief, and she didn't produce any children, however, he was obliged to look elsewhere. Over the years, she ran his whare, keeping his other women busy and still came to him when he wanted her, but they weren't close anymore. He sighed in frustration. Give him a ferocious battle any day over these annoying domestic issues. Rangi commanded Piri to continue his prayers for Rongo's recovery before dismissing him. He went to eat, refusing to acknowledge or speak to any of his women. They shrank from him sulkily, not daring to stir his anger.

It was late when the chief arrived at Rongo's whare. Ngoi bowed her head as he entered, offering him a seat, food and refreshment, so he accepted a hot drink. He turned his focus to Marama and asked her how his cousin was faring. Marama gave him a thorough clinical report and gestured for him to come and see. She was about to remove the voracious maggots from his wound. The chief noticed the stench had dissipated, and the whare now smelt of aromatic herbs. Rongo's colour had returned while he slept soundly. Rangi peered at the wound, now free from gangrene but home to a family of industrious, bloated maggots. Like the other villagers, the chief had never seen this treatment, and he was impressed with Marama's skill so far. Rongo's other wounds were treated and appeared to be healing well. A lucky man in many ways. Rangi was certain Rongo would die. He watched Marama as she showed Ngoi how to remove the maggots and check the flesh of the wound to make sure there was no remaining gangrene.

"If there is any left, we will replace one of the maggots for a few minutes." Ngoi nodded, scrutinising the inside of the wound, determined not to miss anything and risk it becoming infected again. "It's a fine balance between ensuring the gangrene is all gone and not letting the maggots eat away too much good flesh, which would inhibit the speed of recovery." Marama carefully replaced the maggots into their woven basket with some food, just in case they needed them again. Rangi observed her focus, the confidence with which she spoke, and the practised ease of her movements as she treated Rongo. They were similar to those of a warrior who practised with his weapons until action and reaction became second nature.

"The worst is over, but if you want your warrior back to full health, his body will require ongoing care." Marama lowered her eyes. He grabbed her face with his right hand, turning it up so he could look into her eyes. Rangi found he never tired of looking at them. They, like their owner, fascinated him.

"You have pleased me with your work here, Marama. Come, you can return later and check on Rongo," he said as he gestured for her to leave with him. Ngoi and Marama both looked swiftly at the ground. Marama lowered her eyes so he wouldn't see the annoyance in them. Frustration, even after she pleased him by saving his cousin, he still intended to visit her whare. Ngoi kept her eyes down so he wouldn't see the sympathy she felt for Marama, who described herself as a slave for breeding sons. She was acutely aware that the man she loved was recovering because Marama chose to save him. In return, there seemed little she could do for Marama, who the chief constantly selected to share his mat. As they left the whare, a tear escaped the corner of Ngoi's eye. That could have been her fate also, but Rongo never forced himself on her. He treated her with nothing but kindness and dignity, even though she was rude, unwelcoming, often insulting.

Eventually, Ngoi became aware many other women were vying for Rongo's attention and wanted to be his woman. As second in command to a paramount chief, he was well respected. Although ugly to look at, she was horrified to discover he had no shortage of sexual partners.

Ngoi spoke to her mother when she visited regarding her disappointment at being given to such an ugly man. She also expressed dismay to her mother that he shared his affections with half the available women in Aotearoa. Her mother laughed at her pretty but naive daughter and asked her what she intended to do about it. She advised Ngoi that she should remain aloof if she wished to share their whare with several other women. One of his other women would eventually produce some children, possibly a son, and her status as his first woman would diminish. If she didn't want that to happen, she needed to seduce the man with her charms. Ngoi still resisted, sulking for some time about how unfair life was, lamenting she had neither a handsome chief nor warrior.

Then Rongo started to spend more time out of their whare, eating with other people or visiting neighbouring villages. He didn't always come home at night, and while he was still polite, he appeared to have lost interest in her. During a feast, Ngoi noticed the same woman kept choosing Rongo to dance with her. They were having a lovely time together, and he was overly attentive to the flirtatious little fantail, who pulled him ever closer to the edge of the forest. Ngoi experienced a searing stab of jealousy as she realised her man was being stolen away, right in front of her, how embarrassing.

The situation galvanised her into action. She marched up to a handsome youth and practically dragged him up to dance. Ngoi knew she was a graceful dancer, prettier than many of the women in the village, and she flipped her beautiful long hair while smiling brightly to show off her perfect teeth. That had been enough to bring Rongo to her side. He wasted no time in sending the youth packing and claiming his woman. She initiated their sexual relationship, and Rongo took the time to drive her inexperienced body mad. Rongo was patient, loving, able to do things to her that she had never dreamed of. In the dark, she could pretend he was as beautiful as she wanted. The memories made her smile to herself, and she brushed the tear away, but her sympathy for Marama remained like a pebble in her throat. The village women talked among themselves, and while the chief's women were always cautious not to speak ill of him, their bruises, tears, and sour faces were difficult to hide. Ngoi now understood how lucky she was to be matched with Rongo and not the handsome chief. She needed to repay Marama for saving her whānau, but where the chief was concerned, she had no power at all. Or did she, Ngoi mused? Today Marama called on the spirits to help Rongo, so she would implore her tīpuna to help Marama. She spent the rest of the night until Marama returned in fervent prayer and supplication. Ngoi was determined to help their saviour in any way she could.

The days flew by as Marama began to teach Ngoi and Huia the rudimentary skills of healing. They practised on Rongo, who seemed to flourished under the tender care of the people he loved. The rest of the whānau returned to the whare, relieved that their father was recovering and intensely curious about Marama. They failed miserably in their attempts not to stare at her. Ngoi chastised them so often that Marama invited the children to examine her eyes, feel her hair as Huia had done, to keep the peace.

Piri came to check on progress every day, and the chief would come by to see his cousin before summoning Marama to her whare. Now that Rongo was recovering, he could see that Ngoi was troubled and concerned for Marama, who often sported the trademark bruises of the chief's women. He noticed Marama was stoic and didn't cower or shrink away from Rangi, so he remained captivated by her. Like Ngoi, Rongo knew he and his family owed Marama an enormous debt. He knew he was dying before Marama came to treat him. Sometimes he awoke with Ngoi snuggled beside him, and he pinched himself to make sure he was alive. If that miracle wasn't enough, the ancestors chose Ngoi and Huia to learn healing skills from Marama, and they had spoken directly to Piri. Rongo felt proud that the ancestors selected his whānau for this task. He was especially pleased for Ngoi, who came from a tribe where women were skilled and held in great esteem. Her mother was a highly skilled weaver, acclaimed storyteller, and her father was a renowned tā moko artist who worshipped the ground her mother walked on.

Rongo met Ngoi's parents while he was on a trade mission for Rangi, seeking to acquire valuable pounamu and wood to fashion the weapons they needed. He liked Ngoi's parents from the moment he met them. They were assigned to take care of him by their chief, who desired some of the obsidian and whalebone Rongo had to trade. Rongo was impressed by their knowledge, openness, humour and good nature. When he first saw Ngoi from a distance, he completely lost his heart to her. Rongo had never wanted anything in his life as much as he desired her. He confessed to Ngoi's parents that he would be leaving his heart in their village, and they had both laughed heartily, telling him he could have her!

They tried to dissuade him from making an offer for her hand. Apparently under her pretty exterior, she was haughty, messy, ungrateful, too clever for own her good and lacked a refined sense of humour. They loved her, of course, she was their third daughter, but her credentials as a woman for a man of his standing weren't impressive. Initially, Rongo assumed his unhandsome appearance was the reason they discouraged him. As his mission was nearing an end, they both told him – decisions were made together, not just by her father – that if he was serious about Ngoi, he should return for her the following year. They hoped another year would allow her to mature and her attitude to improve. It was a vain hope by her parents. Rongo, however, applied his patience and cunning to win Ngoi, rather than taking her by force when he brought her home. He travelled a lot and observed the softer nature of women who loved or liked their man. A keen observer, Rongo noticed the increased productivity of villages that acknowledged and encouraged the women to contribute to communal life. In some villages, a couple seemed to govern together, or make decisions together, just as Ngoi's parents did. He had also seen women speaking at gatherings. Rongo shared his observations, but Rangi dismissed his stories with a laugh and said he preferred women on his mat where they were useful. Rongo made a concerted effort to include Ngoi in the decision making for their whare and whānau, as he knew this was what she expected. Ngoi's mind was quick, Huia's even more so. They were both well suited to learning a skill that would provide them with duties outside the home, and a chance to serve their people, perhaps earn some respect. He observed Marama teaching them in his whare. She was patient, instructive but also exacting, having them repeat information and testing their learning consistently. Marama had told them she would be doing this when they both agreed to start the training. A healer who chose the wrong remedy, or administered an incorrect dose, could inadvertently kill a patient. Huia's eyes grew wide in horror, but Ngoi just nodded and said she understood. Watching them blossom under Marama's tutelage seemed to ease the pains in his leg and battered body. It meant they soon learned how to deal with patients who believe they have recovered more than they have. Ngoi was quite firm with him, but Huia, who Rongo adored, painted horrible pictures for him of what would happen to her when he lost his leg or died. Guiltily, he would return to his prescribed rest.

With Rongo on the mend, Marama asked Ngoi to let the other women know they could come to speak with them or send their children if they had minor ailments. The story of Rongo's miraculous recovery and the words of Kotuku raced through the village, fuelling the women's curiosity. They brought their children whether they were ill or not. It was an excellent introduction to the broader world of healing for Ngoi and Huia, who were already able to dispense simple herbal remedies for sores, stomach aches, and difficulty sleeping. It all took place under the watchful eye of

Marama, who was cautious about allowing people time to become familiar with her. Young children were drawn to Marama, and she played with the ones whose mothers' permitted them to approach her. It was slow progress but progress nonetheless. While Ngoi chatted to the women, she fed them information about how Marama missed her young daughter, delivered all the babies in her own and the surrounding villages, essentially drumming up some future business so she and Huia could learn more. Marama thought Kotuku had chosen wisely, as Ngoi and Huia could think for themselves. Huia also told her peers about the maggots, washes, and potions that saved her father. She had inherited her grandmother's story-telling ability, and her audience cringed and pulled faces as her story unfolded. The next day, there was a trickle of people with more severe ailments. Chesty coughs, arthritis pains, a sprained ankle, a baby with a horrible rash, and two pregnant women arrived for treatment. They worked together all morning, taking turns to stay with Rongo and help entertain him.

When they all returned to the whare, Marama explained that they would need to replenish their supplies. It would also be an opportunity for her to show them how to harvest the plants and herbs they would need. She asked Ngoi if Piri could tell them where to find what they needed. Ngoi set off to ask him. Marama was still loosely guarded, and they would have an escort when they left the pā. The chief had no desire to lose the son Marama was carrying. Piri arrived and offered to accompany them as he needed to replenish some of his supplies. He was intrigued to see how Marama used the plants she asked for, as he didn't know of any medicinal properties for some of them.

They set off with Piri leading the way, and were able to find most of the plants Marama wanted or something similar. She showed Ngoi and Huia which part of the plant to collect - bark, leaves, seeds, berries, flowers, how to pick them and store them. Marama explained as she went what they would be doing with each part - drying it, boiling it, pounding it into a paste, keeping it in a dry place and giving a brief report on the most common uses for each item. It was a lot of information to take in, but Marama reassured them that she would go over the information time and time again until they could harvest and repeat it all back to her. Piri hoped that if he ever became ill, Marama would be there to treat him as her knowledge was astounding. They were all busily harvesting *mānuka* (Leptospermum scoparium) leaves when Marama noticed a group of fungus, which she picked and dropped into her leaf pocket. She would look at them more closely later. They were drawing near to the hot water stream, and Marama heard the tohunga call her name.

"Here, Marama! The *kawakawa* (piper excelsum) grows here close to the warmth of the stream, where my grandmother planted them for my father. I also use the leaves and seeds for many things. What do you use them for?" he asked. Marama began reciting a long list of uses from teas to washes for the skin, toothaches, chasing away insects. She was grateful to have a supply of such a versatile plant and carefully showed her trainees all the parts they could use. They found a plant each as they didn't want to take all the leaves from one, and Piri also wanted a supply.

Marama was focused on harvesting seeds a little downstream from the others, and as she turned, expecting to find Piri or Ngoi behind her, she came face to face with Roimata. The woman ploughed her fist as hard as she could into Marama's puku. Marama cried out as the blow connected and the guard, who was loitering, distracted and bored with the plants, came running as did Piri. They both saw Roimata's hastily departing figure as she disappeared down the path. Roimata's hatred was bitter, and it drove the self-righteous passion of a woman scorned. Ngoi arrived breathless with her hand over her mouth, unable to believe Roimata had been so vicious as to punch a pregnant woman or try to harm an unborn child. Huia crouched down next to Marama and asked her to take deep breaths so she could to get some air into her body.

"Mama, help me examine Marama, please," said Huia as she shed a garment for Marama to sit on. Marama was still clutching her puku, but the colour was returning to her face.

"Show us where the pain is?" said Ngoi. "Can you sip some water yet?" Marama nodded and took a sip of the water. Huia uncovered the mark from Roimata's fist on Marama's puku. She and Ngoi hoped it would not have any effect on the tiny life inside Marama.

"I think I am just winded," said Marama. "The muscles in my puku are quite hard, and I tensed as soon as I saw her. Thank you, I am already starting to feel better." Piri bent down, concern written all over his face. His ancestors had laboured long and hard to bring this woman to them, to give their chief a son. He checked her eyes, which were as unusual as ever but seemed to be functioning normally. Hovering his hand above her belly without touching her, Piri closed his eyes, searching for the life he felt before. Still there, thank goodness. He didn't sense any distress when he called to his ancestors, only a whisper that the son would be born. The tohunga sighed in relief before turning to the guard and lambasting him as a useless imbecile who couldn't keep one pregnant woman safe. The guard bowed his head in shame. The tohunga's tongue was sharp, but he knew he deserved the harsh words. What cut the guard was letting Rongo down. Failing to protect the woman who brought Rongo back from certain death was unforgivable. Rongo had trusted him, and he didn't deserve his faith.

"I think that I can get up now. Ngoi will you help me?" asked Marama. Ngoi and Huia helped her to her feet, and she gave them both a smile. "Don't worry, the baby is still with me. He is a survivor. I think that's enough foraging for one day. Let's go back."

"When we get home, I need you to lie down for a while so we can put what we have learned into practice and ensure you and the baby are fine," said Ngoi with a stern look. Huia nodded her agreement with her mother, and they set off, with Marama ambling between them and the chastised guard so close behind that Ngoi peevishly scolded him not to tread on her feet.

Chapter 4

Piri went ahead, and as soon as he was out of sight of the women, he broke into a run. Roimata had almost succeeded in ruining the carefully woven strands of fate, so painstakingly drawn together by their tīpuna. Rangi would hunt her down and deal with her harshly. She had violated many of their customs with her actions. He dreaded telling his chief what transpired, but he knew he must do so before anybody else did. Roimata was most probably running to escape Rangi's wrath, and if she wasn't, she had a death wish. Piri arrived breathless at the warriors' practice area where Rangi was drilling the men today.

The warriors were unaccustomed to seeing their tohunga running. The chief immediately called his men to take a break, so he could find out what was so urgent that Piri had become a runner. When Piri asked the chief to have his warriors find Roimata urgently, and told him what she had done, Rangi let out a bloodcurdling scream of rage. He shouted at his men to find Roimata. Whoever returned her would have his thanks and favour. That galvanised all of his men, who quickly split into groups to search different areas. The chief was well known for his ill temperament and fickle moods, but this terrible anger was a tangible force, hanging in the atmosphere and turning his face a shade of purple. His men were anxious to leave his presence, and only the tohunga stood near Rangi, still panting.

"Are you sure that my son still lives?" the chief spat.

"I am positive chief, both the woman and I have confirmed that the boy is still in the womb. I can feel his presence, and the ancestors have let me know that he will be born. Marama has the abdominal muscles of a seasoned warrior, and she tensed reflexively as soon as she saw Roimata. The mark that was left was also high, so it is unlikely to have affected such a new life," he said.

"Why would Roimata do this to me when she knows how much I want a son?" he asked with deadly quiet in his voice.

"A rejected woman can be as unpredictable as a hungry shark and just as dangerous. She most probably feels that Marama has stolen you away from her, and the thought of losing you, of being replaced, has made her angry." Piri hoped to temper Rangi's fury with an obvious truth. The grunt he received in response made him doubt the explanation had any effect. "Where is Marama now? Is she safe?"

"She is returning to Rongo's whare with Ngoi and Huia. I have sent the men I encountered on the way to you, to guard her."

The chief nodded his thanks before grabbing his spear and hurling it ferociously at a target on a tree, venting another angry scream. It hit with such force that it remained vibrating back and forth for some time, and Piri prayed Rangi wouldn't ask him to retrieve it. The chief didn't tolerate disobedience, especially from his women, and he was trembling with fury.

"I once shared all my dreams with Roimata! I allowed her to run my whare, even though she produced no children, and this is how she repays me Piri," he said bitterly. The tohunga realised Rangi had no empathy for Roimata's point of view, so he wisely elected not to try and explain it again.

"She will need to atone for her deeds when we find her. Her actions are unacceptable. An insult to our Gods, tīpuna, and they can affect the *mauri* (life essence) of our hapu, wairua of us all. Roimata targeted the unborn child, and she has violated the *tapu* (protection) of a mother and your son," said the tohunga gravely.

"Roimata can pay with her blood," said Rangi, his voice deadly. Piri closed his eyes for a moment. Atonement should fit the action and as the baby still lived, having Roimata pay with her life was too much. Still, he knew better than to oppose his chief openly. To do so would only make him more determined to hold to his course. Blood didn't necessarily mean her life, so they might yet find a better solution to satisfy the chief. Rangi wouldn't determine Roimata's fate. *Korero* (discussion) to reach an acceptable justice included leaders, elders and whānau - this was their way.

Marama and her growing escort made their way slowly back to Rongo's whare. Ngoi and Huia fussed over her, making her lie down, fetching calming herbal drinks, elevating her feet until Marama laughed in amusement at their efforts. She commended them as they had learned quite a lot in a few days. Rongo awoke, looked across to see Marama lying in his whare being treated by his whānau, and he felt confused. Ngoi went to his side and gave him a brief explanation so he wouldn't worry, and he drifted back into sleep. There was a lot of activity in the village as the men searched every building to ensure Roimata hadn't hidden there.

"They are all looking for Roimata," said Ngoi with a frown.

"What will happen to her?" asked Marama.

"She will be subject to our justice. The chief will be angry. Rangi holds the highest rank. Your unborn child is tapu, *taonga* (a treasure) from Papatūānuku, and you were brought here by our tīpuna, so I cannot begin to speculate on how she will make amends for her actions. Roimata was also Rangi's first woman, his young love at one time so he will feel especially betrayed by her actions. What she did was unforgivable, extremely foolish when she knows Rangi better than most. But I hope her judgement will be fair, as is our custom, rather than making a brutal example of her." That was the closest Ngoi had ever come to criticising the chief out loud, and she admonished herself to guard her tongue more closely in future. Marama paled at her words but was feeling exhausted after the drama of the day, lulled by the relaxing herbs, and she soon drifted into sleep, feeling strangely safe in Rongo's whare with his women. Eventually, she awakened as the settlement erupted in a hive of activity around them. The warriors had captured Roimata.

People made their way to the wharenui to participate and witness the events of the unfolding scandal. The discussion was lively, and speculation was rife. It was the juiciest, most exciting happening to gossip over that had occurred in many moons. Worthy of stories, songs, poems and works of art depicting the events, the villagers' imaginations ran amok as their curiosity piqued feverishly. A runner left to advise Roimata's family of the scandal while she was still on the run. A large delegation of her whānau arrived in haste, with sombre faces, determined to settle the grievance with honour. They were thankful Marama hadn't lost the child, and they weren't engaged in battle with an angry, grieving Rangi. The strategic alliance Rangi and Roimata's match provided her village, meant it was approved wholeheartedly by her people. It also presented an opportunity for Roimata, a bright, beautiful, ambitious young woman, to be with the man she loved passionately.

All that was left of that blazing love now was cold ashes and bitterness. The price of reparation would be extremely high. As the offended father, Rangi would be demanding and bleed them dry, probably enjoying the process to assuage his infamous temper. However, he did have the moral high ground, and they had no idea what the child's mother would expect. Roimata's fit of jealous rage would cost her hapu dearly. She wouldn't be welcomed or loved in her former home, but her relatives all believed in fair justice. Nobody could afford to offend Papatūānuku so badly without making amends, and Rangi was an ally they could ill afford as an enemy. Rumours travelled to them, stories of Rangi's increasing ill-treatment of his women as they failed to produce the son he demanded. The whānau delegation carried a heavy burden of guilt. They should have intervened earlier to plead a case for better treatment of Roimata, the flower of a generation in their hapu, who deserved respect as his first woman. Instead, they had been afraid to risk angering Rangi, possibly losing their alliance, and they did nothing. The leaders wondered if they already offended Papatūānuku by allowing Roimata's humiliation and degrading treatment to continue unchecked. Roimata's mother, and their tohunga, believed that as a whānau, they had failed the girl. Perhaps they were right, and now they would all pay the price.

After the formal welcome, tohunga Piri conducted the first karakia before inviting the tohunga from Roimata's village to speak. To find an effective resolution, they both needed the support of their ancestors and the wisdom of the ages to guide them towards a middle path. The tohunga released Roimata from captivity into the care of her whānau. She was no longer Rangi's woman; he returned her in shame. Her whānau could have argued that as Roimata was Rangi's woman when she attacked Marama, he must also bear the responsibility for her actions. Prudently they chose not to. As Rangi was one of the people Roimata had offended and inflicted pain upon, they knew it would be unwise and possibly unsafe to point the finger of blame in his direction.

Marama sat quietly with Ngoi, behind Rangi. She bowed her head but focused intently on proceedings. The procedure was a new experience for Marama, very different from how they made decisions at home. She asked Ngoi to educate her on what to expect. Ngoi proved to be a diligent teacher, taking the time to explain the subtleties of the negotiations that would take place. What had already occurred couldn't be undone. The gathering and the korero would be focused on reparation, to restore and protect the honour of Roimata's hapu and to make amends to those affected by her deeds. To do this, they would offer the injured parties more than adequate compensation, seeking the goodwill of those in all three realms of existence. A challenging task for Roimata's people when she had offended Papatūānuku, which could affect all of the inhabitants of both villages. The parties focused on fruitful negotiations that would be especially pleasing to Papatūānuku and any tīpuna set on revenge. Rangi's anger, and his position in society, was especially dangerous. His warlike ancestors would answer to his righteous angst, and they would demand restitution. Ngoi asked Marama to think carefully about what Roimata's whānau could do for her, to make amends. As the mother of the child Roimata targeted, Marama would contribute her thoughts to the korero. She would have an opportunity to build wealth and standing for her unborn son. Roimata's whānau would be trying to anticipate what would please her. Ngoi hoped Rongo would be awake and lucid enough to offer Marama his thoughts on what she should expect or what to request. Marama petitioned the ancestors for guidance. Specifically, she consulted Kotuku, knowing the spirits of this village had brought her here.

Roimata's people brought such great wealth to offer, that they must have beggared their village. Rangi sat unflinching and stony-faced while Roimata's whanau lay one treasure after another at his feet. Some of the taonga had their own stories, names and had been in the family for generations. Offering such gifts to Rangi was an enormous mark of respect and commitment to reparation. The process was an intricate weaving of the physical and spiritual to seek approval and the appeasement of the offended parties in all realms. People gave speeches, sang chants, offered prayers to the Gods, and made frequent offerings to Earth Mother. If Papatūānuku ever turned her back on them, they would all be doomed.

Marama watched proceedings as a participant and as a student of etiquette and customs, fascinated by the elaborate ceremony of the occasion. Piri and the village leaders were delighted with what Roimata's people offered them, as the gifts exceeded their expectations. They would gain land, crops, hunting rights, access to artisans, and valuable, tangible treasures such as weapons, jewellery, carvings, canoes, cloaks, weaving, and preserved food. Only Rangi wasn't satisfied, and as the father of the unborn child, he had the right to ask for more. The leaders felt he was asserting his authority and possibly seeking to punish Roimata further, but it was up to Rangi to articulate what he wanted.

Piri was glad his eyes were closed when Rangi demanded Roimata's younger sister to replace her. The visiting tohunga was staring at him when he opened his eyes. Neither tohunga anticipated such a request, which wouldn't please any ancestors or Papatūānuku. Marama experienced an angry buzzing in her ears and shook her head to alleviate the distraction. The rest of the people were silent, apart from Roimata who finally broke down. Her shoulders heaved with silent sobs, hands covering her mouth in horror at the fate she had woven for her sister. Roimata's family couldn't refuse. To do so would bring further shame and represent a declaration of war. They were, however, permitted to negotiate. An approach had already been made and accepted for the younger sister's hand, so arranging a release would be delicate and take time. Roimata's whānau subtly suggested that Rangi should treat Roimata's sister with respect and dignity, befitting her rank. The negotiations poised on a precipice. Rangi set his jaw. His mouth a cruel, brutal, line and his eyes narrowed at the veiled implication he mistreated Roimata, which of course he had. Rangi didn't accept any responsibility for Roimata's actions. With such a self-absorbed nature, he apportioned all the blame to her. He did, however, acknowledge her family divested themselves of every scrap of wealth they possessed to make amends. In the end, he nodded his acceptance of the terms. Roimata's family breathed a sad but collective sigh of relief. They had discussed the possibility of Rangi demanding Roimata's life, perhaps offending Papatūānuku even further.

The quick thinking of their tohunga brought them some time and a little reassurance. Roimata's people only had to face the demands of the strange woman who was carrying Rangi's child. What Marama might ask of them was hotly debated as they tried to anticipate what she would desire. When the visiting tohunga had consulted their village mothers, they were unanimously outraged by Roimata's behaviour. It left him under no illusion that they should expect clemency or forgiveness from this quarter. Only the tohunga indicated he believed the woman Marama could surprise them.

"This woman wasn't born here, and there is no history of quarrels or struggles. She is deeply spiritual, and her connection to Papatūānuku, the elements of nature are strong. For one so young, she has lost much in her life that she loved. Perhaps I don't know exactly what she will ask for, but her nature runs in opposition to Rangi. Our tīpuna urge us to trust her."

It wasn't common for women within their tribe to speak in such a large public forum, but to Marama it was second nature, a skill learned under the leadership of her chief and the tutelage of Nani. She gave silent thanks that she was born during the life of a man she respected, loved and now considered her guardian. Speaking was a considered task, a privilege, but not daunting to her as she was confident in her oratory skill.

"I am Marama, the woman Roimata wished to harm. I am the mother of the son, not yet born, who will one day be chief." Marama paused here for effect as Nani taught her. She slowly panned sharp green eyes across the riveted faces of Roimata's relatives. They felt the hairs rise on their necks and arms, skin prickling and goose-bumping in reaction to something they couldn't see.

"The boy is much stronger than I knew, and he is unharmed. He has already passed the second trial for survival, which prepares him for the many challenges that await him in life. My body is strong, and it needs to be so, to hold him to my womb. I am also unharmed. Roimata is guilty of jealousy, indulging in spiteful behaviour, but she is also a victim of the bitter reverse-blade of love. I have thought long and hard, and there are several terms that I ask of you today." Marama paused again, looking each of them in the eye. The look was considered, weighty, more wise-old-owl than offended mother. Marama's likeness to her grandmother was uncanny at that moment as if Nani also gazed out through her eyes.

"I ask your hapu to swear an alliance in arms, an oath of fealty, in perpetuity, through any change of leadership, to the unborn son and his successors. You will welcome him as one of your own. Roimata, you will become his mother when he visits your village. You will nurture, feed and protect him with your life. He is now your son too." There were a few inhaled gasps, some shocked looks, and Roimata raised her tear-stained eyes in disbelief.

"In return for this, I will take Roimata's sister as my own and into my home. I do this to restore the goodwill of Papatūānuku, who fosters kinship and sisterhood amongst women. She has blessed me with her gift of children, and now she has also blessed Roimata. We give thanks to you, Papatūānuku, for your wisdom, your kindness, the shelter you give us all to make our homes." Marama closed her eyes, and her hands made the flowing moves of the spirit language as she thanked the ancestors for their inspirational thoughts.

The tohunga looked at each other pointedly. It was similar to the language the tohunga used, and Marama communed with the ancestors. Not just her own either, she also spoke with their ancestors. Rangi regarded Marama carefully. He was impressed with her demands, and he wished he had thought of them himself. She was clever. Now she would have control over Roimata's sister, cement her place as his first woman, and she had already secured their son's dominance over another hapu before he was born. Rangi hadn't thought of offending Papatūānuku when he asked for Roimata's sister, but he supposed his thoughts of beating her while breaking her in were unlikely to please. Still, the request had finally broken Roimata. It punished her whole family and brought them to their knees, at his mercy, where they belonged. He liked the prophetic way Marama spoke of their son and his destiny. Finally, he would have a worthy successor and create a dynasty that would last for generations to come. His ego purred with happiness, and he decided he needed to look after Marama better. Here was a woman worthy of his attention.

After the tension of the drama, followed by the protracted

negotiations, everybody was craving food and rest. Roimata's relatives were eager to depart for their home, but hospitality demanded the hosts feed them, and it would be impolite for them to leave immediately. Although the korero resolved the situation without violence, it wasn't a cheerful or comfortable meal for anybody. They departed in haste as soon as they could. Only the two tohunga spoke freely and exchanged a warm hongi before they took leave of each other. Tohunga existed in a class of their own, with one foot in each world guiding the living to the right path whenever they could, and the two men respected one another. Piri and his counterpart had developed a deep respect for Marama. Had she been a man, they would have welcomed her into their fraternity, but women didn't become tohunga. Sometimes they saw the future or were adept healers, but spiritual leadership was the domain of men. The tohunga agreed their tīpuna sent Marama for a particular reason, and the unborn son was a person of great significance to the survival of their tribe. They decided to share information they might receive over time that could benefit them both. This spirit of friendship didn't extend very far between the two groups.

The only other improved relationship, ironically, was between Roimata and Marama. The process had purged Roimata's hatred for Marama, and the thought of being a mother to the boy soothed her wounded heart and empty womb. She realised Marama signalled an intention to try and protect her sister, but in such a way that Rangi hadn't been offended. Her jealousy, the bitterness of Rangi's rejection, had blinded her to Marama's kindness and quick mind. Roimata had felt abandoned by her people in her heart, but she never meant for them to pay such a high price for her foolishness. Now she was free. When Rangi so spitefully asked for her sister, she saw past his external beauty and glimpsed the ugliness of his soul. Roimata asked herself how she could have been so stupid as to love him obsessively. As they prepared to leave, Roimata approached Marama tentatively.

"I am truly sorry Marama, for what I did," said Roimata

with tears in her eyes. "I will dedicate the rest of my life to Papatūānuku, and I will always watch over our son." Marama opened her arms and embraced Roimata as she shed tears on her shoulder.

"I am sorry too Roimata. A long time ago, I lost the man I loved, and I wanted to die." Then Marama whispered in her ear, "you will have children soon, with a true man who will worship you." Roimata searched Marama's face, found only sincerity and hope began to stir inside her that life would go on. That one embrace healed more wounds than the mountain of words that preceded it, and the spirits of Roimata's people lifted. They hoped the strange woman's son would possess her spirit, her qualities and that he would be a better chief than Rangi the Arrogant, for that was the name they called him in private.

Chapter 5

Marama reckoned she could sleep for a week and was surprised when Rangi escorted her to Rongo's whare himself. He asked Ngoi to look after her, Piri for karakia to protect her, and his general fussing caught her off guard. After Rangi departed, she raised an eyebrow at Ngoi, smothered a giggle before making a relaxing tea. Marama wanted to check on Rongo before she passed out. Rongo's face now looked healthy, his wound was healing better than she hoped, and the restorative sleep was working its magic. Ngoi was incandescent with love and the joy of knowing her man would live. He was a man worth saving, Marama thought as she sipped her tea and surrendered to the lethargy claiming her tired limbs. This baby was draining her more physically than the others had, but maybe it was because she was getting older.

True to his word, Rangi organised improved living arrangements for Marama. She was moved to a larger whare right next to Rongo and Ngoi. Marama would have company, Rongo's men's protection, and improved facilities and supplies for her healing work. Piri guarded her and the baby spiritually, but Rangi wanted him to learn about Marama's skills. His warriors were his power base, and he would do everything to keep the most valued men alive. Marama threw herself into teaching, and the healing work, to assuage the constant ache inside for her own family. She saw Aroha and Kai in so many of the children that she often succumbed to tears. Ngoi would hold her and comfort her when this happened. Marama also longed for her belly to pop out, so she looked like a beached whale. She sincerely hoped Rangi would flee her company to his other women. Her longing for her real love, Starman, was tormenting her. At night she would look up at the stars to try and guess which ones he could see, just to feel closer to him for a moment. Homesick, heart-sick and pathetic, she chastised herself in her head. It was no time to indulge in self-despair, or Rangi would crush her.

Rongo gradually returned to his energetic and robust self, much to the relief of his men who valued his excellent judgment and temperament. They had all travelled and fought together for a long time, sustaining few injuries among their group. They believed Rongo valued life so much he always planned meticulously and often took on the riskiest tasks himself due to his superior skills. Rongo's men were careful not to vocalise their opinion. They acted like buffoons so that the other warriors wouldn't take them seriously, and they knew Rongo was a more competent leader than their vicious chief.

Marama worked with Ngoi and Huia on their observation skills. They watched everyone and everything around them. Marama taught them that a healer needed to understand the people they treated, as sometimes their physical ailments were only symptoms of more significant issues that affected their wairua. For example, worry about a child, or a man going into a dangerous situation, often caused anxiety in their immediate family. Infidelity or incompatibility could affect couples' temperaments or actions. Preventative healing was about early intervention. Sometimes a good conversation during a shared task, such as the washing or food preparation, could be more effective than prescribing remedies later. As her pupils adored Rongo, Marama had them watch him going about his duties. They told Marama what they saw, and she supplemented their observations with her own. It was rewarding to see her pupils revelling in their studies as the depth of their admiration for Rongo expanded in new directions.

"Marama, what magic is it that you possess? You have turned my untidy, lazy little household into a well-trained waka crew all paddling in the same direction."

"Well, Rongo," laughed Marama, "I am sorry to say that you have revealed your true self to them. They just needed a good healer to lift their eyelids, to see a little better. Ngoi and Huia are some of the best pupils I have ever had, but you can't treat wounds in a messy whare unless you want your patients to die." She softened her comment with a wide grin.

"I'm glad you enjoy teaching them. Ngoi and Huia seem so happy even though there's a lot of extra work to do. Somehow they seem more content, more appreciated perhaps."

"As a woman, it is sometimes difficult to find fulfilling work that isn't cooking, cleaning, and raising children. Understand me, we enjoy all of those duties, but having a skill, a craft, and being empowered to make decisions can be uplifting for the spirit," said Marama thoughtfully. "My chief, where I am from, is the most humble, respectful man. He values me, my opinions, skills, and in return, I would follow him wherever he led me, without question." Marama's comment was wistful, and Rongo noticed her gazing off into space as if she was searching for something in the air.

Marama was the most unusual person Rongo had ever met. She had saved his life. His family adored her, and he wasn't sure how he would ever repay her. In return, he had delivered her to Rangi, not a very fair exchange in his opinion. Admittedly Marama's pregnancy put Rangi in a better mood, frame of mind, and he was less harsh with almost everyone around him. The women in Rangi's household still looked like they were going to a *tangi* (funeral) regularly. Rongo had recovered enough to supervise the men's training and they were in great shape, no longer sporting injuries or bruises from brutal sparring. When they did sustain an injury, the healers were on hand after drills to patch them up. Rongo also worked with Marama and Ngoi on the men's diet to improve their strength, stamina, reflexes, flexibility. Marama understood a lot about warrior training for a woman, and he hoped to meet the chief she loved so much one day but certainly not in battle. The effort they put in was yielding results, and the men were thriving, gaining skill and confidence, but Rongo needed to take care. He was acutely aware that his men were loyal to him, although they hid it well. He couldn't afford to foster loyalty to himself with all of Rangi's warriors. The problem was they feared Rangi but didn't love him or respect his decisions. Rongo didn't want to survive near-death only to fall foul of his cousin's temper or be sent into battle to die a convenient martyr. He needed to influence his cousin by planting seeds of ideas that Rangi could then claim as his own.

There were issues with the training, wellbeing, morale of the men, but the issue of his treatment of Marama and his women was pricklier. It would require careful thought. The ancestors may have guided Marama here, but physically he was responsible for bringing her to the village. At times Rongo regretted the role he had played in Marama's capture. The injuries Rangi's women sustained, which he now saw regularly, grated on his conscience and ingrained sense of decency. Rongo's respect for his cousin was eroding as his admiration for Marama grew. For the first time in his life, Rongo's loyalty to his chief became divided. As a leader of his people, he didn't always condone Rangi's behaviour. He thought becoming an expectant father of a son would return Rangi to the lively youth Rongo had loved as a brother, but it didn't. Rongo looked up to find Marama regarding him, a frown wrinkling her brow.

"You are a good man Rongo. We cannot always control the strands of flax held in the hands of another weaver, but we must have faith in the wisdom of our old ones." Marama lay her hand on his shoulder in a comforting gesture as she departed. His flesh warmed with a tingling sensation, leaving him wondering who she had been consulting in the air.

When her belly did pop out, even Marama was astounded, for

it was huge. Ngoi giggled so much she could barely speak and tears rolled down her face. It was Huia who gave her a gentle slap, telling her mother to stop. Marama had joined in the hysterics by this stage, and whenever one of them tried to stop, they would set each other off.

"You are both impossible," huffed Huia, who was waiting to examine Marama. Eventually, they managed to contain their laughter for long enough to wipe their eyes dry, and Huia gestured impatiently for Marama to lie down.

"I am sorry Huia, but my little man hasn't had much laughter in his life, and frankly, it's all your mother's fault," said Marama with mock severity. The comment made Ngoi snort, and she started laughing again.

"Out Mama," scolded Huia in her bossiest voice, "you are intolerable this morning!" So Ngoi left the whare, still stifling her laughter with one hand while Huia rolled her eyes.

"I know you warned us this would happen, but it is quite impressive," said Huia raising her brows. "May I feel your puku?" Marama nodded, doing her best to behave well for Huia, who took her healing studies extremely seriously. Huia probed around Marama's swollen belly before placing her ear against it to listen to Marama's breathing and then closing her eyes to listen to her heart beating. She examined Marama thoroughly, checked her eyes, ears, mouth, feeling her temperature under her armpits, asked about the colour of her urine, the consistency of her stool, how she was managing tasks and was Marama breathless. Huia asked pretty much everything Marama had ever taught her. Then Huia wanted to know what else she could check. By this time, Ngoi returned and observed so Huia wouldn't tell her to leave again. Marama had them both examine her back and posture. Pregnancy could sometimes cause extra strain on the spine as the baby grew, became heavy, and the mother's breasts enlarged, especially if they were lifting other small children as well. The purpose of such a thorough examination was to notice the changes that would occur over the coming months and find remedies while problems were minor. They nodded in understanding, and Marama experienced a surge of warmth towards them. She was in good hands.

While most people were astounded and amused to see the sudden change in Marama's physique, Rangi was delighted. Seeing his son growing so large was a tangible, physical step towards realising his long-held dream. Marama was dismayed he still arrived at her whare that evening, apparently more besotted with her than ever. Outwardly she always welcomed him, knowing it would be unwise to refuse his advances. He even stayed in her bed, stroking her belly and talking to the baby of all the lands they would conquer together. The tohunga rescued her, coughing discreetly, calling for Rangi as he strode towards the whare. The two men departed together, speaking as they walked. Marama heaved a sigh of relief, rose to find water to cleanse herself of Rangi's presence, and found an anxious Ngoi at her door with a steaming gourd of warm water.

"Thank you Ngoi. It's so kind of you to anticipate my needs. Now that I am a lumbering sealion, I probably shouldn't go scampering to the bathing pools in the dark," she said wryly.

"I know you hoped your puku would make you unattractive, but many men find it sexy. It makes them feel particularly virile, a manifestation of their masculinity, you might say," she said.

"At least he was more gentle than usual. His other needs may be satisfied elsewhere, I'm afraid." The two women looked at each other forlornly. They knew from the frequent ailments they treated that Rangi inflicted violence on his women regularly. Even worse, he seemed to enjoy inflicting pain which made him a dangerous and unpredictable lover. Marama counteracted him, as he also seemed to enjoy receiving pain, so she often treated him roughly, surprised him, or initiated sex spontaneously. She went out of her way to assert control. It worked most of the time, and when things weren't going her way, she employed the skills Starman taught her to bring proceedings to a swift end. Marama no longer tried to make herself look attractive, but the pregnancy gave her an inner glow. She saw Rangi for what he was, a powerful, violent, vain, selfish tyrant. All her children and her people were alive, well, safe, including her unborn child, but she couldn't stay here forever. Ngoi brought her friend some food, and a soothing drink, before returning to Rongo's arms to be comforted as she lamented her inability to help Marama. As the children snored gently, in whispered tones, the two concocted a plan to cool Rangi's ardour for Marama.

"Come cousin," gestured Rongo, "your men are drilling and want to impress their chief," he said with a grin. This pleased Rangi, as he wanted the men to seek his praise and approval. He was in an excellent mood today, for he had everything he wanted. People had mourned the passing of his father, who was a gifted warrior and born leader. Rangi's father had despaired, telling his son he was a worthless, spoiled brat - but Rangi swore he would surpass his father. People would sing songs about his conquests, and his son would continue his legacy. He didn't believe in his father's dream of uniting everyone as friends and family. It was he, Rangi, who was born with a warrior heart. His vision was to bring people under his dominion and rule over everyone in Aotearoa. A legacy of war, conquest and greatness that his sons would continue. The men moved in disciplined ranks and fell into sparring pairs with a variety of weapons. Their muscles rippled, their movements were supple, flowing, and they seemed tireless. Rangi clapped his cousin on the back in an uncharacteristic show of pleasure. He was glad Rongo recovered to achieve such an outstanding result with training his warriors. Rongo still carried a slight limp himself, but his mind found a way to transfer his weaponry skills more effectively as a result.

"A fine job you have done with my warriors Rongo. I will turn my thoughts to our next engagement, and we should unleash the fighting prowess of these men," he said with a wicked grin.

"Do you think we should consult Piri? I feel the same about such fine men, but after what happened with Roimata, I confess I am reluctant to leave your son unprotected Rangi. By now, knowledge of his importance will have travelled with Roimata's people." Rangi nodded sagely, as he valued the way Rongo thought of him first in all matters. It was a valid point that he made.

"Assuredly, cousin, I am meeting with the tohunga this afternoon to discuss bolstering the unborn son's protection. While I have every confidence in his mother, she is just a woman." He was meeting with Piri about something else, but no point in letting Rongo know he hadn't considered this. All his men needed to have confidence in him.

"A huge woman now cousin!" Rongo laughed heartily, seeing the pride in Rangi's eyes. "Ngoi fears the baby grows large quickly Rangi. She urges Marama to be careful with her activities if she wants to carry the child to full term. He will be eager to come out. It was the same with our second son, although he wasn't as big. I had to ban Ngoi from my bed, as I felt there was no longer room inside her for both of us. She wasn't happy with this initially, as she wanted to have sex all the time when she was pregnant. Ngoi cried, begged, tried to seduce me and even scratched me once," he rolled his eyes heavenward. "My beauty must have been irresistible," he chuckled, stroking his chin animatedly. Rongo's joke elicited a burst of laughter from Rangi. "Poor Marama, she knows these things, but you are more handsome than me cousin. I fear she will be unable to control her desire for you."

"You are right again Rongo. The woman is insatiable, practically throws herself at me as soon as I go to visit her." He loved that about her, and she aroused him with her desires. The most important thing to Rangi, though, was that Marama gave birth to a, healthy son. "I would be grateful if Ngoi is firmer with Marama cousin, on my authority, of course. I will play my part and rebuff her advances. I hadn't considered our passion might compromise the child. There are plenty of other women to keep me entertained, even if they annoy me at times." The truth was they all tried extremely hard to please him, but none of them intrigued or satisfied him the way Marama did. There was a young woman in a neighbouring village who had caught his eye, so perhaps it was time to pay them a friendly visit with a few of his younger warriors. He would leave Rongo with a large contingent of men to protect his family, and he would present him with a gift of some value for his loyalty, achievements and advice before he went.

When Rangi came to Marama's whare in the early evening, she remained seated with her weaving, greeted him politely and offered him food before lowering her eyes.

"How is our son faring today?" he asked.

"Our son is well and demands I eat all of the time to feed his growth," she smiled. "He also requires me to take the best care of him that I possibly can," she said contritely. Rangi lifted her chin to look into her eyes, which seemed a little misty, the green depths exquisitely beautiful under the shimmer of moisture. Ngoi had done her work well, and he was now battling his rush of desire for her. He stood abruptly, mumbling that he must see the tohunga, and bid Marama a hasty good night. Marama waited for a few moments, barely daring to breathe or move a muscle. Ngoi told her of the plan she and Rongo had come up with the previous evening. They were both slightly apprehensive that they were relying on Rongo's acting skills but discussed in depth how Marama should behave. Ngoi felt it would be safest not to tempt Rangi, and they settled on reluctant contrition as the best strategy. Marama was confident these days in her ability to create a believable perception in other people. Nani had taught her that people see what they want to see. If you portrayed the emotions they sought, your audience would make assumptions. The thought that brought on her tears was that she would be spending every night with a man she loathed if she failed. All she wanted was to daydream of the man and people she loved more than life itself. Ngoi experienced the thrill of danger but confided in Marama that it was exhilarating to be influencing events instead of just being dutiful. Marama remembered how she felt when the Chief had spoken to her directly for the first time and asked for her thoughts. From childhood to decision-maker, it started a journey for her, and she was eternally grateful for that. The price for her reprieve from Rangi's unwanted attentions would be treating the injuries of his other women, but the drive to protect her unborn child stiffened Marama's resolve. Rongo and Ngoi played a dangerous game to rescue her. They were good people, and she knew they would have a part to play in whatever their ancestors were planning. For now, she would enjoy the evening alone, spend time giving thanks, making offerings to Papatūānuku and give Huia some spiritual instruction, to allow Ngoi time with Rongo.

As the days trickled by, Marama's life fell into her new routine. Rongo continued to grow in strength as his remarkable recovery continued. Huia and Ngoi honed their healing skills while the life inside Marama blossomed. Ngoi took charge of Marama's pregnancy, manipulating Rangi in such a deferential way, he never even noticed. It made Marama smile inwardly with pride whenever she witnessed such an exchange. She was to be confined early. Ngoi convinced Rangi that his son's increasingly robust nature threatened to bring him into the world too soon. Rangi saw the violent movement of Marama's belly and felt the boy kick, so he agreed at once. Piri issued instructions to artisans to build Marama's birthing whare, and Rongo supervised the arrangements for her physical protection. Either Huia or Ngoi must remain with Marama at all times. It was common practice to isolate the mother and child for some time, even after the birth. The women would burn the whare down when they were declared healthy and returned to the village. For Marama, Ngoi and Huia, it was to be a holiday of sorts from their daily duties, and they were all looking forward to having some time apart from the other village inhabitants. They planned ceremonies, what they wanted to learn, would take turns preparing food to try and impress each other. Marama had insisted she only wanted Ngoi and Huia. She wouldn't risk anyone harming her child, and she insisted emphatically that Roimata's sister must not be anywhere near them until the boy was thriving. Rangi acquiesced readily. Marama rarely asked anything of him but had requested his tohunga weave protection around them. She wanted to ensure the boy was born with the favour of his tīpuna and the Gods, especially Papatūānuku, and so did Rangi.

Of course, Piri began preparations before Marama even arrived, but he included Rangi in some of his ceremonies. Piri wanted to reassure his chief, who was displaying all the signs of an anxious, expectant father. For all their sakes, the tohunga hoped the birth would take place without any drama, and the boy would be everything their tīpuna desired. The women retreated into a world of their own, and a lightness of being suffused them. With all the women from Rongo's household commandeered to look after Marama, Rangi ordered his women to take over the cooking, cleaning, washing and domestic duties for Rongo and his sons. It didn't take them long to discover the calm of Rongo's household, his kindness, or to appreciate his polite, helpful sons. Most of them went from their own home to Rangi's and assumed other families in this village would be the same as his. The women, reluctant to take on extra duties at first, began to enjoy taking care of Ngoi's men. No yelling or beatings and the whanau thanked them for their efforts. Food was praised by the man and boys, enjoyed heartily, and an atmosphere of joviality reigned in the evening. The pity they harboured for Ngoi, at having such an ugly man to share her mat, evaporated and was replaced by begrudging envy.

Marama examined herself regularly, showing Ngoi and Huia what she was doing.

"Here, Huia, place your hand here. You can feel his head today. When the time for his birth arrives, his head will turn down, and he will sit low in my puku, ready to engage in his quest for freedom," smiled Marama.

"What if he doesn't turn Marama?" Huia drew fine brows together in an expression of worry.

"You will do the same thing as I did when we delivered Kapu's baby. Your small hands are perfect for the job of reaching inside me, to find the umbilical cord, turn the baby so I can push him out," she said confidently. Huia still looked concerned.

"Don't forget that I will be able to tell you what to do, and I have delivered many babies in my lifetime. Most of them are easy for the healers as it is the mother who does the most work. Your mother, who has given birth to three children of her own, will also be beside us with her calm presence." Marama held out her arms to hug her young pupil, and Huia responded with a grin as she spread her arms around Marama's mammoth belly. Huia referred to the baby as her little brother in quite a proprietary way, which amused Ngoi and pleased Marama. Sometimes Marama ached to hold Kai, stroke Aroha's hair, feel Starman's familiar arms around her, be mothered by Ari, or sheltered by her Chief. When Ngoi arrived yesterday, she found tears streaming down Marama's face in an uncontrollable flood. Ngoi comforted her with the practised hands of a mother, but with a body flooded with raging hormones, Marama was inconsolable at the time. She often cried herself to sleep as she used to when the island invaders killed Tane.

Marama opened her eyes. She was seated beneath the shady green canopy of a *ponga* (Cyathea dealbata) tree, with a musical, tinkling stream flowing over the rocks below her. The scene was too perfect, and she felt no sensations, so she knew she was dreaming. It wasn't Nani who sat on the rock below her.

"Marama, we have spoken before. I am Manaia, your grand-mother's grandmother. Nani watches over your children. They are well, and she wants you to know this. That is not why I came. You need information. The ancestors here have conspired to bring you and your unborn son to this place. Rangi's mother deceived them and tainted their bloodline. He is not of their blood, and they are infuriated by his low-born behaviour. They want Rongo to lead their people, and you have been chosen to turn the tide to this destiny. They also practice their own deception. Your son is born to unite the people of this region. He will be an exceptional leader, and they seek to form bonds, claim a part of him, and restore the mana and vision of their people. The ancestors brought you here to complete this task. The women of Rongo's line, the true leader's maternal tīpuna,

also ask you to restore the balance, the reverence of Papatūānuku and women." Manaia fixed her timeless gaze on Marama's face sternly, and then she was gone. Marama returned to her deep sleep, enjoying a restful night with the child quietly content in her womb, but when she awoke, the dream replayed itself in her mind as she sat up with a start.

"Are you in pain, Marama?" Huia asked anxiously from her sleeping mat.

"No, Huia, I am fine. I had a vivid dream last night, and it spooked me when I awoke."

"Was it a spirit dream?" Huia propped herself up on her hands and was staring at Marama, goggle-eyed.

"Yes, it was," said Marama quietly. She couldn't lie to her first friend. "They are often cryptic, the spirit dreams, and I must ponder the meaning of the words that the ancient ones speak. Seek guidance to the true path." She shared this information with Huia so she wouldn't ask her about the dream.

"Huia, this must be our secret until I can unravel its meaning." Huia nodded her ascent, intrigued but feeling special to be privy to the knowledge of the dream. To her credit, she didn't pry, and Marama wondered if Huia sensed the presence of the spirits. It was unusual she asked the question. Perhaps she possessed some sensitivity or an affinity with the spiritual world. Marama spent most of the morning meditating while Huia bustled about the whare, fussing over preparing Marama's food. When Ngoi arrived, and Huia went off to do some chores, Marama decided to see if Ngoi knew much about Rangi and his mother.

"Ngoi, I need your help. I must understand more of Rangi's whakapapa if I am to instruct my son wisely. What do you know of Rangi's mother and the maternal line of ancestry?" Ngoi looked around nervously, even though she knew there was nobody else there, before turning to Marama conspiratorially.

"Rangi is very particular regarding anything said about his mother. I only know some of the rumours because I am from another village, and my mother is a storyteller." Again Ngoi glanced around nervously before beginning to speak in little more than a whisper.

"Rangi's mother, Atarangi, was a great beauty. Many men competed for her favour and her father's. Her father was a formidable warrior-chief, and Atarangi was raised as a *puhi* (virgin of high rank) to increase her value. People thought Atarangi's father intended to match her with Rangi's father, who grew in status, uniting the people of our area into a strong power base. An alliance was attractive to both chiefs." Ngoi paused again, even getting up to check around their whare before she continued, her face a little flushed.

"This is only hearsay and gossip Marama, I don't wish to speak ill of your son's father and my chief, but as you ask, I will tell you everything… because I owe you everything. Atarangi was loved, obsessively some say, by one of her cousins. They had been close since they were children, and he always volunteered to protect her. Before she came to this hapu to become the woman of Rangi's father, villagers whispered she was caught in a compromising situation with her cousin while he was supposed to be guarding her. Rangi's father never questioned the subject of her virginity publicly because the alliance was too valuable. The two most powerful men in the land quashed the rumours. When Atarangi became pregnant, then Rangi arrived so early, tongues waggled in private, and the gossip came to my mother's sharp ears. Again I stress that these are only rumours." Marama nodded her head in acknowledgement of Ngoi's discomfort and sense of fair play. "That wasn't the only rumour to plague the match. Some in this village say Rangi's father was privately infuriated that Atarangi wasn't the intact prize promised to him. To save face and the alliance, he always maintained that Atarangi was pure. But - others say, he sought solace in the arms of his brother's woman," Ngoi paused again uncomfortably, "and that Rongo is his son. I overheard my parents discussing this when Rongo first expressed an interest in me. They thought it would be hilarious if I, a third daughter of a carver and storyteller, accidentally captured the heart of a high-ranking chief's son." She clapped her hand over her mouth to suppress a laugh, and she flushed pink under her brown skin. "Some of the old people here claim Rongo's physical appearance is the manifestation of the ugly deeds of his real father and Atarangi's deception. Atarangi did everything in her power to ensure Rangi had the best of everything, and the people acknowledged him as the successor. She worked her magic on Rangi's father to bring him closer to her and held him enthralled. The warriors didn't train Rongo. Instead, he was dedicated to the kūmara by the tohunga and assigned to cultivate the earth. He is an exceptional grower of kūmara, it's true, but Rangi needed someone to spar with, and only his large, ugly cousin could give him a safe but worthy contest. The boys grew close as Rangi had no brothers and neither did Rongo. Atarangi's power grew, her skills with plants and herb-lore became legendary. People were scared of her Marama. If she found out anyone was spreading malicious gossip, they would become ill and die. Once Rangi became the chief and established his authority, she simply disappeared. Nobody dares to speak of these old whispers today. Certainly not to Rangi, who would cut their tongues out, or to Rongo who loved his parents." Marama sensed the threads gathering, weaving the past and the future together. She gazed into space, deep in thought, following the strands of intertwining fate. Could these old rumours be the source of Kotuku and Manaia's messages? It certainly sounded like a plausible explanation. Marama was less sure of how she was going to turn events towards a new destiny. In this village, dominated by men, the likelihood of her influencing who led them seemed highly unlikely. She needed to give it some thought. The words and intent were clear, but they did not reveal a path to Marama and Piri.

"Thank you Ngoi, for confiding in me. I value your trust and won't repeat the information, I swear. I only seek to understand the hearts of the people who came before us so that I may choose the best path for my son." Ngoi was pleased by her reassurance as she tried to avoid gossip and spreading rumours but was acutely aware that others in the village thrived on creating drama. The women passed the rest of the morning in peaceful meditation before Marama put aside future riddles to work on lessons. Huia was studying hard, committing more to memory than Ngoi was able to. She also displayed an aptitude for experiments, fuelled by her insatiable curiosity to understand what worked and what didn't. The older women were delighted with her progress, and Huia blushed and basked in the warmth of their praise. They were both gaining in confidence, not just in their abilities but in themselves. Marama thanked the ancestors and Papatūānuku for blessing her with two such apt pupils to restore balance.

The unborn son was late coming into the world in Marama's estimation, but he was perfectly on time to the rest of the village. Whether by accident or intervention by other powers, she wouldn't suffer the same rumours as Atarangi. Her waters broke, the labour pains began in the night, and Huia woke Ngoi. The trainees had prepared everything for the birth many days in advance. All Marama needed to do was concentrate on her breathing and assist her son in making his entrance. Ngoi and Huia were both excited, Huia especially, as she would cut the umbilical cord once the baby was out. Marama talked her assistants through what they should be checking for as she continued to breathe in and out deeply. The baby's head was in the correct position, she was dilating by increasing amounts, her contractions were becoming closer together, and they bathed Marama's pink, perspiring face with cool water. Marama had informed them that she wished to give birth to the baby while on her feet. As the child was so large, she needed the assistance of his weight to help him out. Having two children already meant Marama was far more relaxed, and her body was well-prepared for the birth. The child was also robust. He would push himself out into the soft cushion and waiting arms of his adopted aunt and cousin. The delivery went precisely to plan, and he was the unborn son no more. He screwed up his red face, drew breath and gave a lusty cry as Ngoi and Huia shed tears of relief and joy.

Ngoi had sent a message to Rongo to advise Rangi and Piri that Marama was in labour. They attended to their post-birth duties with ruthless efficiency, cleaned the baby and Marama with warm water Huia fetched from the bathing pool. When the baby was resting clean and content in Marama's arms, Ngoi left them in Huia's care and departed to bring the good news to the chief. Rongo and Piri remained with Rangi, who alternately paced up and down, then sharpened his weapons, before returning to pacing again. The tohunga made a calming drink for Rangi, which he sipped on distractedly, in between his pacing. Ngoi moved through the men guarding the perimeter around the hut, smiling and nodding at them to let them know all was well as she made her way to Rangi's whare. When she entered the whare, she beamed a huge smile at Rangi, to convey that everything was perfect, before she even spoke.

"My chief, you have a powerful and healthy son," she said confidently, bowing her head in deference. Rangi's face lit up in relief and with pride at the news. Rongo and Piri congratulated him jovially, slapping his back and singing an impromptu lullaby for children in their deep voices, making Rangi laugh. Ngoi couldn't remember the last time she saw Rangi laugh because he was happy, and neither could anyone else.

Marama regarded her beautiful, new, not-so-little baby boy with wonder. He looked like Starman already. Tall, dark, extremely handsome, and she was smitten. Judging by the gaga look on Huia's face, she wasn't the only one, so she made room on her mat for Huia to snuggle in to hold the baby with her. She couldn't bear to let him go just yet. Together, she and this little man had found a path to bring him into this world. His life was already inextricably woven into the fabric of the whenua, and these people, where he was born. Huia was also part of his story, his journey to life. She was his doting cousin no matter whether they shared a blood tie or not, and that was a lovely outcome. Marama drew Huia close, kissed her head and thanked her for the perfect job, delivering the baby. The baby wanted to suckle, and Marama hoped her milk would come quickly to keep him satisfied. Ngoi returned swiftly to let Marama know Rangi was elated by the news. He had even laughed at Rongo and Piri's impromptu antics. Marama suspected fatherhood wouldn't soften him as it did with some men, but she could still hope for a positive change. Ngoi clucked and fussed over the baby so much, Marama realised she would have to relinquish him for a few moments to his aunt. The baby was surrounded by love, warmth and whānau, even though he wasn't in his home village. Or was he she questioned? Chosen by spirits to participate in life here, he now had two whakapapa, two sets of ancestors, and two iwi. She frowned thoughtfully before asking, "Ngoi, how do you name babies here? In my village, the parents decide on the name together with close whānau and often incorporate the name or names of significant ancestors." Ngoi looked down at the ground before replying.

"Here Marama, the name of the child is decided by the father, grandfather when there is one, and the tohunga. Men only make the important decisions in this village." Ngoi rolled her eyes heavenward in exasperation. Now she knew the behaviour was abnormal in this village, not where she grew up; the status quo was an irritating insect bite demanding to be scratched. She thanked all the Gods for giving her to Rongo because he treated her well. Her life was so different to most of the other women.

"A name is an important decision that can impact on the child in many respects. I will ask the ancestors for guidance and implore them to send a sign to the tohunga. Naming the baby isn't a decision for Rangi to make alone," Marama said quietly, already looking to the air for answers. Huia was still snuggled under Marama's arm while Ngoi cuddled the baby to her breast, stroking his arm and cooing. The girl regarded Marama with more than a bit of heroine worship. Although Huia was young, she realised how Marama spoke and behaved wasn't like the women here. She was knowledgeable, spiritual and commanded respect, even from some warriors, like her father and his men. Huia not only admired Marama, but aspired to be like her. The girl already knew that she would never be content to be treated like some man's property.

The time in isolation passed all too quickly for the two women and the girl. Once the baby arrived, the days filled with the joy of caring for the robust child. Marama became concerned he would become demanding because he was spoiled, having three mothers instead of one. He was, however, a contented child, blessed with a cheerful disposition and a penchant for long periods of sleep. Unfortunately, they would have to return to the village soon. Burning the whare that was their domain alone would be a sad day for them. Ngoi and Huia consoled themselves, knowing they would spend more time with Rongo and the boys, but poor Marama would be returning to live with Rangi.

The chief made his plans known to everyone. He would provide for his other women and perhaps visit, but they were sent from his whare to live elsewhere. They could stay in the village or return home if they wished. In his whare, he would have Marama, his son, and when she came, Roimata's sister. Piri and Rongo urged Rangi to consider the alliances made when other villages gave the women. But Rangi believed he had received the poor end of the bargain - an insult almost, by taking them. They gave him trouble, no sons, and consumed the resources of their village. The other men knew they wouldn't sway Rangi's opinion, so they didn't waste their breath trying to change his mind. Rongo understood why he wanted to do it. His own life with Ngoi and his family was such a joy that he couldn't wait to have Huia and Ngoi back home full time. He did know his women had a wonderful time being outside the village's daily life, and he acknowledged there was something wrong with that. Why weren't they all dying to come back instead of prolonging their separation? Was the life of women so bad in their village? Rongo decided he must pay more attention to the lives of women. The ancestors asked for change, and it was up to all of them to make that happen. How on earth they would change somebody as chauvinistic and self-absorbed as Rangi, he didn't know, but he would do his best.

Chapter 6

Rangi asked Piri and Rongo to plan an appropriate ceremonial feast to welcome his son and successor into their midst. Piri indicated the ancestors were whispering about the child's name, and he would come to see the chief after he made preparations.

"My son will be named Maui, after my most illustrious ancestor," announced Rangi. "Of course, he will have many names, so the ancestors can help decide on those." Rongo threw a worried look at Piri, who seemed to have paled a little under his tā moko, knowing well their ancestors shouldn't be spurned, especially after the recent insult to the Papatūānuku. Each man felt Rangi was placing their people in jeopardy with his impulsive decisions. They also knew disagreeing with him head-on or in front of another person would be counterproductive. When they exited the whare, Rongo puffed out his cheeks in frustration and deep thought. Piri raised his eyes heavenward, gave a big sigh, and turned to Rongo with troubled eyes.

"Will you make the practical arrangements Rongo, for the appropriate food, drink and entertainment?"

"Yes, I will Piri. However, it pains me to leave you alone with such a delicate task. I will ask our tīpuna for their tolerance, guidance and blessing. The food prepared will all be appropriate for the welcoming of new life, and a homage to the ever-turning circle of existence that we lead, by the grace of the Gods." The two men turned to hongi before each went about their tasks. They supported and respected each other, not only as individuals but in the roles they fulfilled for their people. As Piri stalked off to the cave, he lamented that Rongo was so well versed in the spiritual needs of the village, such a diplomat, and Rangi wasn't. Rangi's father had been a fearsome warrior and a wily negotiator who tended to put his people first. Father and son were never close. With Rangi coddled by his mother, he missed many valuable lessons in the art of leadership. Instead, Rangi received too much instruction in the art of being selfish. He sincerely hoped Kotuku would speak to him again, as he needed help more than ever. His role as tohunga was to safeguard everyone by pleasing those dwelling in other realms, so it was his job to find the way.

Piri would delegate his protégé preparation of appropriate chants and the ceremony's structure, which would please the young man. He would focus on the naming ceremony, the designs of the ancestors and persuading Rangi to do the bidding of their tīpuna. After the ceremony was complete, he would need to seek guidance on influencing their leader. With Rangi proving so difficult, he needed to start training his junior tohunga in the arts of influence and diplomacy, or when he was gone, Rangi would ride roughshod over them. Aue! If Rongo were chief, life for their village and iwi would have been so much easier. He felt guilty for having the thought, but knew his feelings were true if he looked in his heart. While being honest with himself, Piri admitted the idea had been germinating in his mind even when he had refused to acknowledge it.

Rangi challenged the central core of his role as tohunga. Piri dedicated his life to the spiritual harmony between his people, ancestors, the land, and the Gods. The power of a chief wasn't absolute. The right of leadership had to be supported by the elders, and those of rank. For the first time, Piri questioned whether or not Rangi was the best leader for their people. He contemplated speaking to Marama to see if her communion with Kotuku could shed light on the future. There was far more substance and depth to Marama than he had imagined, so he would need to be cautious. At times he was in awe of her presence, mana, the strength of her feminine connection to the earth. Not to mention her spirituality, which he occasionally found overwhelming. They should be working together as allies. It was time to set aside his pride, the long-held tribal view of the inferiority of women, and talk to her. The tasks ahead would require the efforts of many people, and Marama was proving to be a person of significance. Piri swiftly completed the delegation of tasks to his second in charge, who glowed with pride at his mentor's confidence in him. This uplifting unintended consequence convinced Piri he was on the right track. He should be delegating more responsibility more often, as he wasn't getting any younger, and his trainees wanted to do more. Piri strode off to find Marama, who would be moving to her new home today. It wasn't usual for the tohunga to attend, but he felt compelled to greet Marama and see the boy. When he arrived, Rangi was again sharpening the edge of his mere. It seemed to be a task he found therapeutic. He bowed his head to Rangi as he entered the whare, and Rangi looked up startled.

"Forgive me chief, as I was suddenly overwhelmed by the need to welcome the boy home with you. We can never underestimate the importance of your son to all of us." Piri felt honesty, at least half of it, was the best approach. His chief rewarded his effort with a smug smile. Rangi loved hearing people refer to his son positively, especially regarding how important he would be, as it reflected well on him.

"Tohunga, you are always welcome in our whare. Naturally, our tīpuna want to surround my son. Please sit. Would you like a drink?" Piri nodded, and Rangi fetched the drink himself. Perhaps having fewer women to yell at would be beneficial for him after all, as he seemed almost convivial. Piri sensed Marama arrive back in the village and advised Rangi she was coming. His ability to see and predict happenings always impressed his chief, increasing his influence, so Piri often shared his prescient knowledge.

Marama greeted Rangi as the chief, with suitable deference, presenting the child to him for his examination. She experienced a stab of sorrow at the difference between this son's arrival compared to the celebration she shared with Starman when Kai and Aroha were born. Piri looked at her sharply, quickly masking his pity, and Marama knew she had projected her feelings outward. She sincerely hoped, as she suspected, that Rangi was utterly deaf to her emotions. Rangi was impressed with his son. Marama removed him from his flax carrying basket, gently unwrapping his swaddling so that the chief could look at him. The child was healthy, thriving, alert, everything Rangi hoped for, so when the baby grabbed his finger and started suckling, he was enchanted. Paternal pride overwhelmed him, and both Piri and Marama were astonished to see his eyes glistening as he spoke to his son gently. They exchanged a look that shouted, "can you believe that!" The boy startled the chief when he gave a hearty cry, as he realised the finger wasn't providing him with any milk. Marama knelt beside him and put the child to her breast so he could suckle. The chief inclined his head at her, acknowledging her achievement in delivering him a son. The sight of Marama's swollen breasts also made him determined to sire more sons with her. He couldn't wait to be with her again. Should he send Piri away once the child was asleep, he wondered?

"Chief, I would like to invite Marama and the boy to attend my whare once she has fed him. While preparations are underway for tonight, some rituals need to be attended to at once, for the boy who will lead us. Now that your son is with us, his wellbeing must be a primary concern for me as well as his mother," said Piri gravely. Rangi would have preferred to be alone with Marama, as he was in a state of excitement. He agreed readily as his needs became urgent, and he excused himself to go and visit one of his women. Marama breathed a sigh of relief. She noticed the gleam of lust in Rangi's eyes, and she was dreading his renewed carnal desire, especially as the birth was so recent, and she was still tender inside.

"Thank you Piri," she said. It could have been a thank you for the invitation, but he knew she thanked him for his consideration. Piri brought some water for Marama and sat quietly while the boy drank his fill of milk until he could no longer keep his eyes open. Marama was a natural mother with a well-practised hand when it came to infants and children, but it was the wairua of the boy that intrigued Piri. Here before him was the transformational leader who would save, unite, and advance his people. The boy already exuded calm confidence with his place in the world. It was the tohunga's turn to feel tears behind his eyes as he caught a glimpse of the future this child would shape. Marama looked up and directly at Piri, with a smile playing around the edges of her lips, tears glistening unshed in her eyes.

"I feel the same way when I look at him sometimes, and the mist lifts for long enough to see what lies ahead. I think he has drunk more than enough as usual, and he will sleep now for a long time. We should go to your whare as we have much to discuss," she said, placing the sleeping boy in his basket. Piri led the way, and Marama's heart lightened to be out of the whare she would now share with Rangi.

"Do you have a preference for a brew to aid your recovery from childbirth?" Marama smiled gratefully at Piri and produced a leaf packet from her pouch.

"As a matter of fact, I do. It is a blend of bark to help with the pain, combat infection, leaves to help my muscles recover, dried flowers to boost my health and improve the taste. What do you normally give women after they have given birth?"

"A similar concoction from your description but perhaps made with different ingredients. I will give you some so you can compare the efficacy and taste. Who knows, we may be able to combine them to provide something better," Piri said with arms spread. Marama was pleased with his approach, she had thought the same thing, as she often tested remedies herself.

"Have the ancestors spoken his name to you yet?" Marama decided to open with what she thought was an easy question. The closing of his eyes, followed by a heavily creased brow, told her it wasn't an easy question at all.

"They have been whispering for days about the boy's name. His name must carry meaning, but it also needs to be subtle. Rangi won't want him to be known as a creator of unity, like his father, or acknowledge his place as your third child and one of your people. He wants the boy to be named Maui. Rangi shows little regard for the wishes or designs of our ancestors, and I have yet to propose the name of Maui, which they haven't mentioned."

"If it helps at all, I also have genealogical links to Maui. Perhaps a shared ancestor will be an acceptable choice to the many interested parties," proposed Marama, seeking to alleviate Piri's obvious worry. Marama chewed on her lip as she doubted sharing Kotuku's words would provide any comfort to the tohunga.

"There is no easy way to share this information," Marama said, looking Piri in the eye. "Your ancestor Kotuku, who admitted to diverting my path here, is concerned Rangi is setting your iwi on a path to extinction. They cannot stand aside and allow that. Without their people, they have no connection to this realm. My ancestors sent us across the ocean for the same reason. They not only implored me to save Rongo, but they also assisted my ancestors and me with healing his body so he could recover his full strength." Marama searched the tohunga's face. She could feel the wheels whirring in his brain as he digested the information she verbalised. A pivotal moment had arrived for them. They must choose to trust each other or not. Both were aware that if they took this risk and the other betrayed them, Rangi would kill them. The ancestors were providing information through and to both of them. Did this indicate the ancestors meant for them to be allies? Piri had just received confirmation of the thoughts buried in his head, from Kotuku, through Marama. When dealing with the spirits, they rarely communicated messages so clearly. As he thought, Rongo possessed the qualities of a chief and should be leading their people. All the gossip and rumour that buzzed around Rangi's conception, his mother's artifice, her ability to incite fear, and the dark power she wielded flowed through the tohunga's mind. He was much younger then and still learning the ways of the spirits, although his calling was always strong. Dark eyes met intense green ones, and they reached, instinctively, for each other's hands.

The connection between them was instantaneous and powerful. Marama and Piri were transported, and they remained linked in the darkness of the spirit world.

"You have truly found one another at last," said Kotuku with some amusement. He sometimes reminded Marama of her Nani.

"I am here, Marama. Kotuku is leading the way because so much depends on you both. I know you, and I will always place my faith in you, my protection around you, although I am far away." Nani did seem distant to Marama, but just knowing she was there was unbelievably comforting.

"The truth is not always easy to dig from the dirt, and equally, it is not always what you wanted to find or see. Rongo must be chief. He and his sons must lead until the boy is ready to take his place in the world. It is up to you Piri, and you, Marama, to pave the way for the false chief Rangi to be deposed. Take care. If you seize a katipō (venomous spider), *it will bite you. Better to squash it before it has a chance to strike."*

They opened their eyes together to find they were still clasping each other's hands. Sweat beaded their brows, and they were each turning the words of Kotuku over in their minds. Kotuku charged them with a perilous task. Piri's eyes were troubled, and he scratched behind his ear absently. It was Marama who spoke first.

"We can never speak openly of our task, but we both speak the language of the spirits. Does anyone else in the village understand the signs?"

"The tohunga who are in training are already familiar with the basics, although your signs are slightly different. When you want to speak with me, they will be busy elsewhere. The only other person I suspect has picked some of it up is Rongo. The reason I noticed is when I am communing, Rongo seems to anticipate tasks before I have vocalised them. He is also extraordinarily observant, has been since he was a child, and quite a linguist in tribal dialects. That is why Rangi sends him on the trade missions, and of course, they require diplomacy, patience, as well as being physically dangerous." The depth of Piri's respect for Rongo was crystallising in front of Marama's eyes, while his disdain for Rangi was escaping its tightly constrained bonds. She was certain Piri concurred with his ancestors.

"I normally take time to reflect on the messages, look for signs past and present, before deciding on any actions. Do you think that is a good idea?" Marama looked to Piri to try and gauge his thoughts.

"I think it's a sensible approach. Fools make poor decisions in haste, and we must think carefully, plan meticulously, and work in accord. Please ask Rangi if he will come and see me when convenient for him, as I want us to visit the sacred cave together. I will propose to our chief that I spend more time with the boy to ensure he is well protected. As his mother, by default, you will be involved in his spiritual development regularly. I have a potion for Rangi to drink which will dampen his libido and allow you time to recover from childbirth. The remedy won't work forever, and I dare not risk causing so much frustration it's to the detriment of someone else. Do your best to be a dedicated woman, a trusted companion, a model and a subservient mother." Piri paused as Marama noted his advice. "Perhaps we can find each other in dream or the spirit world if we need to," he said, nodding his head at the thought. Marama inclined her head in agreement before they clasped hands again, sharing a spiritual embrace. Piri reached for the baby, lifted him in his woven bed so that he and Marama could both hold him as he slept. The baby graced them with a smile as he moved through dreams of warmth, nurturing milk, and the smell of his mother, cocooned in a blanket of love.

As Marama strode towards the new whare, she repeated Piri's advice to herself in her head and thought about how to deliver the best results. As the baby slept on peacefully, she made the whare look homely, prepared food she knew Rangi found delicious, and did everything she could think of to anticipate his needs. When Rangi returned, Marama greeted him with a sunny smile, the tantalising aroma of cooking food and a contented baby — the domestic bliss he envisioned.

"How was your day? Can I offer you some food?" Marama asked Rangi the questions she hoped he wanted to hear.

"The warriors are in fine form. I have resolved trivial disputes, and I practiced with my weapons today, which felt good," he replied. Marama noticed he didn't ask her how her day was, probably because he wasn't interested, but she took the initiative anyway.

"Tohunga Piri is most impressed with your son. He asked if I could pass you a message that he wishes for the two of you to go to the sacred cave when you have the time, of course. The tohunga seems dedicated to protecting and guiding the future of our child with care. As a mother, this makes me happy. Perhaps you and he will soon come up with a name befitting the importance of our tiny man," she smiled and looked at Rangi hopefully. Her eyes sparkled, and their unusual allure captivated Rangi. She belonged to him now. Perhaps when he came home from seeing the tohunga, he would have her again. The mood was cheerful as they ate together, with Marama giving Rangi a blow by blow account of everything his son did that day. Rangi savoured the flavours of the fish, the sweet, slightly charred kūmara with *horopito* (peppery herb) and succulent *pikopiko* (young fern shoots) she served. The woman could certainly cook. Rangi decided he could get used to such a pleasant home life and better thank Rongo for the inspiration. On the spur of the moment, he chose to present Marama with a gift. After the drama with Roimata, he now possessed more valuable jewellery than he needed. He got up and returned with an intricately woven pouch.

"I have a gift for you. It is rare, one of a kind. I have never seen anything like it before. It's similar to you in many ways," Rangi said, holding the pouch out to her. Marama was genuinely surprised but pleased he was making such a spontaneous gesture, as it meant she was succeeding. She opened the pouch. Inside was a golden orb of shiny beauty attached to a finely woven necklace. Marama reached in and the smooth, highly polished surface of the *kauri* (agathus australis) tree gum caressed her hand before she gasped in surprise, green eyes wide. Rangi laughed at her reaction, and Marama looked down quickly to compose herself, feigning being emotionally overcome. When she turned the orb over in her hand, trapped inside the resin was a spider. Not just any spider, it was a katipō spider. The venomous spider didn't live in the forest, as they lived on the beach, so Marama was startled to see it there. Kotuku's words were ringing in her ears, and the orb was pulsing in her palm.

"Thank you - I, I am overcome," she stammered, her eyes watering. "It is certainly a unique gift, and it means a lot to me," she murmured. Marama closed her eyes as she experienced the pain of emotional angst lance through her from the pendant. There was a story to be told about this pendant, but she would need to wait until she was alone and the baby was asleep.

Rangi congratulated himself on choosing a gift that moved Marama. In his opinion, she would manage more children without them being underfoot and constantly crying. He could also enjoy his other women elsewhere without having their snivelling brats under his roof. Of course, there would soon be Roimata's sister to torment at leisure. His eyes gleamed with malice as he thought of the ways he would humiliate her family through her. The elders were satisfied, but he wasn't. The sight of his son, the boy he could have lost due to Roimata, poisoned his heart with bitterness against them. He would go and see the tohunga now. Marama was right about Piri, he was highly dedicated, and it had been he who delivered the message about finding a worthy mother. They didn't visit the sacred cave together often, so something important must be afoot. Rangi excused himself politely, eager to see Piri straight away. His decision brought another bright smile to Marama's face, making Rangi realise how grumpy and morose his other women were. Never mind that Marama's smile was due to her successful manipulation of him and his departure. Marama had won a skirmish in what would be a long war, but a victory was a victory, so she must celebrate her triumphs, whether large or small.

When Rangi arrived at the tohunga's whare, he found Piri deep in meditation before glowing embers and wafting fragrant, heady smoke. His eyes snapped open, and for a moment, Rangi saw a stranger instead of the familiar gaze. Piri inclined his head, arose smoothly despite his advancing age, and greeted his chief with a formal hongi. Rangi put it down to a trick of the light or maybe the spirits, as a strange atmosphere filled the space, and his skin was prickling.

"Thank you for coming so quickly, my chief. Our tīpuna called us to the sacred cave. You and your son consume their thoughts, and great deeds await in the future. Fate weaves decisions of significance, and we need to be part of the grand design. Are you ready?" Rangi nodded and followed his tohunga, who grabbed a burning reed torch to climb to the cave. When Piri was ascending the hill, his age wasn't apparent, and he set a cracking pace as if he was in a hurry. Rangi had no problem keeping up, he was a warrior in the prime of his life, but he was perspiring by the time they were three-quarters of the way up the steep path.

Piri crouched down at the entrance on one knee, eyes closed as he intoned karakia, hands gesturing to supplement his words to the ancestors. The tohunga's sense of urgency was infectious, and excitement heated Rangi's blood at the thought of the future pivoting around him and his son. He was born for this destiny, the one his mother foretold. The tohunga of the village kept the cave prepared, so all Piri had to do was light the torches and touch his burning rush to the firewood always set in the cave hearth. The dried mānuka branches flamed brightly, throwing shadows around the walls, licking greedily at the dried sticks and logs until they glowed with embers. Piri removed some dried leaves from a pouch and sprinkled them over the fire, with his eyes closed, muttering his prayers under his breath. Smoke swirled in the cave, drifting through flickering firelight, before being drawn through a crack in the ceiling. Rangi wasn't knowledgeable regarding the spirits, but his mother had called on her ancestors frequently as she brewed her potions and prepared her weapons of stealth, so he was wary of them. Since the spirits paved the way to obtaining his son, his belief had strengthened. He did, however, feel that a man created his own destiny. Rangi felt a finger of cold on his neck, but there wasn't anything there when he turned. When he looked back towards the fire, Piri was standing with his arms up in the air, his head thrown back, and every hair on his head was streaming straight outwards. His eyes rolled back in their sockets, leaving blank whites. Sparks flew upwards from the fire and spiralled towards the ceiling in formation. Nothing like this had ever happened in the cave before. Then the tohunga drifted up off the ground until he was hanging suspended in the air. His head tilted upon his neck, and a voice boomed out into the cave, but it wasn't Piri's voice.

"Rangi! You must change your ways. Your purpose is to protect the boy and his mother from harm, along with all of your people. If you do not heed this warning, we cannot help you. The tohunga has petitioned us on your behalf, so we name the boy Maui tama-i-waho, Maui Waho for now. The right of naming a child is ours, not yours," shouted the voice so loud it reverberated around the cave, like thunder, *"and we will choose his real name when he finds the path."* Rangi clapped his hands to his ears, but the scolding rebounded inside his head still.

Piri's body lowered slowly to the ground until he was once again standing on his own two feet. Rangi was relieved when the tohunga opened his eyes, his hair returned to his head, and he recognised Piri again. The angry ancestor with the thunderous voice had departed, so Rangi relaxed, refusing to show any signs of disquiet to the tohunga. Piri wasn't present when the spirit used his body, so there was no need for him to know what was said.

"Have you been communing with our tīpuna Piri?"

"Chief, I had the strangest experience. I found myself in the spirit world, but I was in a forest, sitting under an enormous kauri, a child of *Tane Mahuta* (God of the forest). I could hear a flute playing the most beautiful music on the other side of the tree. Nobody spoke to me. The music consumed me, and I forgot the questions I journeyed to ask. I am sorry my chief, as I feel the ancestors summoned us here, but I am none the wiser regarding our purpose." Piri scratched his head absentmindedly, somewhat perplexed by what happened and wondering why his scalp was tingling all over.

"No need to apologise, Piri, our tīpuna wanted to speak with me directly through you." Rangi had learned from his mother that applying some truth allowed you to omit the details you didn't wish to share in an authentic-sounding way.

"The ancestors have heard your petition to them and revealed the name of my son to me. He will be Maui tama-i-waho, Maui Waho. Kotuku has also asked me to protect Maui and his mother. It is one of my purposes in life," he said emphatically.

"Thank you for bringing me here urgently, as I never expected that I would be addressed personally on these matters. My son is going to be a great warrior, leader, and the spirits reassured me he would continue my conquests."

"That does explain why my experience was so strange, my whole head is still tingling, and my mind echoes with music," muttered Piri. "Was anything else said? Often, the ancestors speak in riddles. Although Kotuku has been more plain-spoken in recent times, especially when issuing instructions on the path to follow," he said, frowning.

"It did seem quite straightforward, but Kotuku told me, a new name might be given to Maui Waho when he finds the path." Rangi nodded to himself as if he just recalled this information. He could see Piri pondering the words, which was perfect as he didn't want to answer any more questions or share Kotuku's warning.

"Let's finish the evening with a ceremonial drink. One of the tasks our tīpuna asked of me is to cleanse your spirit ritually. To do that, we need to purify you. Fasting regularly, meditation at sunrise and sunset, bathing in the sacred pool under the stars, climbing to the summit of our *maunga* (mountain), and abstaining from fulfilling your sexual desires, will sharpen your focus. This ritual isn't for the faint-hearted chief, and you alone have been chosen in my lifetime. Kotuku was the last of our iwi, to reach the heights of discipline that the ancestors demand." Rangi was flattered he was chosen and was confident he could withstand the rigours of any physical test. What he was less excited about was sexual abstinence.

"For a virulent man, in his prime as you are, the suppression of your desire to breed is challenging. I have an ancient recipe to assist you with this, for the moon cycle of the cleansing." Piri proffered a bowl to the chief, bowing his head. Rangi hesitated but remembering the warning, he took the bowl and drank. It didn't taste bad. The thought of curbing his appetites, however, left a bitter taste in his mouth. Angry ancestors or not, he would send for Roimata's sister at the end of his spiritual cleansing. Thanks to Piri, he got his way with naming his son. In his mind, he prevailed. Piri performed karakia and began the process for Rangi's ritual.

The two men made their way back down the hill, lighting the way with one of the torches. It was now long after midnight, and a half-moon was high in the sky, aiding their ability to navigate the rocky path. They were both hungry after the evening of spiritual activity, so they were pleasantly surprised to find Marama awaiting their return, with invigorating drinks and baskets of nutritious food to restore their bodies. Marama fashioned a woven pouch to carry the baby around strapped to her chest while she worked. The child was awake, his eyes following the two men when his mother's movements allowed him to see them. The tohunga looked at the boy intently, noticing how alert he was for such a young baby. He didn't cry or squirm, merely regarded the world from where he was snuggled against Marama's milk-filled breasts, looking both sage and content. Piri was thinking of reaching for him spiritually, but he found the child reached out to him, probing the edges of his wairua with innocent interest. They could feel each other, and as Marama gave a small laugh, he realised she sensed their connection. She was too clever to pass up an opportunity to win Rangi over.

"Look! He knows his father has arrived home, and he watches you when he can," she smiled at Rangi. Rangi hadn't noticed the baby regarding him quietly, but he believed they were bonding already and returned Marama's smile. Opening his eyes wide at the baby, Maui cemented Rangi's belief when he smiled. The baby probably had wind, but Marama and Piri exchanged a smug look.

"Thank you Marama, it's pleasant to return home, to find you have anticipated our needs, and my son is content," said Rangi inclining his head in thanks. Perhaps there is some hope for him yet, mused Piri. Rangi never acknowledged the work or presence of his women, so Marama had wrought a positive change in him. Piri thanked the ancestors he and Marama were working together, not against one another. She exerted her influence subtly but firmly on those around her. Even his tīpuna embraced her ability to usher in change. If the Gods wove the strands of fate and the ancestors designed the pattern, it seemed Marama was contributing colour. Marama turned the light of her green eyes upon Piri, and the hairs on his neck rose. She smiled, creating the impression she was reading his thoughts, but Marama was reading his body cues. It wasn't difficult for her to guess what was running through his mind, and she was also glad they were on the same side. Rangi began to have some trust in her, but she knew his fickle nature would demand much more. Once the tohunga left, Rangi surprised her by retiring to his mat and snoring gently without man-handling her. The sleep was so deep, she knew Piri had given him something in the cave, and she gave thanks for his kindness. In the morning, when Rangi awakened early, before dawn, she rose to prepare food and drink. Rangi declined her offer, explaining he was fasting, participating in a ritual cleansing over the coming moon cycle and what that entailed. He advised that he wouldn't be able to give her the attention she deserved as his first woman, the mother of his son, and asked her to cover her breasts when she fed the baby if he was home. Marama widened startled eyes but nodded in understanding, appreciating the depth of Piri's sympathy and cunning. She determined to make generous offerings to Papatūānuku when the sun rose and seek information to help with their task. The tohunga bought her precious time, a whole moon cycle, and she must use it well.

Marama meditated and made the offerings at dawn alone, but after the baby's morning feed, she asked her pupils to join her in reverence of Earth Mother. Ngoi and Huia were excited to participate in a spiritual exercise with Marama, especially to Papatūānuku, after recent events. Papatūānuku was the nurturer of life, the champion of the feminine, so they called on her often. The baby slept peacefully in his flax bed, placed in the centre of the two women and one girl, his three mothers. Marama led the women in karakia, her hands and fingers flowing through the set movements. They joined hands, Ngoi and Huia intoning a chant Marama taught them with her. Their hands began to tingle with warmth, and they became one with the earth as her energy suffused them, cradling them with her love and power. They all felt refreshed, full of vitality, and their blood thrummed in their veins. Marama's senses heightened. She felt her hair and nails growing, milk swelling her breasts, so she reached for the baby, who appeared to have grown since she put him down. Huia turned shining eyes towards Marama.

"I think he has grown since this morning, Marama and I feel, I feel fantastic." She held her hands up to her face, looking at them as if she had never seen them before.

"Today, I want to plant the whole garden, run to see the ocean and cook enough food for a moon cycle or perhaps have another child," said Ngoi, her eyes luminous.

"Such is the power of Papatūānuku. She can make us more than we are," said Marama with an inscrutable smile. The baby was already nursing hungrily, enjoying the milk that flowed out of his mother without him having to suckle.

"We three have been imbued with power from Papatūānuku to make the desires of the ancestors come true. Today, you will both run a clinic for the women and children. The healing powers you are learning will be enhanced by the mother. Your hands soft and soothing, guided by everything nurturing that we possess as the earthly representations of her. Let us share all of the love she has shown us with those in our care," said Marama.

"Will you and the baby be coming with us today?" Huia looked hopeful but was already organising herself to leave.

"No, I have a task that requires a lot of energy, so today, while I have so much, I must apply myself," said Marama, rumpling Huia's hair. Ngoi looked at her quizzically, curious about what Marama would be doing but far too polite to pry, so she took Huia's hand. They both kissed their fingers and touched the baby before heading off to set up the healing supplies. Marama watched them go, feeling the love between them expanding, like a flooding river that has burst its banks. Inside the love, sharp darts of pain resided. They needled her whenever she thought about Aroha, Kai, Starman, Ari, her Chief and all the people at home she loved and who shared her life. But that pain made her feel alive. When she looked at the baby, she promised him they would return to their natural whānau. Now Marama needed to focus on the task at hand if she ever wanted to leave. She took the baby back to the whare, and he barely stirred as she placed him on her mat. His good nature made her smile, and she knew how lucky she was. Before she began her meditation, Marama decided to tidy away her personal belongings as they were still in disarray from her isolation period. Instinctively, she pulled her hand away as she moved a garment. The katipō spider startled her as it stalked her from inside the necklace. Such a strange gift Rangi gave her. Before she knew it, her hand snaked out and grabbed it. Almost it seemed, of its own volition.

Marama was bathed in golden light as she sat high above the ground in the branches of a magnificent kauri tree.

"Don't be afraid. My name is Hana, and I have followed this trinket for generations, Marama. I was patiently waiting for when I could tell somebody my story and perhaps restore the balance of my existence. I was relieved when Rangi gave you the gift, for I can now speak to you. Where are my manners! Please forgive an old spirit who has not spoken to a living person for so long. When I lived, I was the best friend of one of Rangi's maternal tipuna. May I speak to you of the past Marama?" Marama pondered how to respond, as spirits didn't usually ask for permission to speak. She wondered why Hana did.

"I am honoured that an unknown spirit would choose to speak with me. Do you require something of me?" Marama only knew of one reason permission would be sort, and she was reluctant to be given another task without understanding what this spirit wanted. Nani did, however, monitor the spirits who sought to speak with her.

"You are a smart woman to ask Marama. Your Nani and Kotuku both told me I would encounter some polite but insightful questions from you." Hana chuckled gently to herself before continuing.

"Yes, Marama, I do want something from you. I want your help. Kotuku's desires are not dissimilar to mine. I need to share my story with you for you to understand them. So, I will first tell you the story, then make my request, and you may have some time to consider it before you accept or decline. Does that sound fair?"

"That seems fair to me, and I must confess my curiosity sacred one."

"My best friend was Ngaio, and we lived in a village by the sea. We were so close growing up that people thought we must be sisters. I was drawn to the spiritual world, while Ngaio was interested in medicinal remedies, so we were both curious and quite skilled by the time we reached womanhood. We were also youthfully beautiful and pursued by many boys and warriors. The first challenge to our relationship was when we were both attracted to the same handsome young man. My father was the chief at the time, so it was he who

would choose a man for me. He had promised me to the youngest son of a chieftain from far away. My heart broke when my father told me I must let Ngaio have the man we both loved. What I didn't know was that Ngaio had already seduced him and become pregnant with his child, so I had lost him already. Although I was extremely miserable, I put on a brave face and tried to be as supportive of Ngaio as possible. At the time, the cost of my false cheer and sharing her happiness seemed unbearable. There were many nights when I cried myself to sleep. I was young and tragically imagined I would never be happy again. Ngaio shared all the details of the wonderful relationship she had with her man. The truth was she seemed to enjoy poking my raw wounds, compounding my misery, and destroying my self-confidence. Secretly I was glad when her belly began to swell, and she became ungainly, waddling around the village like one of the lumbering seals on the beach. I knew it wasn't nice to think that way, but I couldn't help myself.

One day Ngaio's man came to see me while I was weeding the kūmara by myself. He told me he had always loved me. That he was sorry, and there was no explanation for why he lay with Ngaio. He could remember nothing of the night he and Ngaio became a couple. There were tears in his eyes as he told me these things, and I believed him. It was, however, too late for us. I thanked him for letting me know but told him I was promised to another, that Ngaio was my friend and we could never be together. I was tearful as I told him. My heart felt like it was breaking all over again. We didn't dare to touch. The only thing to do was to let each other go, painfully and finally. I did feel better, knowing that he had returned my love for him. Slowly, I began to heal and become myself again. A few months later, my betrothed arrived in our village accompanied by his older brother. My Kauri, for that was his name, took my breath away. He wasn't just a gorgeous man. Kauri possessed an easy magnetic charm that made my heart skip. The mountain people of his mother were fairer than us, and his breeding tinged his skin with the hue of kauri wood. He was also eloquent, polite and an accomplished warrior. My father was almost as delighted with him as I was, and my mother was openly impressed. I thanked the Gods, the ancestors and everyone I could think of for delivering such a man to me. Excitement replaced my former unhappiness and the giddiness of physical attraction. The only person who wasn't happy was Ngaio's man. While I supported Ngaio when she found a man, she was highly critical of my match. Surprisingly, she found constant fault with Kauri. His looks were strange, his accent weird, more pretty than masculine in her opinion, and she avoided spending time with us when we were together. Everybody else in the village loved him, and before long, so did I. As the love between Kauri and I blossomed, Ngaio and I grew apart. Her life descended into unhappiness as her handsome man became surly, unkempt and spurned her affections. He even questioned whether he was the father of her child. When a warrior neglects himself, he doesn't survive long in battle, and so it was that his reckless disregard for his safety ended his life. I think I mourned his loss more than Ngaio did. Once, she and I were the greatest of friends. I felt sorry for Ngaio, and I regretted my former bad thoughts, so I reached out to her. We became close again and began spending a lot of time together, reminiscing about our youthful antics. She and her daughter often ate with us as Kauri doted on the girl. I realised he would make a wonderful father one day, which made me happy because I believed that I was pregnant. Then I became ill. At first, I thought it was just morning sickness. I wanted to wait until I was sure about the baby before telling Kauri, so I asked him not to summon the tohunga. Ngaio was lovely, offering to look after me, make food for all of us and bathing my forehead. As the days progressed, I started feeling more and more ill. I developed abdominal cramps, began sweating profusely and eventually, I even had difficulty breathing. Kauri did summon the tohunga, and my parents came to help nurse me, but it was too late. The tohunga knew something, or someone poisoned my body, but he couldn't identify what was causing the symptoms. It made it difficult to find a remedy. Within a few days, my life was an ebbing tide, coming to an end, and I knew the future of the child in my womb would never be." Hana paused here. Her papery voice became a soft, husky whisper. The trauma of her emotions hadn't faded much through the years, and Marama experienced sadness welling inside her as she felt Hana's enduring pain. Marama didn't prompt the spirit. She just let Hana take her time, gather her thoughts; she would resume when she was ready.

"It wasn't until I was here, in this realm, that I began to see the design and the ruthless malice in Ngaio, which drove the life from my body. When I died, she appeared distraught. The whole village took pity on her. First, she lost her man and then her best friend in quick succession. At first, Kauri was lost in his grief and pain. Ngaio used her daughter and her manufactured distress to draw herself closer to him. They found a common bond in their hurt, the gap I left in both their lives. Ngaio made sure she was the shoulder Kauri would lean on in times of weakness with extreme patience and cunning. She fostered his dependence on her by cooking and taking care of his whare as well as her own. He, being a decent man, provided food for Ngaio and her daughter. They eventually became a family, in every sense of the word, and nobody begrudged them this comfort. Even my parents welcomed Ngaio into their home as my father and Kauri were close. What I could see from this realm astounded me. Ngaio had found, then hunted, katipō spiders on the beach, and she knew they were venomous, with a painful, poisonous bite. The katipō became her weapon against me. She didn't want anyone to see multiple bites upon my skin, so instead, she began adding the spiders to my food. With each meal I ate, I ingested more toxins. Soon, I was so weak I didn't notice the taste of what I drank either. Ngaio killed me because she wanted my man, my status, and a provider for her child. In her mind, I destroyed her life because her man never stopped loving me. She justified the taking of my life, unborn child and man as utu (revenge/redress of wrongdoing). I was merely the first obstacle Marama, as she also killed my brother. He was chosen to be the next chief but died the following year in mysterious circumstances. His men discovered his body at the bottom of the cliff, broken on the rocks when he fell. A strange death for a sure-footed warrior in his prime. Especially a warrior who ran every path in the land as a child. There was no explanation for his death, but I know it was Ngaio who

pushed him. I was unable to prevent it from happening. She lured my brother to the cliff, pleading with him to rescue her daughter, who she claimed had fallen over the edge. Faking distress, she cried for his help. As he leaned over to see where the girl was, Ngaio caught him completely off guard and shoved him with her foot. With my brother out of the way, Kauri was next in charge of the men. Ambitious Ngaio cleared the way for him to become the next chief. My father respected Kauri immensely, so with his support, the whānau of Ngaio backing him and the love of his men, Ngaio became the woman of the next chief. To immortalise her triumph over me, she fashioned the necklace with the katipō inside it. The very one that Rangi chose to give to you. The necklace has passed through many hands over the years. It has travelled far and wide. Sometimes it is admired, on other occasions, it has incited revulsion, but it often finds its way back into the hands of Ngaio's venomous bloodline. The necklace was freely given to you by a direct descendant, and I have waited a long time for someone I can speak to."

It was a tragic tale. Marama felt a connection with Hana once the spirit had shared her story. Marama had almost lost her own life and everyone she cared for to a much stronger foe. If it hadn't been for the spirits, she would be one of them. Hana created a delicate situation. After waiting so many years, Marama was sure Hana would want to alleviate her pain by exacting vengeance. The ancestors of Rotowhā wanted Rangi removed from power. Kotuku made that point clear to her and Piri. Once, in defence of her people, Marama had taken a life. The taking of that life resulted in the loss of all but one of his men. Those deaths weighed heavily on her shoulders. When she was home and could see her people thriving around her, it was a balm to her wairua. Without that justification, in front of her every day, her conscience prickled. It tortured her in the dark, even though she would make the same choice again if she had to. Perhaps it was that thought which grated her soul.

"Tormented spirit, I feel your pain across the years. What would you ask of this humble woman?" Marama didn't want to jump to

conclusions. The spirits were often fickle, and their requests could be riddles, open to interpretation by the receiver.

"I want to honour the will of the ancestors who dwell here. Your ancestors look for a path also Marama, for you, and the boy. The way is there, I can see it, and I want you to follow it. There will be signs."

Marama blinked in the midday sun as the baby gurgled to himself. The morning over, she remained seated, the necklace in her palm. Her legs protested after being in the same position for so long. She stretched her limbs to rid them of the prickling sensation as blood-flow returned before reaching for the child. Hugging the baby to her breast, he let her know he was ready to nurse. While the baby fed, Marama repeated the story and the request Hana made. It wasn't the guidance she had looked for or anticipated. The tale gave her much to ponder, but she must ensure her treasured child received everything he needed. She hoped Piri would send for her again soon. If he didn't call for her, she would make an excuse to go and see him.

Ngoi and Huia arrived with food for her. They were animated and overflowing with stories of what they encountered during the clinic. It was a satisfying sight, and the baby gurgled his approval as Huia scooped him up, cuddling and rocking him while dancing around the room. Her eyes shone with pride in the work she and Ngoi did. They made a difference to the village's health, and the women's wairua and self-respect were growing daily. They treated a toothache, menstrual cramps, a baby with a fever, a broken toe, the list went on and on. Marama was sure the female tīpuna of the village would be pleased with this subtle but tangible transformation. Rongo asked if they could check the health of the warriors. They wanted Marama to go with them and show them what to do. Checking people who were already healthy wasn't something they were familiar with, so Marama agreed to accompany them after kai. Huia pleaded to carry the baby. She loved the smell, the warmth and the company of the baby against her. They were well-fed and in a lively mood when they set off for the training ground.

When they arrived, Rongo and the seasoned warriors gave lessons in hand-to-hand combat to the younger men. By looking at the bruising some youths were wearing, there was still a bit to learn. Rongo replaced himself with another man and waved to his approaching whānau. He thought of Marama and the baby as part of his family now. More to do with saving his life and befriending his women-folk than her family connection through Rangi. Little mama Huia had claimed the baby, as usual, he noticed. The truth was, they all loved the boy. There was something unique about the child that drew people to him and brought out the best in them. Rongo was a spiritual man who perceived the magic around the baby, and he wanted to protect him with every fibre in his body. He couldn't have felt more protective of him if he was his child. When he thought about it, he hadn't experienced this primal instinct with his sons. The boy looked into his face with solemn eyes, almost as if he was assessing him and then smiled, and Rongo experienced a surge of love for him. Rangi hadn't been so happy for a long time either. When they were boys, then young men, Rangi and Rongo had had a lot of fun together. Playing tricks, chasing girls, getting into the occasional fight, they schemed together on how Rangi could win Roimata. Those were carefree days when Rongo was close to his cousin. Now Rangi just scared him. He was so unpredictable and violent at times. The cloak of leadership didn't sit well on his shoulders, and Rongo often found himself stretched, filling the gaps in duties Rangi left.

Piri had aged since the old chief died. The tohunga also laboured under a massive workload of additional duties without Rangi's aid. Fortunately, Marama brought them all a respite. The tohunga and his trainees had less daily medical work to do. Ngoi and Huia were thriving in their new roles, and even Rangi's women were getting a rest from his attentions. There had been a shift for Rotowhā into a more positive and wholesome frame of mind. The warriors were in peak condition. Rongo only hoped Rangi didn't send them on some fool's errand, resulting in casualties. He crouched to hug Huia and the baby in her arms, with a wide grin on his face.

"The light of my life and her entourage," he teased Ngoi gently, pulling her close to him.

"Indeed, Rongo, you summoned us to check your men." Marama grinned, waving her hand at the men with a flourish.

"Where would you like to start?" Rongo returned her grin. He enjoyed the light-hearted banter she brought to the village. Once, he had asked Marama if her people considered teasing and jokes an art. She erupted with a full throaty laugh and explained to him what happened when you became a couple. Rotowhā had become sombre over the years, but it wasn't always like that. Ngoi's hapu was far more lively, less morose. It astounded Rongo that Marama, who he had captured to be Rangi's woman, appeared to be one of the most caring, light-hearted people in the village. Ngoi told him Marama had two other children, including a young daughter, who she should be raising, while the child's father and son were on a voyage. Rongo was highly observant, but he struggled to see past Marama's external demeanour. Occasionally he glimpsed the depth of her pain, as it flickered across her face when she looked at Huia and thought nobody was watching. The cold annoyance she masked when Rangi was approaching, she hid carefully. Rangi told Rongo he was abstaining from intimacy for a moon cycle, and the news made him glad for Marama. Marama frowned in concentration as she regarded the men before turning to her trainees.

"Tell me where you would like to start and why." Ngoi and Huia both chewed their lips as they thought about it. A charming trait they shared when they were searching for answers. It was Huia who spoke first.

"I think we should look at the men one at a time. The young men are taking a beating so I would start with them."

"And you Ngoi?"

"Well, my thoughts run in a different direction to Huia. I thought to start with the more seasoned warriors first and see them by status. As they are older, they have seen more battles and will likely suffer from more ailments than the young men.

Also, we haven't done this before. When the younger men see us examine the most senior warriors, it will reassure them." Marama regarded them fondly.

"A good effort from both of you, applying sound reasoning skills. There is no right or wrong answer because, as you pointed out Ngoi, this has never been done before. Decide whose approach we will adopt for today."

"Mama's reasoning offers more depth and consideration than my idea did, so we should follow her suggestion." Marama nodded in agreement. Huia's ability to recognise Ngoi's well thought out idea pleased Marama. The girl wasn't only a natural healer, she was bright and humble. Ngoi was quite spiritual, and while she didn't remember the medicinal learning as efficiently as Huia, she took decisions with a great deal of care. Rongo enjoyed watching these exchanges between the teacher and her pupils. Marama's methodology wasn't unlike his approach to training the warriors, and it made him laugh.

"Fantastic Rongo! As you are in charge today, you will be first," said Marama motioning for him to sit on a log. Now it was Ngoi and Huia's turn to suppress a giggle.

It was an excellent choice to start with Rongo, as the examination was thorough. Marama showed them how to check his whole body and what she was looking for during the inspection. As it was an instructive lesson, Rongo's examination took the longest. It started with checking his head for parasites, bumps and bruises before returning to the routine diagnosis of his eyes, ears, breath and tongue. Marama also showed them how to check teeth, bones, joint movement, look for lumps or lesions, what questions to ask, including body functions and diet, old injuries, examine nails. It was quite an exhaustive process. Once the healers finished, Rongo realised the task would take several days. Marama wasn't entirely happy with the treatment of some of his old wounds. She asked him to begin taking a tonic daily to improve his joint movement. While Rongo was still moving well, Marama explained his joints were wearing out over time.

Huia clapped her hand over her mouth. Her eyes were brimming with suppressed merriment when Marama suggested it would be beneficial if Rongo lost some weight. She looked pointedly at Ngoi, who she knew doted on Rongo, with a tendency to overfeed him. Rongo looked sheepish as he strode back to the men, but true to his nature, he told them exactly what to expect. At the end of his briefing, the more senior men hooted with laughter while the younger ones tried to hide their grins. The examiners knew Rongo shared the advice to lose some weight, entertainingly for the amusement of the men, to alleviate any nerves. The initiative proved to be a worthwhile exercise as the healers unearthed a myriad of health issues. Each treatment made the warrior inspected feel the the aroha of the healers. The advice and treatments given were confidential. By the third day, the warriors were sharing any problems freely. Several people came to visit again, with more information they had recalled. Marama re-broke the fingers of one of Rongo's best men. Whoever treated them hadn't splinted the fingers, and his grip on his weapons diminished, which meant average warriors were now besting him. The restoration of his fighting prowess would allow him to reclaim his place on the sparring field. The work was equally rewarding for the healers. They were transforming themselves, and they were resetting the people's wellbeing and the village's life force.

Piri observed the healers and their effect. He and his trainees worked to enhance or augment their efforts. Papatūānuku seemed to smile upon their deeds and rewarded them with her bounty, while the spirits murmured their approval in his ears. Today he told Rangi preparations were being made for the baby's naming ceremony, and he would require time with Marama and the child. Rangi was pleased with Piri's planning diligence, and after his daily rituals, he set off to enjoy drilling his men. The warriors had grown in stature and prowess. Rangi credited the change to his contentment and outstanding leadership. The tohunga set his trainees an array of complicated tasks for the naming ceremony that he knew would keep them occupied for the entire day. The younger men shone with the trust, and faith Piri placed in them. They truly believed they were stepping into Piri's footsteps since the last moon and were discovering their spiritual paths. The tohunga thanked the ancestors for guiding his hand. While he wanted to have time alone with Marama, his tīpuna also showed him how to be a better teacher. Once the allocation of tasks was complete, Piri tidied up and prepared to go and get Marama. When he stepped outside, Marama and the baby were already approaching. She greeted him warmly with a smile, and Piri ushered them into his whare. Perhaps Rangi had told her to come to him. He checked around the perimeter of his whare, even though it was effectively off-limits to everyone today. People were superstitious, so it was unlikely anybody would flout the tapu of spiritual preparation, but Piri's training had ingrained caution in his nature. Once they were seated, Marama produced the necklace and held it out to the tohunga. She told him of her spiritual journey with Hana and the story of Hana's life.

"I have thought long on her tragic tale. I am a healer. We give our lives to saving the lives of others, but it also gives us power over life and death at times. Once, my Nani and I used our knowledge to protect our people. I couldn't conceive of using healing knowledge for personal gain or revenge," said Marama with tears standing unshed in her eyes. Piri nodded, deep in thought himself. The complexities of Rangi's whakapapa, and the despicable deeds of his ancestors, were a constant source of worry. A chief who wasn't a chief led the tribe, and his ancestors frequently offended the rule of order across the three realms.

"There is a reason Hana has shared this story with you, Marama. Thank you for telling it to me, as I can add her words to my own in the search for the way forward. Kotuku frequently comes into my dreams and urges me to look for the signs, but he has reverted to the riddles of the spirits. He asks me to look to Papatūānuku for the answers and follow the path from the past that will lead to the future. I confess I am no closer to understanding the meaning of his sage words. Do they mean anything to you, Marama?" His eyes looked black and thoughtful in the shaded gloom of his home.

"I wonder now if Hana's story is part of the path from the past, but where it is leading perplexes me as well. I know the days are passing, and the respite you have won for me won't last forever. My ancestors have never been so quiet. They also urge me to follow the path, but it eludes me," she confessed with a frown.

"I have my trainees preparing the ceremony for the child. It will be his preliminary naming. The ancestors have demanded a subsequent naming, at a time they will choose, and they have warned Rangi that he has impinged on their rights. They spoke to him directly in the sacred cave Marama. Rangi didn't have the good sense to be shaken by the warning, and he only justified his decisions. The only concession he made was agreeing to the spiritual cleansing rituals that I have set for him. I am afraid he is devoid of any spiritual abilities as he has no empathy for other people. The mauri of my people is in jeopardy, Marama, and I must find a solution. May I please hold the boy for karakia while he sleeps?"

The frank opinion Piri conveyed emphasised the spiritual weight resting on his old shoulders. It was almost tangible to Marama. Perhaps it was because they shared the task or linked spiritually more closely each time they met. Marama unfastened the bindings of the baby carrier. She was returning to her former shape, which pleased her and amused Ngoi. Today she was able to wear her own garment again. That comforted Marama as Ari made the garment for her. As Piri took the baby, she smoothed her hand over the side of the garment and felt a bulge in the concealed pocket. Marama usually stored delicate items gathered for medicinal purposes in this way. When she extracted the contents, she knew exactly why she had forgotten them. These were the fungi she collected on the foraging expedition just before Roimata appeared. The following hours, then days, were so chaotic Marama had, uncharacteristically, forgotten about them. She froze with the dehydrated mushrooms nestled in the palm of her hand.

"I forgot I harvested these on the day Roimata assaulted me. They are a rare fungus. Do you know of them?" She fixed her gaze on the tohunga.

"I know of many uses for fungi, but I have never seen these growing in this area before. What do you use them for?" Marama looked a little pale, he thought.

"These don't grow near my village either. I was shown the fungi, on a voyage that I made, by a tohunga who used them for baiting vermin that tried to invade the storehouses and...." Her voice trailed away for a moment. "The tohunga used them to bring about a swift end when the drawn-out suffering of a slow death became too much to bear."

Green and black eyes locked for a moment. Each mind was racing through a labyrinth of possibilities. Were the fungi a gift from Papatūānuku? Had the path just been revealed to them? The way to achieving the outcome the ancestors wanted and to exact Hana's longed for revenge? It seemed so convenient a solution to all of their problems. The only issue was that Marama and Piri were both dedicated to the wellbeing and protection of their people. Neither of them could imagine utilising poisonous fungi against Rangi. The thought was repulsive to each of them. Piri looked as pale and distraught as Marama did.

"This cannot be the way," he croaked. "We are both equally dedicated to the preservation of life and the rules of nature. Let's think about this. Perhaps it was just a coincidence," he said. It sounded as unconvincing in his ears as it did in Marama's, but she nodded at him anyway.

They were saved from their dilemma by the baby. He opened his eyes sleepily. The infant regarded them sagely before stretching his little arms towards his mother, already making sucking noises. They cradled the boy between them, a precious new life gifted to them. Piri felt a surge of protectiveness towards the baby, just as Rongo had. He also heard his ancestors whispering that clearing the path for the child's future to unfold was the most critical work of his life. The tohunga knew Marama would play a role in their future, but he was unaware of how many strands of fate would be weaving or the intricacy of the pattern. He shivered as the katipō necklace caught his eye. The evil of Ngaio's deeds cast a long, dark shadow, even in the light of day after so long. The child managed to soothe the frazzled nerves of both adults, and they turned the conversation to the naming ceremony—a much safer topic. The rest of the day passed pleasantly as the two spiritual guides discussed details. When it came time to go, they clasped hands, wrist to wrist, for a moment. Reluctantly Marama picked up the katipō necklace, which she liked even less since Hana entered her dreams.

"Can I leave those with you for the moment?" The mushrooms sat in a mixing bowl. A threatening cloud, hanging sullenly in a blue sky.

"That may be best for now. Were there more where you foraged for these?"

She nodded, her eyes shiny-bright in the gloom. Marama's eyes reminded him of a nocturnal animal, moving warily in the forest at night. Again, the baby restored equilibrium to their world as he talked to them in his unique language. They laughed at his antics, feeling the mood lighten in response.

When they left, Piri began to feel cold. It was a numbing chill that started in his feet but was progressing steadily through his body. The ancestors delivered a solution and sign that suffocated Piri. Although every fibre of his being was rebelling at the thought of harming or taking Rangi's life, he dared not quail. Shirking his duties to his people was unthinkable. The weight of this task was crushing his lungs and squeezing his heart. Still, Piri stirred himself and harvested more of the mushrooms from the place where Marama found them. Today he felt old.

Chapter 7

Rangi was in a jovial mood when he returned from his exercises in the afternoon. Marama prepared a meal of succulent wood pigeon, seasoned with peppery horopito. While she missed the seaweed from her village, there was a good supply of palm hearts and greens to supplement the kūmara she was roasting in the coals. She knew Rangi enjoyed her cooking, so she made an enormous effort to feed him well. The baby was always clean and fed, in a state of contentment before his father came home. Marama was meticulous in her planning to ensure that was the case. She relinquished her child to Rangi to play with, without showing any of the angst she felt in doing so. It stretched her emotional self-control to its limits. When Rangi handed the baby back to her, she was always overwhelmed with joy, and the whare seemed to light up. Rangi had never experienced a happy home as a boy or as a man, so every day was a surprise. He looked forward to the day he could lie with Marama again. A messenger left for Roimata's village in the morning and demanded they send her sister before the moon cycle ended. They were stalling, and Rangi knew it. He would soon finish his rituals and be free to enjoy the pleasures of his women again. The thought cheered him, and he ate heartily. Even if Marama grew old and fat from bearing his children, she would still cook for him, he decided.

The naming ceremony would be a celebratory occasion, and the villagers threw themselves into the preparations with wild, reckless enthusiasm. A mood shift was evident, with people emitting loud peals of laughter while preparing the food or gathering wood. The child they could have lost was taonga, and he represented the triumph of light and life over darkness to them. Marama no longer feared for his safety. She was still cautious around the chief's other women, but they had warmed to her as she treated their ailments with tender care. They were also thankful, because the boy's birth put their chief in a better mood than usual. The ceremony was a roaring success for everyone. After the formal rituals were over, there was feasting and dancing well into the night. Rangi was glowing with pride as he held his prized son, who his people adored. Only Marama and Piri retired early. Marama to take care of the child, who was tired after such a late night, and Piri to continue his endless duties. Rangi noticed the old man looked tired and urged him to take more rest. He didn't want to lose the tohunga who supported him so well, and certainly not before he commenced his campaign of conquest and vengeance.

The evening didn't go well for one of Rangi's women. While he was abstaining from sexual relations as instructed by Piri, he decided to take his frustrations out on a former favourite. The woman was beaten black and blue by Rangi. Their daughter cowered in a corner, hands clamped over her ears, attempting to block out her mother's whimpers. It was a setback for the women of the village. Eyes were downcast but not just in fear and pity as they once would have been. The women hid both anger and frustration at their chief. He now had everything he desired a beautiful son, an accomplished woman who took care of him and his people, even though Rangi abducted her. The Chief was wealthy, in prime physical condition, good looking, with a large contingent of fighting warriors. Why on earth did he need to beat his women, they wondered? While nobody dared to discuss the flaws in their chief's nature, it didn't stop people from thinking about them. An undercurrent of discontent was building amongst Rangi's most oppressed people. While Rangi was sleeping off the effects of the prior evening, Marama went to see Ngoi. Ngoi told Marama of the beating as the woman's distressed daughter came to fetch her once Rangi departed. After giving Marama a thorough, clinical description of the woman's injuries and the daughter's anxieties, Ngoi collapsed sobbing in Marama's arms. The woman was Ngoi's friend, and they gardened, washed and wove together. Ngoi had often seen her bruises and accepted her explanation she was clumsy.

"Marama, she will lose her sight in one eye. Rangi split her lips and broke several teeth. I feel so helpless," sobbed Ngoi once she was able to speak again. Marama held her like a child, stroking her hair and comforting her. She just listened and empathised with her emotions. "I hoped, like many in the village, once Rangi had his son and you, his happiness would improve his nature. It seems we were all mistaken. I dare not voice my concerns to Rongo as it would place him in an untenable position. He already carries so much responsibility, and I can't burden him with my growing loathing for his cousin. What would happen if they were to clash?" Ngoi shivered at her question as the blood drained from her face.

Ngoi was finally articulating her real feelings and the genuine fear she harboured of Rangi. Marama's stomach turned as Ngoi described the particularly vicious injuries inflicted. The tohunga would be aware of what transpired by now, but she would go to him and give him the details of the woman's injuries. Traumatising his daughter and the callous disregard of doing so was unforgivable in Marama's eyes. She picked up the sleeping baby and placed him in Ngoi's arms to distract her and give comfort.

"Thank you for sharing your innermost feelings with me Ngoi. It means a lot to me that you trust me. We must continue to protect Rongo for as long as we can." She held Ngoi's pretty, tear-streaked face between her hands and let the weight of her gaze communicate everything she couldn't say. Ngoi was always transfixed when she was so close to Marama's unusual eyes. Today they were as serious as they were beautiful, but it was reassuring for her to know Marama shared her fears. Ngoi never suspected she would come to share such a close friendship with Marama. That bond warmed her like a fire on a winter's night. Ngoi climbed out of the pit of despair she had plummeted into, determined to face the future resolutely. She lifted her chin and nodded slowly at Marama.

"If I feed Maui, would you be able to watch over him Ngoi, while I go and speak with the tohunga?" Ngoi nodded again, smiling fondly at the baby in her arms. She loved him, he was part of her family, and he stirred every maternal instinct in her body. Ngoi and Marama squeezed hands. Marama strode out of the whare in search of Piri.

Marama was furious with Rangi. She used the energetic walk to try and muster her anger into some semblance of order, but she acknowledged her abject failure as she approached Piri's dwelling. The tohunga came out to greet her, aware of the emotional maelstrom in her wairua. Her anger was pounding him in spiritual waves, and his grandmother whispered that Marama needed him now. They were walking a delicate tightrope together. The success of any action they took depended on their ability to maintain a harmonious status quo with Rangi. One of Piri's trainees arrived at his whare this morning in distress, as the beaten woman was a distant but loved cousin. Piri suspected Marama might come to him, so he beckoned her to enter and took both her hands in his. The tohunga closed his eyes for karakia, calling on the ancestors to wrap themselves around Marama. He asked them to heal her wairua, to dispel her anger and pain, with their spiritual love. Marama felt the roiling inside her, building to a tidal wave since she left Ngoi, transform into a tranquil pool. In the pool swam the faces of those she loved and had lost. They all seemed to reach for her and bathe her in love until she was awash with serenity. As Piri brought the karakia to a close with thanks, he saw tears rolling down Marama's cheeks. After everything this woman had been through, he had never seen her cry. In that fleeting moment, he glimpsed the vulnerable girl she once was. The inner self was cocooned behind an indomitable will, a wall of intelligence, a cloak of spirituality and skill. The ancestors chose well. He placed his hand on top of her head to let her feel his respect and regard but spoke no words. They communed on the cusp between the physical and the spiritual.

"Thank you for being here for me. I am rarely overwhelmed in such a way," she whispered.

"I know this, but I also understand the catalyst. As a protector of women and children, you are in unknown territory. Together we must hold fast. To do what I must do, I will need the best of you Marama." Marama regarded his ashen face and realised he had made his decision.

"It has to be me, Marama. It cannot be you. You are foreign, recently arrived, and may come under some suspicion as you prepare all his meals. You will need to eat everything you prepare first because I will insist on it. I believe it would be dangerous to be obvious. Sickness is most often slow in progress, and you and I will do everything in our power to effect a cure. The Gods and ancestors are calling an errant son to account. People must have time to come to terms with the new leadership, and we dare not risk destabilising the region. Rangi has made many enemies for us. It will take a concerted diplomatic effort to ensure we aren't invaded by those seeking vengeance in a time of weakness. You will be tested further by our chief Marama. I found out yesterday, Rangi has sent for Roimata's sister. Her people will not refuse his demand. Every visitor has noted the strength of our warriors, and Rangi likes people to know how formidable his men are. You and I are standing on the edge of a vast precipice, with only a narrow and dangerous path to follow. Marama regarded him solemnly. Part of her was relieved the spirits wouldn't call on her to take another life. The other part of her was committed to helping the tohunga restore the balance of power but craved justice for the women.

"How do we best protect my son and Rongo?"

"Rongo is our leader in all but title. In a short amount of time, he will restore life in this village to the way it should be. We don't need to involve him at all. His sincerity, loyalty, and commitment to following the appropriate protocol will protect us all. Rongo also owes you his life, and he will adopt your son." Marama swallowed deeply before raising her eyes to Piri.

"You know my son is not Rangi's son." Piri looked searchingly, for a long time, at Marama's guilt-stricken face.

"The ancestors, more particularly our ancestors, chose your son Marama. Whether or not Rangi is his father is irrelevant to them. The man Maui will become can usher in much-needed change. It will enable us to survive in a world that will transform in ways we cannot imagine. My ancestors share knowledge with me. Your ancestors come to our aid even when they want to wrest you from our clutches." He smiled as he shared that information, and Marama quirked an eyebrow back at him. She knew Nani had been reticent to share information with her. Often she hovered in the background, rather than taking the lead as was her custom since shifting realms. Nani believed she shouldn't, or was unable to, influence Marama's choices.

"Is there anything else you need me to do? Anything that will aid you in this task?"

"All I need you to do Marama is to be true to yourself. I don't fully understand how all of this will unfold, but I have faith. Is there anything else you need from me?" Marama shook her head, and the tohunga, who was showing his age, intoned another karakia. This time he called on their ancestors to bring her peace of mind and protection. Marama suspected she would need all the help they could give her in the coming days. The end of the moon cycle was fast approaching, which meant Rangi's rituals were concluding.

The baby was still asleep when Marama returned to Ngoi. Huia finished her chores and was hovering around, hoping the baby would wake up. The women decided it would be nice to go to the pools and bathe. Their lives were always busy with the additional duties they had taken on, so the healers treasured any free time. Marama found the warm water luxurious. It reminded her of the shallow pools she and Tane would wallow in at low tide on the island of her birth. A familiar pang of loss stabbed her as she thought of Tane. He died so long ago now. Time dulled the pain, but it never really left her. Kai was a constant reminder of his spiritual father. They shared so many personality traits, and when he was practising with his weapons, he was more Tane than Starman. That thought made her ache for both the men in her life. How lucky she was to have found two men who loved her and treated her with dignity. She tried not to dwell on the fact she would be returning to Rangi this evening, determined to enjoy her time with Ngoi. They held hands and almost skipped along the path as they anticipated washing each other's hair. Ngoi's infectious, bubbly nature lifted Marama above her pain, and she promised herself she would be tough.

It only took a couple of days until she had to make good on that promise to herself. Rangi began to complain he didn't feel well. He berated Marama for her use of herbs and cooking him too much rich food. Marama dropped her eyes contritely and apologised for any pain she might have caused him. She asked what he wished her to make that would please him. Rangi demanded meat broth which she later found out was what his mother used to make him. Marama diligently made the broth while Rangi was at home so he could see what she put in it. She also took a bowl for herself in front of Rangi, explaining she would taste it first to ensure it was palatable. Rangi watched her sip the broth before gesturing for her to give him the bowl. He was being cautious and making sure she wasn't giving him compromised food.

Marama liked to think she had won his confidence, but he was inherently distrustful by nature. Each day Marama reported what happened to the tohunga. Sometimes orally, when he called on her and baby Maui, at other times using the subtle sign language of the spirits, when in the company of untrained people. The tohunga also called on the chief to discuss village business and to check on his health. Piri brought various remedies and sometimes invited the chief to come to his whare or walk with him to the sacred cave. In this way, Marama was also aware of what was going on. The tohunga only ever brought genuine remedies to their whare. However, what he served the chief in his whare or the sacred cave, was often laced with small amounts of the dried mushrooms or other toxins from his supplies. The chief complained to the tohunga of night sweats and stomach pains. He wanted to know why he wasn't feeling better when his spiritual cleansing was almost at an end. Piri patiently explained this was often the effect of purging your body and mind, of earthly transgressions built up over time. He reassured his chief that he would feel euphoria and well-being unlike anything ever experienced as the ritual came to an end. Rangi began to feel better over the next two days. His vigour returned with a vengeance, and he stunned his men with his speed and stamina on the training field. Rongo clapped him on the back, complimenting him on his prowess, with all the enthusiasm they had shared as youths. Piri extolled the benefits of the cleansing ritual to Rangi, and now they were beginning to manifest in his fighting Rangi forgot about his former ailments. Rangi also eased up on Marama. She was a model woman in many ways, and he was reluctant to upset the harmonious sanctuary they shared at home. His son was growing and learned how to do something new every day to amuse his father. The boy, his Maui, was always content in Rangi's arms. The paternal bonds pulled persistently at Rangi's hardened heart, demanding his love. Maui was, after all, his creation. A part of him resided in the child's developing body, so it was natural for him to feel protective. Maui was his son, who he would train to be a formidable warrior, leader and chief. Rangi would achieve immortality, build an ongoing legacy through the deeds and achievements of his bloodline.

The day before the rituals were to end, Roimata's sister arrived in the village. No relatives accompanied her as she left the tearful goodbyes at home, only a lone warrior. Roimata was distraught, and in the end, their tohunga sedated her. Her family, although not oblivious to her pain, occupied a world of hurt of their own. They were losing yet another daughter to Rangi. It was difficult for them to forgive Roimata for her actions and the consequences they caused. One rash moment of anger cost the village so much. They would all endure hardship and poverty for some time, but it was Roimata's family who would suffer the most. You couldn't just replace a beloved member of the family.

The warrior left the outskirts of the village as soon as the girl was delivered. It was a shameful task to leave her, but he drew the marked stick as an unrelated man. There were no niceties, no polite rituals exchanged. It was mildly insulting, but so was asking for the girl. It was the old tohunga who approached them. Everybody else stopped what they were doing to stare, and the warrior turned on his heel before the tohunga arrived. The girl stood alone. Piri couldn't imagine how she must feel. He read sympathy on the faces of many in the village as he passed them, especially the women. She was disturbingly young, not yet a woman. He performed karakia over her outside the pā to banish any malign spirits or intent that might accompany her.

Piri sent one of the women to fetch Ngoi and Marama. The girl would need to be cleansed by the tohunga before he could present her to the chief. Marama had offered to take the girl into her home as a sister. The tohunga was under no illusions regarding how dangerous the situation was likely to be. She would want to protect the girl, but Rangi intended to punish her for Roimata's misdeeds. Aue! He called on all their ancestors for strength and wisdom. To provide the power, they would need to overcome the darkness and the fortitude to follow the spiritual path. By asking the chief's and Rongo's woman to take the girl to bathe, he was at least affording her the status as Marama's sister, not that of a slave. He felt it would be prudent to establish some rights for the girl if she was to have any chance of surviving. The girl's arrival would bring out the worst in Rangi. The startled look on the girl's face let him know Marama was approaching behind him. He had grown accustomed to Marama's strange looks as they spent so much time together these days. Not so long ago, he remembered, he tried not to look as shocked as the girl did.

"What is your name?" the tohunga asked, softening his voice in a kindly way.

"Arihia," she said. Her eyes were scared, but she raised her chin, determined to be as brave as she could be.

"This is Marama, and this is Ngoi. They will accompany you to the women's bathing pool before I present you to our chief." The girl's bravado faltered for a moment at the mention of the chief, but she nodded stiffly.

"Greetings Arihia. I am Marama, the woman of the chief and the mother of his son. I have pledged to your people that you will live in my home, and I will treat you as my sister. Please be welcome," said Marama with a smile as she stepped forward to embrace the girl. Arihia swallowed, not sure what to do, but she was saved by Ngoi stepping forward to introduce herself. Ngoi was pretty in a traditional way, not imposing in stature, and her bright smile soothed Arihia's fraught nerves, somewhat. The two women helped Arihia with her belongings and led her away towards the women's bathing pool. They chattered along the way, asking Arihia how her trip was and discussing the weather, the crops, and anything else they could think of to calm her.

Rangi stood at a vantage point above the village. He was the first to be informed of the girl's approach, and he wanted to observe her from a distance. She wasn't the fiery beauty Roimata once was, but she was young, and he would completely dominate her. A cruel smile tugged at his lips, as he would subject her to his darkest desires. He could take her into the forest or across the lake, where nobody would hear her scream. Now his happiness would be complete. Rangi tried to suppress the slight shudder of excitement inside as his imagination ran wild. It was only the extra-strong potion Piri gave him in the morning, which held him in check.

The tohunga regarded his handiwork critically. It had been

a long time since he learned how to prepare the hallucinogenic dreaming drink, and it should steep for another day. He was a young man when his mentor allowed him to try it to understand the effects. If he prepared it correctly, it would induce the euphoria Piri had promised Rangi at the end of the ritual. Should Rangi succumb to a craving for the feeling of release, it would provide him with a bargaining tool and power over the chief. Piri was giving himself as many opportunities and avenues to success as he could. Last night he and Rangi discussed a warning from the ancestors. Trouble was brewing in certain villages, and they were planning to mount an offensive against him. Piri suggested they send Rongo on a mission of diplomacy in earnest. That way, when they turned on Rangi, he would be justified in calling all the other villages to his aid, cutting the losses of his warriors. The tohunga cunningly suggested it would be good for Rangi to take command of the men now. While Rongo had done an excellent job in preparing them, Rangi was the chief. The slight implication, it might be prudent to send Rongo away to assert his authority over the men was enough to goad Rangi into action. He had noticed the easy camaraderie between the men and Rongo. It was good to have a strong second in command, and he was sure of Rongo's loyalty, but he needed his men to follow him. The tohunga offered to make the spiritual preparations and brief Rongo if Rangi wanted to take control of the men immediately. Rangi thought this was an excellent idea. All of a sudden, he couldn't wait to be in charge of his men and get ready for a good, bloody battle. Fighting was his forte. He lived to flex his muscles, dance to the music of his weapons and inhale the smell of blood in his nostrils. It was nearly time to begin his campaign.

Rongo was surprised when Rangi strode across the practice field and relieved him of his duties so he could visit the tohunga. He saluted Rangi with a grin, feeling confident the men were up to whatever drills he would put them through. As he left the field, though, he sent up a silent prayer that none of the men would be hurt or maimed. Rangi wasn't always careful to avoid serious injuries during the fighting exercises. Perhaps the brutality gave their men an edge in battle. Rongo sighed to himself as he didn't think it did but tried to console himself with the thought. He loved the men, his brothers in arms. The jokes and friendship they shared, the skills they practised together, were all designed to know each other. All the better, to protect one another in battle. When they fought, they fought as one, and they fought for each other. Rongo would lay down his life for his men as they would for him. Their chief was a formidable warrior. His unpredictability often caught the enemy off guard, but it surprised his men sometimes as well. It occasionally exposed them to more risk, so Rongo always tried to anticipate Rangi's moves to avoid any chaos in the ranks. When Rangi was in battle, he occasionally lost all awareness of those around him as he sowed death in the enemy ranks. Protecting him from isolation was challenging at times, but Rangi possessed an uncanny instinct for survival. Rongo wondered if his witch of a mother Atarangi had woven her dark protection around him. It was a sombre thought that crossed his mind as he approached the tohunga's whare. He hadn't thought of his aunt for years.

"Greetings Rongo," said the old man as he entered, "and the answer to your question is yes. Atarangi's darkness surrounds our chief." Rongo was startled for a moment, thinking he must have spoken the question aloud. Then he realised he had just reached the doorway and it was only a thought. He regarded the old tohunga warily, pondering what else he might know.

"Don't look so worried Rongo. I only perceive what is necessary or influential to the pattern of life the spirits weave. Please sit, and I will prepare us both a brew." The old man bustled around for a few minutes and presented Rongo with a herbal tisane. It was one of Marama's recipes with a few additions of Piri's own to suit his tastes. The benefits were marvellous for tired muscles and aging bones.

"This morning, the chief and I discussed increasing our diplomatic efforts as our tīpuna have sent us a warning. Some villages are planning an offensive against us." Rongo was hardly surprised by the news. Over the past two years, Rangi had succeeded in unravelling many of his father's alliances and made a host of enemies. One reason Rongo worked so tirelessly with the men was to ensure he prepared them for war. The survival of their village and families were dependent on the strength of their warriors. While the pā's location was strategically good, it also had weaknesses if he were attacking it.

"There is a reason you are the diplomatic envoy, Rongo. You are a reasonable and persuasive man who is both well-liked and respected. Your people truly need you now, but these missions will be risky."

"I understand," said Rongo, "and I will do whatever it takes to try and prevent the coming attacks." Piri nodded gratefully. Rongo was always quick to grasp the political situation.

"You have done well training the men, Rongo. Nobody could have readied them for battle as well as you have. Now, you must relinquish their leadership to your chief," he said pointedly. Rongo's face coloured a little under his swarthy complexion. The tohunga perceived more of his thoughts, and he was right. Rangi was the chief, and he owed him his full support. He considered himself chastised and humbly accepted the criticism as the reward for his disloyal thoughts. The tohunga watched him intently with dark eyes. It pained him to treat Rongo this way, but ultimately it was for his protection. Rongo must be loyal to Rangi in the days that would follow to place him above suspicion and reproach. Not an easy position to maintain when the cracks in Rangi's leadership were growing into gaping chasms. Piri doubted any woman in the village would be able to squeeze out a genuine tear for Rangi. He ruled with fear, and the women despised him more with each passing day. Piri felt the whispering in his head. The rustling of anger and agreement from the tīpuna who were reclaiming mana for their female descendants.

"Let us discuss the arrangements Rongo. What will you need to persuade them to give us another chance at diplomacy?"

The discussions lasted well into the afternoon. The tohunga possessed a lot of information gathered by spies and ancestors. Rongo was astonished by the level of detail Piri shared with him. They debated the best gifts to take, the weightiest trading commodities to bargain, and who should be in the diplomatic party. Neither of them believed a show of strength would contribute to a successful mission. While it would be risky for Rongo, they could send his head back to Rangi in a kete, the benefits of a non-threatening party offered the best chance of success. Piri proposed to send his most senior tohunga for additional protection, and to each village, a woman with relatives there would also join the party. Rongo would take two of his most trusted men with him to assist with travel and supplies.

"Please know Rongo, the will of all our ancestors is bent on aiding your mission. They were adamant you must lead this effort. Is there anything else you need from me?" Rongo looked thoughtful for a moment. The crinkled brow indicated the worries running through Rongo's mind. A debate was occurring regarding how to express what he needed. Rongo was a decisive man who could make quick judgements in all kinds of circumstances, so Piri focused on being as receptive as possible. What Rongo wanted could be significant.

"I need you to protect my whānau while I am gone. I have always kept my domestic life, happiness in the background unnoticed and unremarkable. That is no longer possible, with my woman and daughter so busy in our community. Ngoi is a beautiful, loyal woman who has taken extreme care, not to incite envy. There is also Marama and Maui, who we hold dear. We couldn't love them more if we shared blood. I feel responsible for bringing Marama here, a burden of guilt I must carry every day for the rest of my life. I cannot explain or express how protective I feel towards Maui. He has captured my aroha as surely as I captured his mother. Perhaps the Gods have decided it is a kind of justice. I know I need to lead the mission, but I also feel like I am leaving my lookout post. There is an uneasiness, a kind of misgiving that I feel inside," finished Rongo with a sigh. Piri was highly aware of Rongo's spirituality and the intuition that guided his decisions. He couldn't afford to take his concerns lightly.

"Your feelings trouble me also, Rongo. I will commune with Kotuku in the sacred cave tonight and try to uncover the cause of your misgivings. At the same time, I will seek to boost the spiritual protections around your family. We have enclosed Marama and Maui in a veritable fortress. It will also be my duty to take care of them all while you are gone, but I will pay special attention to Ngoi. I do not take this duty lightly," he said, meeting Rongo's worried gaze, his own dark eyes now filled with concern. Rongo's loyalty wasn't blind. He didn't shy away from his cousin's faults. Instead, he found strategies to mitigate his problems, and to Piri, it seemed he had done so for a long time. Piri ended their meeting with karakia. Without speaking the words, he accepted Rongo as his chief, in sight of their ancestors, and pledged his support for him. Piri called on the ancestors and the Gods who Rongo honoured to bless and protect his family. Tonight he would make offerings and deepen the ritual he commenced. The tohunga let strength and respect flow freely between himself and the next realm, to pass to Rongo. When Rongo opened his eyes, he felt fortified and full of hope. He promised himself he would visit the old tohunga more often. There was much he could learn from Piri.

Ngoi prided herself on being a good woman to her husband, but she could not hide the distress his impending departure caused her. Rongo didn't hide the risks or realities from Ngoi. If the negotiations turned sour, there was a slim chance he wouldn't return. He would prepare his family for that eventuality. If the other hapu didn't respect the trade rituals and killed him, Rongo wanted Ngoi to take one of his men into her whare immediately.

"You cannot risk the future of our children Ngoi, by allowing Rangi to take you as his woman. Both you and Marama would be at his complete mercy," he whispered in her ear. Ngoi's hand was over her mouth to stifle the sob that threatened to bubble out. She looked at him, her eyes pregnant with unshed tears, but eventually gave an almost imperceptible nod. Rongo enfolded her in his arms, reassuring her he always considered the worst-case scenario but had no intention of dying. Ngoi gave him a tremulous smile. She needed to be braver for Rongo, but faced with losing him, Ngoi truly comprehended how much she loved him.

"Ugh, you two! Most parents barely talk to each other, and here you are canoodling like teenagers in the dark. You are so embarrassing!" wailed their younger son, pulling a face.

"Get out, you little upstart," said Rongo, shaking his fist comically at his son. "If I want to canoodle with your mother in my whare, you will just have to live with it." He picked up one of Huia's *poi* (a small ball suspended on a woven string, twirled while dancing) and launched it at his son. It hit him with a thump on the chest, and he turned and fled, laughing.

"They have no respect for us Ngoi. What is a father to do?" He rolled his eyes upwards, making Ngoi laugh so hard she finally released her tears. With Rangi in charge of the men, and all the village children probably aware they were together by now, Ngoi and Rongo made love in peace.

"Perhaps we will be blessed with another baby," murmured Ngoi as she snuggled into Rongo's bulky shoulder. Rongo raised his eyebrows at her. They had lost two babies before they were born, after Huia, which traumatised Ngoi.

"Do you feel ready for that, my love?" Rongo asked the question gently, as Ngoi's mother reluctantly gave her daughter the remedy she requested to prevent pregnancy.

"I have learned so much from Marama, and little Maui makes me feel so broody again. The smell of him, his quirky smile, even his cry for milk is stirring my maternal instincts. I have never felt so ready Rongo. I hope I am pregnant now. We need to make love as often as we can before you go, as I want to be sure." Rongo threw back his head and laughed. It was a loud throaty roar of merriment.

"What's so funny?" asked Ngoi indignantly.

"I listen to constant whining from my men, all day every

day, that their women are too tired for love-making. Here I am, practically ordered into my woman's bed to get her pregnant. I am the ugliest man in the village, but I am such a lucky bastard." He giggled, pinning her underneath him with a grin. Ngoi pretended to protest, but she was secretly pleased he was still so attracted to her. He would leave this whare too exhausted to be interested in the unattached pāua who would make eyes at him, and try to cling to her rock when he travelled.

After Ngoi and Marama accompanied Arihia to the bathing pool, they returned her to the tohunga and his trainees. Understandably the girl was subdued by the thought of meeting their enemy. Although she answered any questions the women asked her politely, responses were coolly concise. When he couldn't put it off any longer, Piri took it upon himself to present the girl to his chief, observing the appropriate rituals. Tonight she would be safe, as Rangi would still be completing the cleansing ritual. Tomorrow, she should be safe because the effects of the potion the tohunga brewed would last at least a full day and night. The chief would be too caught up in the dreams and magic to worry about anything else.

Rangi was aloof with the girl, and he treated her like a fish presented to him as part of the daily catch. He poked and prodded her, squeezing her mouth open so he could inspect her teeth, subjecting her to a humiliating physical inspection. The chief didn't bother to hide his cruelty from her or his intentions from the tohunga. Rangi made every effort to intimidate and criticise her. To her credit, Arihia didn't cry or flinch from his prying fingers.

"You present me with such a disappointing specimen Piri. I thought she would, at least, look a bit like her sister. What to do with this timid little girl?" Rangi sighed, advertising his displeasure with her.

"Have her taken to the guest whare where I once housed Marama. I'm sure I will think of some use for her. Get somebody to take her some food," said Rangi turning away.

"My chief, do you recall Marama promised Arihia's people she would take her into her home as her sister?" Piri knew it was always a risk to question Rangi, but the formalities around fulfilling pledges made in negotiations were strict. It was his role as tohunga to ensure they met all the commitments they had negotiated.

"Certainly she did. You are correct. The small whare was Marama's home, and my whare is my home. I will, however, tell Marama to prepare some food for her new sister," he stated with mock sincerity and a wolfish smile.

The tohunga knew he needed to push ahead with his plans a little faster than he wanted to. Piri didn't dare to stand aside and allow Papatūānuku to be affronted again or have his ancestors desert them. Rangi's attitude would make life difficult for Marama and Arihia to bear.

Marama kept her face neutral when Rangi ordered her to take her new sister food. He smirked to himself in amusement.

"You can find her in your first home. I conceived Maui there, so perhaps I can produce another son."

"As you wish, my chief." She bestowed a benign smile on Rangi before busying herself at the fire. Inside, Marama was seething. Years of training enabled her to maintain an external air of calm as she refused to satisfy Rangi's sadistic sense of humour. The poisonous mushrooms flitted through her mind, and the katipō necklace pulsed calm against her skin. She hummed cheerfully to dispel her black thoughts, soothe the baby, and prove to Rangi she wasn't upset.

"Maui is sleeping. Would you like me to take him when I drop Arihia her food?"

"You better take him. I need to visit Rongo to give him instructions for his mission."

Marama was relieved to be taking Maui with her and pleased she would have an opportunity to speak to Arihia alone. Perhaps the baby would help to thaw Arihia's icy resolve and loosen her tongue. They needed to work together, and time wasn't a luxury they possessed. Marama packed the food in a flax basket, secured Maui against her chest and set off. Emulating the tohunga's first visit to her, she coughed gently to announce her arrival. Arihia was sitting stiff and upright on her mat. The girl looked lost, young, and so alone.

"I have brought you some food Arihia." Maui stirred at his mother's voice, and he opened a sleepy eye before shoving his fist in his mouth and sucking. "Let me introduce you to Maui, my son and Roimata's. I hope he will behave nicely for his aunt." Marama smiled gently and kissed the baby's head.

"Thank you for the food, and he is a nice baby." Arihia picked at the food absently, staring into the basket. Marama frowned, as she had hoped the conversation would flow more naturally between the two of them. Tonight could be the only opportunity they might have to speak openly. Marama took a deep breath and sat beside Arihia.

"Not so long ago, I was brought to this whare as a captured slave." Arihia startled, then looked up at Marama. Marama placed her hand on Arihia's and searched her face with concerned eyes. "You cannot face Rangi alone. He is a cruel man who will use you to punish your family. Roimata resented me because she loved him, but she saw him for what he is in the end. We are nothing to him Arihia. Women are only for cooking, childbirth and sexual pleasure to Rangi. Worst of all, he doesn't honour Papatūānuku or the ancestors. I pledged to take you in as my sister, but he twists the words I spoke to suit himself and places you in what was my first home. I don't know how I can protect you from him, but I must try." It was a risk to speak so plainly, but honesty always served Marama well. She patted Arihia's hand as she stood to leave.

"Thank you, Marama. Roimata told me her hatred and jealousy of you drove her to misjudge you. You have a good heart, but I fear nothing can save me."

"In times of trouble, I always turn to my ancestors for succour and hope. They have never let me down. Here I stand, alive, with three children. I am still breathing after losing the man I loved, plumbing the depths of despair, sailing an ocean to escape certain death. Only you can determine your fate Arihia. Rangi has built his power over others on fear and abuse of his status."

Marama didn't want to spend too much time with Arihia lest Rangi became suspicious they conspired against him. It was easy to rouse Rangi's mistrust, and she needed his trust to support Piri. How best to achieve that outcome she mused? Instead of heading home, she decided to go and visit Ngoi and Huia. One of the most positive influences on Rangi was the new experience of whānau life. Rongo's whare was a temple to familial love and support. As soon as she arrived with Maui, Huia and Ngoi descended on them, but even Rongo's sons gathered around to fuss over him. Maui responded by stretching his arms, yawning and waving his arms in the air. His extended whānau giggled and cooed, marvelling at his every move. Huia volunteered to change his swaddling, and there was a great uproar of laughter as Maui shot a stream of pee into the air. The two men glanced up from their conversation in response to the hullabaloo. Rongo grinned as he was used to the antics of his whānau. Rangi, however, was enchanted by the unfamiliar warmth of whānau aroha. A smiling Marama looked at him, her eyes glowing with pride in their son.

An only child, Rangi's life was devoid of nurturing. Atarangi gave him to another woman to nurse as a baby to preserve the appearance of her breasts. As her son grew, his life was devoted to warrior training, with a succession of tutors. His mother raised Rangi to place himself above other people. Only Rongo, his ungainly, ugly cousin, dared defy Atarangi and include Rangi in his juvenile pranks. Her tolerance of Rongo was a calculated strategy as every aspiring chief needed supporters. Rongo's buffoonish but loyal nature meant he was an unlikely threat. Rongo also adored his cousin, and Rangi had few friends. Atarangi was less pleased when Rongo Kūmara, a nickname inspired by his stout lumpy body, became Rangi's sparring partner. She argued that the kūmara boy wasn't an appropriate match for the chief's son, but the instructor and her husband disagreed. In the end, it was Rangi who convinced her. He wanted to best everyone in his generation in combat. This group included older, larger boys. Sparring with Rongo improved his strength and speed. The fighting and tutelage enhanced the skills of both boys. Rongo was born with intuition, sharp ears, and he knew better than to beat his cousin at anything. If he wanted to survive, second best wasn't so bad.

It was a magical evening in Rongo and Ngoi's whare. Rangi grasped both happiness and contentment for a moment in time. The camaraderie and aroha that existed between his family and Rongo's were beautiful. He relaxed, basking in the adoration heaped upon his son. Briefing Rongo was an easy task as Piri did most of the work, and they soon moved to join in the fun. Marama held out her hand to Rangi, pulling him closer, to watch Maui at play. The boy was chortling as his cousins tickled his feet, blew on his puku, made all sorts of noises or pulled faces. Maui waved his hands and kicked his legs in approval. His parents exchanged proud looks, and Marama squeezed Rangi's hand, still captured in hers. She fantasised it was Starman's warm hand.

"Isn't he amazing? I love him so much. Everybody adores Maui." Marama's love for her child radiated out of every pore in her body.

"The most wonderful child I have ever seen. My son is a special boy, destined to be an exceptional man." Rangi mused he was starting to sound as prophetic as Marama. On impulse, he kissed the top of Marama's head tenderly. The gesture surprised them both for different reasons. It also caused Ngoi and Rongo to raise their eyebrows at each other secretly. Having his son, a real family, was an elusive dream for so long it frustrated Rangi. Tonight, he felt triumphant. This family was unique, incredible and his. Love stirred in his breast, rising from neglected cold ashes. Ngoi insisted they stay to share food and drink before taking 'their' Maui away for the night. It was a fun evening, and Rangi and Marama strolled home hand-in-hand, later than planned, with a sleepy Maui snuggled against his mother.

"My ritual is almost over Marama. In a couple of days, we can resume a proper relationship and perhaps give little Maui a brother." Marama brought her mouth close to Rangi's.

"Maui would love that." She let a hint of a smile cross her lips, playfully. The thought of resuming their sexual relationship was depressing, but the spirits had assigned her a task. The rituals Piri set were often physically taxing, and Marama was relieved when Rangi was snoring gently. Drawing Rangi close physically was fraught with risk, but he maintained his abstinence.

Chapter 8

Rangi awakened in the cool darkness well before dawn. Today was the final day of his trials, and he needed to greet the sunrise atop the peak nominated by the tohunga. He was fasting so Marama could enjoy some sleep this morning. She usually made him food and a warm drink before leaving, no matter how early he was up. It amazed him how organised and easy his life was with Marama and Maui. The bickering, constant noise and stress of his former home was now a distant, unpleasant memory. He made an effort to be quiet so he wouldn't wake Maui. Not that the boy cried. When he opened his eyes, he amused himself by talking and waving his tiny hands. The boy wanted for nothing as Marama seemed to anticipate his every need. Rangi smiled as he set off to complete his last day of tasks before completing the final cleansing ritual.

As he walked through the sleeping village, Rangi passed Rongo's whare and imagined Ngoi's shapely form snuggled against his cousin's lumpy body. He decided he would visit the unlucky Ngoi when his ugly cousin was away. She was good-looking, excitingly off-limits, and he imagined the feel of her long hair on his skin. A woman worth having. He paused outside the whare where Roimata's sister slept. A sinister grimace replaced the contented smile. Anticipation stirred in his lower belly, spreading to his groin as he imagined the satisfaction awaiting him at the end of his trials. He stalked on an apex predator in the dark. Adrenalin coursed in his veins, and he broke into a run as he hit the path leading away from the village. The burning in his lungs and muscles, providing the physical release he craved.

At the first hint of light invading the night sky, Piri made a solitary trek to the sacred cave. His feet knew the way. Once, he even made the ascent blindfolded. A foolish undertaking in his youth that resulted from his boasting. The lesson Piri learned was etched as a deep scar on his knee. The tohunga chuckled, shaking his head as the memory flooded his mind. He would teach his successor how to make the dreaming potion when his task was complete, but now he must remain focused. Although he knew the potion he was carrying was unusually potent, he wasn't exactly sure how strong it was. Two nights ago, he tried a minuscule amount and experienced the most bizarre dreams. Tonight he would be serving a whole bowl to Rangi, and he wondered what the effects would be. Piri didn't anticipate any harm would befall Rangi, but it could incapacitate him for a couple of days. Piri would spend the day preparing for the final ritual. He would greet the rising sun with a lament to the ancestors, offer prayers and gifts to the Gods.

The fire needed to be lit, stoked hot to warm water and oils, for anointing Rangi's body. When Rangi returned from his morning task, he would bathe in the sacred pool. Two trainee tohunga would wash him while invoking the ancestors to guide the village, with specific karakia prepared by Piri. The tohunga trainees were drilled mercilessly by their teacher. Every phrase and nuance of the karakia was imbued with purpose by Piri. They probably recited the words in their sleep as well, but Piri was now confident they were up to the task. Seated cross-legged, in the mouth of the cave, he opened his arms to the colour-tinged tendrils of predawn.

Piri sat in a waka in the middle of the lake. The water sparkled around him.

"Kia kaha (have strength) Piri. All the events you fear will become a reality if you do not act. You have found the way, and you must save the girl. Arihia's ancestors are incensed, and they implore Papatūānuku to save her. I have asked them to aid us. There is no time to delay your plans. Marama must champion Arihia's safety, and we cannot fail Papatūānuku again."

It was Piri's grandmother who came to warn him this time. Feminine energy was amassing throughout the realms. The tohunga swallowed nervously. Although warm, loving and nurturing by nature, Earth Mother's anger could reshape the world in a few short breaths. He closed his eyes as the weight of the task settled heavily, crushing the air from his lungs. They couldn't fail, and he prayed he and Marama would be worthy.

Rongo and the diplomatic delegation left the village at dawn as Piri sat in the cave mouth and Rangi performed a haka atop a rocky peak. The strands of the future weaved apace now, as texture, colour, and pattern took shape. When Marama awoke, she rushed to comfort Ngoi, whose suppressed fears for Rongo's safety were bound to surface. Huia would be distracted by Maui, thankfully oblivious to the danger her father was about to face.

"I know you are worried Ngoi. You must have faith in Rongo as your ancestors have entrusted him with this mission, and they watch over him."

"I know Marama, but I can't bear the thought of losing him."

Ngoi blinked her eyes furiously, trying to avoid another fall of tears. Marama pulled her friend close.

"That man who captured your unwilling heart, and my uncooperative person, can accomplish miracles. Those village negotiators don't stand a chance of doing anything other than what Rongo wants them to." Marama quirked an eyebrow at Ngoi, shrugged her shoulders and laughed. The best she could do for Ngoi was to share her confidence in Rongo's abilities. It worked, and Ngoi chuckled while nodding her head emphatically in agreement. With Ngoi settled, Marama prepared her and Huia some food. Maui hungrily nursed until the sounds of his whānau eating around him lulled him to sleep. Marama knew Maui would miss them when they returned home, and so would she, but she ached for Aroha and Kai. Their absence was a gnawing pain in her belly which kept her awake at night. She must soon find a way for her and Maui to return to their village. They couldn't maintain the ruse with Rangi indefinitely. Eventually, she would slip up, or they would clash over his behaviour, and she would be physically in danger. There was also Arihia to consider. She would be at Rangi's mercy every day of her life. Marama was suddenly overwhelmed and asked if Ngoi and Huia could watch the sleeping Maui so she could meditate.

The necklace hung like a stone around her neck. She was hot and suddenly breathless when she stepped inside. As she sank to the floor, darkness closed in.

"Marama, it's Nani. We don't have much time, so listen carefully. Rangi will stretch your self-control. If you want to protect the weak, you must not lose your temper. I am sending help."

Marama's eyes flew open, and she gasped for air. She was desperate to hold on to Nani, to ask her questions, but repeated her words until they became a mantra. There was tension in her muscles, and her mind was flitting through the messages received over months. Events were running out of control. To ground herself, she lay on the earth floor and asked Papatūānuku to guide her heart and hands. The earth enfolded her. The sound of the tree roots growing around her filled her ears. Birdsong filled her mind, and water lapped at her toes. Calm descended upon her once more, as Papatūānuku cradled her soul, nurturing her inner strength and feeding Marama with love. Fluttering her eyes open, she was unsure how long she lay on the floor, but her mind was as clear as a summer sky. Fortified, she hurried to retrieve Maui, to bathe him in the remnants of the gifts from Papatūānuku.

"What happened Marama? You are covered in dirt."

"I have been in the arms of Papatūānuku Huia. Is Maui still sleeping?"

"He has barely stirred since you left." The disappointment in her voice was palpable. Playing with Maui was one of Huia's favourite pastimes.

"Thank you so much for watching him Huia. I love you, and so does Maui." Marama kissed the top of her head and let the love inside her wash over Huia. The girl turned wondrous eyes upon Marama before skipping out the door to dance in the forest. Marama lifted Maui and cuddled him to her breast. His eyes flew open, and he began to laugh and gurgle with joy. When Ngoi returned, she found them dancing and laughing. They enfolded Ngoi in their bubble of happiness until tears ran down their cheeks as a feeling of euphoria surrounded them.

"Hold on to this love," a papery voice whispered to Marama.

Rangi was triumphant as he made his way to the sacred cave. He had done it—the first warrior since Kotuku to complete the cleansing ritual. The tohunga called for him as he ascended the winding path. The villagers below him watched his progress. They knew their chief was selected and found worthy. His chest swelled with pride. It had been challenging to maintain discipline, especially abstaining from sex, but he accomplished what other men couldn't. Curiosity gnawed at him. Piri had prepared a special potion, and he was impatient to try it, but first, they must bring the rituals to an appropriate close. The tohunga held fast to tradition, and Rangi acknowledged the tohunga was instrumental in fulfilling his plans. He did feel stronger mentally and physically, so he would complete the rituals correctly.

Piri greeted Rangi with a formal speech and hongi. Once Rangi was inside the cave, he knelt as Piri began a complicated karakia. Rangi's eyes grew heavy as the tohunga threw herbs and powders into the fire. The tohunga invited Rangi to lie on a bed of reeds and soft grasses covered by an ancient cloak. The tohunga rubbed warm scented oil into Rangi's cleansed skin. Piri intoned prayers as he worked, paying particular attention to the tā moko that told a version of Rangi's life story. A tingling sensation ran over Rangi's skin where the tohunga touched. He understood the words spoken at times, but Piri often muttered low unintelligible prayers as tohunga were wont to do. The ministrations transported Rangi to another place, where his body pulsed with energy, even as his muscles melted in relaxation. The sensation was almost sensual. Piri's mutterings were summoning the feminine ancestors to their cause. He invited them to look upon Rangi's tā moko, seduce him, and taste his skin so they would know him. They sighed in Piri's ears, for they knew their time was approaching.

The potion, prepared with care and ceremony over many days, was proffered by the tohunga.

"My chief, you have earned the most sacred rite. This potion allows you to walk and dream with the Gods and Ancestors."

Piri knelt with a bowed head as he held the bowl. Rangi reached for the bowl, excited to experience what it offered. He drank the draught greedily but didn't spill a drop, then lay back down on the bed as instructed and closed his eyes. The old man began singing softly, and the smell of sweet herbs filled the cave. Rangi slowly drifted into the welcoming arms of the narcotic potion as its euphoria enveloped him. It would be two days before he emerged from the cave to be reborn. Piri bought them two more days. Two days of safety for Arihia, time for his preparations, Rongo's negotiations, and Marama and Maui to build strength. He shook the age from his limbs as there was no time for rest.

When Rangi stirred from his dreams, he was reluctant to return to the real world. Craving for more potion plagued him, but he was also ravenous. The villagers had prepared a feast to welcome their chief back to the village, and Rangi's hunger was so keen, he thought he could eat it all himself.

"Your mouth will be dry. Take some spring-water, then this, the recovery brew."

Rangi grimaced slightly at the taste of the recovery brew, but it did make him more alert.

"Congratulations chief, it is an astounding feat you have accomplished. Let your people welcome you home with the accolades you deserve. I have blessed the kai already, and I imagine you are famished."

With a laugh, Rangi clapped the old tohunga on the back. He made a show of his descent, dancing with warrior steps, protruding his tongue and widening his eyes—a fearsome but graceful sight. Once Rangi was greeted by the elders and warriors, he made his way to Marama and Maui. Maui put on his entertainment. He grabbed Rangi's fingers and talked loudly, waving the other hand in the air. It looked like karakia, made the villagers laugh, and signalled the feast should begin. Food never tasted so good to Rangi. He fasted during the trials, but the two-day energy burn of the dreaming, left his body starving. Marama and Piri understood his needs, as they experienced the same sensation when they entered the spirit world. Marama had once revived her chief and Nani with special cakes after a challenging battle in the spirit world, so she refilled Rangi's basket with nutritious food each time it emptied. As the feast wore on, it became rowdier, with singing, dancing, competitions and jokes. Arihia was seated as far away from Rangi as possible, but once hunger was satisfied, his eyes sought her out. They skewered Arihia, a fish on a spear, as his mind turned to other appetites.

Marama had dressed with care. Her breasts were heavy with milk, and her figure more voluptuous from recent childbirth. Black rimmed eyes glittered green as she positioned Maui to suckle. That succeeded in diverting Rangi's attention from Arihia. When Marama rose to take the baby home, Rangi trailed after her. She barely placed the baby down before Rangi pounced. He was clumsy in his urgency, but Marama didn't flinch from the rough handling that often preceded sex. Rangi screamed in frustration when he couldn't maintain an erection, but Marama placed her fingers gently over his lips.

"Didn't you tell me Piri gave you a potion he mixed to suppress your desire?"

"Yes, he did, but there was no mention of it lasting after the trials."

"The more virile you are, the more it affects you, so it may take a little time to wear off. Come, there are other ways to share pleasure until we can make Maui a brother."

Marama's suggestion did nothing to comfort Rangi, so he pushed her away and opted to return to the feast. Piri had added more of the abstinence potion to the recovery brew. Arihia had left the party already and was staying in Ngoi's whare for the night with Huia. The first day of risk was averted, but they all knew they must remain vigilant. With the help of a sleeping draught the tohunga brewed for Rangi, everyone slept well.

It wasn't easy to settle on the best strategy, but Marama decided to keep Arihia with her when she could and send her to Ngoi when Rangi returned. It worked well for a couple of days because Rangi wanted to be sure he was functioning normally before seeking out a woman, especially Arihia. He also didn't want to fail sexually in front of Marama again. A slave girl was carrying fish back from the lake on the third day. Rangi was feeling a little nauseous. Piri warned him this could be a side effect of the dreaming potion. Instead of joining the fishing party, Rangi followed the girl, dragged her off the path from behind, and raped her. There was no longer a problem, but the girl didn't satisfy him. He bathed in the hot pools until he was ready for more sport. On his way to the village, he spotted Arihia gathering food in the forest, so Rangi hid behind a tree and watched her surreptitiously. She would think he was out on the lake fishing, like everybody else. The girl was nothing special, but the allure of punishing Roimata was an aphrodisiac. He stalked her on silent feet, positioning himself behind her. It was as easy to grab her as the other girl. If he knocked her out, he could paddle up the river and enjoy her for the rest of the day. Poised to move, he saw a flash of movement to his left. He froze, as it was Marama and Maui. Rangi withdrew to his hiding place. Marama looked in his direction with a frown, sniffing the air.

"How are you doing Arihia?"

"My basket is almost full Marama."

"Have you seen anyone else in the forest today?"

"No, it's like we are the only people in the world here. It's so peaceful. Why do you ask?"

"I thought I..... Never mind, probably just imagining things, us tired mother's do that sometimes. That's enough for our meal Arihia, and it's time to get Maui home."

Marama looked hard at the spot where she thought she saw movement. The fine hairs on her body were prickling, and she stayed alert on the journey home. Rangi exhaled slowly. It wouldn't have mattered if Marama caught them, but he found the secrecy added to the excitement. He enjoyed the hunt and the chase. While he hid in the forest, he decided to visit one of his other women as soon as he returned. There was enjoyment for him in self-denial. He would wait for Arihia.

After satisfying himself with two of his women, Rangi made his way to the tohunga. Piri needed to assess how he was recovering. Perhaps he would ask him to make more of the dreaming potion. It was mind-blowing, and he wanted more. For now, though, he needed something for the nausea. His sexual energy returned to normal, but the queasiness was beginning to bother him. The tohunga examined him, paying close attention to his eyes and his breath.

"Are you feeling nauseous at all?"

"Yes, I am. Can you give me something for this?"

"Of course. I thought that might be the case, as the brew was a little stronger than I anticipated making, I could tell by the depth of its colour. Still, you are a powerful man, and it needed to match you so, perhaps it is just as well."

Piri brought a bowl of a pleasant smelling concoction and urged Rangi to drink it all. There was a sweet flavour to the remedy.

"Is your strength and sexual desire returning chief?"

"Not at first, but I feel up to impregnating every woman in the village now. My martial skills have improved as well, and I feel faster and stronger."

The old man nodded his head in approval. So far, his plan

was working. He was controlling Rangi's intake of substances. Dispensing most remedies himself, but he gave strength boosting mixtures and sleeping draughts to Marama as well. They needed to move swiftly but without alarming anybody.

"Can you make more of the dreaming potion, old one?"

"The ingredients are not easy to come by chief. I also wouldn't recommend taking more potion so quickly. You must fully recover and reap the benefits of the cleansing ritual for your body and mind."

"Yes, yes, I understand. Give a list of anything you need to the young tohunga or Rongo when he returns. Then you will make more. I want to walk with the Gods again."

Piri bowed his head in understanding as Rangi had issued a command, not made a request. He would share his concerns with the younger tohunga. As the spiritual leader, he needed to remain above reproach. Piri was correct in gauging Rangi's addictive nature, and the potion's strength was adding to his obsessive longing for more.

Rangi shared a pleasant meal and evening with Marama and Maui. The boy was gripping his father's heart in his tiny fists, and Marama was proud of him. Small he might be, but he was playing his part in their charade. His birth father would be proud and enchanted when they met. A pang of loss pinched at Marama, so she busied herself while Rangi enjoyed Maui's lively entertainment. Marama was surprised when Rangi retired early. He said he was still feeling some of the effects from his trials, he wanted to rise early to take charge of the drills, and could she leave him out some food. It wasn't long before he was snoring gently, so she fed Maui before putting him to bed. Marama was surprised Rangi hadn't made any sexual advances. She did know a slave girl arrived distressed after an assault on the path, and one of Rangi's women sustained injuries in the afternoon. Instinctively, she knew it was Rangi in the forest this morning. The whiff of his scent, after sex and bathing, confirmed it. It didn't surprise her when Rangi moved stealthily off his mat in the dark. She waited for the sound of him relieving himself, but the night was silent. Marama rose quietly and tip-toed outside, glancing back at Maui, who was sleeping soundly. Maui would be fine, but Arihia was in danger. If Rangi desired the girl, she would live through it, but he wanted utu. To punish Roimata and her people, he would crush Arihia in the cruellest way he could imagine. The thought made Marama shiver, and she reached for the love of Papatūānuku. As she approached the small whare, she could hear scuffling noises. Rangi was on top of Arihia with a hand clamped over her mouth, while the panicked girl writhed and bucked underneath him, trying to break free.

"How dare you insult me like this Rangi. I am your first woman, and I should be first in line!" Marama hissed the words out with all the venom she could muster.

She grabbed Rangi's arms and yanked him backwards with all her weight before pushing him sideways to catch him off balance. Arihia wriggled out from underneath Rangi, but his reflexes allowed him to get his feet underneath him in a crouch.

"Get Maui and take him to Ngoi's, you insolent girl!"

Marama shoved a shaking Arihia out the door before Rangi launched himself at her with a growl. He grabbed Marama, squeezing her throat to restrict her air supply. There was no way she would be able to fight this man, but she hadn't travelled so far to die.

"Hold on Marama, I am here with the female ancestors."

It was Tane. Her lost childhood love. He no longer spoke to her, so maybe she was going to the next world. She felt a surge of heat coursing through her body and seized Rangi's arm, forcing it away from her neck with a groan.

"That's my girl," Tane whispered.

It wasn't just her strength that enabled her to do this, but she must not fight with Rangi. Quick as a moonbeam, she pushed Rangi to the mat while the ancestors were still with her and straddled him, arms pinned overhead. Her strength shocked him. Marama longed to kill him with the spirits and Tane's aid, but she fought the primaeval surge of self-protection valiantly. That wasn't the plan.

"You offend Papatūānuku. The Gods gave me to you, and you are mine first."

Marama used him roughly, biting him hard enough to leave marks, and he loved it, responding to her passion with gasps. Mercifully, he passed out. Marama gave thanks to Papatūānuku, the female ancestors of Rotowhā and Tane.

"I love you always." It was a faint echo in the back of her mind, but there was no doubt it was Tane. Was he the help Nani promised? Marama poked a finger at Rangi. He was unresponsive, out cold, but breathing deeply. She wondered what Piri gave him tonight, and the musing raised the corners of her mouth. Now she must decide what to do. She went to Ngoi's to check on Arihia and Maui. Ngoi and a concerned Huia were examining Arihia's bruises. She hadn't sustained any serious injury to her body, but Arihia raised scared, tear-filled eyes to Marama.

"Maui is still sleeping. Did Rangi hurt you? Where is he?" Arihia was staring, fixated by the finger marks on Marama's neck.

"Thank you for fetching him. I don't like to leave Maui alone even though he sleeps through everything. I am fine. Like you, I have a little bruising, and Rangi is sleeping soundly in your whare. Ngoi, can Maui and Arihia sleep here? I think it's best if I stay with Rangi as I need to wake him up early tomorrow." Marama smiled at their frightened faces, desperate to make them feel better.

"Of course they can. No need to ask really. Will you be - comfortable?" Ngoi wanted to say safe but didn't want to alarm the girls. She searched her friend's face but only saw reassuring confidence there. Marama nodded and kissed them all goodnight, lingering over Maui to gaze adoringly at him.

To her surprise, Marama did sleep soundly. At the first hint of light, she prepared food for Rangi and awakened him with a kiss.

"That was an amazing night of passion Rangi. Maybe we should fight regularly and come back to my old home more often," she purred, biting his ear. Rangi's memory of the night was somewhat foggy, so he shook his head to clear the fuzziness in his brain.

"I am sorry for defying you, Rangi, but I wanted to be with you last night, as there is a slight chance we may have conceived another child. That skinny little girl can wait. You need a woman with enough passion for growing your seed." As Rangi's memory put together the pieces of the night he remembered, he laughed.

"You are a greedy, insatiable woman Marama. Don't clash with me again." He grabbed her buttocks and ground his groin against her.

"Do you have to do the drills today?" Marama smiled at him coquettishly.

"Unfortunately, I do. With Rongo gone, I don't want the men losing condition. Perhaps we will come back here tonight." Then he was gone. Marama breathed a sigh of relief. There had been a chance he would beat her badly this morning, but she was still in his favour. Nani was right. The temptation to kill him was almost her undoing. She shied away from that action, and now the old tohunga bore the weight of death on his shoulders. Maui would be waking and wanting his milk, so she hurried back to the comfort of Rongo and Ngoi's home. Arihia looked hollow-eyed from lack of sleep. Marama paused to cuddle her and stroke her hair as Ari had always done with her.

"Don't worry, little one. Your ancestors have come to protect you, as mine are here to protect me. The women of this village from the next realm, and Papatūānuku herself, are on our side. We can prevail."

Arihia looked up at her sharply. At home, she studied whakapapa and was keenly interested in spiritual matters. She and Huia shared much in common. Like Huia, Arihia was slightly in awe of Marama, grateful to learn from and be protected by her. Last night, Marama's bravery had saved her from a fate she didn't want to face.

Chapter 9

Rangi drilled the men brutally. They ran until they almost collapsed, and the sparring was bruising and bloody. The haka left them hoarse, purple-faced, pink chested and their thighs burned with lactic acid. Rongo's exercise regime strengthened muscles increased speed and health, but Rangi enjoyed pushing them to the edge of endurance. It prepared them for battle, and he enjoyed exerting his power over them. His nausea settled after the tohunga's remedy, but in the middle of the afternoon, Rangi's stomach began to cramp. Pain lanced his abdomen, and he finished the exercise, much to his men's relief. He sent a runner to fetch Piri. The tohunga ran to the training ground as fast as he could. Only Rangi remained there, seated on a log. When he saw Piri, he allowed himself to double over in pain as another cramp gripped him. Piri screeched to a halt in front of Rangi, and he held his hands out in front of him and began karakia. The tohunga seemed to probe the air around Rangi, moving his hands in circles.

"Give me something for the pain."

"Where is the pain chief? Describe how it feels to me."

"It is here and feels like a hot spear in my puku." A sweat broke out on Rangi's forehead as he forced the words out.

"Chief, there is a dark stain on your wairua. Have you been in contact with anyone who might wish you harm?"

"For the love of the Gods man, just give me something for the pain." Rangi's face was red and contorted. The tohunga mixed a powder for the pain in a bowl of water to alleviate Rangi's cramping. The chief grabbed the bowl and gulped it down, lumps and all.

"It might help if you lie down on your side."

"I don't want my men to see me weak. Help me up and get me home while they are bathing."

The pain subsided for a moment, so Piri did as he was told. Rangi made a show of standing alone whenever they encountered anyone along the way. Once they arrived, Rangi collapsed on his sleeping mat. Marama and Maui weren't at home, so Piri stirred the fire into life and warmed some water for a sleeping draught.

"The treatment for the pain should begin to work soon. I need to get more of my medicines to improve the treatment of your symptoms, but we also need to get to the bottom of this ailment."

Piri returned with several pouches. He examined Rangi thoroughly while chanting to himself, clucking his tongue as he prepared a steaming bowl and told Rangi to drink it all.

"I am most concerned chief with the spiritual presence that surrounds you. Did anything out of the ordinary happen today or yesterday? Did you find any objects? Argue with anyone? Clash with any of the men?" Rangi greeted his questions with silence. "Please try and think of everything chief. The most insignificant piece of information might be of importance."

Rangi saw no reason to mention it was he who raped the slave girl. Surely it wasn't that, as the girl was nobody.

"Yesterday, I argued with Marama. I chose to steal away to Arihia last night, and she was jealous."

"Arihia, aue! The girl has many protections around her. I went through all her belongings, but her people despise you. You must be careful with that girl. Can you avoid her for now, please?"

Rangi nodded his agreement. He was reluctant, but another cramp made him more flexible.

"What else?"

"Marama said I offended Papatūānuku by not choosing her first. She pushed me away from Arihia. I had no idea she was so strong. Marama wanted me for herself because she thought we might make another child last night."

"Aue! We are already on shaky ground with Papatūānuku, and even our maternal ancestors are unhappy with us. I begin to perceive a problem. Anything else?"

Rangi furrowed his brow in concentration once the cramping stopped, and he could think again.

"This morning, I sparred fiercely with several of the men, but I drew blood from Tahu." He had enjoyed drawing blood from Tahu. The young man fought well, a little too well for his own good today. Rangi taught him a harsh lesson about landing painful blows on his chief. While he liked a good fight, his status afforded him some respect. The tohunga looked thoughtful as he recalled the warrior.

"Tahu wasn't born here. He only came to his uncle and aunt after enemies killed his father in battle. The hapu he came from is trying to break its alliance with you. You have given me a lot to investigate. Each of these issues you have raised with me could be the cause of your ailment. I must find the correct one to enable me to cure you."

The tohunga was almost talking to himself as he turned the information over in his head. Rangi's eyes were beginning to feel heavy as the pain dissipated.

"Sleep well chief. Sleep is the best remedy for the body. I will ask Marama not to disturb you, and I will return." The tohunga barely moved before Rangi sank into a deep sleep, leaving Piri free to search for Marama. Marama was at Ngoi's with Maui, and so was Arihia.

"*Tēna koutou katoa* (hello everyone). Marama, I was hoping you and Maui might join me for karakia?"

"Thank you for always thinking of us. Shall we come with you now?" Piri nodded with a smile and turned to a frightened-looking Arihia.

"Your ancestors will always take care of you Arihia. You have displeased our chief, and you are not to go near him, understand? Ngoi, can Arihia stay with you for a few days?"

"Yes, Huia will be excited to have another girl in the house." Ngoi gave Arihia a beaming smile to let her know she was pleased as well.

"Now might be an opportune moment to collect her belongings from Marama's old whare."

Ngoi inclined her head in thanks. The old tohunga was fastidiously polite, always conformed to the correct protocol, but today she perceived care and kindness under his stiff exterior.

Marama walked behind the tohunga, to indicate her subservience to him. They must ensure people did not suspect they were conspirators. Rangi's confessions would allow Piri to seek out Marama, Arihia and Tahu, of course. Piri was under no illusions Rangi was honest with him. He had experienced his ability to be economical with the truth already when Kotuku warned Rangi in the sacred cave. No doubt there was far more detail to the stories than he knew. Settled in Piri's whare with a soothing drink, Marama told the tohunga what happened during the night. Piri listened attentively, a bit like Nani used to. He shook his head at Rangi sneaking out to Arihia, frowned at Rangi's treatment of Marama, but widened his eyes as he heard of the spirits and Tane's intervention. The tohunga nodded sagely at her as she confessed the conflict the urge to kill him caused her. He patted her hand in support of her decision to stick to the plan.

"I asked Rangi if anything out of the ordinary happened yesterday. I was unpleasantly surprised by what he told me but suspected there was much more to it."

"I think he was in the forest yesterday, spying on Arihia, but I was nearby. He didn't go fishing as planned. There was a girl assaulted on the path from the lake to the village yesterday. She was grabbed from behind and roughly used. One of Rangi's women also came to Ngoi with injuries."

"Aue Marama! Papatūānuku may be stirring the earth as we

speak. The chief is currently asleep in his whare as he has fallen ill. You and Maui may soon need to move into your old home. Will you trust me blindly in the coming days? I dare not confide in anyone."

"You have my faith and trust. Maui and I are grateful for the sacrifices you make for.... for all of us."

"Speaking of Maui, I want to hold him and feel how he is growing. There are words of wisdom and prayers for him from our ancestors. Maui will be a man of the people Marama, and he will be wise, just, a true leader. The ancient ones speak of his future, and he will be renowned for his mind and martial skills. Although he won't be named Maui forever, his clever inventiveness will pay tribute to his tīpuna and first namesake. When he is finally named, his name will reflect the complexities of his origins and role." The tohunga closed his eyes and began to chant, moving his hands gracefully through the air while Maui smiled up at him. There was a bond between the tohunga and the child. The gifts of the village ancestors flowed to Maui through Piri, enhancing them both, and Marama sensed the energy and spirits around her. While the exchange didn't include Marama, the spiritual warmth comforted her. The familiar sensation was an echo from the past, her childhood memories, and she smiled as she sank into reverie.

"Ah, you perceived the gifts Marama."

"Not the gifts exactly, but I experienced the warmth of the flow. The ambience of your whare reminds me of my childhood home and my Nani. She often lived as much in the spiritual as the physical world. Her primary guide was her grandmother, and they seemed to be connected all the time. There was rarely anything I did that Nani didn't already know." Marama rolled her eyes and laughed just thinking about it.

"That must have been frustrating for a young girl."

"It was at times because my abilities didn't manifest until quite late in life, whereas it came naturally to Nani early. Once I was able to talk with the spirits, I understood her much better." Marama's voice trailed off wistfully. The tohunga experienced her loss and the sadness she carried, hidden from the rest of the world.

"Your Nani sounds an intriguing woman. I would have liked to meet her. You miss her, don't you?"

"Yes, I do. We have always been together in life, and after she passed to the next realm. It was Nani who raised me after my parents disappeared. Our tasks at present are many and varied. I have three children and people I love, scattered across the land and sea. Maui's future was always veiled, so it was up to me to ensure he lived. Nani is the custodian of everyone else I care for, including my young daughter. We are often separated now, for the first time in my life."

Piri placed Maui back in his mother's arms as he knew it would comfort her. Maui laughed and made noises for his mother before nuzzling at her breasts to let her know he was hungry again.

"It appears Maui's greatness will be grown on an endless supply of milk." She laughed at the baby as he became serious about nursing.

"I will return to check on Rangi when the sun is lowering in the sky. Best to let him sleep undisturbed. Is there anything you need from the whare?"

"Nothing really, we spend most of our time at Rongo's whare with Ngoi and Huia anyway. We keep all the healing supplies there, and Maui has everything he needs. Should I prepare food for Rangi, or do you want me to check on him?"

"Yes, I think some broth might be good, but I will attend to his ailments myself. Some offerings to Papatūānuku from all of you and supplication to our ancestors might also be a good idea, in light of recent events. How is the slave girl?"

"Mihi is her name. Not just a slave, somebody's treasured child and relative. She is used to such treatment and is only surprised and wary that we are kind to her. The low value placed on women, combined with Mihi's low status as a captured woman, has left her with an abused body. This treatment is cruel and counterproductive as she isn't even strong enough to complete a day's work. I suspect she will die because she no longer has any will to live and be of no value to anyone. Can you speak to the men of these practical considerations Piri? I doubt we can change attitudes formed over generations in a few days, but this behaviour is madness."

"I must try Marama. When your ancestors demand change, you obey. From what you have told me of your story, you know this to be true. Rongo is the man who can help me affect change."

Marama thanked him and readied Maui in his carrying basket. The tohunga tickled Maui under his chin, clucking his tongue at him. Impulsively, Marama hugged the tohunga for a moment in farewell. She was the only person who understood his burden and stoic courage.

The day passed in an unremarkable fashion. Marama made broth for Rangi and helped weed the kūmara beds with Maui fastened on her back. It was enjoyable to do some physical work with her adopted family. She was amused when Huia and Arihia quizzed each other on the use of remedies while they worked. When there was a disagreement, they both came to Marama to ask her opinion. The girls displayed a solid foundation of knowledge, and often, they were both correct, just utilising remedies in different ways. It was good to see Arihia talking animatedly with Huia, even when she knew what her future would hold.

"What is that around your neck Marama? Is it a spider?" The pendant drew Arihia, a moth to the flame, and she exhibited a slightly horrified fascination. Huia giggled at her gawking.

"It's a katipō spider. A venomous creature that lives on some beaches amongst the driftwood."

"How did it get inside?"

"I'm not sure Arihia. I received it as a gift recently from Rangi, so I don't know how they made it. There is a tragic story attached to the pendant." Now she had everyone's attention. The prospect of a story stirred the girls' curiosity, and they loved a good tale.

"Will you tell us the story tonight?" Huia was practically hopping up and down with enthusiasm. Ngoi looked hopefully at Marama, and Hana whispered her approval, so she agreed as long as Maui behaved himself. The baby laughed at his mother right on cue, sending the girls into a fit of giggles.

Marama saw Piri pass by on his way to attend Rangi. She waited long enough to allow the tohunga to perform karakia, make his examination and prepare a remedy. Maui was busy playing with his nursemaids, so Marama balanced a large bowl of steaming broth and set off to Rangi's whare. She was never able to think of the whare as their home. In her mind, it was a shelter for them while they travelled. Before she arrived, Marama cleared her throat to alert Piri to her presence.

"May I come in? I have brought broth for Rangi as you asked."

"Enter please, I think the chief would benefit from something nutritious. Taste it to make sure it isn't too hot."

Rangi was propped up on his mat and looked pale beneath his brown skin. Marama tasted the broth. It was good, and her stomach growled as she hadn't eaten yet.

"It seems you are hungry too, Marama. You may sit with Rangi and share the broth with him." The tone of Piri's voice was cold and condescending. Marama hesitated, appeared confused for a moment, then went to Rangi's side.

"How are you feeling Rangi, you look a little pale?"

"I haven't been feeling so good today, but Piri is plying me with remedies. The broth smells good." Marama took a smaller bowl, filled it from the vessel she brought, and handed it to Rangi.

"Taste it first, Marama." Piri was making sure everything Rangi ate was safe. She sipped from the wooden bowl, gulped it down and smiled at Rangi before holding the bowl out to him. The broth was hearty, full of the flavour of smoked wood pigeon, salty fish, fresh herbs, and thickened with starchy kūmara. Rangi didn't share the rest of the bowl with Marama. Whatever ailed him wasn't affecting his appetite as he asked for more. This time Marama tasted the broth without being asked. She also served a bowl to the tohunga and took one for herself, returning to sit next to Rangi. It would be prudent if she also remained above reproach.

"Is there anything else I can do?" She looked to the tohunga for the answer as he had taken charge.

"Make the whare tidy. The chief's son must be kept safe by Rongo while his father recuperates. Make arrangements to sleep elsewhere for the moment."

Piri returned to Rangi's side and began another chant. Marama did her housekeeping efficiently and quietly. She threw a concerned look at Rangi before she departed but didn't dare to interrupt the tohunga. Once the tohunga ceased his chanting, he felt Rangi's brow.

"Are you suspicious of Marama Piri?"

"I am suspicious of everyone chief. Your sickness is affecting your wairua, which in turn affects your body. Enchantments can be placed on objects by a skilled tohunga, and food can be tampered with by anyone, not just the person preparing it. Somebody wants to cause you harm. I need to find out who it is, and until then, I can't trust anyone. Today Marama just made you delicious food and seems genuinely concerned, which is good to know. You are also the father of Maui, so harming you would harm his future. It would be useful to have Rongo here. He would lay down his life for you, and he is the one person we can rely on. Let's hope negotiations go well, and he returns to us soon."

"My pain has eased, and I am hardly ever ill. I'm sure there is nothing to worry about."

"I do worry chief, as I am perplexed by the source of influence. We cannot take offending the Gods lightly either. We must take steps to improve the lives of our women because our ancestors have told us we must do this. Somebody assaulted a captured girl yesterday, and it must have been a man from the village. Our relationship with Papatūānuku is tenuous at best, and I can only hope she punishes the perpetrator, not the rest of us as well. I have much to do, chief. Please take this sleeping draught when you feel tired. I will come back to check on you before I retire, and I am posting a guard."

The tohunga bustled out the door, already calling for his assistants. Rangi felt his stomach churning, and he began to feel hot again. All of this hocus pocus wasn't real. He probably trained too hard in combat and injured himself. A stab of pain made him wince. The life of a slave was worth nothing. Another cramp made him double over, so he took the sleeping draught and gulped it down. What he needed was to walk with the Gods again. The tohunga must prepare the potion for him so he could resolve any spiritual issues with the Gods. His mother told him Papatūānuku favoured him. She had endowed him with his healthy body and good looks. Let Piri make peace with her in this realm, and tomorrow he would probably be better. Rangi closed his eyes and welcomed the oblivion, where his pain didn't exist.

Piri was meticulous in briefing his young tohunga. He wanted them to keep their eyes and ears open. Their teacher reminded them of their oath, which bound them to keep information shared confidential and to always act with discretion. Any secrets were to be brought to Piri alone. In this case, gossip was of interest to him, especially the whisperings of the women and girls. He also asked the tohunga to attend to the spiritual needs of the warriors when they exercised today and report back to him. His successor remained after the others left.

"I have already heard gossip, and I intended to seek your advice before you called us to meet."

"It's good you are alert. Noticing what is happening is a critical component in caring for the well-being of your people. One day soon, you will wear my cloak, and you must be ready. We will navigate this latest challenge together. I fear our chief consumes my time, and I may neglect the needs of our village as a consequence. The next phase of your training will be intense. I will take you into my confidence Tamati, and I would be grateful if you could share your thoughts with me. You have reached a point where I value your opinion as much as my own. The chief has instructed me to prepare the potion given to those chosen to complete the cleansing ritual. I will teach you how to make the potion and how to set the tasks. You may never have to do this in your life, but you must pass the knowledge to your successor. I have cautioned our chief against taking more potion, as our tīpuna designed the ritual to test the mind and will of the staunchest men. There has never been anyone who has taken the drink more than once. The tohunga who passed the recipe to me warned me not to try more than a little to gauge its strength. It is seductive and leaves lesser men with a yearning for more."

Tamati regarded his mentor with serious eyes. He took an inward breath and puffed out his cheeks. Piri knew he was thinking and making a decision.

"The gossip I have heard is regarding the chief. I fear we have many avenues to explore, as Rangi has many enemies. Where to start? Yesterday I saw Huia inspecting bruises on Arihia's body on their way to bathe. I understand from their conversation, Arihia was visited by the chief and handled quite roughly. Arihia has no love for our chief and most probably would do him harm if she could. Her people would celebrate his downfall. Is it possible we could have missed something when we welcomed Arihia into our midst?"

"I have asked myself the same question, and we must be vigilant. I have urged the chief to stay away from Arihia for now, and he has agreed." Piri let out a sigh.

"That isn't all. My cousin, one of Rangi's women, told me Rangi came to their whare yesterday. He wanted to relieve his sexual desires and chose two women. Rangi beat one of the women, and the other was left crying. The chief isn't a gentle man when it comes to his women, as everyone knows. They thought he seemed more aroused than normal, and they wonder, in whispers of course, if it was he who raped the girl on the lake trail."

Tamati lowered his eyes. The man didn't gossip. He would never say anything about the chief except on the instruction of his mentor.

"Thank you for sharing this with me Tamati. I know this task isn't easy for you. Like me, you are loyal and careful, but information such as this is what we need. I too heard a rumour the chief was in the forest around the time someone assaulted the girl. Ngoi also treated the beaten woman. The more incidents we have, the further our net widens, and with Rongo absent, people will also look to us for leadership while the chief is ill."

"There is one other matter regarding the warriors. This gossip I overheard myself when a group of men were resting by the lake after a swim. They weren't aware I was fishing behind the rocks in the next bay. One of the men wished Rongo would hurry and return from his mission. The gist of the conversation was that Rangi punished the warrior who gave him such good sparring practice by injuring him. A few of the men grumbled that nobody wants to spar with Rangi. If you don't fight hard enough, he thinks you are useless and gives you extra practice. When you fight well, you can't land blows, or he loses his temper and unleashes his wrath until he beats you. The consensus was they would rather follow Rongo, and his men are the lucky ones. I waited until they all left before I took the long way home. If the men knew I overheard their conversation, they would be mortified."

"Aue! Not the men as well. I have also been approached individually by our village leaders since the incident with Roimata. Our eldest *koroua* (elderly man) is concerned our chief lacks the mental stability to guide our people wisely. There are also questions regarding whether the alliances made by our former chief are squandered, without good reason. The difficulty is, people are becoming too afraid to voice their opinions and oppose Rangi. Our elders and those of high rank are accustomed to being influential, but at the moment, they don't feel respected. We have shared many worries today Tamati, but it feels good."

Piri placed his hand on Tamati's shoulder and gave him a heart-felt hongi. It was like wading into a stormy sea together, but at least they were supporting one another. The younger man was overcome by the trust and faith Piri showed him. The weight of responsibility settled on his broad shoulders, and he welcomed it as a sign the door opened to his calling.

Piri was shocked by how much gossip was circulating. His sources flooded him with information. Apart from a handful of children, almost everyone harboured a grievance against Rangi. From deflowered daughters and women to slights, errors in adhering to protocol, the chief's transgressions mounted steadily. Tamati sometimes gnawed at his thumbnail in thought when he and Piri were alone.

"You are so deep in thought Tamati, that your ears are turning red. Tell me what you think?"

The younger man flushed a little. He hadn't realised his ears betrayed him, as did his cheek-puffing and nail-biting. Piri urged him to be honest, but he was used to being prudent as well.

"Well, there seems to be a lot of gossip with recurring themes. There is a pattern of behaviour, which implies much of the gossip is true. Our chief isn't a popular man. People don't respect him, but they fear him." Tamati paused for a moment, deciding how best to articulate his thoughts. "A chief is a leader of people. A man isn't always born to be a chief. The welfare of the people, the whenua, the mauri are the primary responsibilities of any chief. Does Rangi fulfil those duties, I ask myself? If not, what can we do about it? A chief is accountable to his people, and our hapu leaders should contribute to the decision-making for our village. We have the right to address grievances and, in extreme cases, to choose a leader. Do I speak like an inexperienced man who doesn't know his place, or am I correct?" Piri smiled at Tamati, who was stepping into uncharted territory. Piri needed to give him a response that respected the honesty of the question.

"You are correct, I can see you speak from the heart and thank you for your trust in me. Our histories, the stories in our whakapapa, tell us we have been in situations like this before. Each situation has its own unique set of challenges. We know our people and should ask ourselves, can we influence this person? Most of the time, the answer to this question is yes. Our role as spiritual guides allows us to earn respect. As tohunga, we petition our ancestors and the Gods for answers or guidance. This guidance will usually move events in a favourable direction. At times the ancestors may intervene directly to influence a stubborn person." Piri shook his head from side to side, his face crumpled with sadness. "We have taken all of these actions, and the Gods have answered our prayers. Guidance has been given, specific guidance, without interpretation or signs. A direct intervention has been taken by Kotuku himself, to no avail. You are right to ask what we can do."

Piri recounted to Tamati the details of his visions and the words of their ancestors. The search for Marama to complete the chief as a man and allow him to become the leader they needed. He repeated Kotuku's words of warning to Rangi, delivered in the Sacred Cave. The message that was given to Marama, from their ancestors, to restore the mana of their women. Tamati's eyes widened further and further in surprise. He grasped the vast number of signs they received and how clearly the ancestors had communicated their messages. His own experience of the spirits created the impression they mostly spoke in riddles. Often when his great-grandfather came to him in dreams, he didn't understand what the message meant until he was in the middle of it, like now.

"I too received a message from my guide. It was cryptic, and I have been contemplating the significance of the words. My tīpuna told me to 'follow the true leader, my instincts for justice, and to hold to my values. Turbulent times are coming to test you all.' His words came to me now as you were talking." Tamati's abilities were developing apace. Piri decided to share with him the forbidden gossip surrounding Rangi and Rongo's birth, but to his surprise, Tamati already knew the story, which pleased him.

"My kuia used to regale me with tales as a child, and I know every bit of gossip that was circulating before you were born." Tamati grinned mischievously as he even knew a few stories about his mentor.

"Is that so Tamati? She was a sharp woman, your great-grandmother, with an extraordinary gift for recalling whakapapa and gossip, it seems."

"What do you need me to do?" Tamati raised his eyes to Piri again.

"Our ancestors have laid out the path. Our chief carries a dark stain on his wairua, but he hasn't been honest regarding his deeds or followed the directions his tīpuna have given him. I need you to watch over the village in my stead, and particularly Rongo's whanau. My place is by Rangi's side, and I must endeavour to follow the will of the Gods and ancestors. If I need you for anything, I will send someone for you or come myself. I expect the chief will order me to prepare the potion soon, even though I have advised him against taking it. Please continue to gauge the mood of the people while my eyes and ears are engaged elsewhere."

The two men embraced. They shared a common purpose to serve their people. Working together redistributed the burden of responsibility, and Piri felt lighter of spirit for it. He turned to his fire, preparing a mixture of berries, dried flowers, herbs, honey, narcotic plants and deadly, powdered mushroom. This burden was his alone.

Maui and Marama settled quickly into their new abode. It was cosy, intimate and they enjoyed having time alone together. The bond between mother and child deepened with each passing day. Marama carried Maui with her whenever she could, fastened to her body. She stooped over the fire, careful not to let the smoke waft in Maui's direction. For Rangi's dinner, she prepared a rich fish stew with fresh greens, peppery horopito and salt from her medicine pouch. The salt helped remove leeches, but it also enhanced the flavour of the tasty fish from the lake. Tonight she would take Maui with her to visit Rangi. It would please him to see his son and help to keep her in his favour. At times she longed for a less complicated life, but she only had here, and now, so she fussed over the baby to console herself. She was fortunate Maui hadn't transformed into a demanding monster because he was over-indulged. Again she watched for Piri and planned her visit to Rangi. When she arrived, Rangi was looking much brighter. He was sitting up, sharing a drink with Piri and finishing a sweet cake. Piri offered the last cake to Marama as he finished his. Marama thanked him and offered him some fish stew, which he accepted. Carefully, Marama followed the same routine as the day prior, tasting the food in the bowl before handing it to Rangi. She knew this was one of his favourite dishes as long as the fish was fresh and succulent, added at the end to avoid overcooking. As soon as Rangi finished eating, he wanted to hold his son. His eyes glowed with pride as he noticed the double chin and chubby cheeks Maui had developed. He was a good looking, healthy child. Maui's eyes were a lighter colour brown than his own but not green like his mother's, and his skin was fairer than most but looked like it would tan. Maui kicked his legs and talked to Rangi in his own language, eliciting a chuckle from his father.

"It is good to see my boy. He seems to grow fast, and he is strong for his age." His comment made Marama smile. She doubted Rangi ever paid any attention to children, but he was right. Maui was active when he was awake, with strong limbs. When he was in her belly, he had kicked a lot more than his siblings. Marama cleaned up diligently and tidied the whare before bidding the men a good night.

On the way home, Marama and Maui stopped in at Ngoi's. The night before, Marama recounted Hana's tragic tale to Ngoi, Huia and Arihia. All three of them cried, moved by the tragedy of Hana's untimely demise. Huia was adamant she would always look for signs of foul play when healing people in future. It was a valuable lesson for the healers. Not everyone had good intentions, and some people thought only of themselves. Huia had also told Arihia, in whispers, the story of Rongo capturing Marama. That tale had softened Arihia towards Marama even more. Ngoi asked a lot of questions about the symptoms and effects of spider venom. Large, slow tears rolled down Arihia's face. She was touched by the love story and empathised with Hana's feeling of helplessness. Marama explained not all spirits were powerful or vengeful. Hana was sad she lost her baby and the man she loved, but she never begrudged him a family or finding happiness after she was gone. A gentle soul in life, Hana's only crime was being a trusting, loving friend and devoted woman. If the pattern of evil behaviour hadn't emerged, generation after generation, Hana may have found forgiveness and peace. Alas, it wasn't to be, so she lingered to try and arrest the evil, as she has a legitimate reason to seek redress. It was an unusual twist of fate, the necklace coming to Marama, and Hana could finally communicate with the physical realm.

"Do you think we are supposed to help her Marama? Is that why she came to you, and you are telling us?" Huia asked her questions with naked sincerity.

"Perhaps it's so Huia. We must search for the path and let the spirits guide us. It isn't for us to seek revenge on Hana's behalf, but spirits may require assistance from this realm."

Arihia wanted to examine the necklace, and she stroked it as if trying to offer comfort to Hana by sharing her pain. Marama wore it again tonight. Arihia found a distraction from her fears by connecting with Hana's emotions. Rangi being so ill was probably helping Arihia emotionally as well. It certainly made Marama feel better. Maui was the centre of attention as soon as they arrived. The boys had kai but still jostled with the girls to make the baby laugh but were distracted by the leftover fish stew. The lively home gave Marama and Maui a bit of joy in an otherwise terrible situation. While everyone was fussing over Maui, Arihia came to sit by Marama.

"May I look at the necklace again, Marama? I think I dreamed of Hana last night. Maybe it was the story playing over and over in my head that made me dream I was watching her."

"What did you see?" Marama was curious, as dreams often contained messages.

"I saw her happiness with Kauri and how in love they were. I also saw her sick and dying while Ngaio smirked in the corner." Arihia shuddered.

"Did Hana speak to you?"

"No, she just looked at me. It was as if she was begging me to help her with her eyes. I knew I couldn't save her because she died long ago. When I woke up, I was crying."

"Please let me know if you remember anything else, have another dream or if Hana speaks to you. It might be important to her."

Arihia nodded and reached for the necklace as Marama took it from her neck. Hana might want Arihia to play a part in her vengeance. They both harboured a grievance with Rangi and his ancestors and Marama decided to monitor the interactions between the two of them. Hana wasn't malicious, and perhaps she might afford the girl some much-needed protection.

"Sorry to intrude Marama, I cannot speak to Arihia, but we share blood, as well as a tragic fate. I am forgotten in our whakapapa because my brother and I were erased by Ngaio and her descendants after she replaced us. Before I am gone, I will send Arihia a dream to find me, and they will remember us. She is innocent, and I cannot let her die too." Hana steeped her words in sadness, and she emitted an ethereal sigh.

Each morning and evening, Marama led the women in supplication to Papatūānuku. As they sat outside to be closer to Papatūānuku, some women approached them to see what they were doing. Tonight they would be joined by several women who also wished to pray to Papatūānuku and honour her. After Maui was exhausted by play and sated with milk, she lay him to rest in his woven pouch. She liked to have the baby close when they honoured Earth Mother, and Marama hoped this would endow him with a sensitivity to the feminine world. Huia and Arihia helped her prepare herbs and floral tisanes for the ceremony. Ngoi watched and learned too, but indulged the girl's enthusiasm by letting them complete any tasks. The two women exchanged satisfied grins as the girls discussed whether they had ground the herbs finely enough. Arihia was no longer the sullen girl who arrived in the village. With preparations complete, they moved outside to the large fire Ngoi's boys had built for them.

As the women arrived, they lay their mats on the earth as Marama did. Marama led a prayer of thanks to Papatūānuku for the many blessings she bestowed upon them every day. She asked for guidance in nurturing life and forgiveness for any transgressions against the order of nature. Marama invited the women to offer personal prayers silently or aloud. Ngoi commenced her supplication. She thanked the mother for her children, their home and implored her to assist Rongo in finding peace and returning him home safely. The sincerity of Ngoi's simple words opened the women's hearts and lips. They were all thankful for what they had, asked only for essential favours, and unanimously committed to honouring Papatūānuku. Huia and Arihia shared the prepared offerings with each woman. Marama closed her eyes, her lips moving silently, before she scattered her offering in the fire. Each person followed suit, allowing a more personal moment of worship.

"Thank you, Marama. I don't know why we have stopped honouring Papatūānuku openly. My grandparents performed such rituals daily. She nurtures us all, and we wouldn't exist without her." The woman embraced Marama with tears in her eyes. The rest of them followed suit and stopped to bestow blessings upon the sleeping Maui. The women's shift to embrace Papatūānuku moved Marama, as did the affection they showed her and Maui. Upon return to their whare, Marama slept peacefully for the first time in many days.

During the night, Rangi's condition became worse. Fortunately, Piri stopped to check on him quite late. The chief was drenched in sweat, severely dehydrated and racked by diarrhoea. Piri awoke a trainee who lived nearby, sent him to get Tamati and bring fresh water. The illness hadn't improved the temperament of the chief.

"Whatever you have done didn't cure me. Give me something for my puku now!"

"I can see that chief. These are different symptoms from yesterday, and I need to make a remedy. I am warming water to bathe you, but please sip some water now. You have lost too much fluid." Piri's manner was brusque and professional. Tamati arrived, and he asked him to steep herbs for a sleeping draught. The freshwater arrived, and Piri instructed the boy to take the warm water and cleanse the chief. Halfway through, the chief lurched to his feet and ran outside. He didn't get far before another bout of diarrhoea overtook him. When he stumbled back into the whare, his face was pale, and his body was shaking. Piri took the warm water from the scared boy and sent him back to his whare. He bathed Rangi himself, drying and chafing his limbs to warm him up before covering him with a cloak. Cradling Rangi's head, Piri asked him to sip the remedy he mixed, and Tamati came to his side with the sleeping draught.

"Before you take the sleeping draught, we need you to drink some more water to replenish your body." Rangi regarded him with baleful eyes but did what Piri told him. His dreams were wild, nightmarish and disturbing. Roimata had been chasing him, then striking him with his battle mere, while she laughed maniacally and the slave-girl clapped her hands.

"Did you have any dreams, chief?" Rangi was startled. Was Piri reading his thoughts now, he mused with irritation?

"No, I didn't. I just feel lousy."

"Please let me know if you do. The cause of your illness may reveal itself in your unconscious mind. It could be vital to making a speedy recovery." While Rangi was sure Roimata would like to harm him, he didn't believe she had the power to do so. Perhaps he ate something disagreeable before he fell ill.

"I took food with the men when we were sparring. Could it be something I ate?"

"That is possible chief. If that is the cause, what I have given you will clear it up completely in a couple of days. I am not convinced, however, that your illness is just physical. The darkness of your wairua has deepened, and I have asked Tamati to assist me as I seek answers in the next realm. The assaulted girl died today, one of the fishing waka overturned on the lake, and for the first time in my life, the men returned with no fish. The Gods show their displeasure with us."

"What I need is the dream walking potion. I will speak to the Gods myself Piri. Stop stalling. I order you to make it."

"But the ingredients chief... and it takes days to make it. It isn't wise to consume such a potion in your weakened state. It is powerful - "

"I don't care! Just make it. I earned it." Rangi shouted at the tohunga before grabbing the sleeping draught and gulping it down.

Tamati bowed his head. He couldn't bear to see the chief treating Piri, an accomplished, respected tohunga and his mentor so poorly. The chief was always volatile, but Tamati thought he was at best delirious and at worst mad. It was no wonder the men preferred Rongo. He was tough but affable and even-handed with dispensing praise or criticism. The men who surrounded Rongo and travelled with him went to great lengths to win his praise. There was authentic leadership, residing in their midst, cloaked in an unattractive, hulking body. Even his beautiful woman, who initially didn't want him, adored him and produced a brood of lovely children. The more time Tamati spent around the chief, the less he respected him. He puffed out his cheeks and began tidying up. Piri rolled out a sleeping mat, deciding he should stay with Rangi for the rest of the night to ensure he didn't deteriorate. Perhaps a smaller pinch of mushroom powder next time.

When Marama rose to greet the day and commune with Papatūānuku, half the women and girls of the village turned up. People were in shock after the death of the assaulted girl. News of the previous evening and how the women who attended felt spread rapidly through the village. Ngoi suggested they move to a more open area to accommodate the growing crowd. They chose a glade by the stream. The women sang, lifting voices to the trees, paying homage to all the plants and creatures of the world. They danced, swaying like the trees in the breeze and closed their eyes as the sun kissed their upturned faces. The women dedicated the morning to thanks and considered what they might do to honour Papatūānuku. Many women brought gifts and placed them at the base of a magnificent *rimu* (dacrydium cupressinum) tree. The women shed tears and bowed heads as they reconnected with the earth. Marama sensed it was essential to seize the moment. Many of the men were curious about where the women were going. It was a vital reconnection to Papatūānuku, which needed to occur for everyone. She urged the women to walk with a spring in their step, to smile as many smiles as they could today for Papatūānuku, and to nurture their families by lavishing them with aroha. Earth, nature, home, whānau, kai and *tamariki* (children) were all beloved of Papatūānuku. The activities of the morning uplifted the women. As they went about their business, an undercurrent of joy and happiness pervaded the village. The men wanted to know what was happening.

"We are following the will of our tīpuna, to reclaim our mana and reconnect to Papatūānuku. She has already bestowed many gifts upon us which we share with our whānau, and I want to take care of you as Papatūānuku nurtures us."

The men were delighted. Food tasted sweeter. The behaviour of the children improved, and couples rekindled old passions. The village was transforming into a happier place. The elders constructed masterclasses in favoured disciplines and taught strategy to the warriors. Nobody missed the chief, but they couldn't wait to show Rongo what they learned. Rangi was sick for several days. One day, he came to the practice field, assisted by Piri when he felt better, but he hadn't returned since. As Rangi shouted at everyone and made them fight until one warrior overpowered the other, the men were relieved when he didn't come again. His health often improved one day but had a setback the next. The ongoing treatment was taking its toll on the old tohunga, and Tamati worried about him, which meant everyone else did as well. Tamati also let slip that Rangi shouted at the tohunga. The men were shocked, but the elders were horrified. Piri was the spiritual guide of the village and frequently stood between them and the wrath of the Gods. Quite often these days, that anger was caused by the chief. Piri's efforts to find a woman to produce a son for Rangi were well known. He had laboured for a complete cycle of seasons. Little Maui was a delight, and his mother pleased the chief, made his whare a home. There was much head shaking, trying to understand why Rangi rewarded the tohunga with abuse instead of praise. The village leaders decided to hold a *hui* (meeting) in the wharenui, where wooden carvings immortalised generations of ancestors. They asked Tamati to join them as he had assumed most of Piri's duties.

Tamati went to Piri, and as Rangi was sleeping, he invited him to his whare to share food. He lived alone so they would be able to talk in private, and his sister brought him a tasty smoked eel in the morning. Piri loved smoked eel. He licked every morsel off his fingers with gusto, which always made Tamati laugh. The only delicacy he enjoyed as much as eel were gelatinous fish eyes. Mind food, he called them. The two men strolled to Tamati's whare in companionable silence, bathed in the golden sunshine of a perfect day. Piri clapped his hands in glee when Tamati presented the smoked eel. He looked more like a small boy than a tohunga. Tamati performed a simple karakia, and they ate heartily.

"I have news." Tamati started the conversation while Piri picked over the remains of the eel.

"Please tell me it's not another offence by our chief against the Gods?" Piri rolled his eyes to the heavens but continued to lick his fingers.

"No, no gossip this time. It's positive news. Marama has managed to galvanise most of the womenfolk in the village to worship Papatūānuku twice a day. This practice is having a transformational effect on the mauri of the village and the wairua of our people. The men are in awe of how loving and happy their homes have become."

"She is a good woman, clever too. Somewhere, a good man is lamenting her absence. Let's hope her people don't come seeking vengeance on us." He let out a long sigh.

"That isn't the only news. The village leaders have called a hui this evening. People are scandalised that the chief has shouted at you as he yells at the men. I don't know what they want to speak of, but they have invited me to take your place as you are busy. The karakia must encourage their thoughts to flow out in their words. In the presence of our ancestors, in the wharenui, I hope they will make decisions. What would you do?"

Piri looked thoughtful, stroking his chin to tease out the ideas before scratching his head and laughing.

"The question isn't what I would do, Tamati, but what will you do? I entrust this karakia to you. Deliberate on it carefully but know I have confidence in you. The path offers us all a chance to make changes for the better. Make sure they have the opportunity to grab that chance with both hands. They must know the ancestors and Gods will support them when they do what is best for their people. Thank you for a wonderful lunch Tamati, now I must return. Tonight, after the hui, we will check on the potion we are making, and you can let me know the outcome."

Tamati spent the rest of the afternoon working on and reworking the most important karakia of his life.

With Rangi ill, Marama and Arihia were enjoying newfound freedom. Marama still prepared his food, but the tohunga tasted it himself and shared it with Rangi. He sniffed at everything and everyone who entered the whare. Eventually, people stopped bringing gifts of food and stood outside to ask how Rangi was. Protocol drove the inquiries. It would've been impolite and unwise for any whānau to snub the chief. The longer the illness dragged on, the more cantankerous Rangi became. He nagged the tohunga to finish his dreaming potion and frequently berated him for his incompetence. After one such outburst, Piri offered to send for another tohunga.

"I can't deny your illness lingers chief. Both Tamati and I labour to identify the root of the problem. If you feel you would like a second opinion, I can send for a tohunga from another village."

Rangi refused to admit any weakness to another village. If news of his sickness reached his enemies, they might choose to strike while Rongo was away.

"No, that won't do at all. I don't want to advertise my weakness to the world."

"I could ask Marama to take a look at you. She did work a miracle to save Rongo's life, and he has made a full recovery. Perhaps she will see something we haven't."

"Is that wise Piri? You still don't trust her with my food, and we did capture her."

"I don't trust anybody with your food. While we aren't making progress, Marama is the best healer in the village, and you are Maui's father. I am inclined to see if she can at least alleviate some of your many and ever-changing symptoms."

"Very well, send for her, but make sure you finish the potion. If I need to petition the Gods, I must walk with them again."

Tamati was in the wharenui early, preparing for the hui. He meditated, finding comfort and support from his ancestors. This situation was the most delicate he had ever faced as a tohunga. All his instincts were driving him to champion change. Knowing he was following the wishes of his ancestors made him determined to coax the leaders into taking more control of the village. They began to arrive early as well. Some made their quiet entreaties to the carved ancestors who inhabited and protected the wharenui. There was a nervous undercurrent to the meeting. While it was perfectly normal for the village leaders to meet, they rarely did so these days without their chief. It was unlikely he would approve of them making any decisions without him.

Nevertheless, their status required them to lead the people, and at the moment, there was a void to fill. Each person harboured many concerns for the spiritual and physical well-being of the community. Tamati began his karakia with a formal greeting and acknowledgement of the Gods. He greeted all the ancestors represented in the carvings, speaking of their deeds, leadership qualities and bravery when facing adversity. The essence of Tamati's message was to invite those attending to step up to past standards set by tīpuna. It was subtle, but he hoped it would inspire them to shed the caution necessary to survive around Rangi. Tamati decided to lead by example.

"In the sight of our esteemed tīpuna, I tell you all that I am concerned for our people. Kotuku told us to restore the status of our women, but change is slow. Women are beaten, assaulted, raped. The offences committed against Papatūānuku, the mother of us all, are mounting. Incompetent leadership unravels the alliances formed over generations without any benefit for our people. Rongo is risking his life to broker peace with those who have traditionally been our staunchest supporters. The men bask in the respect you show them when you share your knowledge and treat them with dignity. The lack of mana in leadership sows seeds of discontent in our finest warriors. The village needs direction. A dark stain has invaded the chief's wairua, and despite our best efforts, we have been unable to isolate the source yet. You are our leaders. I open the floor with the blessing of all our ancestors and a message from Kotuku, 'kia kaha'. They urge you to speak the truth with their protection. We have a slim opportunity to influence the future weavers in our favour."

As Tamati left the floor, silence echoed in the wharenui. The eldest koroua in the village looked around the circle of burdened faces before struggling to his feet.

"I am old. My time here is nearing an end, so I will speak plainly. This hapu is a disgrace. We who are leaders in name only cower in the shadows instead of helping to lead our people to prosperity. It is time for real leadership. The Gods know it, the ancestors know it, and we know too if we look around us. Can we afford to continue indulging the self-centred nature of one man at the expense of everyone else? You know the answer. My age allows me to recall the stories and rumours we are not permitted to speak of surrounding the chief's parentage. It is clear to me that Rongo possesses all the qualities of a leader. Our current chief is unfit, in too many ways to mention. I feel a duty to replace him. The mauri of our people, our whenua, must be rescued from a tyrant. If I pay for my opinion with my life, I will die with honour."

Tamati couldn't have hoped for a better opening speech. Piri would be pleased. Some bowed their heads, others nodded in agreement, but the spectre of Rangi's anger carved fear in the features of many. There was a void of silence. It lasted so long people began to shuffle uncomfortably. Finally, another speaker rose to greet them, the youngest of the group, Muru.

"I hesitated to speak next, as I consider myself junior to most of you. It shames me it took the eldest amongst us to speak the truth. I feel derelict in my duty to our people, and we hesitate because we are afraid. To remove a chief is also an enormous decision to make. Nobody wanted to be the first to articulate such a dramatic step, lest they brand themselves as disloyal. The eldest of us is the bravest man here. I salute you, old warrior. We are leaders, but I see fear and uncertainty still amongst us. We must stand together if we are to follow the path our ancestors choose. My tīpuna have visited my dreams, and there is no need for bloodletting. I propose when Rongo returns, we ask him to assume the leadership of the village due to Rangi's illness. For a man to be chief doesn't require a title. He needs mana and the support of his people. Let us all see for ourselves what happens to the mauri of our village and whenua. When and if Rangi recovers, I doubt anyone in the village will want to return to where we are now."

The speaker scanned the faces of those around him and saw he had given them an idea to ponder. His proposal was endorsed unanimously. It was a neat solution and decreased the risk to any individual while garnering the support of the people. Muru suggested sending runners to find Rongo and ask him to return as soon as possible. They all agreed what they decided at the hui would be kept confidential within the group—no discussion with anyone else. They granted one exception for Tamati so that he could brief Piri in the sacred cave. Tamati assured the participants they had Piri's support to do the will of the ancestors. The tohunga laboured in earnest to find a remedy for Rangi, but he must dig up any grievances against the chief to do so. The sheer volume of conflict and transgressions which came to light was draining the old tohunga's resources. The elders shook their heads in dismay, as they didn't want to lose their tohunga.

Piri's reputation commanded the respect of their enemies. The relationship shared with the old chief meant Piri participated in the peace negotiations and alliances formed. Tamati impressed them, but the longer he spent with his mentor, the better his preparation for assuming his mantle one day. Despite the revelation, when the group disbanded, they were lighter of heart and spirit. They had made a necessary decision. It could cost them their lives, but they could die with their pride and rank intact, serving their people.

Chapter 10

It transpired the man sent to find Rongo easily accomplished his task. Rongo successfully concluded his negotiations and was on the river, not far from home. Piri knew he would be returning, thanks to Kotuku, and sent Tamati to greet him. He organised for Rangi to be violently ill when Rongo came to report to him. It wouldn't hurt Rongo to see how incapacitated his chief was, as the leaders would meet with him as soon as possible. Piri wanted to take Rongo to the sacred cave, where he and Tamati would enable the spirits, to share with him their vision for their people. Rangi was in a particularly foul mood today, and Piri would be happy to give him a potent sleeping draught. He sent a message to Marama not to bring Maui to visit his father today. The tohunga decided to minimise the boy's exposure to Rangi's negative energy at his tender age. Maui was spiritually sensitive already, and Piri wanted to shield him from the world's ugliness for as long as possible. Tamati briefed Rongo on his chief's illness as they climbed the hill. He asked Rongo's men to organise the travel equipment while he took Rongo straight to the village. The men were curious but knew better than to question the tohunga. Rongo was alarmed Rangi was so ill. His cousin was unusually robust and had never lost a day to sickness Rongo could recall. The village gossips speculated Atarangi fed him all sorts of magic potions to ward off illness as a child. Although he ached to see Ngoi and his children, Rongo hastened to Rangi's side. He could smell sickness before he entered the whare and heard Rangi berating somebody for their incompetence. To his surprise, it was Piri inside with the chief. Rongo frowned as tohunga were a class in their own right. He respected Piri and his pupils. The road to their role was long and arduous, both physically and spiritually. Earning a place amongst the tohunga was difficult, and his fraternity revered Piri for his knowledge, skill and spirituality.

Rangi looked terrible. He had lost weight and condition. The skin on his face was taut and pasty. The whare was scrubbed and cleaned but still managed to smell of faeces and vomit. The old tohunga looked gaunt, his face as drawn as his patient's.

"Rangi, Piri, what can I do to help?"

"Yes, Piri, you must tell my cousin what he can do to help me." Rangi's voice was condescending, scathing even.

"Spiritual enemies plague our chief Rongo, and despite efforts from both Tamati and I, we are unable to isolate the cause of harm. There is a darkness on the chief's wairua, and the enemy still has the upper hand."

"Or my tohunga don't have the skill to fix my ailing puku." A fit of vomiting racked Rangi's body, and Piri was there with a bowl in an instant.

"Rongo, can you hold this please, so I can prepare a remedy." There didn't seem to be much point in sharing the outcome of the negotiations with Rangi, so Rongo held the bowl steady. Rangi continued to curse and abuse Piri whenever he wasn't retching. Marama arrived, and her face split in a wide grin when she saw Rongo. Ngoi and the kids would be ecstatic at his safe return. She examined Rangi, but concurred with Piri that his illness was of a spiritual rather than physical nature and beyond her capabilities to heal. Marama offered to bring some remedies, to alleviate nausea, suppress vomiting and diarrhoea and help with rehydration. As a healer, she was perplexed by Rangi's many symptoms. This illness was more than the work of mushrooms, and although she tried to alleviate symptoms, nothing seemed to work for long. Rangi became angry with her as well, hurling a bowl that just missed her head. Piri suggested she should return to delivering broth so if Rangi became hungry, he would have sustenance. At times Rangi allowed Marama to dribble soup into his mouth. If he was to recover, he knew he must eat. The sight of Rongo reminded him Marama had saved his life, so perhaps he should give her another chance. Although the tohunga gave him many cures, they only provided a brief respite from his illness. Thankfully the dream walking potion was almost ready, and Rangi convinced himself he would cajole the Gods into curing him.

"You have at least returned cousin, so I assume all is well?" Rangi's eyes were closed, but he was finally able to speak.

"It all went perfectly. I can tell you the details when you have recovered, but we achieved everything we wanted and more. They pay tribute to you again and sue for peace."

The details were incredibly complex. The greeting in some villages had been openly hostile. However, Rongo charmed, scared, won respect, prayed to Gods and ancestors, laughed, ate, drank, and negotiated until he hammered out a deal. The results were stunning. He had made firm friends out of Rangi's enemies. Rongo was a humble man, but even he was proud of his achievements. The chief didn't acknowledge the news with anything more than a nod, but Piri and Marama beamed grateful looks at Rongo. They were both aware of the dangers of his mission. Rangi snatched the latest remedy and gulped down a strong sleeping draught.

"Rongo, drill the men hard tomorrow. Who knows what those old fools do in my absence. Leave me now, all of you. I want to rest."

The trio was relieved Rangi dismissed them as Rongo wanted to go home. Maui needed Marama, and Piri wanted fresh air, so they all hurried to Rongo's. Piri asked him to come to the wharenui as soon as he had greeted the family, eaten and bathed.

Although they were all in a hurry, Rongo deserved a proper homecoming. He had saved them from inevitable conflict. The tohunga would summon the leaders to the wharenui after kai. Rongo's children ran to meet their father, launching themselves at him in a rowdy competition to hug him first. He picked Huia up and hugged her close, tousled the boy's hair commenting on their growth, and their faces glowed as they all talked at once. Ngoi was ecstatic, scooped up in his arms, and she showered Rongo's face with kisses, eyes shining with tears of joy. The thought of losing him had gnawed at her until she became wan and listless.

Fortunately, Marama was there to notice and help her friend manage the fears which had plagued her waking hours. Ngoi's spirituality developed and deepened as Marama guided her to find comfort. Her many prayers to the Gods for Rongo's safety were answered. It was a merry meal, and everyone wanted to hear stories from Rongo's travels. They were disappointed he needed to bathe, then attend a hui, but the boys quickly volunteered to scrub their father's back and wash his hair. Huia's lip trembled, but Rongo promised to tell stories in the evening. He noticed Arihia eating quietly with his family, so he greeted her warmly too. Ngoi would tell him what was going on when he had time. His only disappointment was Maui slept through all the noise. He stopped to admire the sleeping baby he loved before he went to the pools, and Maui rewarded him with a smile in his sleep.

Scrubbed clean, with a full puku and wearing clean garments, Rongo felt refreshed. He was greeted enthusiastically by the elders when he arrived at the wharenui. It was good to be home where he could relax. Diplomacy was a demanding task. Every word and action was carefully scrutinised, especially outside the official hui, and you couldn't afford to offend anyone. After seeing Rangi and how ill he was, Rongo assumed there would be tasks that needed attending to urgently. After seeing his whānau, he could take on the world. Piri opened with karakia, asking the Gods and ancestors to have patience with their village. There was also karakia from Tamati, reassuring their tīpuna that what they demanded would be done. Rongo wondered what he had missed. The eldest of the leaders was extremely old now. He hadn't been actively involved in village politics for a few seasons, attending only the most important hui. Rongo was surprised to see this koroua, a man who he respected greatly and who deserved rest, take control of the hui.

"Rongo, welcome home. You have seen the chief and have no doubt figured out for yourself that you need to take on his duties immediately. Please tell us of the diplomatic mission."

The koroua smoothly accomplished the transfer of power without discussion or question, and they appointed Rongo as the interim chief. Their tīpuna rewarded them with the news of the successful negotiations. Rongo exceeded the expectations of the most optimistic among them, and the sense of relief was tangible. Instead of facing the coming season with broken alliances and new enemies, they had renewed the bonds of trade and friendship. The elders were lavish in their praise of Rongo's efforts, and he admitted to himself he was enjoying the positive response to his mission. Rangi wasn't someone who displayed any appreciation of effort on his behalf. When he gave you a task, he expected you to produce a good result. The most enthusiasm Rangi ever displayed was when they brought Marama to the village.

"The village has urgent need of leadership Rongo. Piri, can you explain to Rongo our most pressing spiritual needs." The koroua was still a plain speaker, Rongo noted.

"Our tīpuna want us to restore the mana of the women Rongo, but we have done little. Only Marama and Ngoi work on change with the women. The attitudes of many men are slow to adapt. The spirits didn't grant us generations to effect change, so please turn your thoughts to make this happen. There is also the matter of offending Papatūānuku, seriously, on multiple occasions. While you have been gone, there have been beatings, assaults and rape, committed against our women. Again, Marama leads the women in worship and supplication to the Papatūānuku twice a day. I should be aiding this effort, but I am trying to find a cure for the chief. Somebody wants to harm him. There is darkness in his wairua. We have tried to find the culprit, but our investigations found so many people who have a grievance with the chief that it's a slow and painstaking process. It's a matter of urgency that we stop offending Papatūānuku, lest we find our village at the bottom of the lake. Tamati has taken on my duties, and he and the younger tohunga will assist you."

All eyes were on Rongo. Now he understood why Piri looked so drained. The beatings were most likely Rangi's handiwork, and with Arihia staying at his place, possibly the other issues as well. Aue! Rangi could be an idiot sometimes.

"I will think on these issues and discuss strategy with the tohunga and Marama. We can do this, but I will require the assistance of everyone in this room. People will follow when we lead them in unity, in the right direction. When we depart, the subjects of restoring the status of women and honouring Papatūānuku must be the topic of conversation in every whare. You are our leaders, and we have the power to sow the seeds of change. Is there anything else?"

This time it was Rongo's friend Muru, the youngest of the elders who spoke.

"I know you will take charge of the warriors again Rongo, but please be aware discontent is brewing within the ranks. The chief pushes the men to breaking point and beyond. He has his reasons, but he also drew blood from a young warrior who was sparring well against him. There is muttering, and the injured warrior Tahu has left to live with a cousin in another village. Our warriors must be committed to their leader if they are to defend or battle successfully."

"These are good men. This task is the easiest of the jobs we have discussed so far. Give me a day, and I will restore morale. Anything else?"

"You have broad shoulders, Rongo, but we have laid enough burdens upon them for now. Please call us back here when you need us."

The stoic carvings appeared optimistic, and the leaders were filled with a sense of hope. Rongo reassured them. He was an impressive leader, and they filed out of the hui, confident in their decision.

"Come Rongo, we want to take you to the sacred cave, these are leadership tasks, and you need spiritual support and protection. We will collect Marama and Maui on the way. The cave was tapu to women, but we have lifted it. We will create an example of change. Marama is effectively a tohunga in her village, and our tīpuna speak to her. I hope it will assist in restoring the women to their rightful place." The two tohunga and Rongo wasted no time, striding off as soon as the hui closed.

Marama was waiting outside Rongo's whare with Maui.

"I have informed Ngoi we will be with the tohunga for some time." Marama fell into step with them, and Piri nodded his thanks. His legs seemed to be moving swiftly on their own. The ancestors were driving him to reach the cave. If Rongo was weary after his journey, he didn't show it. Tamati ran ahead to meet them and welcome Rongo and Marama into their most sacred spiritual site. Closing her eyes, Marama's lips parted slightly as the distinctive character of the cave wrapped around her. She thought the pools were magical, but this place was a beacon lighting the gateway to the next realm. A sigh of ecstasy escaped, and when she opened her eyes, she found Tamati staring at her, curiosity shining in his eyes. Maui blinked, gazing around the room as he blew bubbles, waved his hands and made his noises. Piri gestured for Marama to place Maui in the centre, where he could see them all. Once he had positioned everyone where he wanted them, he began chanting. His hands moved, sometimes flowing but also with jerky staccato motions. During some of the movements, Tamati joined in, adding his voice to the refrain of the chant. As the call to their ancestors went on, Marama and Rongo also raised their voices. Marama wove her silent language, in gestures, around the message of Piri. To Tamati, she added harmony in a spiritual voice. The ancestors pressed around them as they brought their instructions to Rongo.

"Give your chief everything he desires so that you can lead our people back to the light. The strands are weaving, and the five of you must choose."

Rongo didn't know who spoke the words. The voice was ancient, laden with time. He shook his head from side to side, to still the whispering inside. Marama stared into the smoke that wafted upwards, arms spread wide, and found Nani.

"Stay the path Marama. There is a way for you and Maui to come home. Aroha from Papatūānuku enfolds you all."

Their ancestors succoured Piri and Tamati as they had answered the tohunga calling and were up to the task.

"What message from our tīpuna Rongo?" The tohunga looked expectantly at him. First, he repeated the message to himself silently to make sure he remembered it. Then Rongo relayed, word for word, what the spirits told him.

"What does it mean Piri? Everything Rangi desires could encompass a lot." Rongo stroked his chin while he thought.

"You will know what to do when the situation arises, and so will we." Marama and Tamati both nodded in agreement. The dreaming potion stood in the corner, waiting to be delivered. Piri knew Rangi desired the brew, and now he must give it, against his better judgement. Rangi also wanted Arihia. Tamati committed to following Rongo, knowing he would make intuitive choices. Calm descended on them all. Even the baby stilled, his features composed in contemplation. Piri finished with karakia, and they tacitly made their way down the hill. In the village, the women quietly rejoiced, for Marama was the first woman to be invited to the sacred cave. The men glanced up and were relieved to have Rongo back amongst them. Before they completed the descent, a positive shift in the mood was already in motion.

Rongo hailed the first people he saw with a loud, enthusiastic greeting. He slapped backs, swung children, complimented women and exchanged hongi with the warriors. His jovial nature was magnetic, and the ease of his leadership was never more pronounced. Boys ran through the village to call the warriors to the practice field. The pā buzzed, and people laughed. Their ugly first warrior had returned in a cheerful mood and they marvelled how one man could make such a difference. The tohunga and Marama all wore knowing smiles as those in other realms recognised the new chief, and his people followed suit.

"Do you think you can bring Ngoi and Huia to the training ground Marama? I want you to be there. Also, any of the women who have been honouring Papatūānuku can come too. Everyone must acknowledge the change in status."

"Welcome home." Marama embraced him quickly and strode off to do his bidding.

"I will return to Rangi. He shouldn't be left alone right now. Would you like Tamati to join you as well?"

"Yes, that would be helpful. If we want the chief to recover, we must pay more attention to observing spiritual traditions. We should always have tohunga present when we commence training and close the session. Our tīpuna will watch over us only if we ask them to. Now I think about it I can't recall when or why we stopped doing that."

The company scattered with purpose, and the village rippled with a wave of positivity. Piri looked up to the sky and welcomed his ancestors' approval as it rained down on them.

It was only a matter of minutes before the men mustered. The leaders came to join them, enthusiastically discussing how great it was to have Rongo back. They also talked about how successful his mission was, in earshot of everyone. The village gossips were delighted to have good news to share with anyone who would listen. The runner boys and their friends hung around the field, eager to be a part of whatever was happening. They would be training here one day, with Rongo, they hoped. Rongo invited Tamati to open proceedings with karakia. He delivered a rousing entreaty to their tīpuna to make them strong of body and mind, aid them in all their endeavours, and he recalled the glories of illustrious ancestors. When Tamati finished, Rongo thanked him for his spiritual contribution and turned to address the men. Ngoi,

Marama, Huia, Arihia and a large host of women had just arrived.

"Battle brothers, warriors and protectors of our village, I am grateful to return to you. The chief is ill, but our tohunga labour to improve his health. Leaders and tohunga urge us to reclaim our spirituality. We will retake the gifts our Gods and tīpuna once bestowed upon us. I am only one humble man, but when we stand together, we can achieve anything. Our ancestors instructed us to restore the mana of our women. To my shame, we have contributed nothing to progress this. Instead, we have done the opposite and offended the Earth Mother. The women have taken the initiative to restore our relationship with Papatūānuku. I invited them here today to thank them and offer our pleas to the Earth Mother for her favour. It is up to all of us to treat women with the respect they deserve. Without a mother, we cannot exist. Without a woman, we will have no tamariki or mokopuna. We would have to care for ourselves and feel the cold embrace of loneliness at night. My woman is the heart and soul of my home, the source of my strength and she cares for my wairua. Papatūānuku is the earth we live on, train on, fight on, take food from, and we must honour her. We exist because of her and at her mercy. This relationship is not something we can take for granted."

Rongo began to sing. It was a homage to Papatūānuku and the creation of life. The villagers all joined in with set movements and voices. Everyone knew the song, and it was uplifting to join their voices as one. When the last notes faded, the women drew together and began a chant. It was hauntingly beautiful. The chant described the unfurling of life, nurturing for growth and the seasons. Feet tingled as life pushed its way up, from the earth, into the bodies of the villagers. They collectively experienced the joy of life surge within them. As the chant faded and people opened their spiritual eyes, they began to greet each other, and an air of festivity permeated the field. Rongo lay face down on the earth at Ngoi's feet and fervently thanked Papatūānuku for her patience and love. Where Rongo led, his warriors followed, and so the healing began.

"Tonight we will hold a feast, in honour of Papatūānuku. And now, I want to see how well you have all trained while I have been gone!" Rongo led the warriors in a rousing haka. Stomping feet shook the ground, and veins popped in temples from the effort exerted. It was the perfect warm-up before exercises began in earnest. As they were drilling and sparring, Rongo moved through the ranks, taking the pulse of his men. In his mind, they were his men, and that is how he treated them. He always felt responsible for them and their families. Rongo laughed with them, dispensed encouragement and praise where it was due. Some of the men sported bruises, cuts and injuries, so he avoided contact sparring. Their bodies needed time to heal. Battle offered many opportunities to sustain damage, so Rongo saw no need to inflict harm on one another, on purpose, before you went to fight. He and Rangi disagreed on his approach. It was easy for Rangi to speak of men understanding how to fight as if their life depended on it. Rangi was a fierce, exceptionally gifted warrior, and during his practice, he allowed nobody to strike him with any force. Even if you could challenge the chief, a wise man didn't. Rongo lamented the loss of the young warrior Tahu, one of his protégé. He must find a way to lure him back home.

Rangi was stirring when Piri arrived at his whare. The tohunga threw sweet-smelling herbs into some hot water to improve the smell inside. He took cool water to the chief to quench his thirst, followed by warm water for washing.

"Rongo has taken the men in hand, and they exercise as you would want."

"Good, one less worry for me. I feel better today, and I am hungry."

Piri brought a bowl of steaming broth to the chief, blew on it, then sipped tentatively before passing it to Rangi.

"Is the dreaming potion ready Piri?"

"The potion has matured, but is your body prepared? Time is different across the realms. The illness depletes the reserves of your body quickly."

"This is excellent news. Bring me some stew, and I will fill my puku before I drink it."

"I will bring what you desire, and prepare the ritual."

"No need for rituals Piri. I have already been through a moon of preparation, and I don't want to deplete my strength before I start."

The tohunga nodded his acceptance and left. Once outside, Piri looked for Tamati. He was instructing a group of older children in the art of spiritual protocol.

"Aue Tamati! The chief has called for the dreaming potion, but those on trial should only take it once in a lifetime and after meticulous spiritual rituals. It overpowers those without the strength to resist its pull. He is the chief, but I have my misgivings about breaking protocol. I have been unable to dissuade him. Can you assist me? I must do my best, always, for our leader."

Bystanders and the children overheard and they could see how upset the old tohunga was, as Tamati shook his head in resignation. The villagers now knew Piri didn't support the wishes of the chief. The children ran off to tell their parents. Tamati was in the middle of a lesson regarding the importance of following the correct spiritual procedures. The children were burning with questions. Was it different for a chief? Could a leader ignore the proper protocol without repercussions? When could you disregard the advice of the tohunga? The tohunga climbed the slope once more to the sacred cave. People below noticed Piri was slightly stooped, and there was much concern for the stern old man. He diligently cared for the chief, almost alone, for many days without complaint. The elders observed his diminishing energy and mulled over what they could do to prevent his decline. The knowledge and experience of Piri was an asset to the village and the iwi. Muru believed he wouldn't swap one Piri for ten Rangi's. He had made his choice.

Tamati was grateful he learned to brew the potion with Piri. The preparations alone were incredibly complex. Whoever made it would air-dry some ingredients, grind others while fresh and make some into pastes before baking them. The fermentation and maturing process required careful attention and adjustment during each day. Colour, smell and consistency, were all indicators of how the potion progressed. Piri urged Tamati to take a tiny quantity of the immature brew. It affected Tamati dramatically. The vivid and bizarre nature of his hallucinogenic dreams scared him. He wondered what happened to the chief when he drank the whole lot. Despite Rangi's insistence that the rituals weren't necessary, Piri spent time muttering incantations and communicating with their ancestors. The tohunga put all his trust in their tīpuna and delivered to Rangi what he desired. Hollow-eyed and weak, Rangi guzzled all the potion down at once. He lay down on his mat, eyes closed, and Piri covered him with an ornate cloak. Once outside the whare, Tamati turned to hongi his mentor. His admiration for Piri's dedication increased with each challenge he saw his mentor face. They decided to find Marama and Ngoi to ask if they could assist with spiritual preparations for the feast to honour Papatūānuku.

People pillaged the food stores. Papatūānuku must be honoured with the best of everything the village could offer. The men prepared a *hāngi* (food cooked in a pit dug in the ground). The river stones were heated until they glowed in a hot fire. They heated the stones, placed them in the pit, then placed the wrapped food in the hole. The stones were doused with water, then covered with earth. The steam would slowly cook the food, while the mānuka wood added a distinctive smoky flavour. Hours later, the cooks would dig up succulent, tasty food to delight the taste buds of the villagers. Everyone worked together to make the hāngi, men, women and children. Marama led the women to the bathing pool, where she and Huia performed rituals of thanks to Papatūānuku. Ngoi and Arihia anointed the women's feet with oil and dressed their hair. Four of Rangi's women accompanied them. Ngoi and Marama had treated injuries for all of them. They made a special effort, on behalf of the women, to invoke the protection of Papatūānuku. They stared hopefully into Marama's bewitching eyes. It was their belief, Marama was a gift sent by Papatūānuku herself. The women sang together, weaving intricate harmonies with their voices, while the land seemed to sing with them as the Earth Mother transformed them. The women tingled, feeling somehow different, more positive and carefree.

The feast was magnificent. People ate, danced, laughed, sang and gave praise to Papatūānuku. Women looked more alluring to their men. The festivities included the children, so they were on their best behaviour as nobody wanted to go home early. Rongo was in fine form, telling stories of his travels. The warriors relaxed, enjoying the camaraderie and slight ache of well-used muscles. Content elders watched and participated, gratified to see their village coming to life, and they asked Marama to allow Maui to stand in for his father. Marama laughed and clapped her hands. Maui was already fulfilling his first duties to the village, and she was proud of him. The baby laughed back at her, adding to the merriment. His sunny nature encouraged everyone to dote on him, so Marama just accepted his popularity as a boon from the Gods. Ngoi watched Rongo like a love-sick teenager. She was sure even her mother would have been impressed with his stories. His animation captivated his audience and squeezed her heart. Perhaps tonight, they would be blessed by Papatūānuku and conceive another child. Rongo looked straight at her and grinned as if he had read her mind, bringing colour to her cheeks. It was a fabulous night and the life force of the village hummed as it should and could. People realised that their chief was stifling their community. Nobody discussed it. People were enjoying living in the moment and basking in the love of Papatūānuku. The villager's thoughts, however, were a different matter altogether. Discontent planted a seed. Imagine if Rongo was the chief all of the time, they wondered, what would life be like for them?

"You have done well Piri, as our people can see the future as it could be. Trust in me for a little longer, and we ask nothing more of you. You have given us everything, although we have tested your beliefs to the extreme." Piri felt a little faint with the strength of Kotuku's

message. He also felt a tremendous sense of relief. It had fallen to him to administer the mushrooms to Rangi. Taking a life went against all his beliefs, but he proceeded as instructed, keeping his options open wherever possible. The first dreaming potion was powerful with narcotics. He exposed Rangi's selfishness to Tamati, and the leaders, while highlighting Rongo's attributes. The rumours of Rangi's parentage were recirculating. The frustration with them stirred in Papatūānuku, was being assuaged, and they could feel the difference her favour made. Marama caught his eye and raised her bowl to him. Once, he had acknowledged her cleverness and vowed not to underestimate her. Today she did the same to him. He walked a dangerous road, primarily alone, these past few days. Marama was relieved to see Tamati assume more duties, and respect for him grew exponentially in the village. The more cruel Rangi became, the more noble Piri's selfless care appeared. The status of Ngoi and Huia as healers was rising, and it was no longer just the women who sought them out. The warriors often called on them as well. Women were becoming more than servants and chattels. When Marama retired with a sleepy Maui for the night, a deep sense of satisfaction bloomed within her. They played a part in effecting change. Although she arrived as a captive, she refused to be crushed by the chauvinism or brutality that reigned in the village. Most of the villagers were good people. Maui stroked her face and smiled at her as if to say well done, so Marama laughed and cuddled him to her. He was a light in her life.

When Piri and Tamati stopped to check on the chief, Rangi was trapped in the dreaming world with the maternal ancestors. His body twitched, and he made sounds, but they had no idea what he experienced. Rangi's face appeared shadowed and gaunt, partially from his illness but also from the potion's energy burn. The tohunga retired to their whare. There was nothing more they could do for now.

As people left the feast, Ngoi seduced Rongo away from his faithful men, who reclined with full puku and light hearts. She whispered in his ear.

"About that baby Rongo, I don't think I can make it by myself. You have been away a long time." They left the feast accompanied by much whooping and teasing, but they just grinned as they slunk off into the night. Huia and her brothers rolled their eyes in unison.

"We can't go home yet Arihia. We might as well have some more food." The boys, who were always hungry, grumbled but filled baskets with leftover wood pigeon and kūmara. They also searched for the special drinks some of the elders had left in their bowls. They all giggled and ate, well into the early hours of the morning, noticing who was sneaking off together. In the morning, they would be the source of much friendly gossip.

Chapter 11

Marama and Piri were both up to greet the new day. Dawn welcomed new beginnings as life was renewing in the village. They gave thanks for their transforming world, and Piri climbed the path to the sacred cave. Marama chose a glade by the stream to complete her ritual to Papatūānuku. Maui watched his mother serenely, filled to bursting with nutritious milk. The day progressed in the same buoyant mood as the day before. Jobs seemed easier as people helped one another, and the craftsmen and women awoke inspired. Couples were affectionate with each other, their children, and life in the village hummed. Rangi remained in a drug-induced stupor for almost two days, allowing everyone a respite from his temper and demands. His illness removed him from daily life, so Marama, Arihia and his women enjoyed freedom. Thanks to the dreaming potion, the old tohunga slept soundly in his whare. Tamati took his place while Rangi was unaware of who was with him. Rongo was everywhere, working with the men, helping the women, playing with the children and meeting with artisans, fishermen and leaders. He made time, twice a day, to worship Papatūānuku with Marama and the women. Other men joined him. They all hoped to gain the favour of Papatūānuku and experienced a newfound peace since Rongo reinvigorated the old ways. The elders nodded and smiled at one another, discussing in hushed tones, in private, the undeniable truth. Rongo was a born leader who cultivated the people as naturally as his kūmara. The men made subtle comments at first. More honest conversations followed the mutterings between those who trusted one another. The warriors thrived under Rongo, and they felt united and able to take on anyone. Their mana shone through in their deeds. Murmurs reached the keen ears of Rongo's second in command, Nikau. It amused him that the other men were only now acknowledging what he had always known, but it also concerned him. Instead of bathing with the other men, he waited until Rongo was by himself.

"I hope you still have time for an old friend with all your current duties?"

"Nikau, you are a welcome sight for my weary bones." Rongo laughed and threw his arm around Nikau's shoulder, leaning on him playfully.

"Whew, I forgot how heavy you are Kūmara!" Nikau chuckled. He enjoyed teasing Rongo.

"How are you Nikau? And how are our men? I have hardly stopped since we arrived home. Here I was thinking the negotiations were going to be the difficult challenge." Rongo shook his head wearily but grinned.

"We are fine Rongo, enjoying the training with everyone else. You have taught us to be flexible and resilient. It's not us I want to speak of, but you." He paused for a moment until Rongo raised his eyebrows at him.

"I am your man, no matter who is chief. It's the same for all those who travel with you, whether we acknowledge it or not. We know it's better to keep our loyalties to ourselves because nobody is offended that way. The issue is, all the other men start to feel the same devotion to you that we do. They are beginning to speak of their loyalty to you, amongst themselves at first, but increasingly openly. Rangi's men admire you Rongo. They are starting to look to you for leadership. Even worse, they acknowledge Rangi's faults, compare him to you, and it isn't a favourable comparison for the chief. You are on dangerous ground Rongo. The chief's men have all become your men, whether you intended them to or not."

Rongo stroked his chin thoughtfully. Nikau was always honest with him, and he did look worried.

"I have always worked the men more than the chief Nikau. I am second in command, and that is how the men see me. You know I am less of a task-master than Rangi, someone who doesn't punish them as much. They probably like me more, because I am one of them. Rangi has no cause to doubt me, and he knows I have always been loyal to him."

"That may have been true in the past Rongo, but something has changed. While we were on our mission, our chief hasn't endeared himself to anyone. There is an appetite for change. The chief is observant, and I believe he will find fault with you when he has recovered. You know where my loyalty lies, and I will always have your back." The two men shared a respectful hongi as they clasped each other's shoulders. Whether they fought together or negotiated trade and peace, they trusted each other unreservedly. Nikau gave Rongo advice for thought. He closed his eyes and let the mauri of the whenua surround him. His skin tingled, and his muscles felt refreshed as he prayed to his ancestors to guide him.

"Hey Rongo, I am going to bathe. It looks like you could do with a soak." It was Tamati, beckoning Rongo to join him. A soak did sound good, so Rongo waved and ran to the trail. By the time they reached the pool, the last men were departing, leaving them alone to enjoy the steaming water. Tamati murmured karakia before they entered the hot pool. Rongo bowed his head, joining in when appropriate and inviting Tamati to climb in first. The respectful gesture warmed Tamati. They must have been blind to take this man for granted for so long. Both men languished, eyes closed, up to their necks in water.

"Can I ask you for a favour Tamati?"

"Of course Rongo."

"I am wrestling with a problem, recently brought to my attention." Rongo puffed out his cheeks and exhaled slowly. "This afternoon, I asked the ancestors for guidance. I don't want to disturb Piri as I notice he has aged these past few weeks. Would you be able to make an offering and add to my request? You are also extremely busy, but I feel I need assistance."

"Of course Rongo. The spiritual well-being of all our people is also my responsibility, and I am proud you have asked me. Perhaps the Gods sent me your way in answer to your prayers. I will do this for you Rongo."

"Thank you. I want to do my best for everyone."

"You serve our people well Rongo, our alliances hold, and the land can know peace again. You lead with your heart and head in consort. I feel the positive shift in mauri, the brightening of wairua of our people since you returned. It is a privilege for me to serve you. Our ancestors speak of you, and they have been guiding you your whole life."

Tamati left the pool to do Rongo's bidding and to give him time to reflect alone.

Rongo was greeted at home by the hustle and bustle of his family as they prepared a meal. Ngoi was glowing, beautiful and fluid as all her movements flowed like a dance. Perhaps she was carrying another child, or maybe her worship of Papatūānuku was enhancing her femininity. He still couldn't believe she was his woman sometimes. Papatūānuku had given him a precious gift, beyond compare. When Marama and Maui arrived, with fragrant meat cooked over glowing coals, Rongo took her aside.

"Marama, I want to make an offering to Papatūānuku tonight. Can you help me?" Marama nodded enthusiastically.

"It suddenly struck me that the Gods have blessed me beyond my dreams. I have Ngoi, and she loves me. Don't you think I am the luckiest, ugly man in Aotearoa?" He grinned as he whispered to Marama. Her hand flew to her mouth to stifle a childish giggle, but Maui began to laugh.

"After we eat, I have a ceremony and offering in mind."

Marama gazed off into space, smiling as if she shared a joke with someone else.

The meal was chaotic, happy, and a welcome relief for Rongo from his many duties. Ngoi and Marama put their heads together, a more mature version of Huia and Arihia. Marama whispered of Rongo's request and shared her belief Ngoi would soon feel life stirring within her. Nothing could have made Ngoi happier. She floated on air, radiating warmth, the embodiment of Papatūānuku in their whare. Her whānau turned their faces to her, like flowers to the sun. The children were excited when Marama invited them to her whare to hear stories from her homeland. She also promised to show the girls how to make a special tea and told the boys it would make them more popular with girls. Both Ngoi and Rongo threw her grateful looks as they desperately wanted some time alone. Marama smiled conspiratorially. By the time she and Rongo finished the ceremony, the children would need to be elsewhere as the fertility offering she was planning would be potent.

In Rangi's whare, the atmosphere was oppressive. He twitched and mumbled constantly. To Piri's ears, it sounded as if he walked with demons rather than Gods. The tohunga's observations weren't far from the truth as the female ancestors extracted their dues.

"What have you done to my son, you old fool?" In the doorway stood Rangi's mother, Atarangi. Time had streaked her hair with grey, and her cheekbones were more prominent in a lean face, but she was still a striking woman. Beautiful to behold on the outside. Piri rose from his place by the fire and faced her.

"You, a nobody who abandoned her son, dare to come here and question me. What you need to ask is, what have I done to my son? He demands whatever he wants, just as you taught him to do. There is violence in him and no respect for anyone. Your false and foul deeds pollute your wairua and his. Our cuckolded ancestors are angry, the Gods are insulted, and I should kill you now." She turned on her heels and ran. This welcome wasn't what she expected here, she had always commanded grudging respect, and her son was chief. When Rangi awakened, she would demand he cut out the old tohunga's tongue. Now wasn't the time to place herself in danger. She saw and smelt enough to know Rangi's body was drugged and riddled with toxins. The old fraud probably had no intention, or ability, to save her son, but she did. Atarangi departed for her secret cave to work on a cure. She summoned the spirits of her venomous ancestors as she went, calling them to protect their bloodline. Piri, however, was way ahead of her. The village ancestors were ever-present, ever watchful, weaving the future they had planned so carefully. Tamati rushed in.

"I saw a figure leaving the whare but didn't recognise them. Is something amiss?"

"The visitor was Atarangi, and she is as arrogant and rude as ever. She sows discord wherever she travels Tamati, but our ancestors have been awaiting her arrival. They have a score to settle with her. Please remain vigilant. She is both cunning and unpredictable. Tomorrow Rangi will stir again because he has depleted his body, but he may still be under the influence of the hallucinogenic. We need to prepare for anything and everything. His mother will most likely demand my head or my balls, possibly both, if she awakes in a bad mood. Please stay close by if you can, and look for signs."

The ancestors informed Piri well. His words were almost prophetic. Late in the morning, Rangi groggily opened bloodshot eyes. He was parched. His tongue stuck to the roof of his moisture-deprived mouth.

"Water, I need water," he croaked. Piri raised a bowl to Rangi's lips, but he gulped the water too quickly and began to choke. "Are you trying to drown me?" Rangi drew his lips back in a sneer, and his eyes rolled back in his head.

"Of course I'm not chief. You are drinking too quickly. Try and sip the water slowly. Your body has been under the influence of the potion for almost two days."

"Where is the girl?"

"Which girl?"

"Roimata's sister, the skinny girl. I want her, and I want her now!" Rangi's eyes bulged in his head and distorted his face in anger.

"I will send someone to fetch her as soon as you have recovered chief."

Rangi pushed himself up to a seated position, then attempted to stand. He wobbled and fell to his knees with a thud, where he laughed maniacally. After a few minutes, he succeeded in coming to all fours and eventually, he struggled to a standing position. Leaning on the wall, Rangi sucked air into his lungs, swaying slightly. He talked to himself, laughing again, before skewering Piri with a baleful glare. "No more stalling Piri. She is my reward and vengeance. I will find her myself."

"My chief, I only worry for your health, but you must have whatever you desire."

Rangi was stretching his limbs to stimulate his sluggish circulation. Piri moved to help him, rubbing his legs to assist the blood flow and make sure he didn't fall again. Once he felt steady, the chief stepped outside the whare where he could feel the cool breeze on his face.

"Do you have any idea where she is?"

"The girls were tasked with weeding the kūmara today."

The tohunga stood stiffly, watching the chief lurch in the direction of the gardens. Piri closed his eyes and heard Kotuku's voice, *'give him whatever he desires'*. Though he feared for Arihia and anyone who might intervene, he must hold fast and trust his ancestors.

Tamati saw the chief leaving his whare from afar and headed in his direction, maintaining a discreet distance. Heads bowed as Rangi passed, looking more like a corpse than a chief. People stared or greeted him, but he didn't acknowledge anyone. Rangi fixated on his mission. The men tended lovingly to their weapons, on the other side of the village, after an enthusiastic morning of training with Rongo.

The elders and leaders had departed at first light to debate elevating Rongo to the position of chief in the shadow of their maunga. It was a unanimous decision, but how to effect the change required? Much discussion with so many details to consider. How to avoid Rangi slaughtering them, or Rongo, was foremost in their minds.

Marama's hand flew to her breast as the katipō necklace released a surge of intense heat, and the spiritual world grasped her. Baby Maui frowned, looking intently at his mother.

Huia raised her eyes for a moment and saw Rangi approaching them. She placed her hand on Arihia's shoulder so she would look up too. There was something about the look on Rangi's face that made Arihia shudder. All her instincts urged her to run for her life. With a frightened gasp, she turned and fled as fast as her legs would carry her. Rangi laughed demonically, frightening the rest of the girls in the kūmara garden. The sound of it made Huia shiver as her eyes followed Arihia streaking down the path. A sob tore from Huia's mouth, and she ran to get her father. He would know what to do.

Rangi should have run Arihia to ground quickly, but he was weak from illness and the days spent drugged. He believed the chase would make his reward even sweeter, so he jogged after her, falling into an easy ground-eating stride. Muscle memory propelled his limbs. Even when his mind was elsewhere, his body responded to a lifetime of training. The girl was sprinting, and he knew she would be unable to sustain the pace for long.

Arihia ran until she felt a stitch in her side, and her legs were heavy with lactic acid. Knowing she couldn't outrun Rangi, she prayed to Papatūānuku for inspiration. She remembered the story Huia told her of Marama's capture by Rongo. There was a steep drop to her right. The cliff fell to the edge of the lake. When she rounded a corner, she sent a shower of stones off the side, then darted into the bush to crouch and hide. Rangi wasn't far behind her, though he appeared to run slowly. Arihia saw him cock his head to the side, listening to the loose stones still bouncing down the cliff face. His face was something from a nightmare as his red eyes turned to the edge, his grin more of a lopsided grimace. Rangi halted at the edge of the cliff.

"Come out and play Arihia. I have waited a long time for you, but we can spend days together!" Rangi brandished a small sharp cutting implement as he spat out his words. Arihia suppressed a sob by clamping her hand over her mouth and biting the edge of it. The pain reminded her, she still lived. She held her breath so she wouldn't make a sound. Rangi craned his neck to see over the edge, but there was no sign of the girl.

"My patience is wearing thin, Arihia. The longer you make me wait, the worse it will be." He cursed profusely at the girl when she didn't appear and leaned out a little further. Yelling profanities, then what he would do to her when he found her, Rangi was consumed. He spewed vitriolic hate until veins bulged in his temples and forehead.

"You share my blood and carry my pain Arihia. We can triumph over evil this time," whispered Hana. Arihia snapped. She launched herself from her hiding place and shoved Rangi with all her might, just as Ngaio had done to Hana's brother. Rangi teetered on the edge, arms wind-milling to try and stop himself from falling. Papatūānuku crumbled her soil from under his feet, and he screamed as his body plummeted toward the rocks below. There was a dull thud as he hit the ground. Papatūānuku embraced his irreverent body to her stony, unyielding breast as the impact drove life from Rangi's broken body.

Chapter 12

Tamati skidded to a halt as he rounded the corner. He heard Rangi's screamed threats, his depraved promises, and he was just in time to witness Arihia shoving him over the edge. If he arrived a few seconds later, he would have seen nothing. Arihia's head whipped around as she heard Tamati's laboured breathing. Stark, unadulterated, fear stood in her eyes, but his ancestors sighed in contentment around him. He had to make a choice. Tamati opened his arms to comfort Arihia. She was a victim, and it was Papatūānuku who crumbled the earth from under Rangi's feet. Hana embraced her descendant Arihia spiritually, for they had accomplished a balancing of the scales, together, in a most befitting fashion. First Marama, then Rongo, came thundering around the corner, with Nikau hard on their heels. He was struggling to keep up and had never seen a woman run as Marama did. Tamati gestured towards the cliff. Rongo walked to the edge and lay down so he could see to the bottom without falling himself. He shook his head as he saw his cousin's body, twisted and lifeless.

"I am sorry, Rongo, I was unable to catch the chief when he pursued Arihia, as I was too far behind. He was still under the influence of the potion. The potion Piri begged him not to take so soon and without the appropriate rituals. My mentor asked me to be vigilant, and I fear I have let him down." Arihia blinked back tears as she heard Tamati's explanation, which made no mention of her role in Rangi's demise.

"You are too hard on yourself Tamati. This event was the work of Papatūānuku, your ancestors and a spirit named Hana. They all had scores to settle with Rangi and his bloodline. We are only mere mortals. The future weavers have a plan and a purpose for the survival of their people. That is why the ancestors brought me here." Marama looked from Tamati to Rongo and also encircled Arihia in her arms. Once in Marama's embrace, Arihia's tears burst forth in heart-breaking sobs. They were tears of fright, guilt and relief. Rongo was stunned. He didn't know what to say, so he fell to his knees to ask his ancestors to help him see clearly through his grief. Tamati and Marama each lay a hand on his shoulder to allow Kotuku to speak with him.

"Rongo, you are the true chief, chosen by the people and in blood. Atarangi cheated you of your birthright. Though you loved him, Rangi wasn't your cousin, and he wasn't a leader. He has revealed his true nature over time. You will lead our people until Maui is reborn and returns to save us from approaching darkness. Teach him well and bind him to us closely. He is not of our blood, but he is one of us. Our survival rests on the shoulders of the man he will become. You must protect him from the forces of evil. Beware Atarangi, for she means to do us harm."

It was overwhelming for Rongo to have his ancestor speak to him directly. Marama and Tamati bore witness to the words, and they raised Rongo to greet him as their chief. A winded Nikau also pledged his alliance to the new chief. Arihia bowed her head in deference to Rongo while furiously swiping away her tears while Tamati led them in karakia. There would be formalities later, but the five of them bowed to the ancestors' wisdom, as leadership settled permanently on Rongo's shoulders.

Other people began to arrive. Rongo's men and some warriors appeared along with an ashen-faced Huia gasping for air.

"Aue! Rangi has fallen to his death on the rocks of the shore below. Nikau, please choose some men to return his body to the village. Tamati, can you go with them to ensure the men observe all spiritual necessities? The rest of us will return together to bring the news to our people." Rongo spoke softly, but there was no mistaking the authority or command in his voice. Tamati nodded in agreement, again noting Rongo's grasp of spiritual rituals. They were all tired from the break-neck run and straggled home sombrely. The reality was they acted appropriately, as someone had died. However, there were no tears or the wailing of loss due to Rangi's ill-treatment of his people. In some cases, people gave prayers of thanks, as secretly they were grateful to be rid of their brutal chief. Huia and Arihia held Marama's hands. They tried to suppress their sense of relief, exchanging glances when nobody else was looking. Marama was aware of their buoyant mood but didn't chastise them, as it only reflected her own. Soon, she would find a way to return home. The thought of seeing Aroha again made her feel dizzy with hope, and her boys may have returned home by now. Her only worry was the significance of Maui to these people because she would never leave her child behind. With Rongo taking his rightful place, she hoped they would come up with a suitable compromise for raising Maui. Villagers were still running out to meet them, and although nobody said anything about what happened, Rangi's absence was noted, along with the sombre faces. Gossip preceded their return, and the entire village was on the marae with Piri. A sea of quizzical, upturned faces greeted Rongo. Piri commenced karakia as soon as he could see them approaching, and Rongo stood in front of his people, ready to address them.

"Our chief has fallen off a cliff today, and he has joined his tīpuna in the next realm." Rongo searched for their leaders, but not a single one was present. It wasn't unusual for them to meet, but it was strange they hadn't let him know they were leaving the village. "When our leaders return, I call on them to meet and discuss the future of our village. Tamati leads a contingent of men, handpicked by Nikau, to retrieve the body and bring it home." He turned to the older tohunga, shared an emotional hongi, and handed proceedings over to Piri.

"We must look to our tīpuna and our Gods to guide us, especially in times of trouble. They guide our spiritual waka, through times of change, with love and care. It is not for us to question their grand plan for our future but to stand resolute in our commitment to them. Rangi's time has suddenly come to an end, but Papatūānuku is reinvigorating our hapu and iwi. There is a light in our wairua. Our whenua flourishes, and we can navigate this change together. We are blessed. Rongo returned to lead us when Rangi was ill before this happened." Piri began a song of praise.

There would be time for lamentation later. Now, people needed to let the Gods uplift them, and their ancestors deserved their adulation. Instead of an outpouring of grief, which generally occurred when a chief died, the oppressive taint of their world lifted altogether. The mood of the people was an overriding feeling of relief. The ancestors were patient with Rangi until it became apparent he would never be fit to lead. It was a relief to Piri, as he was dreading administering a lethal dose. He committed to carrying out his ancestors' wishes, but his humanity, commitment to the sanctity of life, had prickled at his conscience. Piri now understood Marama's feelings regarding saving her people. While others dealt the final blow and were justified in doing so, he was equally responsible for the outcome. Piri would carry this burden to his grave, but he would do it again just like Marama.

As the day surrendered to the inevitability of dusk, the leaders crested the approach to the village. The climb from the lake was steep, so Muru carried the eldest on his back. Their faces were implacable, and their hearts were proud, for they had made a difficult decision. Rongo took up the dormant mantle of leadership, and the purpose of the hapu long suppressed by Rangi, re-emerged invigorated. The tohunga held watch on the gate. Piri and Tamati walked out to greet and brief the leaders as soon as they appeared. The eldest climbed down to hongi Piri first. Before the tohunga could speak, the koroua held up his hand authoritatively.

"A decision has been made. Rongo will be chief. Rangi must pay for his misdeeds. His role as chief doesn't render him immune to making restitution. Our people must be permitted to thrive, not cower in fear as we have done. The ancestors have spoken, and we will obey." The stern faces gathered around the tohunga all nodded in unison. The tohunga shared a glance of satisfied approval.

"Your wisdom and authority proceed you. Rongo has called a hui upon your return, and he has invited our kuia, Marama and Ngoi, to represent Papatūānuku. Earlier today, Rangi fell from the cliff to his death on the rocks below. Shall we proceed to the wharenui?" A myriad of emotions flickered across the leaders' faces—shock, surprise, relief and disbelief but again, no sign of grief. They thought on the way to the village. There were muttered thanks to those in the next realm who had delivered the elders a solution. The group who arrived at the wharenui, presented an outwardly stoic demeanour. Inside, thoughts were racing at the possibilities opening wide before them. They began to comprehend how restrictive Rangi's rule was. He was a tyrant who enjoyed conflict and war. For the first time since Rangi's father died, they inhaled sweet freedom into their lungs. The eldest was determined to set right the wrongs of the past.

"*Tihei mauri ora* (call for the right to speak). Today we made a decision - Rongo, you are the leader our people need. We took this decision before we knew of Rangi's demise. You need to know that, and so do our people. Our tīpuna knew Rangi wasn't the son of our chief, and he wasn't even of our blood. Perhaps this is the reason he treated our people so poorly. Rangi's descent is from a long line of ancestors who align themselves with evil. The truth is difficult for you Rongo. Your heart is pure, and you have been loyal to the man you believed was your cousin. Before she died, your mother confessed to me your father was the old chief.

She begged forgiveness for stealing your birthright, but she was afraid Atarangi would kill you if she believed you were a rival to her son. The people who love and follow you deserve to know the truth. You are, and always have been our true and chosen chief."

Rongo's face was pale. Children had whispered, teasing him, but he never paid any attention to the rumours. He assumed they were hurtful childish taunts, not the truth. The man he believed was his father was actually his uncle. Everyone was watching him, awaiting a response. Ngoi moved to his side and squeezed his hand, so he would know she was there to support him. Marama moved to Piri's side and asked if they might speak. The tohunga took Marama's cue to buy some time for Rongo to absorb the shock. Piri reiterated the words of their tīpuna to him and Marama. The more reinforcement the leadership decision received, the more readily the hapu would embrace the change, and the better everyone would feel. When Piri finished, he opened the floor to Marama. He led by example. Women hadn't spoken at hui for many years, but today that would change. Marama was used to public speaking, so he couldn't think of anyone better equipped to pave the way. Ngoi, who was the woman of their new chief, could observe her mentor, and Piri was sure she would also speak out on women's issues in the future. Marama appreciated the significance of the moment, and she intended to make an impression. She began with her karakia, complete with the flowing movements of her spiritual language.

"We stand before you, Papatūānuku, the instruments of change, to do your will. Your aroha is a gift that we will never take for granted. Every man, woman, and child in Rotowhā will endeavour to keep you in their hearts." In a strong, clear voice, Marama sang a *waiata* (song) she composed in praise of Papatūānuku. Her body moved gracefully in carefully choreographed honour of Papatūānuku. Marama slowly made eye contact with every person in attendance. Each person was reminded of her differences as her unusual eyes searched theirs.

"Your tīpuna demand you restore the mana of women. I stand

before you, accompanied by esteemed kuia and the woman of the true chief, as a speaker in your wharenui. We cannot undo the past, but we can seize the future, to fulfil the wishes of our old ones. The winds of change blow favourably, for those who love and honour their ancestors." A warm gust of wind swirled into the wharenui. It lifted dried flowers from a bowl, showering everyone with petals. Nani whispered in Marama's mind.

"Entertaining enough for you, my dear?"

Marama released a lump of smouldering coal into a bowl of ground bark and minerals. It flared, in a bright burst of light, warming the oils inside the rim. Smoke and an intense fragrance of flowers wafted through the meeting house. Nani chuckled in pleasure, and Marama sensed Kotuku's approval. Holding the bowl aloft, Marama entreated the Gods and ancestors to accept the humble thanks of the people. Ngoi and kuia joined their voices to Marama's for her closing chant. Both tohunga were impressed, as her words reinforced Piri's message. The ancestors' contribution was tangible, and combined with the passion of the women, the ritual was perfect for the occasion. Rongo had regained his composure by now, and Marama pledged her loyalty to his leadership of the village. She also entrusted to his care the flowers of Papatūānuku, the women and girls of the village, before leaving the speaking place open for him. Tamati admired, not for the first time, Marama's ease and instinctive response with a ceremony. The spiritual was also her domain. Piri was right, she was one of them, and her skills were awe-inspiring. Rongo performed a passionate haka to the Gods and his tīpuna. He swore to Papatūānuku he would honour her until the breath left his body. Only then did he turn to his people.

"I am the chief, but you are the heart of our people. You put our people first, even though you could have forfeited your lives. I salute the bravery of you all, for together, we have learned a harsh but valuable lesson. Never again should one person be permitted to wield so much power, especially when it is detrimental to our collective well-being. Henceforth, we must respect our whenua, mauri and wairua. I usher in a new age of spiritual harmony and dedication to peace. My role is to safeguard our people until turbulent times arrive and Maui is reborn to unite us all. We will lead together. I would like to ask two of our warriors to join us and for Ngoi and Marama to choose two women to represent Papatūānuku on our council. Does anyone object to this or have any ideas?"

"I would like to propose you consider Nikau as one of those men. He has always been loyal to you, and the men respect him. They respond well to his calm, competent manner, and I notice warriors often approach him for advice or assistance." Muru seated himself to allow the next person to speak.

"Thank you Muru. I also think Nikau is a good choice. As he has travelled with you, Rongo, he is well versed in spiritual customs and used to diplomacy. When we retrieved Rangi's body, his authority was evident. I think it would be prudent of us to allow you to pick the second man. It is likely you will need someone you can rely on in battle besides Nikau, and you know the men best." Tamati returned to his seat.

Rongo surveyed the room as he was greeted with a chorus of yes' in agreement. Marama rose when nobody else stood to contribute.

"My proposal is unusual in some ways but logical in many others. Please consider Huia as one of the women. Although she is young and the daughter of Rongo, Huia has already become an accomplished healer. She also displays a propensity for the spiritual. To have a healer, who can work in the physical and the spiritual realm, provides an enormous benefit to the village. To have two healers on your council from two different generations provides continuity of knowledge over time. Exposure to considered decision making at an early age will allow her to develop a unique set of skills. My education was similar, and Huia's mind is as quick as her nature is caring. She dedicates herself to Papatūānuku and is beloved of the Earth Mother."

There was much nodding in agreement, and the Leaders

accepted Marama's proposal. Due to their obvious bias, Huia's parents, Rongo and Ngoi, didn't participate in the decision. The council selected Huia unanimously. Rongo steered the conversation to practical matters such as announcing the new leadership and arrangements for Rangi's funeral. A shadow appeared in the doorway.

"How dare you sit here discussing the *tangihanga* (funeral) of my son without me!" Atarangi's face was puce with rage. "You have murdered my son, your chief, and you are a fraud Piri. I know you poisoned him, tell them all what you did. Kūmara, lumpy as ever, how can you sit there in my son's place when these people killed your cousin?" She spat the words at Rongo with such venom some of the elders flinched. Rongo, however, was deadly calm.

"Aunty, what a pleasure to see you, and you are as polite as ever. You have no place at this hui, as you abandoned your son and our hapu many years ago."

"You insolent, imbecile! Give me my mokopuna, and I will go."

"Your mokopuna isn't 'your' mokopuna. Maui belongs to us all, a gift from 'our' tīpuna." She flew at Rongo but was intercepted and restrained by Muru and several of the leaders. Atarangi tried to bite and claw at them. Once again, it was the eldest who spoke.

"Atarangi, you are filled with malice. The deceitful deeds of your past have returned to haunt you. You did this to your flesh and blood. With all due respect to your close relationship with the former false chief, I believe it would be best to send his body home with you to his real father." Atarangi's face blanched at his words. How did this old man come to possess her secret? She had returned to Rangi's father, her cousin, but they lived in isolation together. They travelled far when they wanted company and used different names. Her ambitions to be headwoman, give birth to a chief were realised long ago, so she returned to the man who loved her. There was no love in her for these simple people, only contempt at how easily they cowered. They didn't love her either, but they did fear her. The skills of her family were beyond their comprehension, so she crushed anyone stupid enough to get in her way. The leaders ignored Atarangi's outburst and removed her from the wharenui. They secured her to a tree under guard to discuss the eldest's proposal in peace.

In the end, they all agreed on a course of action, and only Rongo expressed a desire to say farewell to Rangi. He offered to dress him and place Rangi's fine weapons, along with those from his mother's whānau, with his body. Any taonga belonging to their ancestors would remain in Rongo's care to be handed down by Rongo to his sons or Maui. They would need to choose and brief people to return Rangi's body. Taking Atarangi with them would be dangerous, but she might escape if they didn't take her, and then they wouldn't know where she was. They decided the warriors would first take Rangi's body to Atarangi's people. A second group would follow with Atarangi. It would be up to her people to decide what to do with them both. The eldest urged them to be diligent in restraining her, and whoever escorted her must be careful. She would use all her wiles and poisons to obtain freedom or exact revenge. They debated how wise it was to let her go, but as they didn't want to keep or kill her, the choices were limited.

"I have an idea," said Marama. Everyone turned to her, eager to hear any ideas concerning the prickliest issue of the day. "If we select an escort for Atarangi, it needs to be small, incorruptible and committed. Tamati would be wary, and your ancestors will help him. When Rongo captured me, Nikau guarded me so Rongo could sleep. He was both vigilant and trustworthy. Perhaps the warrior who left us when Rangi injured him can be coaxed back. Rangi has mistreated Tahu, so it's unlikely he will have any sympathy for his mother. My last suggestion may be controversial, but I believe if Arihia travelled with them, the spirit Hana would watch over her as will Papatūānuku. She and her family have been punished by Rangi enough. Rongo, would you consider returning Arihia to her whānau as a gesture of goodwill between your people?"

"Your ideas are well-considered, Marama. It was only Rangi who insisted they must give Arihia to him. The rest of us were impressed with the generosity of reparation offered by Roimata's whānau. I, like Marama, believe we should return the girl to her whānau. Roimata and her people were also cheated by Atarangi, just as we were. Rangi won the flower of a generation by deception. My sense of fair play urges me to return the gifts we received when Roimata came to us. Life for Roimata will not have been easy when she returned. She spent much of her life here, and perhaps we should offer her a place amongst us. Marama, how would you feel about that?"

"I agree with you Rongo, Roimata and I made peace before she left."

Tempted to broach the subject of a return to her whānau, Marama opted to wait. It had been a challenging day already. She wanted to speak to Rongo and Piri about it first as well. There was some discussion amongst the group regarding what they should return to Roimata's hapu, but they all favoured sending Arihia home to her people. Without exception, they were sorry for Arihia and embarrassed by Rangi's treatment of her. Through Hana, only Tamati and Marama knew the high price Arihia had paid to earn her freedom. Tamati thanked his tīpuna for answering his prayers and supporting his decision to keep the full circumstances of Rangi's death to himself.

The villagers were all summoned to a hui on the marae. Eldest koroua and his kuia told the villagers everything they knew. Piri and Tamati also told portions of the story when called upon to do so, but they never mentioned Arihia's push. There was joy and relief when they heard Maui, the child they loved, wasn't Rangi's son but was instead chosen by their ancestors to save them. No taint of foul blood or dishonesty would reside in their hapu, to return to haunt them. Marama was relieved by the acceptance of the people for Maui and her. The telling reminded Marama of her journey from Hawaiki when the people she loved also chose to be open and honest with their people. The villagers gasped, covered their mouths, cried silent tears or became angry. It was an emotional journey they all shared. Muru presented the leader's plans for Rangi's return to his mother's people. They wouldn't show them any disrespect, as it was Atarangi who had disgraced them.

All protocols to the dead would be observed and overseen by Piri. The eldest singled out Piri, Tamati, Rongo, Marama and Ngoi to offer thanks on behalf of everyone. Arihia received an official apology for her treatment. Marama asked her to escort Rangi home as a representative of Hana and Papatūānuku before returning to her family. Arihia accepted the apology and mission graciously. A return to her whānau was an outcome she never dared to dream of when she arrived in Rotowhā. Each elder offered their view and sage words on leadership. They asked the people if those qualities existed in their village? Rongo's name was called out by men, women and children, starting a chant.

"Rongo, Rongo, Rongo, Rongo," until the eldest held up his hand for quiet.

"We are glad to know what you want, and we are all in agreement. I invite our chief Rongo to address his people."

Rongo was moved by the support and aroha he received so enthusiastically. Kneeling before them, he pledged his life to serve them. Guided by the ancestors and Gods, he would strive to safeguard their mauri, wairua, whenua and increase physical and spiritual prosperity. He shared his vision for peace and unity. They were fierce, well-trained, formidable, but battle and war would be tools of necessity rather than the reason for living. Most of the villagers had close whānau in other hapu, so his words were a balm for frayed hearts. There was no feasting that night, but once they returned Rangi and Atarangi to their people, there would be huge celebrations throughout the iwi. Rongo sent out carefully crafted messages and invitations with runners to deliver the news, and invited Ngoi's parents to come early to participate in his elevation to Chief. He had an ulterior motive, for he knew Ngoi's mother would craft the tale into an epic story with songs and actions. The lesson would be immortalised and shared across the land.

Chapter 13

It was a day filled with drama and excitement. Marama collected then cuddled Maui to her breast as most of his day was spent with Huia and the boys. She could not bear to be separated from him for long. Maui was her only child right now, and that hurt. He was content, well-fed and sleeping soundly when Rongo's head appeared in the doorway.

"I was hoping you would still be awake. Can I come in?"

"Of course chief, it's an honour." Marama's cheeky grin belied her flowery words as she was teasing him. She placed Maui gently on his mat and set about making a warm drink for them both.

"We didn't speak today about your future Marama. I sensed you wanted to discuss it when we were talking about Arihia. Rangi was also the reason you were captured and brought here."

"I did think of raising it Rongo, but I wanted to talk to you and Piri first, rather than to add another issue to a growing pile. I am also conscious Maui is precious to all of you. As his mother, I will never leave him." Tears sprang to her eyes at the very thought.

"Nobody expects you to leave Maui with us Marama, least of all me. I know how much you love him, and I am a father. You need to return to your whānau. I know this. Ngoi and I have been discussing ideas for how we can make this happen. Maui is special to us, and we have glimpsed his future. My proposal is for Maui to belong to both iwi. I will be his father here, and when he is old enough, he will come to us for one moon cycle every year. We would like to form bonds of friendship with your people as well. Trade, share knowledge, make matches, and visit one another. I may have captured you, but you and Maui have captured the hearts of my whānau and people. We all love you and the boy Marama. Ngoi can't bear the thought of never seeing you again, and we haven't mentioned anything to Huia yet." Rongo made a face and rolled his eyes heavenward.

"The feeling is mutual. I can't imagine our life without all of you in it. Will everyone agree Rongo? I am desperate to go home, see my children, my man, and loved ones." Marama fought to hold back her tears, swamped by the emotions walled inside her for so long.

"The tohunga will support my proposal, and I think other people will too. We owe you a lot Marama, you have helped restore balance to our lives. I feel especially responsible as I brought you here, even if my tīpuna orchestrated it. If you can wait a few days, I will escort you home myself, and Ngoi will journey with us."

"Oh Rongo, you will make me the happiest woman in the world if you can just take me home to my whānau." She hugged him tightly, eyes closed to hold back her tears.

Marama drowned Piri in her emotions on the other side of the village, and his ancestor answered her call.

"Marama must be taken home Piri. We promised her ancestors we would only divert her to create an outcome we all desired. She has suffered enough and given us much. Her people require allies, and we must honour our debt."

"It will be done Kotuku. Our lives are richer for her presence here, and I wish to know her people. Rongo feels the same."

At first, Marama was too excited to sleep but eventually, she succumbed, falling into a deep slumber. In her excitement, she was still wearing the katipō necklace. It was the searing heat of the necklace that woke her.

"Quickly Marama, the boy is in danger." It was Nani.

Marama's eyes snapped open in the dark and her ears tuned for vibration. She heard a rustling sound and perceived a presence in the gloom near Maui. Muscles tensed before she launched herself from her mat, body smashing into someone, crushing them against the wall of her whare. Breath whooshed from the shadow, but it slithered from Marama's fingertips, lurching for the door. Marama was torn. She wanted to give chase and find out who it was, but Maui was her priority. At the risk of scaring Maui, she let out a loud, bloodcurdling scream before clutching the wailing baby to her breast. The commotion awakened everyone around them.

"Somebody tried to steal Maui!" Marama yelled at the top of her lungs. The baby just laughed at her now that he was awake. Her cry stirred a hornet's nest of activity. People emerged from their whare and hastily lit torches while listening for sounds of anyone fleeing. Warriors grabbed weapons, knowing they could be under attack and needed to defend Maui. Sleepy but outraged mothers searched the darkness for anyone unfamiliar. Atarangi was tied up, so Rongo ran straight to her, but all he found was an unconscious guard and cut bonds. He cursed under his breath. They had underestimated Atarangi, and all assumed she came alone, but Rongo was no longer sure of that. Calling the names of his most trusted warriors, he sent eight of them to guard Maui. Huia and Arihia followed the warriors, determined to protect the baby as well. A beacon was lit. It alerted the perimeter guards that enemies were inside the pā. Rongo despatched reinforcements to the palisades and gates. He was sure she was still here. Piri materialised at his side.

"We need to take her alive. She poisoned the guard, and I need to know what she used. I want Marama to look at him." Marama manifested out of the gloom behind them.

"Maui is safe. My tīpuna surround him, and the spirit Hana hunts Rangi's kin. They are hiding, but we must be careful, as the weapons they carry are deadly, and they are desperate. Where is the guard? I have an antidote for him." She moved quickly to administer the remedy Hana whispered to her. The necklace throbbed against her skin, and the connection with Hana held.

"Atarangi's man is with her. We need to go this way." She gestured to Rongo and Piri to follow her. Marama crouched low, placing her feet carefully as she stalked into the darkness, a huntress herself. She frequently stopped to listen. Hana was magnifying the sound of Atarangi's heartbeat to guide Marama.

"I am with you Marama." It was Tane.

Once her first love told her, he would always be with her, even after he died. Then, he said goodbye, leaving her distraught but free to live and love again. In her time of need, he still came to her. The knowledge of his protection strengthened Marama's resolve. Atarangi's poisons were no match for the spirits, and she could feel Kotuku and Rongo's ancestors massing around them. The heartbeat was speeding up in her ears but becoming fainter, so she knew they were moving away swiftly.

"Faster Rongo, they are running."

"I know where they are going, Marama. Piri, send the men outside, to the western palisade, with torches and guard all the paths to the lake." Rongo took the lead, and Marama knew he was going the right way because the heartbeat became louder. As children, Rongo and Rangi used to sneak out of the village. Rangi had seen his mother, using a secret exit, a tunnel under the palisade. A woven mat covered with earth hid the entrance and exit from view. You could walk right past it every day and never know it was there. He guessed this was how Atarangi's man gained access to the village and freed her. Rongo sprinted now. They could only wriggle through the tunnel one at a time, and it wouldn't be easy for a grown man. Atarangi's heart was pounding in Marama's ears now. She was either panicking, exerting herself or both.

"Hurry Rongo. They are escaping!"

Rongo found a burst of speed in his legs. The moon, Marama's namesake, burst from behind the clouds and lit the shape of a man huddled against the palisade. Without breaking his stride, Rongo launched himself at the figure. The man struck out, but Rongo dived low to avoid weapons or poison. Rongo's shoulder and fist struck the figure's kneecaps a mighty blow. He whipped his mere around and slashed the invader's Achilles tendon to disable him before jumping out of reach. Marama could see Atarangi worming her way through the tunnel. Of course, she went first. She grabbed Atarangi's retreating ankles and pulled with all her might. Atarangi tried to kick and twist from Marama's vice-like grip, but her mouth filled with dirt as her face scraped the bottom of the tunnel. Her fingers clawed at the ground, but Papatūānuku rejected her grasp, turning the ground to dust under her fingertips. Marama hauled a choking Atarangi from the tunnel in one fluid motion with Tane's strength in her arms. Hearing the cries of pain from her man, Atarangi struggled desperately. With a knee between her shoulder blades, Marama used her body weight to pin her down. Rongo darted over and stomped on Atarangi's right hand to stop her from wielding any weapons. A panting Tamati ran to secure her left side.

By now, more warriors were arriving. They surrounded the prone invader, spears against his throat. Piri returned and carefully bound Atarangi's hands, looping the rope around her neck so she would choke herself if she moved them. The old tohunga intoned a chant to his ancestors as he bound her. She was spitting dirt and cursing foully. He gagged her so she wouldn't spook everyone with her threats before binding her ankles together so she couldn't kick or run. Finally, they pulled her to her feet. Atarangi threw herself at Marama, trying to head-butt her, but Marama was too quick and jumped back out of reach. Somehow, Atarangi's head connected with the katipō necklace. Did it fly up to meet her, or was it just the result of her trajectory? Nobody could be sure. Atarangi screamed like a wounded bat when the necklace seared her brow. Heat, light and energy, radiated from the golden orb as Hana satisfied utu and the ancestors meted out punishment. Sinking to her knees, Atarangi breathed heavily, and everyone stepped back for their safety and gave her space to breathe. When she looked up, the contact had imprinted an angry red mark on her forehead. It resembled the red marking of the katipō. Atarangi stared at them with innocent eyes.

"I couldn't leave her to poison the minds of future generations or seek to harm any of you. Your tīpuna supported my actions. Thank you, Marama, my descendants, and I can now find peace." Hana slipped away quietly.

"I will always love and protect you, Marama, but I must return to our son." Marama felt a stir of air, like the brush of lips on hers, then Tane was gone as well.

Atarangi blinked and looked around, frightened. Malice, and her evil deeds, were wiped from her memory, replaced by the uncomplicated mind of a child. After everything she endured, Hana still chose not to take Atarangi's life as well as Rangi's.

"She will harm us no more. The spirits have rendered her black soul impotent." Piri stated the facts with a set mouth and satisfied gleam in his eye.

"No! What have you done? Aue! My beautiful Atarangi, what have they done to you?" Her man was distraught, and he pushed himself onto the spears surrounding him with brute force. Although the warriors swiftly retracted their spears, he had ruptured his jugular vein. His body ebbed, a crimson pool of life. Papatūānuku gathered up his offering, absorbing all into her nurturing womb.

"What shall we do with her Piri?" Rongo looked to the tohunga.

"We must return her to her people. Those of her own blood should determine her fate. At least now, she poses no risk to our people."

"Atarangi's deeds make an amazing story—one of lust, greed, power, the spurning of Papatūānuku, the Gods and ancestors," said Marama. "Perhaps Ngoi's mother can weave this tale into her repertoire as well. There are many lessons to be learned. I must return to Maui, but I am grateful to you all for coming to our aid when we needed you most." Marama broke into a jog as soon as she was out of sight. She needed to hold Maui and anchor herself to the physical world. With Tane and Nani on the other side, being away from her family - sometimes she longed to be there with them.

Returning two bodies and a woman-child to another tribe would be a delicate matter. It mattered little that Atarangi and her man hadn't returned to their hapu for years. Atarangi's people committed a historical insult when they gave an impure Puhi to a chief. They were, however, all deceived by Atarangi and her cousin. They also returned a false chief, who had died under unusual circumstances, and replaced him with a chief who didn't have blood ties to Atarangi's tribe. Fortunately, they were familiar with Rongo. It was always Rongo who fostered trade and peaceful alliance. They barely knew Rangi, but they did know of his warlike reputation. Whether they would mourn him as a lost son and great chief or as an embarrassment best forgotten was their choice. There was a lengthy discussion and debate about how best to return them. Some preferred to bury the dead and take the woman close to her village, where she could wander home. Others argued deception always bore bitter fruit, and honesty was the best option. A delegation would travel south to Atarangi's people. The travel party selected by Rongo was Tamati, Muru, Huia, a woman from Atarangi's tribe and a contingent of seasoned warriors. Piri, Ngoi, the elders and Nikau's capable hands would guide the village while Rongo was away.

"I know we have asked much of you already, but I would be grateful if you joined us, Marama. One day, Maui will unite us in our time of need. You are intuitive, a wonderful distraction for placing people on the back foot, and Maui will be known to them. The tale we have to tell will be more realistic if you are both present. We travel in the wrong direction to return you to your people, but if you do this, I swear to return you myself as soon as we conclude negotiations." Rongo looked hopefully at Marama. Although Marama longed to bolt home in a borrowed canoe as fast as she could, Maui's future might depend on this alliance.

"I agree to accompany you Rongo, with Maui."

This woman was an enigma to them all, brave and selfless. Returning bodies was never without risk. With her agreement, Marama secured the undying loyalty of the entire village to Maui and herself.

"What of Arihia Rongo? Can we now send her directly home to her people?"

"Yes, I think that would be best. Will you speak to Arihia Marama? I cannot think of anyone better than Arihia to convey such a woeful tale to her whanau. We can organise an escort and messenger to accompany her.

"Consider it done Rongo. You are a good man. We have the chance to salvage the lives of two good women from an unhappy existence, and that will please Papatūānuku."

Marama was already taking up her cloak, and Maui's carrying basket as Rongo took his leave. She hurried to Arihia, determined not to let her suffer any longer than necessary. Maui was left in the capable hands of a curious Huia when Marama arrived and asked Arihia to join her in giving thanks to Papatūānuku.

"Arihia, you are truly favoured by Papatūānuku. Rongo visited me a few moments ago, and you are to return home to your whānau immediately."

"Oh, Marama! I – I can't believe it. My whanau, I will see my whanau again." A sob escaped as Arihia's brittle exterior melted in tears of relief. Marama held her for a moment, letting her vent her pent up emotion. "I don't feel like I deserve this. Rangi didn't-"

"Shhh, no need to fret. The ancestors' designs are beyond the comprehension of us mere mortals. Do you know Hana is your ancestor? You have only aided her in exacting retribution. In return, when she comes to you, you will reinstate her and her brother in your whakapapa. There is also your future as a healer to fulfil. Your calling is strong, and you will lead the way in improving the health and well-being of your village. I also have a task for you. Rongo will send an escort and messenger with you, but I feel your people will best receive the news of what has transpired here from you, but never mention your part in aiding Hana." Arihia nodded in understanding. "Today Rongo and the leaders have agreed to return much of the wealth Roimata brought with her. We feel Rangi and his scheming mother cheated all of us. Rotowhā is Roimata's home. Your people won't have welcomed her back under such unfortunate circumstances. These people are her people, and they would welcome her return if she wishes. There is a man in your village who has always loved her Arihia. They could return here together if they want to. Can you please convey this message to Roimata from Rongo and me?"

Arihia regarded Marama through misty eyes. In truth, she hadn't forgiven her sister yet, and here was the injured party offering Roimata another chance at life.

"You are a better person than I am, Marama. I will convey the message, and I will reinstate Hana and her brother in our whakapapa. She saved my life." The two embraced, and Marama began a soft song of love and renewal to Papatūānuku.

It felt good to Marama to be on the move after months confined within the village. They travelled for two days by canoe, before shouldering packs, to trek through the bush trails. Transporting the bodies was heavy work, and Rongo rotated the bearers frequently. There were two teams for each body, so the men got adequate rest between shifts. Rongo worked alongside his men. His example was good for morale, building strength and stamina. They camped, hunted, and ate well from their supplies at night, lightening the load for the next day. Tamati and Marama took care of spiritual needs as they trekked through unfamiliar whenua. Huia tended to the voyage ailments of the delegation and looked after Atarangi. Her brothers were jealous she was accompanying their father at first. When Rongo explained he was leaving his whare and entrusting their mother to their care, there was a shift in attitude. All his children were proud to play a role in Rongo's plans. They glowed, basking in his trust and their allocated responsibilities. Most of the injuries were minor, and Huia rarely needed Marama's help, so she and Rongo shared the task of carrying Maui with Marama. While Marama never showed signs of tiring, they both enjoyed the company of the baby and the stories Marama told when they walked beside her. Soon Marama and Maui would return to their people, but neither of them wanted to think about it just yet.

Once in the proximity of Atarangi's village, Rongo sent a runner to request a formal welcome for Rongo, Muru, Tamati, Atarangi and Marama. It would be dangerous to arrive, with a large contingent of warriors bearing bodies, without first explaining why they were there. The runner returned swiftly, with cordial greetings for Rongo and an invitation to the marae. Initially, Rongo planned to leave Maui with the warriors, but both Marama and Tamati were confident, he was protected. Huia argued she should accompany them as well. If Marama needed to speak, she could hold Maui, reassure Atarangi if she was scared, and a party with children was less threatening. Tamati and Marama agreed with her, so Rongo relented, knowing she was right. He noted Huia and Ngoi learned far more from Marama than healing, but it pleased him to know they could think for themselves and articulate opinions.

The call of welcome floated through the air. The women walked onto the marae first. A murmur ran through the curious bystanders who gathered as they recognised Atarangi, but as Marama drew closer, jaws dropped in silence. Huia held Atarangi's hand and smiled at her. The woman's childlike eyes were startled as she took in the unfamiliar faces. Atarangi did recognise her wharenui and began to search for other familiar landmarks. The two parties greeted each other, and the elders welcomed them. The speaker traced their genealogy to common ancestry, shared victories, arriving at the union of Atarangi and their chief, and the birth of Rangi. When it was the turn of the visitors to speak, it was Muru who addressed them. They decided first to bring the news of Rangi's illness, death, and Atarangi's condition. Muru then requested an urgent private audience with the leaders to discuss matters of importance to them all. Although honesty was a good policy, Rongo thought it prudent not to put any leaders on the spot, in public, in front of their people. They had decided they should share the details with the leaders first. It wasn't difficult for the hosts to work out there was more to this tale. They were also intensely curious about Marama and darted surreptitious looks in her direction. The current chief was only distantly related to Atarangi. He remembered how beautiful she was when he was a boy. His own family thought she was arrogant, demanding and cruel. When she left the village, many people were relieved to be rid of her. There were always rumours surrounding her, her cousin, and her unnatural magic. Atarangi's return was unlikely to be positive, so he was more comfortable speaking in private. The chief liked Rongo, and from what he had heard of Rangi, he sounded a lot like his mother. He didn't feel any grief when he learned of Rangi's demise. One less ambitious, blood-thirsty chief to contend with was always good news. What concerned him was if Atarangi's behaviour would cost them in reparation. Like it or not, this was her hapu, and Rongo's reputation as an astute negotiator was well known. The hosts invited the guests to dine after the formalities were satisfied. A tohunga blessed their meal before asking Tamati to do the same. The tohunga were eager to speak and sat together.

Muru shared the news they had chosen Rongo as their next chief. The hosts were pleased to have Rongo visiting them and shared congratulations. They hoped to form closer ties and discuss trade.

"Thank you for your hospitality. As you have probably guessed, there is far more to this story. I thought it best to discuss the happenings of the past few months with your leaders. It is a strange tale. The will of our tīpuna, and the hands of the Gods, have guided us to where we are now. Tohunga Piri has remained to watch over our people, but we are fortunate to have tohunga Tamati with us. As the tale begins with Rangi's desires and a prophecy from the spirits, with your permission, I would ask Tamati to begin." There were nods of assent from the hosts as curiosity was gnawing at them. It sounded like there was an intriguing story to be told, and they liked nothing better. Tamati told them of Rangi's desire for a son and his fury when all his children were born female. The ancestors revealed a way to achieve Rangi's desire to Piri, and the search for the foreign woman began. They all turned to Marama and the baby, finally understanding her significance and presence. It also gave them a chance to look at her without being rude, as she fascinated them. The guests observed Marama, unable to resist the magnetic pull of her uniqueness. Maui found it all extraordinarily amusing and let out one of his trademark laughs, waving his fists in the air. The kaumatua and kuia were enchanted, and they clapped their hands, encouraging his boisterous babble. Rongo took up the tale next. He spoke of finding Marama, capturing her to return to his chief, how Marama had eluded him and then introduced herself. Rongo explained how Marama won their respect on the trek home. They had felt reluctant to give her to Rangi due to the violence he inflicted on his women.

Tamati told of Marama's connection with their tīpuna, the instruction to restore the mana of the women and her request to share her healing knowledge. The hosts were riveted and regarded Marama with a healthy respect, as they revered spirituality and healing skills in their village. Women also participated in decision-making for their people, so there was admiration for the boon requested. Rongo guided them through the emotion of the pregnancy, the drama with Roimata, Rangi's demand for Arihia and the birth of Maui. Maui, a gift from their tīpuna, sent to save them in their time of need. He also spoke of the training of Huia and Ngoi, Marama's input into the health of the women, children, his warriors and her leadership of the women to honour Papatūānuku. Tamati resumed the tale of the rituals. Rangi's failure to heed the warning of their tīpuna. The offences Rangi committed against Papatūānuku and the impact that had on the mauri of the village. He spoke of Rangi's illness and how the tohunga searched for the cause, to find a cure, in vain. When he outlined the many grievances people held against their chief, people gasped or covered their mouths in horror. Tamati told them of the many demands made on Piri, his mentor, and how the tohunga took care of Rangi but received abuse in return. Rangi's insistence on breaking with protocol and its effects, which Tamati believed, led to his untimely death. He told them of Rangi's crazed pursuit of Arihia and falling off the cliff. Rongo picked up the thread of the story again. Atarangi had returned to their village, but when she was too late to save her son, she blamed Piri for his death. Piri battled for weeks to save Rangi's life and their village. He told them of Atarangi demanding Maui, her abuse of the leaders, her removal and subsequent imprisonment. They were intrigued as Marama spoke of waking in the night to find somebody in her whare, near her baby. Marama loved to tell stories, and her oratory skills were well-honed. Her voice moved from soft and loving mother to affronted warrior defending her child, and the realisation Atarangi wasn't alone. She shared the story of the katipō necklace and Hana, how Hana guided her towards Atarangi until Rongo guessed where she and her accomplice went. Marama told of the capture of Atarangi's man by Rongo and how she pulled Atarangi from the tunnel by her ankles, assisted by Papatūānuku and the spirits. Marama recounted the binding of Atarangi by Piri and her attack on Marama in a quiet voice. She raised her voice as she told of the searing mark on Atarangi's forehead as Hana took her revenge, and Atarangi's lover's actions when he realised Hana had altered Atarangi's mind forever. The hosts could see the mark, and they were horrified. Atarangi and her cousin were both originally from their village. The blood drained from their chief's face, leaving him pale with worry.

Muru shared with their hosts how they had chosen Rongo as chief and the painful backstory of Atarangi's artifice. She had tricked everyone. Rangi wasn't the son of their chief, and was not their leader. The ancestors were patient, hoping he would become the leader their people needed. When his true nature emerged, even after his son was born, and his behaviour became unacceptable, he was doomed. Even before Rangi's death, the leaders had decided Rongo would be chief. During Rangi's illness, the village began to come to life and heal. Rangi wasn't only a fraud but a brutal dictator who affected the wairua of everyone around him. Over time, he stripped away the ability of almost anyone else to make a decision.

"We bring back to you the bodies of Rangi and his father. Atarangi is once again a child. They are of your blood, and it's appropriate that we return them to their whenua." Muru paused here, trying to gauge the feelings of his hosts. Rongo decided to build a bridge with these people.

"I want to be open with you. This delegation isn't seeking reparation for any misdeeds past or present. Atarangi hasn't lived here for many years. You are blameless. We came to return the bodies to rest in their rightful place and Atarangi also needs a home. They are not of our iwi, but we don't dishonour people in death. We hope, out of the horrors of their deeds, to find friendship and trade with your people." They were the words, Atarangi's village needed to hear. It was inconceivable to give nothing to Rongo's tribe, but he gave them the right to choose what they thought was appropriate, without formalities. It was a manoeuvre to win friends and allies rather than seek wealth or foster enemies. The old chief of Atarangi's people had shared his suspicions about his daughter, with his successor, before he died. He prepared him for the day someone might call them to account.

It was a fantastic story, perhaps even close to being the whole story. With so many enemies, he doubted the Gods alone caused Rangi's illness and death. Somebody had helped them, as a fall was suspiciously convenient. It was, however, unlikely it was Rongo. People spoke of his loyalty to his cousin and chief. The man possessed mana, a born leader in his opinion, and a valuable ally. If this boy grew up to be of such significance, he could also be a future ally.

"You have given us much to discuss, Rongo. We thank you for

your generosity and the spirit which brought you to our marae. Atarangi will be taken care of by her relatives. Would you and your people like to stay with us tonight while we deliberate?"

"It would be best if we return to our camp. You must have the opportunity to make decisions for your people in private. We will return tomorrow, officially, to discuss trade and alliances but also to hear what to do." The two men shared a long hongi. It conveyed the respect, trust, and hope they shared for the future.

Maui was doted on by the elders whose admiration he won with his lovable nature. If the ancestors were correct, one day, their mokopuna might fight beside him. They perceived the weight of his destiny in his tiny, strong fingers.

Rongo brought smoked fish, exotic feathers, whalebone, fine stone tools and intricate weaving to discuss trade. The two delegations met in the wharenui. They decided to gently tell their people the story of Atarangi, her cousin, and her son. Such a tale would spread rapidly, so it was better if they heard it from their leaders, and it was important they didn't feel ashamed. The actions of wayward whānau on the wrong path, in the end, yielded a positive alliance. Tohunga and elders wished to commit the bodies of the wayward sons to the bosom of Papatūānuku. There were caves on their sacred maunga, and the site would become tapu. No parents or siblings besides Atarangi lived to mourn the loss, but the tohunga would adhere to the appropriate rituals and return with Rongo to take charge of the bodies. Atarangi's people presented preserved gigantic eel, intricately carved hard-wood weapons, including taiaha of the highest quality, bowls, utensils, woven flax baskets of all shapes and sizes, prized kiwi feathers, a variety of dried berries and medicinal herbs to trade. Marama and Huia left with a tohunga and kuia, in complete excitement, to investigate the medicinal stores. Huia was impressed by the role of women in this village and the atmosphere it created. Her natural curiosity and ability to ask analytical questions delighted the healers, as did Marama's depth of knowledge. By the time Rongo's party was ready to depart, they had formed firm friendships with their hosts. Twice a year, they would trade formally, visit each other's village, and informally whenever anyone accumulated excess goods.

"We have gifts of friendship for you and your people Rongo. Our people will present these to you before you leave. Maui, the son of your village, we adopt as a son of our village also. He will always be welcomed, sheltered, and offered alliance by our people. We invite your daughter Huia to visit and study with our healers each year, and we hope you will bring your sons to choose weapons of their own. To you, Rongo, we pledge our friendship, and we will take up arms against anyone who attacks you without just cause."

Rongo's forfeit of reparation was rewarded handsomely with gifts of considerable value. A kiwi feather cloak, weapons, a supply of medicines, crafted tools and utensils, all stowed in beautiful baskets. Atarangi cried as Huia waved farewell, but a distant cousin held her close to calm her.

The warriors were relieved when Rongo returned and astounded by the wealth he brought. Tamati and the tohunga conducted the rituals and prayers necessary to hand over the two bodies. The atmosphere surrounding the travel party was lighter, having returned the corpses to their rightful place, with their people. Although the day was half gone, they set out on the return journey. Marama wished she could run all the way back to the village. The sooner they got there, the sooner she could go home.

Chapter 14

The villagers prepared an enormous feast when Rongo and his travel party returned. Everyone celebrated Rongo's elevation to chief with dedicated enthusiasm. Food, singing, haka, dancing and general merriment were all in plentiful supply. Ngoi's parents arrived, so her mother entertained them with a vast repertoire of stories and jokes. A happy Ngoi collapsed down next to Marama and Maui after a particularly strenuous round of dancing.

"You know you are getting older when you can't dance all night anymore. Did Rongo tell you I am coming with him to take you home?"

"Yes, he did. I can't think of anyone I would rather travel with, and in the early stages of your pregnancy, it should be fine. I am going to miss you Ngoi."

Ngoi's eyes crinkled with joy. She thought she might be pregnant, but Marama was always right about these things.

"Piri is going to come too. Much of the journey is by canoe, and we stayed home last time, so it's only fair." Ngoi flashed her toothy grin at Marama.

"We feel very special to have such an escort. It will also make leaving my new whānau behind a bit easier. I'm not looking forward to saying goodbye to Huia. She was my first, and for a while, my only friend here." The two women clasped hands and huddled together. They had accomplished a lot and now cared for each other deeply. It seemed an unlikely friendship at first, but now Ngoi was the sister she'd always wanted. Later that night, Maui was tucked up in bed, and Marama lay on her mat. She was lost somewhere between thinking and sleeping.

"Marama, I am close. Everything is well. Tread carefully and stay alert." It was Nani, a much stronger connection now. Marama sat upright in bed, repeating the words like a mantra.

True to his word, Rongo gave Marama and his men a mere day to pack for the journey. They departed the following morning as soon as it was light. Huia cried a lake of tears while her brothers blinked at the ground, trying not to look at Maui. The women performed songs asking Papatūānuku to watch over Marama and her whānau. The tohunga wove protections around them, made offerings to all the Gods and petitioned the ancestors to guard the precious travellers well. Piri regained the vim and vigour he possessed before Rangi blanketed the village in his darkness. There was more grey in his hair, deep lines on his face, but spiritually he was more powerful than ever. The canoes launched into the lake. Marama recalled her first glimpse of Rotowhā when Rongo removed the headcover. It was a long time ago, she thought as she stroked Maui's hair. Against all odds, she held the spark of life inside her, and they were returning home together. Gliding smoothly through the water as the paddlers settled into a rhythm, Marama raised a hand in farewell to the faces who were now friends, whānau and Maui's people. Marama sensed a probing curiosity, brushing against her conscience, more interested than invasive. The sensation she had felt on arrival, and experienced again now, was unlike anything else she knew. A presence pulled her eyes downwards to peer into the waters of the lake.

"Ah! I see you have made the acquaintance of the taniwha who guards our lake. Our people have abbreviated Rotowhā's name over the years to protect our secrets. The sacred name of this body of water is Rototaniwha." Piri nodded sagely to himself.

"He must recognise you and Maui, so when you return, he will grant you access to our village. On the surface, our pā isn't the most heavily fortified. However, the occupant of the lake provides a whole different dimension to defence. There has never been a successful invasion of Rotowhā from the water." The tohunga spoke to Maui now, and the child grabbed his nose, fixing his eyes intently on Piri. Marama thanked the taniwha for their safe passage, introduced herself, and began a chant of thanks to the Gods. It was an ancient ode, taught to her by Nani, handed down through generations of spirit guides. Piri listened with interest and an attentive ear. He could understand most of it, and he hummed along, enjoying the melodious lilt. They made camp before dark and ate the cooked food from the village. Tomorrow they would fish or hunt, but today Rongo wanted to travel swiftly. He owed Marama his life, gratitude for her support, and little Maui needed to meet his other family. Losing Maui from their daily life would be difficult, but Ngoi having another baby would comfort them. The travel companions were lively in the evening, as they were all released from the responsibilities of the village. A carefree attitude pervaded the camp. They talked, debated, sang, told stories, played games and laughed a lot. Ngoi was learning as many of Marama's recipes as she could, which pleased the other voyagers. Tasty food and warming drinks were a luxury on such an adventure.

Rongo selected a route they could navigate by canoe instead of returning the way they brought Marama. He and Piri decided to carry gifts to Marama's people, and Rongo wanted to save the tohunga days of strenuous walking. Marama paid close attention to their route and mapped the position of the stars and moon when she could.

"What are you looking for each night when you gaze up at the stars?" Rongo raised his bushy, black brows at Marama.

"I am making a star map in my head, so we can always find you. Maui's father is a navigator, a sea voyager from Hawaiki, and he taught me some rudimentary skills on our journey to Aotearoa."

"Just as well we covered your head when we were travelling." He grinned at her mischievously.

"Actually, it was a complete waste of time Rongo. I could feel the direction of the sun, the current movement, and I memorised the tributary turns all the way to the river that flows into the lake. If I needed to escape, I wanted to be able to find my way home. You must take more care in the future." It was Marama's turn to admonish Rongo, with a quirked brow and a cheeky smile. Ngoi's hand flew to her mouth, but not in time to smother a snort of laughter, earning her a petulant look from Rongo.

"I never suspected you would be able to do any of those things." He scratched his head, frowning.

"That is the point Rongo. You need to expect the unexpected."

"I want to ask you something Marama. Did you let me find you the day I captured you?"

"Yes, I did. I knew from your conversation by the stream, you were looking for me, and I wanted to lead you away from my people. The only way to do that, and guarantee you didn't return, was to go with you. Slipping through your men and laying false trails was simple enough. If you weren't with them, I might have had to give myself up. Ironically, you are now taking us home, and I will show you the way." Marama shrugged her shoulders. This time, they all laughed, but Rongo took her words to heart. He and his men couldn't afford to underestimate an enemy as badly as they underestimated Marama. If Marama had escaped, she might have returned with a contingent of blood-thirsty warriors seeking revenge. The responsibility was Rongo's if lives were lost. Rongo puffed out his cheeks as he mulled over what he could learn, as his strategic mind was always working. Marama saw a reflection of her Chief and parts of herself when she looked at Rongo. Having him as a leader would benefit his people in so many ways.

A wave rippled into Marama's dreams, tugging insistently at her unconscious mind.

"We are coming for you Mama, and we are searching."

When Marama opened her eyes, the voice of Kai's whale

brother was still awash in her head. It was the sound of water moving deep in the ocean. The whale said, 'we' so Marama believed Kai, at least, had returned to Aotearoa. Nani wanted her to be alert, so she must remain vigilant. Today they would be travelling by sea, along the coastline. She wondered if the whale would locate her and decided to tell Rongo of the message. People would be scared if the whale breached close to the canoes, and she didn't want anyone to harm Kai's brother in a moment of panic. If her people were searching for her, they would do so stealthily. She had been missing a long time, and they would assume she was a captive. They must avoid a clash between the two groups.

"Rongo, my people are looking for me. Potentially, this could be a dangerous situation as they will believe I am a prisoner. They know I can find my way home. We must stay alert, and if a whale approaches us, we must not harm him. My oldest son rides with his brother, but I don't know if anyone else travels with them." Rongo was slightly mystified by Marama's belief they might be approached by a whale, but he hoped her son would be reasonable.

"You know your people best Marama, what do you think they will do?"

Marama thought carefully before answering. What would she do, and would they do the same?

"I can't be sure Rongo, but I would first locate me. Then I would watch from a distance to find out the strength of the party and its routine. I would send in a scout to check my situation and see if I have a baby. The choice of plan is a more difficult question. If they have superior strength, they could attack you and rescue me, but I think this is unlikely because they won't want to risk harming Maui or me. It would make more sense to try and steal me away in the night. They could also ambush us and demand you hand me over, but again that is risky. My first choice would be to create a diversion or situation where we are in chaos or disarray, that would probably provide the optimal opportunity to take us and escape without conflict."

"Sometimes Marama, I am glad you aren't a warrior or a chief. I would choose the ambush if a perfect location presented itself, but the diversion is a better option. If we both have the same ideas, however, will they choose to do something more unexpected? Everything you have told me about your Chief, the esteem you hold him in, urges me to tread with caution."

It was Marama's turn to be surprised by Rongo's insightful comments. She didn't think she revealed much about herself or her people, but Rongo was right. Marama tapped her crooked tooth with her fingernail while she thought.

"You make a good point Rongo. They will choose an unpredictable approach. We are most vulnerable, and they will be much stronger at sea. Can you give me a few minutes before we depart? I want to consult with my spirit guide, my Nani. None of my people can walk with the spirits, but perhaps we can search for them."

"That would be unpredictable from us. If we do that, it would be prudent to reduce the size of our party to you, Maui, me, Ngoi and Piri. We will be at a disadvantage, so less of a threat." Marama liked Rongo's idea. He was a brave and selfless man to propose taking Ngoi, the woman he loved and the mother of his children. Two women, including her, a baby, an old man and one warrior, wouldn't appear dangerous to a search party. She nodded emphatically and hugged Rongo before excusing herself to find Nani.

Sitting cross-legged on a rock by the ocean, Marama retreated inward. She reached the void, where the physical gave way to the spiritual.

"I am here Marama. The ones who seek you are drawing nearer every day."

"Nani, I need to find them. There are too many unknown variables for us to meet by chance. Kai's brother has echoed in my mind, and he told me they are coming, but we need to avoid a clash between us. Can you help me?"

"I cannot communicate with any of our people as I do with you

Marama, but I can lead you. There are also signs we can deliver to them, which will bring you together."

"Rongo has proposed he, Maui, Ngoi, Piri and I, set off alone. Do you approve of our plan?"

"He diminishes the threat to our people, a good thought. Tane will watch over you, and now I have work to do."

Marama's head jerked up as she returned to her body. Never a straight answer from the spirits, but good enough for her. She went to Rongo and Ngoi, holding her arms out for Maui.

"We have our guide Rongo."

"I have already briefed the men. They will give us a one-day head start before setting out themselves to follow the coastline. If we can't find your people in three days, we will rendezvous at a meeting place. We can send a messenger to them, carrying a specific token if we find your people, or they will search for us."

Excitement was prickling Marama's skin, and her heart was racing as she was desperate to see her family again. She had fantasised about this moment to keep her spirits up when she was living with Rangi. So close now to bringing Maui home, but she cautioned herself to remain focused. After surviving their many trials and prevailing over a much stronger enemy, Marama craved a peaceful reunion with her people. They re-packed their provisions and belongings hastily, eager to be upon the sea while it was calm. Maui nestled against his mother, content with his milk, confident in the people who surrounded him. They decided to take one more paddler, a cheerful young man who sang beautifully, a nephew of Rongo's. Rongo could hardly expect Piri to propel the canoe with him. Ngoi and Marama both knew how to paddle as well and when they were at sea, they would do whatever Rongo asked of them, as would his nephew. The men were somewhat unsettled. They didn't expect their chief to leave them behind, but Rongo's authority meant nobody questioned his decision. His second on the expedition took charge of the men and was proud to do so. He and Rongo clasped each other's arms and shared a hongi before Rongo launched his canoe. The water was glassy, curling away from the bow in a blue-green salute. Marama's hair whipped in the breeze as the exhilaration of being at sea washed over her. She travelled a lot with Starman on his voyages. His ancestors had elevated her senses and sea-craft due to her relationship with the sons of the sea. Tangaroa enfolded the waka in his arms, propelling them into the deep, where the current set their course. Starman's grandfather whispered to her to relax and let the sea take them, so she passed the message to Rongo, and he flicked her a boyish grin. Kūmara grower he might be, but his love of the ocean was plain to see. They were a company of adventurers, eyes shining with the allure of the unknown. The day passed swiftly, and they made good progress but made no contact that day. They rode an incoming tide to the shore and found a cave to shelter in for the night. Rongo and his nephew scouted the area, but there were no signs of inhabitants. The canoe was pulled ashore and hidden amongst the undergrowth, above the high tide line. It wasn't safe to light a fire, so they ate the provisions they carried. They had no desire to draw attention to themselves when they were such a vulnerable party. When it came time to allocate the watch, both Marama and Piri felt one of them should stay awake while the other four would each take a turn at keeping them company. The tohunga and Marama assured their companions they would nap the next day, but Marama doubted she could sleep. Her nerves were taut with anticipation, body and mind tuned, searching for signs from the spiritual world. Ironically, when Piri relieved her, and she closed her eyes, the whale song sounded in her mind. Marama swam with Kai's brother in the realm between waking and dreams as he sang of the place they would meet once more.

In another camp, Marama's people dreamed. They awakened in a tense state of excitement. Some people recounted their dreams to each other, or Kai, as Marama wasn't there to interpret what they saw or the spirits told them. Today could be the day they would find her. How they would rescue Marama wasn't yet decided, but they had an advantage at sea as the whale travelled with them.

They all knew it would be unwise to underestimate an unknown enemy. Marama was a resourceful woman, and it concerned them she hadn't escaped to return to them herself. Nobody believed she had perished. It was a thought they wouldn't entertain. Kai dreamed he and his brother were swimming past underwater mountains, through kelp forests, towards his mother. She was hovering above them, her hair streaming in the wind, laughing. Marama threw an umbilical cord into the water, and he climbed up it to be greeted by a baby. Kai hoped this meant his baby brother was coming back to them with his mother. There were clear signs for setting the course, with fast-flowing currents and prevailing winds, so, with the elements directing them, Marama's people followed their instincts.

Once Rongo's little band were at sea, Ngoi proposed four paddlers might be better than two. While it wasn't their usual way, perhaps Piri could petition the Gods. Marama was drawn so taut, Piri feared she might snap. Paddling was traditionally the domain of men, but Piri knew a story of a woman who saved the great canoe of her people. She had implored the Gods to allow her to be a man. Four paddlers would improve their progress, and his female ancestors would be pleased if the Gods approved. He awoke with a feeling they must hurry, so he closed his eyes and began his prayers.

"Allow them to paddle Piri. We, your ancestors, have asked the Gods and Papatūānuku to champion these women. They honour us, and you must increase your speed."

The tohunga opened his eyes with his grandmother's words still in his ears. He nodded at Ngoi and Marama, who wasted no time in grabbing a paddle each and positioning themselves. To distribute the weight evenly, Ngoi paddled behind Rongo and Marama behind his nephew. Piri took charge of the sleeping Maui and hummed gently to him. The exercise was a blessing for Marama, and it helped settle the nervous energy burning inside her. She turned her head constantly, scanning the ocean and glimpses of land, searching for the meeting place. The morning waned, and the paddlers took turns to take a break to eat and drink while the others paddled on. Marama turned her face to the sun and closed her eyes as she paddled, catching glimpses of mountains and the waving forests of the deep. She pulled up her paddle, signalling Ngoi to do the same and hurried to the front of the canoe. There was a rocky outcrop protruding from the waves, pointing to a high mountain on land. This scene was the place she dreamed of last night. She leaned forward, peering into the sparkling ocean, her head full of wave-song and heart thrumming with joy. The whale breached. Water sprouted from his blow-hole and his tiny eyes locked on Marama before he dived. Up ahead of the canoe, he leapt from the water and splashed his tail in greeting. Marama was ecstatic. She saw his markings but already knew this was Kai's brother. Behind her, Maui was squealing with excitement and bewilderment was stamped on the faces of her companions. Piri clapped his hands in delight, reminding Marama of her Nani.

"I am here too. They are coming for you," whispered Nani.

"What does it mean Marama? Why has the whale come, and what should we do?" Rongo turned shining eyes to her, eyebrows raised to his hairline.

"We will wait here, Rongo, and my people will come to us. My Nani is with us Piri. All will be well."

The waiting was interminable, so Rongo decided they should fish instead of twiddling their thumbs, and Tangaroa rewarded them with a hoard of tuna. The tohunga returned the first and largest fish to the sea, including Maui in his ritual of gratitude. Marama's face hurt because she couldn't stop smiling, no matter how hard she tried. She squinted as the whale appeared again, swimming on the surface. As he drew closer, she saw a speck astride his back.

"It is Kai, my son and Maui's brother." Marama's voice was suddenly husky with emotion.

"You are already the mother of a whale rider?" Piri asked, incredulous.

"Was ever a mother so blessed Piri? My middle child Aroha is already earning a reputation as a healer."

Ngoi hugged Marama, crying tears of joy for her friend, while Rongo encircled them in his brawny arms. The tohunga was already absorbed in his karakia, Maui still cradled in his sinewy arms. Marama stood at the front of the canoe, waving her arms and laughing as Kai's brother delivered him to his mother. Kai had seen the canoe through his brother's eyes. The whale conveyed the message that Marama paddled with four people who appeared to be friends, although one was quite fearsome-looking and a baby. The whale saw a much stronger contingent of warriors on the water, armed and potentially hostile, but they were at least a day behind. The search party agreed to Kai's request to go ahead with the whale, as they knew his brother and spirit father wouldn't let any harm come to the boy. If necessary, the whale could carry Kai and Marama to safety, but they hoped this wouldn't be necessary. The bond Kai and his mother shared strengthened as he moved closer, and the vision of the umbilical cord from his dream flowed through Kai's mind.

"Mama," sighed the whale to Marama.

Kai stood atop the whale's back, grinning from ear to ear. His teeth were white against deeply tanned skin, he already looked like a voyager, and his hair had grown long, bleached lighter by the sea and sun. He leapt lightly from the whale's back to the canoe, into his mother's waiting arms. They just held each other, savouring their reunion. Eyes were closed in the ecstasy of the moment, reconnecting. Finally, they broke free and looked at each other, grinning madly. It was as if they never parted.

"Come, Kai, I have some people to introduce you to. I have gained a new family while you have been on your adventures." She tousled his hair and hugged him to her side. Marama formally introduced Kai to Rongo and Ngoi, but as Marama took him to meet Piri, Maui couldn't wait his turn. He held out his chubby arms to Kai, chattering and laughing. Kai scooped his baby brother up and, much to Maui's delight threw him up in the air and caught him gently on the way down. The whale turned on his back and waggled his enormous flippers in the air. The two brothers looked at each other, thrilled to be meeting, and Kai snuggled a wiggling Maui against his chest. They loved each other.

The tohunga greeted Kai with a hongi. He was fascinated by this boy whose spirit sparkled and shone like the sun on the ocean. His destiny radiated around him, merging with the aura of the whale, and Piri predicted fate would weave many stories around the legends these two would create. He cackled to himself, as today he seemed extraordinarily ordinary.

"Mama, do you have any food? I am hungry." Kai patted his concave puku with his free hand.

"Forgive us, Kai! Of course, we have food." Ngoi was beside herself that she hadn't offered him anything to eat and jumped up to fetch food.

"Don't be silly Ngoi, it's not every day a boy arrives on your waka riding on the back of a whale, is it?" said Marama laughing. "I am sure my son will forgive you once he is stuffing his mouth with every morsel of food you can find. Unfortunately for him, both his parents have voracious appetites, but he can out-eat us both." She raised her eyes to the heavens, shaking her head as if to ask the Gods why it was so. It was a merry meal, and Kai did lend some weight to Marama's words when he ate more than Rongo, who had been paddling all day.

The great canoe specked on the horizon. Each stroke of the paddles drew them closer to Marama. Her heart thundered in her chest, and her breath was uncharacteristically shallow, literally panting. Kai lay his head on his mother's shoulder and stroked her arm to calm her as he did as a baby. His whale brother sang a lullaby to her to assuage her highly strung nerves. With a son in each arm, Marama waited, poised to see her people again. It had been so long. They glided into focus. The Chief stood proud at the front of the canoe, and navigating the waves from the rear was her love, Starman. Ari waved both arms in the air before bringing her hands to her mouth to hold in her relieved sobs. Starman handed the steering to one of the other navigators and ran gracefully on sure sea-legs to join the Chief. It was her. They had found Marama, and tears built behind Starman's eyes. He was so afraid he had lost her and their son. Squeezing his eyelids together, Starman offered silent prayers of gratitude to the Gods. The Chief placed an arm around Starman to support him. They never spoke of losing Marama, but both were aware of the risks. When they returned from their voyage, they were ecstatic to arrive home to their loved ones. For Starman, the homecoming had rapidly descended into a nightmare. Guilt flayed him for leaving his pregnant woman alone. The possibility the woman he loved, and his unborn son, were gone forever tormented him. He was unable to sleep. Aroha informed the Chief and Ari she was adding sleeping herbs to his food and drink at night. She was a perceptive child Aroha and she played up her dependence on her father to give him something else to concentrate on besides Marama. The Chief was furious with Tau's stupidity at leaving the village unprotected and his lack of action to find Marama. He hadn't known where to start a defensive Tau had stammered to his father. The village leaders convened an urgent hui, and Tau stepped down from leadership in shame. The Chief assumed command of the village and Marama's rescue. Now here she was, his adopted moon-daughter, standing in a canoe in the middle of the ocean, waiting to greet them.

"Isn't she a magnificent sight?" The Chief hugged his friend warmly and tousled his hair in a fatherly gesture.

"Yes, she is that." Starman didn't dare to take his eyes off Marama, or his boys, lest they disappear. As the canoes came into proximity, Rongo and his nephew manoeuvred the smaller vessel to board the great canoe. Marama was the first to clamber aboard, and Starman pulled her straight into his embrace. He buried his face in her hair, inhaling her scent and moulding her body into his. Then he showered her face with kisses, the tears flowing freely. Marama leaned into his chest and knew she was home. Her body trembled with the torrent of emotion, released from the dam built inside herself. They were laughing, crying, hugging, kissing and the world around them dropped away for a few moments. There was only the two of them, magnets returned to their opposite, at last, green eyes locked to brown. Ari could contain herself no longer, and she threw her arms around them both, sobbing openly now. The Chief joined them, then Piki, Koha and pretty soon they were enveloped by everyone in the canoe except the navigator steering. Fanning her face with her hands and wiping away her tears, Marama turned to the side of the canoe and hoisted Maui aboard.

"Let me introduce you to our son, Maui."

Starman reached for the baby, who went straight to his Papa. He looked just like Aroha when she was his age. Maui grabbed Starman's nose and his hair, flexing his legs and blowing bubbles. Starman's heart lurched with joy, another precious child. He lifted Maui above his head, which made the baby chuckle with glee. Everyone on the canoe melted, and they all wanted to make Maui's acquaintance.

"I have some special people I want you all to meet. They became our whānau while we were away. Their nurturing and care sustained us during dark times, and now they have delivered me home. Please let us greet them with the hospitality they deserve." Marama's eyes pleaded with them to trust her.

Rongo, Piri and Ngoi all came aboard while Kai and Rongo's nephew looked after their canoe. Greetings were warm, and they regarded each other with much curiosity. The Chief was everything and more than Rongo imagined. Marama's man was even more handsome than Ngoi was expecting, and she felt a little flustered, whereas Ari she could have picked from the crowd, so accurate was Marama's description. They afforded Piri much respect. The tohunga discerned the deep spiritual bond these people shared with their ancestors. It emanated from them, shone in their wairua. These were indeed Marama's people.

With the greetings out of the way, the two leaders decided to go ashore for the evening. Kai and his brother scouted a safe place for them to spend the night, which could only be reached by sea. Everyone was itching to hear Marama's story, but they knew it would be a long one. They needed to make camp, prepare food, and hope she wasn't too tired for the telling. Having a chief, his woman, nephew and a tohunga as guests also added spice to the company. They were interested in new ideas and asked the guests about how they did everything they were doing. It was an intensive cultural exchange, as the guests were just as curious to learn about the ways of Marama's people. Although her whānau didn't know it yet, the guests would be entrusting the future leader of their iwi to them. Rongo could see immediately where Marama's sunny disposition came from, as all her people were carefree. They laughed and joked with each other as they went about their activities and would spontaneously burst into song or dance. Teasing was a universal pastime for young and old. Marama and Starman provided material for many a smutty jest, and the sexual innuendo was enough to make a grown man blush. Ngoi was enjoying it immensely, it reminded her of her home, and she joined in both the singing and dancing. Rongo and Piri noted how dour they had become and how much more efficient completing tasks was when men and women worked together. There was work to be done when they got home. Rongo dispatched a messenger with his whalebone pendant. It was the token to let his men know he was safe and with Marama's people. Rongo's nephew and two of the Chief's men would wait for Rongo's warriors and lead them to the village.

Starman and Marama couldn't get enough of each other or share enough cuddles with their boys. Maui held court for his two newest admirers, his father and his brother. They were hopeless, and Maui was going to become the most spoiled, over-indulged child in Aotearoa - aue! The only person missing from their perfect world was Aroha, who they hadn't wanted to bring into potential danger. Aroha was also quite a healer already and took her responsibilities of filling in for her mother seriously, so she remained at home without complaint. Before the evening meal, while Maui was with Kai and Ngoi, Marama and Starman sneaked away for a bath. There were no steaming hot pools here, but the bathing was only an excuse to be alone. They gravitated toward one another as soon as they were alone. If they could have, they would have melted into one person to be closer. Starman kissed Marama tenderly, her eyes, her ears, her face, and finally, her lips. Marama pulled away.

"There is something I need to tell you-"

"Shhh, there is only me and you, the love we share."

"But I feel dirty, unclean, I was claimed by an-"

"I don't care Marama. You have done everything you could to protect our child, and I will only love you more for the sacrifices you made. Unless, of course, you enjoyed it, then I will demand you pleasure me every night for the next year." He grinned wolfishly and waggled his eyebrows at her.

"You really are impossible!"

"Impossibly starved of your affection." He kissed her again as if she hadn't interrupted at all.

"What did they feed you on those islands of yours? You have returned home a horny old man." She giggled and ducked down to scoop a handful of cold water at him. The result was a childish water-fight, followed by a passionate re-acquaintance, which made them aware the separation only made them want each other more. When they arrived back, the teasing was so lively, they took a bow and applauded each other. It reminded them of *Rangitahua* (the Stopping-off Place or Kermadec islands), where they stopped on the journey to Aotearoa when they first committed to their relationship and had been teased mercilessly.

When daylight faded, the company gathered hopefully around the fires with warm drinks. Nobody wanted to press Marama for the story, as she might prefer to tell her close family or the Council first. Still, curiosity and the enjoyment of a good tale gnawed at them. Marama smiled to herself as she knew exactly what her people wanted to hear. She had already spoken to Piri,

Rongo and Ngoi. They would each tell a portion of the story, the tradition now in both villages for epic tales. From start to finish, Marama's people were captivated. The orators spoke well, their emotions colouring the often tragic story, allowing the listeners to journey with them. Tears sometimes streamed down people's faces or hands clasped in horror. Marama held Ari's hand more than once, and the Chief stroked her hair. There was cheering at Rangi's demise and Atarangi's defeat. Late in the evening, when the stars were burning bright, the listeners stumbled to their mats, shaking their heads in disbelief - Marama and Maui were home.

Starman and Marama strolled to the beach instead of going straight to their mats.

"I'm afraid to go to sleep, Marama. What if I wake up and find this was all a dream?"

"It is real enough, my love. I couldn't invent a story such as the one Maui, and I have lived. At least now you know everything. Our youngest son is going to be as special as the eldest," she sighed.

"No growing old and grey in boredom for us I fear," he said, grinning. They cuddled together, contemplating the future. It was miraculous they had a future to contemplate. Together they had brought three beautiful, gifted children into the world. Sons and a daughter who would keep their knowledge alive, remember the ancestors, worship the Gods and weave the future.

"Want to find where your island home was my love?" Starman touched his forehead to Marama's.

"No, my home is right here with you." She took his face in her hands and claimed his lips, just as she had when she was a young girl. The same moon shed her silvery beams upon them while the eternal stars shone their distant light upon their heads, and the ocean murmured its contentment in its never-ending pursuit of the shore. Papatūānuku sighed as the circle of life turned in balance once more.

Chapter 15
The Homecoming

The light was a mere hint in the night sky of the day's arrival.

"Come, we must hurry." Aroha stood in the doorway, dressed, fed and impatient to be gone. Ari let her stay with Marama's dear friend Kani. Marama delivered Kani's daughter Tuakana Marama on the voyage to Aotearoa. The older girl doted on Aroha in the same way, Marama always fussed over her, and Kani was grateful to do something for Marama.

"What is happening Aroha? Why are we in a rush this morning?" Kani stretched and yawned sleepily, but Aroha had a point. It would soon be light.

"My whānau are coming home today, and I want to meet them before everyone else." For a child of only a few seasons, Aroha was both articulate and intuitive. While her mother was gone, Aroha stepped into her shoes so naturally, it was apparent to everyone she was answering her calling. Kani was excited to hear the news, so she hastily splashed her face with water, stuffed some food in her mouth and put on garments for walking. Aroha was young, but she hiked up hills and through the bush at a fast pace. Keeping up with her wasn't always easy, especially when she walked under low-hanging branches where adults couldn't fit. Tuakana slung a water skin over her shoulder, and they set off, following Aroha's lead. Aroha chattered to Tuakana as they walked, showing her interesting plants and extolling their healing properties without missing a stride. She also foraged for things to eat as they went, which Kani was grateful for as she became hungry as the morning wore on. They paused at a stream to drink and refill the waterskin but didn't stop to rest.

"Aroha, I fear I am lost already. Do you know how to get home?"

"Of course Kani, I promise not to lose you or Tuakana in the forest. My Mama would be disappointed with me if I did that!" Aroha pulled a face at the thought before beaming a cheeky smile at Kani. It was refreshing to see Aroha behaving like the child she was, so Kani chuckled at her funny face. The responsibilities of being the villager healer, spirit guide, and the only member of her family in the village were too heavy for one so young. They trudged upwards, sweating in the warming sun, before cresting a rise to find a plateau. The view was magnificent. Treetops stretched endlessly before them in one direction and the ocean blended into the sky in the other. Aroha nodded her satisfaction.

"You can take a short rest here before we climb down," she announced casually.

Aroha stood poised on the front edge of the plateau, staring out across the ocean intently, before closing her eyes and beginning to chant. It wasn't a chant the others had ever heard. The cadence, melody and phrasing seemed quite complex. They wondered who taught Aroha the chant, and then she began a song of welcome in a voice so loud, it seemed to boom across the ocean. The great canoe rounded a point in the distance, hugging the coastline as they drew closer to home. In response to Aroha's welcome, the paddlers raised their voices in song, and the waka changed course towards the bay below the plateau.

"Come on, it's time to go down so we can travel home on the canoe," said Aroha. She was already clambering down the steep descent, surefooted and full of energy. Kani cast her eyes upon Papatūānuku, giving thanks she wouldn't have to walk all the way home.

Marama was drawn towards the front of the canoe as soon as light appeared in the sky. A restless yearning blossomed in her breast, and her mind was questing, drawn to the spiritual. She could hear the whispering of spirits when she closed her eyes, but it was like eavesdropping from afar, and she couldn't make out what they were saying. By mid-morning, she reached for Nani in frustration, but she wasn't there. Starman could see Marama was preoccupied and joined her with Maui balanced on one hip. Piri also ventured to join them.

"What is it Marama? I can feel the disturbance of the spirit world, it is quite powerful, and it reminds me of when you came to our village." Marama clapped her hands and hugged the old tohunga, tapping her finger against her head.

"How silly of me not to perceive that." She rolled her eyes and laughed, shaking her head. She now knew what was going on, but Piri was none the wiser. Chanting began to echo from the spiritual, becoming louder and clearer to their external ears. Rongo also came to the front of the canoe, shaking his head.

"What is that sound Piri?" Rongo asked.

The tohunga and Marama exchanged amused looks. So they were correct about Rongo's spirituality, and Huia most probably inherited his sensitivity. Before they could answer Rongo's question, a song of welcome rolled across the ocean, pulling their eyes to a plateau above them as they rounded the point. Standing high above them, booming out her song, was Aroha. Tears rolled down Marama's face, but they were tears of happiness. She was overjoyed to see the child she left hidden in a tree. Starman threw his arm around her, and they both burst into song, responding to Aroha. The entire crew erupted in a jubilant round of singing, and they nudged closer to the shore as the figures clambered down.

"I didn't want to ruin Aroha's surprise," cackled Nani. *"She has learned much while you have been away."*

Starman, Marama and Kai, clambered aboard Rongo's smaller canoe and paddled to the shore. Aroha jumped up and down on a rock waving, so excited to see her parents, especially her beloved mother, who she missed terribly. Tuakana scrambled down the last bank to join her and finally Kani, who was gingerly picking her way down with care. Kai manoeuvred the canoe close to the rocks, so his father could brace them and help the welcome committee aboard. He waved and called a greeting to his little sister, who had grown so much physically and spiritually since they went away. A lump in her throat seemed to choke Marama as Starman swung Aroha aboard into her waiting arms. They clasped each other for a long time, eyes closed, as emotion washed over and through them. Marama sensed a change in Aroha, a new spiritual depth.

"Let me look at you, Aroha, how you have grown! I have missed you so much and thought of you every day since we parted."

"I missed you too, Mama. If my spirit guide hadn't come, I don't know what I would've done." She shrugged her shoulders and turned wide eyes to her mother.

"You have found your spirit guide already? That is wonderful, Aroha. Now I understand my sense of you better."

"I have learned so many things, Mama, about healing and the spirit world, but you make it look so easy and it's hard work." Aroha's mouth turned down as she drew her eyebrows together in a frown of displeasure.

"Oh my darling, I am so sorry. I never meant for you to replace me!" Marama shot a distressed, guilt-laden look at Starman.

"You are like two seeds from the same pod Marama, so I wasn't surprised at all. Aroha is, however, much bossier than you, and she slips her poor Papa sleeping potions in secret."

Aroha raised amused eyes to her father. She thought she got away with her deception, but apparently, she hadn't. Marama enfolded her namesake and Kani in her arms as well. It was good to be amongst her people, and she couldn't wait to introduce them to Rongo, Ngoi and Piri. They began the paddle out to deeper water to join the crew of the great canoe.

"Who is your spirit guide Aroha?" Marama regarded Aroha fondly, proud of her sense of responsibility.

"You know her, Mama. My guide is Manaia, the grandmother of your Nani. She stayed with me while you were gone so that I wouldn't be lonely and I would always know what to do. I love her, and she knows an awful lot about everything."

Marama breathed a sigh of relief. Manaia had also spoken to and looked after her in the spirit world. When Nani was alive, it was Manaia who screened the other spirits seeking Marama. Nani also told her Manaia was exceptionally gifted, as she was connected to each realm even when she was alive. Marama sent silent thanks to her ancestor. She was a spirit who would guide Aroha through the trials of life with care.

"Aroha is gifted Marama. She was born with a wisdom beyond her years, and we are well-matched," murmured Manaia.

"Oh!" said Aroha. "I can't wait to meet that old man on our canoe reaching out to me. Who is he?"

"That is the tohunga Piri, who is the spirit guide of the village where I have been - visiting." Marama knew she would have to tell Aroha the whole story, but she just wanted to be her mother for now.

"I like the big man with the hidden stories in his tā moko. He has a colourful aura, but is that my baby brother with Papa?" Aroha's voice became a high pitched squeal of excitement. Her eyes became fixed on the baby. She blinked back tears as she perceived the beauty and light of his wairua as it twined around her own. At that moment, they bonded. It was to be a bond forged in stone, weathered over time, to endure throughout their lives. Piri glimpsed the future. Maui's power base was already building around him, and his sister would share his shining destiny. While he was only a tiny baby, three villages had already pledged their loyalty to him, and he was yet to meet the people of his parent's village. The tohunga chuckled to himself and hoped he would live long enough to see the boy become a man and the woman his sister would become. When Aroha climbed aboard, she greeted everyone with the perfect protocol. Her Chief introduced her formally to Rongo, Ngoi and Piri. She charmed them with her polite dignity and genuine curiosity. As she clasped hands with Piri, a warmth flowed between them, just as it did with Marama, and they smiled knowingly at one another. However, with formalities over, Aroha squealed and hopped up and down until Starman relinquished Maui to her. As he did with Kai, Maui held his arms out to his sister. He put a tiny hand on her face tenderly and snuggled against her body, gazing into her eyes adoringly. Marama, Starman and Kai, were moved by the sight of the two youngest members of their family together. They were so sweet but strangely captivating as well, and the entire crew of the canoe stopped what they were doing to watch them. The spell broke when the Chief detected a changing wind stir against his skin and called his paddlers to action.

"The wind God favours us! Let us make haste, and we can sleep in Kāingatipu tonight." The Chief grinned as the crew leapt into action. Starman kissed Marama before running to the navigation area in glee. They were heading home to their village, their people, their ancestors, and they were all together. Marama hugged Ngoi and Ari, her cheeks aching from smiling so much.

The karanga rang out in the scent-laden evening air, calling the four visitors onto the marae. Ngoi walked ahead of the three men, fittingly and to the pleasure of Rongo's female ancestors, the first person from their iwi to set foot in Marama's home. The smell of the food for the feast wafted tantalisingly on the sea breeze. Formalities were brief as a chorus of rumbling puku began to resonate from all directions. With a laugh, the Chief invited Piri to bless their food before anyone fainted from hunger. The visitors were thrilled to find themselves amongst so many light-hearted people who enjoyed humour and laughter. This atmosphere was what Piri, Ngoi and Rongo wanted to create in their village when they returned home. Ngoi became misty-eyed when she saw how relaxed Marama was with her people, and she noticed how beloved her friend was. Maui rapidly wrapped the villagers around his little finger, but Ari was firm with everyone about letting his close whānau have time with him first. For Marama, the feast brought her and Maui's adventure to a close. They were back where they belonged, with their whānau and in their spiritual home. At least Marama's spiritual home. In truth, Maui was born of two iwi, so he would always be at ease in any of his adopted villages. Kotuku admitted he diverted them from their path but never mentioned any change to Maui's destiny. They simply wanted Maui to be part of their future, to save their people. For now, he was a sleepy, chubby, over-indulged baby and needed to rest. Aroha and Tuakana materialised next to Marama, with outstretched arms, announcing they would sing him to sleep. The feast lingered long into the night as the villagers wanted to hear Marama's story, so they regaled the villagers with their tale. Starman was able to pay more attention to the account the second time around, and he began to comprehend the intensity of Marama's struggle for survival. He would be reluctant to voyage without her again. Their eyes met as Rongo and Piri completed the tale. They stole away to the beach, always their special place.

Starman placed a cloak around them both, and they snuggled together, seated on their favourite log.

"I am sorry you endured such treatment, Marama, but you succeeded in bringing our son into the world. You are wonderful, and I never want to be parted from you again." He kissed the top of her head and pulled her closer.

"I never appreciated the social structure of our village, the openness of our culture, and our cheerful natures more. I have truly learned to cherish the love we share, the respect we have for one another, in a whole new way. To be treated as the property of someone else and afforded such a low status was – enlightening at best. Sometimes we can overlook the things you take for granted every day, but I see the lives we have built for ourselves so positively now." Marama placed a hand on Starman's cheek, stroking his face with her thumb. She could feel the warmth radiating from his body, smell his scent as his unbound hair mingled with hers in the breeze. His lips were warm against hers, expressing his love and longing for her in more than words. Together again, they felt complete, whole once more in body and spirit. They smiled into each other's eyes, leaned their foreheads in until they were touching, savouring the sensation of breathing the same air as their reconnection deepened.

"Do you think we should try and have one ordinary child?" Marama's eyes crinkled in amusement.

"I do so enjoy the trying Marama, but I fear we have failed to produce any normal offspring so far. I do not know how we will cope with the destined lives of the three children we have. I am eternally grateful we are three parents, at least for Kai, and we have watchful ancestors." Starman's teeth were white in the moonlit darkness as he grinned.

"Hey, you haven't told me about your journey yet! How was your real home? How long did it take to get there? What was Kai's initiation like?"

"I am sorry, Marama, it is a long tale, and you will have to wait until tomorrow. We are alone, together, and I have become fixated on trying to father another child with you." He raised his eyebrows at her and grinned with eyes full of mischief.

Starman pulled Marama into his arms, smothering the questions which longed to bubble from her lips. As her body responded to his touch, she conceded perhaps he had a point. The tale could wait for another day.

*If you enjoyed this book please write a review on Google,
any good readers site or rdewolf.com*

Glossary

Māori words often have multiple-meaning, dependant on the context of their use. These are not dictionary definitions, merely the author's plain English explanation of what a word means in that particular sentence in this book. There is no 's' in Māori so words can be singular or plural.

aroha	love
hāngi	food cooked in a ground pit
hapu	a settlement of people who share a marae and lands of a smaller region within a tribe, a subtribe or clan (can also mean pregnant)
hongi	sharing the breath of life, is a traditional Māori greeting in which people press their noses together. (In this book, the hongi also represents high regard, respect and shared responsibility. Interestingly, hongi were shared between men and women before European settlement.)
horopito	peppery herb used in cooking and healing, pseudowintera colorata
hui	meeting/gathering
kai	food
kaimoana	seafood
kaitiaki	guardian
karakia	prayer or ritual
katipō	venomous spider native to NZ latrodectus katipō
karanga	call or summon at the commencement of a welcome ceremony
kauri	huge long-living tree agathus australis

kawakawa	medicinal bush piper excelsium
kererū	wood pigeon
kete	woven flax bag
kina	sea urchin
kiore	Pacific rat, rattus exulans
korero	talk, chat or discussion
koroua	an elderly man
koura	crayfish
kūmara	sweet potato
kuia	an elderly woman
mana	spirit/heart/standing/strength/ability to give unstintingly or unselfishly (look for context, this word has many layers of multi-faceted meaning and represents many desirable qualities and traits)
mānuka	teatree leptospermum scoparium
marae	a complex of buildings and grounds belonging to a tribe, subtribe or family
maunga	mountain
mauri	life essence
mere	flat, hand-held striking weapon often made of jade, wood or bone
mokopuna	grandchild
pā	a fortified settlement
Papatūānuku	the mother of the earth and Gods
pāua	abalone
pikopiko	young curled shoots of ferns
poi	a ball on a cord, twirled and spun (also a form of dance/storytelling)
ponga	native silver tree fern, Cyathe dealbata
pounamu	greenstone, the jade of New Zealand
puhi	virgin of high rank
puku	stomach/belly
rimu	large native tree dacrydium cupressinum
Rotowhā	Fourth Lake, an abbreviated name of

	the lake masking its real name (fictitious place)
Rototaniwha	Taniwha Lake, the original sacred name of the lake, home to a taniwha
taiaha	long wooden Māori weapon
tamariki	children
tā moko	tattoo
tangi/tangihanga	funeral or funeral ritual
Taniwha	mythical creature/beast that lives in the water
taonga	treasure
tapu	forbidden/off-limits/protected
tipuna	ancestor singular
tīpuna	(with macron) ancestors, multiple
tohunga	spiritual leader, priest, healer
utu	redress/reparation/revenge. A word with layers of complex meaning.
waiata	song
waka	canoe
wairua	spirit/aura
whakapapa	genealogy/family tree
whānau	family, both close and extended
whare	house
wharenui	meeting house/communal hall for meeting or sleeping

Phrases

Kia kaha	have strength
Tēnā koutou katoa	Greetings everyone
Tihei mauri ora!	call to claim the right to speak

Thanks

To my husband Ieme de Wolf, William Ngarimu for advice on Te Reo Maori, Katrina Reedy Editing Consultant, advanced readers Makere Ngarimu-Ngatai, Paula Kearns, Katerina Kupenga, Taranga Kent Proofreader and the authors of he-hinatora-ki-te-ao-maori for producing such an informative resource.

About the Author

R. de Wolf is a Māori author from the East Coast of New Zealand. After many years living in Australia and abroad, she now lives in Tūranganui-a-Kiwa (Gisborne) with her husband.

The Inspiration for the Spirit Voyager series, The Future Weavers is the second of six books, was people's curiosity to understand where, how and why Māori people came to Aotearoa (New Zealand). The stories are fiction but draw on aspects of history and Pasefika culture. R. de Wolf's novels incorporate themes she is passionate about – equality, empowerment, the balance of nature, the acknowledgement of ancient wisdom, and the importance of women's rights